TONY DUVERT

ATLANTIC ISLAND

SEMIOTEXT(E) NATIVE AGENTS SERIES

© 1979 by Les Éditions de Minuit, 7, rue Bernard-Palissy, 75006 Paris.
© This edition Semiotext(e) © 2017

Published by Semiotext(e)
PO BOX 629, South Pasadena, CA 91031
www.semiotexte.com

Translation revision: Noura Wedell

Cover and Frontpiece: Louie Otesanek
Design: Hedi El Kholti

ISBN: 978-1-58435-177-1
Distributed by The MIT Press, Cambridge, Mass. and London, England
Printed in the United States of America

TONY DUVERT

ATLANTIC ISLAND

Translated by Purdey Lord Kreiden & Michael Thomas Taren

1

Julien sat up in bed: the church bells had just sounded; it was half past ten. The wall behind his head was humid and smelled like moldy fabric or mushrooms. The child didn't dare turn on the light: he wasn't sure his parents were asleep. They would see the light under the door adjoining the two bedrooms.

"It's coming down harder and harder. I don't know if I'll go. No, I'm not going. It's not gonna happen, it's raining too much. No, it's not gonna happen."

No wind. The waves battered the shore under the downpour. It was the end of April.

Julien pricked up his ear. They were sleeping, now. The snoring that ascended steeply, abruptly interrupted by a hiccup, then resumed as a slow whistle, was his mother's, Simone Roquin.

"What's the old man waiting for? He's jerking off, the bastard."

Julien himself had his hand nestled on his genitals, his ten-year-old boy's genitals. The thought he just had disgusted him: he removed the hand.

"There it goes, I hear him."

The other snore, his father's.

Julien hesitated to get up. But he didn't want to stay either. He didn't feel tired.

"Ok I'll go for it. Maybe Guillard went. Maybe René'll be there. Alright, I'm going."

He was now standing, sure of his movements in spite of the darkness. The bedroom was tiny; there was the bed, the dresser, and the chair. Julien quickly groped along the wall: he knew that the two squeaky floorboards were just one step after the corner of the dresser. He took a long stride over the slats, as if they were a sleeping watchdog or the blade of a scythe.

After that, it took Julien almost five minutes to open the window and the shutters, inch by inch. He wasn't worried about the hinges; he'd greased them this morning. It was the wood itself that whined and squealed as soon as it was touched. Salt and squalls had rotted it.

"Shit."

A gust of wind tore the shutter from him, and it slammed against the outside wall. The little suburban house trembled.

Julien froze, his breath caught in his lungs. Here, at the window, the rain prevented him from hearing his parents snore.

"What happened? There's no wind. Not a fart. This one on the left. Careful."

After a moment he was reassured. Now he could get dressed. He set his shoes on the windowsill. He'd put them on outside.

The rain made him change his mind and he tied them on in his room. They were the tough shoes of orphans or peasants.

He stood back up. He scanned the darkness of the garden. His eyes adjusted. Soon he could make out details. The lights in the streets were out; they were cut after ten. Squat homes scattered about, whitewashed, on flat treeless terrain.

The downpour was less heavy now.

"Yeah, Guillard'll be there."

His rain slicker was hanging in the kitchen. No way of getting it. He slipped his pajama top over his sweater. The shirt-sleeves bulged out, tied off at the joints.

Julien bounded up to the windowsill, then immediately down to the ground. He started running on tiptoe, avoiding the puddles. None of the gardens here had a fence on the street side.

They were meeting in the Thérets' boatshed.

Alain Viaud lived at his grandmother's. He was nine. The kids called him Millipede because he was a little cross-eyed. He'd escaped from his house as early as ten o'clock: Grandmother Viaud went to bed early and he liked the rain.

His house, like Julien's, was in the western suburbs of Saint-Rémi, where the truck farming began. Down under the cliff, the water was black, disturbing, and stunk even more than the port water. No one looked at it, and no one ever went down there. The pretty beaches were to the southeast, on the other side of town, where the rich lived.

Viaud got to the shed first. He was wearing a cyclist's cape of smoky plastic, a little transparent. It hung down to his ankles, but it was torn in front. The rain lashed against his bare knees. Under his armpit, Viaud was holding a pâté sandwich that, despite the cape, gave off whiffs of garlic and greasy liver.

He dived under the shed, climbed into a small boat that had been pulled up onto the gravel, sat down and started eating without pushing back his hood, wet, smiling from cheek to cheek at the fat piece of bread.

Old lady Viaud found her grandson's pilfering insufferable. She would yell, scold, slap when she caught him. Once, when the orphan was five or six, he had done something stupid that had so infuriated her that she'd had a neighbor chase and punish him. The neighbor had pulled his pants down and whipped him until he bled, right in front of the house. One good whipping for the fifty he'd gotten away with.

The other children laughed and said that Alain Viaud had been cross-eyed ever since.

Now he'd learned how to avoid the blows, he'd never get caught again. He stole right in front of the old woman; he taunted her with that one eye of his that didn't look perfectly straight. He didn't talk much and was useless in class. But he was intelligent.

His grandmother tried to civilize him; she screamed:

"Why don't you ask, instead of stealing?"

Viaud didn't have a clue. It was true he didn't like to ask, not her or anyone. It was true that he only liked what he stole. The meals his grandmother made, that hard and bitter little mummy, gave him no pleasure. He wolfed them down mechanically. His delights happened at night, when he devoured, alone in his bed, what he had pinched. An oil-drenched piece of bread, the shriveled butt-end of a terrine, the ribcage of a rabbit congealed in its sauce, a raw egg, and best of all, pork skin. His grand-mother removed them and set them aside for soups, but he watched out for them, he tracked them down, he made off with them with the patience of a rat. The smoked, amber skin, the grease white and gristly, riddled with gashes, the stiff hairs that prickled like the chin of an old woman, it all drove him wild. He munched on the rinds on his pillowcase, his fingers smeared in oil, and fell asleep in it. He didn't care about the meat around the fat.

Grandmother Viaud explained to her neighbors that squinty was not such a bad kid; he just couldn't help it. Lack of sociability.

Dr. Ambreuse, a young woman, asked her if she had ever stolen when she was a little girl. Never, answered old lady Viaud. Her parents would have squashed her. The pains in her spinal column were from a thrashing she'd gotten sixty-four years ago. The family used to be honest, they didn't steal—only criminals did that.

Dr. Ambreuse explained that Alain's eye would be easy to operate on. Mrs. Viaud refused brusquely, aggressively, as revolted as if someone had threatened her with becoming young and beautiful.

Once in a while the doctor let the little boy have a syringe that she was throwing out. She didn't seem to worry that he might hurt himself. He played right in front of her. He squirted out streams of water; he gave injections to apples, carrots, hearts of cabbages, and rags.

He scratched a finger on the beveled edge of the needle on purpose, he let it bleed, and he looked at the young woman with defiance. She didn't react. Satisfied, he sucked on his wound and resumed injecting everything in his grandma's place. Soon the needle broke. The Doctor smiled, spoke, didn't threaten, didn't yell, didn't hit, didn't apply a Band-Aid, didn't whine, and didn't slam the doors. Perplexed, Alain Viaud forgot to steal for the rest of the day.

For a week now René Théret had been catching up on his algebra. He had turned thirteen and being the eldest, had made serious resolutions.

From now on he'd swallow garter snakes, crunch cockroaches, drink venom, caress spiders, and kiss a mountain of frogs on the mouth. In other words, he hardly masturbated, tolerated his parents, had stopped smoking, listened in class, washed every morning from nose to navel, didn't bully his two little sisters, exercised his abdominals on his bedside rug, and sweated over his mathematics.

Inflicting all of this upon himself seemed important. He had even vaguely weighed the idea of going back to mass. But the priest annoyed him. Saint-Rémi had twenty-six thousand inhabitants and other parishes and other priests; René prudently ignored this detail. He had judged it more expedient to scorn the Church based on a single man, the one he knew.

Théret had yet to discover any sort of advantage to his new behavior. If anything, he had a feeling that people were taking advantage of it. Cruelty came to light, stimulated by his gentle nature. Ever since he'd corrected his failings, he'd had to suffer those of others helplessly. He was boiling over: one more day of garter snakes and he'd burst.

"René, what on earth have you done with your shorts, I can't find them."

His mother, a character out of a novel, was yelling in front of the washing machine. The Thérets ran a popular enough delicatessen in old Saint-Rémi. The husband knew his stuff, the wife put on airs, and the clientele quibbled. They made a humble living.

"I put them in the hamper," René answered dully. He sensed a humiliation to come, hunched over. His mom and her shorts. He'd slit the throat of everyone on earth, mother after mother.

Mrs. Théret liked to do her household chores after dinner so that her entourage got a better sense of the slavery she suffered. The husband plunged into his accounts. The children gave one another silent looks. Then Louise Théret put the little girls to bed and turned on the TV. René then had the right to flee.

"Well, I can't find 'em," Mrs. Théret repeated through the sloshing of the water. "You sure you changed your shorts? My little friend, are they still under your bed, or will you come and look for them yourself, I don't have all night!"

At the store, Louise Théret was well polished, didn't wear a smock, even played at being elegant. They said she was a natural blonde. She knew how to be congenial when it could serve her, subtly. Everyone thought the world of her. She was one of the better-looking adults in the neighborhood. But, once the store was closed, she took on the wilted duds and bad moods that can only come out with family.

According to her reveries, she should have been the long-gloved lady from the Champs-Elysées in the advertisement for the *Soir de Paris* fragrance, in *Sélection*. That desirable destiny should have been hers; she despised her loser of a husband and the loser's litter. The clients, their foie gras, their Chinese wines. She despised it all. She hated herself; she loved no one but herself.

"René, I'm waiting! I need my quota of underwear! I won't start a new load just for you."

René had to leave the kitchen, the mathematics textbook, the reassuring symbols, and enter the bathroom, sort through the whole family's underwear with his eyes. Her cheeks hot, her sleeves rolled up, and with a sideways look, Louise Théret hid her pleasure under an air of industriousness.

"She stashed it on purpose," thought René.

In such moments, although only a pubescent child, he felt himself becoming an adolescent, a piece of garbage, something like them. Why have a ridiculous fit of virtue if not in the hopes of escaping all that. But no, who'd escape? He was cornered; they had him, rubbing his nose in it. It was his turn; he had to take it, too. It would've been too easy.

René, blushing, pointed a finger at his dirty shorts, suddenly identified among the several lacy stains, curly like pink, shitty jellyfish, of the girls' underwear. He instantly analyzed the details of each smear, front and back. There was his little dribbling dick, his yellowish asshole, and some gray at the waistband, there, for everyone to see. A revelatory imprint, an abject negative.

With an enormous gesture that mimicked exhaustion, Mrs. Théret shoved the mound of laundry into the machine. Her eyes sparkled with satisfaction. She did a big load every week and wouldn't tolerate her males changing underwear more often. They weren't babies anymore; at their age they shouldn't be dirtying themselves any longer. If her husband or son dared change twice instead of once, she bombarded them with suspicion, questions, and reproaches. They must be leading a double life, or have a shameful disease. They were overloading Mrs. Théret with work; she'd show them she was no servant.

To prove it, she gnashed her teeth, bawled and quarreled like a slovenly maid giving notice. Sometimes she complained so much that someone offered to do the laundry in her place. She trembled with indignation at the thought of this matricide; she refused, harshly and with curt reasons. The machine would break down, they'd mix everything together, they'd waste detergent, and the laundry'd be torn to shreds. She was looking after a tribe of incompetents, her ordeal was unending. Mrs. Théret's reign was total, and her moans irrefutable.

René Théret had grabbed his rain slicker, a trench coat too short at the legs, and he mumbled some words. He was going to the Guillard's to watch the film on the other channel; it ended at eleven thirty or forty.

They trusted the Guillards. Ever since he had become a widower, the father had been rubbing elbows with the police; they'd let him do the painting work. Marc, fourteen years old, helped him after class. He was skilled and a good son. Old Guillard wasn't stingy when he paid him. They didn't have workers, but they had a stash squirreled away. No one knew that after dinner Old Guillard shut himself up in his room with a flask of cognac or aged rum. Marc and René did, and they took advantage of it.

On his birthday, René's first resolution had been to break it off with the others.

He had missed a meeting even though recently they'd been taking place on the land his parents had in the suburban markets (they called it the gardens). There was a soft, narrow, fairly clean river that went down to the sea and to their boat shed. A dilapidated fence delimited the edges of the land without closing it off. It was a fallow vegetable plot. The small boats were never used; the Thérets had gotten them from God knows who when they'd bought the land. They were letting them rot away.

René would go to tonight's get-together with Marc. He couldn't wait any longer. His familial and scholarly virtues had lasted a week: seven days too many.

His bike seat was wet. He wiped it with a slap, climbed on, and set off in the rain.

Raymonde Seignelet brought out the pasta and, with the stammering shriek she used for a voice, she threatened:

"This's real spaghetti! The Italian way! A real sauce! Not from a can!"

"Just look at the meat in it!" she added. She set the dish down and eyed the spaghetti as if daring it to say otherwise.

The four boys facing the trouble-brewing dish displayed slow lolls of circumspect necks, and slight stirring of cautious shoulders. Submissiveness, disquiet lurked, and a faint hunger for burnt fat.

Mrs. Seignelet sat down curtly, belying her oozing shape.

Robert Seignelet, a lumbering chief subaltern at the electric company, considered the pasta drowned in brown and lumpy sauce. He tipped a quivering nose, like a gourmet won over, and let out a peremptory rumble of approval.

The children relaxed too soon; Mrs. Seignelet was in no mood to be satisfied with so brief an homage.

"It's not like all that garbage from the store," she added sourly.

She explained the dish's merits. Jean-Baptiste Seignelet, eleven years old, shot a mocking glance to his brother Dominique, thirteen, and examined with a biologist's astonishment the blackish meatballs bogged down in the sauce. He was pretty, with a cheery disposition. He got a hold of himself before his mother noticed his goings-on.

Mr. Seignelet had no opinion on factory-made sauces and helped himself, intensifying his mask of familial and gastronomic solemnity. In reality, he was an alcoholic and ate very little, without appetite, without desire. His swollen belly, his bulging chest, his thick neck were all impressive and led one to overlook his wasted limbs. What's more, he would slap his children like a homicidal butcher. They were calm, theatrical executions.

The boys' plates were filled to the brim; they needed to grow. Raymonde Seignelet stuffed them with lard and didn't let them talk back, which is to say, leave anything uneaten.

"Mmm, mmm," emoted Mr. Seignelet, gulping down a big coil of spaghetti that he'd formed around his fork with a roll of the elbow, pomposity, verbose precepts, and touristy verdicts. His progeny did likewise.

Once his palate was clear, he fulfilled his conjugal duties.

"Mmm, mmm," he affirmed. "They're so much better than in Italy. It makes sense, complete sense. Since a French cordon

bleu made them. French! That is, the best in the world! …
Mmm."

The table chewed over this notion. Robert Seignelet ate
another mouthful, which emptied his plate. He uncapped his
second liter of wine and said:

"My dear, it's, mmm … It's, I'll say it, it's … luscious! It's luscious! Dear, your sauce is luscious!"

The children exchanged anxious glances. In their comic strips,
a lush was someone who drank too much wine, and despite the
ample and moist lower lip with which their father had illustrated
the adjective, they sensed danger in it, a gaffe. They waited for
Mrs. Seignelet's reaction but didn't dare to look in her direction.

She was eating, as it was. And the custom was to avert the
eyes, to simulate indifference, for Raymonde Seignelet was a
repellent glutton. She wasn't aware of it. She liked to think of
herself as having manners, style, a petit-bourgeois education; you
would have assumed that she was neat and quiet during dinner.
But food threw all that out the window.

Mrs. Seignelet took her spaghetti without any fork rigmarole.
She sucked them up seven or eight at a time, like a kid with a
cold snorting back parallel strands of snot. The pasta followed a
single curve from the plate to her stomach, but slurped, lapped,
severed on the way.

When she heard the word "luscious" behind her oral fanfare,
Raymonde Seignelet merely rolled her eyes to the ceiling, and
then shot a sharp black look towards the bottles and her husband. She checked to make sure her sons were eating properly.
She glared at the youngest, Philippe, a slightly frail seven-year-
old child, who was dillydallying; and then she returned to her
praying mantis mastication.

Finally, rather pleased, she put on a pernickety, finicky,
falsely disgusted look and, with the she-rat nose that was part of
her motherly ritual, she chirped:

"No! No! No way around it! It don't look like no Ragú! Pff! Prrrf! Uh uh! You can't say mine isn't the real thing!"

She sniggered pityingly. Immediately, the whole table sniggered pityingly, but without conviction.

Offended, Raymonde Seignelet insisted.

"No! No! Not the real thing!" she chirped.

She took another slurp, right ear tilted to her plate as if she was listening to the pasta agree and grovel. When she lifted it up to her mouth, she gaped, exposed her teeth, and stuck out her tongue. She had eyes like a blind man, and snapped up the pasta brutally, grimacing like a puking dog and making a plughole pop. Then she formed her mouth into a muzzle again:

"And mine doesn't even have meat! Not in my sauce! … It ain't no Ragú! Roasted meat, you must be joking! That pigswill … As if I roasted it myself!… No! It's meatless!" She chirped again as she sucked away. "None at all! Pff! Pff! Mine!"

She pointed to the meatballs with a thrust of her chin, and sniggered pityingly. The table sniggered pityingly. Bertrand, the eldest, fifteen years old, an oaf with a fat ass, a fat neck, a fat chin, and square cheeks inflamed with yellow-tipped zits, protested with a malicious smile and a hoarse voice:

"Good, mom! It's a real good one! Heck yeah!"

With an assured swipe of his palm, he readjusted the gold-rimmed glasses on top of his nose, a boxer's nose speckled with oozing black heads. He wore a mask of deliberation that mimicked his father's. He tapped his plate, turned the overcooked pasta in their pond of vaguely tomatoed flour, scorched in oil. He sopped everything up with four fingers and a big shovel of bread. He smiled again, chewed. He liked having peaceful relations with his superiors.

There was a satisfied silence; they swallowed; they were all in unison.

Then a high-pitched voice whispered:

"My tummy hurts."

It was Philippe. His late birth, his slight build, and his presence never ceased to be a surprise.

Everyone gave a start. Philippe, who was really ill, didn't notice the stir he'd caused. He wanted permission to go be sick, but didn't dare ask. He was afraid: you weren't supposed to vomit what mommy had provided. He would have liked to hold it in, but his stomach refused to obey. He was what housewives called a sensitive kid, a difficult child, a fussy eater, a nuisance, and a headache.

Mrs. Seignelet meditated on a retort, hesitated quickly between two attitudes, her eyes screwed up.

With a dangerously low, slow voice, she said:

"No, no, it doesn't hurt Philippe. I know you. Did you go poo at school?"

"Yes," whispered the child.

He was turning white.

"I haven't seen you go poo since then, though, have I?"

"No," admitted Phillipe.

He knit his brow pleadingly; he was going to vomit at the table. There was a showy, duck-blue nylon oriental rug underneath it, full of flowers.

Mrs. Seignelet realized that her son wasn't going to hold it in. She seemed to think for a moment. She grew sugary, took on a contralto tone:

"Ok, go now. Hurry up. That's enough already. You want me to take you?"

"No," whispered the little boy, rising. He fled.

They heard him launching an enormous stream of thick mud into the water of the toilet bowl. They envied Philippe a bit. They swallowed back their saliva. They were nauseated: little ones were really nothing but bowels.

They were all quiet. Mrs. Seignelet shrugged, and resumed in her inane, yelping voice:

"He never goes to the bathroom! All he does is play! He doesn't even take the time to do his business! And he doesn't go at school either! He's lying! His teacher told me! He's telling fibs! Or he wouldn't be sick after two or three noodles! He didn't even finish his plate! … Look at that! What a waste of time! … And you," she continued, "you aren't going to leave me with that, are you?"

She grabbed the serving dish where her grub was congealing. The children held out their plates again.

"Truly luscious, dear," repeated Mr. Seignelet tiredly, as if he just had a painful little reflux of compliments. He poured himself some wine. His gestures were growing fuzzy. There were some drops on the tablecloth. He was hammered.

Philippe flushed the toilet and went back into the dining room. Mrs. Seignelet gave him a stern reception and decided to put him to bed without delay since he was sick.

She waited, exasperated, as he drank a bit of water. Philippe was a nuisance to his mother. His sensitive digestive system systematically refused and denounced meals made by shrews and cafeteria food. His scrawniness was enough to shame people who had social standing, people who took up space, who were respectable mommies. When they'd been so see Dr. Jurieux, he'd prescribed fresh, light, carefully-chosen food: what the child wanted to eat, and no more. Mrs. Seignelet had felt accused of not knowing how to feed her children. She reacted badly. She slapped Philippe whenever she got a chance; that would teach him to have a normal stomach. She went on feeding him as before, threatening him with purgatives, enemas, paraffin, and even worse retaliatory measures. The little boy would obey, swallow, turn pale, throw it all up, get punished.

"Your brothers never made a fuss like this! Never!"

Raymonde Seignelet snarled as she put the sick child to bed. She couldn't take it anymore. It was torture, having this child every evening at the dinner table. What a fuss he made. Things had to change. Now. If he tried it again he'd get a real spanking. And he'd go poo in front of her, like a little kid, if that was what it took. Maybe he'd eaten something on the sly, bought himself candy? Junk food, that was for sure. And with what money? Was he also turning into a thief? And he promised he hadn't stolen anything. Right! She'd go check her wallet.

She tucked Philippe in the way you'd buckle a straitjacket and left. The child stayed alone in the dark. He was ice-cold from vomiting, his teeth chattering. He loosened the bed sheets a little by wriggling his shoulders, and curled himself into a ball, burrowed up to his ears.

Jean-Baptiste Seignelet never had any trouble sneaking out of the house at night. He wasn't a worrier by nature; he enjoyed himself, wheedled, and played tricks. He shared a room with his older brother, Bertrand. The latter, an industrious high school student, went to bed at half-past ten, read or chatted for a few minutes, then turned out the light. A small glimmer would remain at Jean-Baptiste's nightstand, who'd put it out shortly after. Bertrand masturbated with the sheets up to his neck, wriggling as if he were changing his shorts under a bath towel at the beach. He'd soon be snoring, after wiping his genitals off with a special hanky—stiff, crackly, gluey, yellow and greenish—that he kept hidden away. Sometimes he'd wash it.

Mr. and Mrs. Seignelet, even if they stayed up late to watch a film or make a scene, would forget their children's existence as soon as they retreated to their bedrooms. The doors were closed. Each was in his proper place: Raymonde and Robert, Jean-Baptiste and Bertrand, Philippe and Dominique. The parents would never have gone on a nightly inspection, or even eavesdropped, spied on or deciphered the imperfect silences. They seemed to believe that well-trained children didn't have a will of their own. At night, you stored them in puppet boxes after use, where they remained dumb, immobile, and frightened until the following day—when they were taken out and manipulated all over again, like ventriloquist dummies.

The Seignelets lived in a house with a small garden that they owned. There was still seventeen-years left on the mortgage. This house was located to the north of Saint-Rémi, at the periphery where constructions of a kind previously unseen around the island had been sprouting up for the last twenty-five years. This was housing for office workers, low, cube-shaped, and already dilapidated buildings, individual prefab houses that were pretentious, piddling, planted crookedly on plots of landfill, each with its own lawn, its own lawn-mower, and its own withered and expensive-looking Thuja trees.

Without even waiting for his brother to fall asleep, Jean-Baptiste rose in the darkness, grabbed his clothes, and went out. He locked himself in the bathroom and put his clothes back on. He hid his pajamas behind the toilet tank.

He slipped into the garden via the kitchen. He didn't have a bike: he was meeting up with the older Cormaillon who was giving him a ride on his Solex.

The night was nice. The rain felt pleasant. Jean-Baptiste, well protected and warm, hummed a tune. He forgot they could hear him from his house. Anyway, that house there, that neighborhood, those parental barracks, those battered plots of land weren't his home,

One of the boys, to the left of young Lescot, kept repeating: "My knife's not a joke! It's a Loubinox!"

Lescot was the youngest at eight years of age. They'd never seen him at their nightly meetings before. His thirteen-year-old cousin Hervé Pellisson had brought him. He had taken advantage of the fact that Mrs. Lescot was overwhelmed with work: a widow in her thirties, she ran a humble café by the canneries near the port. She cooked a few dishes, mussels, omelets, stews, and vegetable casseroles. She stayed open late. The clientele of her café was lively, plentiful, mostly families. Hervé, who liked the vibe, often came over to help. He was a good boy, her nephew Hervé, always in good spirits, a helpful, good Christian, and he idolized the little one.

"Did you see that?" Joachim Lescot asked him, pointing at the beams of the boat shelter suddenly illuminated by a flutter from the lamp.

"See what?" Hervé asked.

"Up there," little Lescot whispered respectfully. "You didn't see? Well, it's full of spider h-hairs! …"

Hervé laughed and kissed his cheek:

"It's 'webs,' not hairs!" he corrected. He leaned to the boys sitting in front of him:

"Hey, check out what my cousin just said! …"

A bigger boy was getting everyone to turn off his flashlight and quiet down. Joachim Lescot recognized him: it was Guillard. The child separated the bigger boys into two categories: those who talked to him and those who despised him. Marc Guillard and Hervé made up the first kind: all the others formed the second. Joachim listened.

But he was sleepy. He had trouble understanding their sentences. He was bored. The small boat on which he was sitting was dipping slightly into the water, and some boys were rocking it back and forth with their butts.

Joachim put his thumb in his mouth, curled his index finger around his nose and began to sleep with his eyes open, nodding gently. The only remaining light came from a candle stub around which they'd constructed a pebble cage.

Later, Joachim closed his eyes. He was slumping. His cousin took him on his knees, leaned him against his chest, held him with one hand, put the other hand between their thighs, and kissed him noiselessly. Joachim brought his head closer and let himself go.

Later still, there was a movement of damp and panting boys who entered the shelter with a gust of cold air. Flashlights were briefly turned on. Lescot opened his eyes and asked what was going on.

"It's Théret and Roquin and the others," Hervé explained. "Coming back."

He still had his hand on Joachim's stiff little pecker, and was tickling his palm with it. The child didn't ask another question.

But it wasn't over. They talked for a long time. Someone had mentioned Roche-Notre-Dame. They uttered the word "girls." Several voices protested. What followed was said in hushed tones. An agreement was reached; Joachim went back to sleep; Hervé soon woke him and they left. The boys scattered. Joachim found himself back in his bed without knowing how he'd gotten there.

Laure Boitard taught literature at the mixed high school in Saint-Rémi (which also had a public middle-school), and for fifteen years now had been Maurice Glairat's lover, a philosophy teacher in the same school. They were born on the island.

Both single, they lived together, had two children, were a scandal, mingled with the upper crust of the island, were going on fifty. They covered culture for *The Reunited Republican*, a government opposition daily, which was widely read in the county to which the island belonged.

Glairat penned opinion pieces. Laure Boitard wrote book reviews and critical reviews of music and local art.

She was no longer happy. Maurice Glairat drank too much, smoked too much, and pontificated too much in the cafés with his court of high school seniors. He boasted of an unstaged play, actually never finished, and of an unwritten philosophical summa that he drooled about everywhere, glass after glass. He was aging.

Nevertheless, Laure and Maurice, dressed, styled their hair, copulated, read, spoke, and thought *young*. They were not a day late. They were the intelligence of the place and they didn't hide it.

Their two children, a boy and a girl, were well treated. Even so, an ongoing puberty sharpened the benign character of the twelve-year-old François-Gérard.

Laure Boitard glanced at the time. Midnight soon. Maurice would come home drunk, desperate, soulful, and marvelous. She had to finish writing her piece for *The Reunited Republican* by tomorrow morning. She counted the lines. She'd expressed her admiration for three novels; she couldn't take it any longer, but she was still missing a good chunk of text.

She left her desk with a sigh. She dug into the pile of review copies with a vague appetite for the medical. That would perk her up. She noticed a softcover devoted to diabetes for the general public. What a relief. She could review this without having to think a thing. She opened it, sat back down, set it near her type-writer, and began to write the article, randomly fishing about, as was her habit, for sentences that she linked together with the aplomb for which she'd gained a reputation of competence.

Her hips were aching, she felt exhausted, beautiful, mature, heart-rending. Very beautiful perhaps. Very. Maybe a vodka later on, very strong, very cold, in a very handsome glass, very simple? An orange juice? A pain to take out the appliance. Check if any in a carton.

"… The answer is a resounding yes … And too bad for the morning croissant! For, indeed, Dr. Prot will frankly confess that in the case of diabetes the issue of sugar arises, because of the presence of a lack of insulin, which the pancreas is, alas, no longer secreting.

"Even still, is that a reason to warrant the villainous word of diabetes? Alas, the answer is yes, once again! Fortunately however, any rush towards disquiet would be unwarranted haste! For, indeed, this illness can be easily treated when detected early—heredity (in which pregnant women play a determining role) is far from being a decisive factor in all cases.

"Such is what Dr. Prot affirms. For he does not hesitate to affirm, indeed, that this illness can indisputably be cured if it isn't detected too late. Under the condition, of course, that such authorizing conditions be strictly fulfilled by the affected person himself, who must play a significant role in this instance. Good advice to follow, without a doubt."

Shoot, and prepare her class on *Phaedra*. She abominated that play. Did the author like women? Those writers. The curriculum. It must all be changed.

"Nevertheless, even so, one must take up a strict diet and restrict all fruit intake, both being essential. Such is the virtue of this precious little book accessible to all, and which shall certainly serve to all those men or women that it will help. Perhaps you, tomorrow!"

Laure Boitard loved her playful, congenial tone: she knew her job. She sensed that her sentences were a bit jarring, but that was journalism, you had to overlook certain imperfections. You had to be on time.

Besides, no one ever read her articles. Not even the typographer who set them. She received compliments; she had her reputation. They simply checked that her signature or initials were there each week; otherwise, the sort of greetings she received wouldn't have been quite the same.

She went to the kitchen and fixed herself an iced vodka-orange, light. She returned to her armchair with dreamy elf footsteps. She felt like composing a very beautiful poem, very pure, very silent. Oh, and that mummy of a Racine! No, her prep would have to wait. Enough with chores for now. She drank the vodka and suddenly felt good. (… A light and icy vodka-orange, if you are weary … for you must know that … she began mentally typing out in fragments.)

She prepared herself a second glass, stronger.

She snuggled in a corner of sofa, feet folded beneath her, like a little girl, like a cat. She was being interviewed for *The Reunited*

Republican after Glairat's suicide, the rebel prophet, mentor to a generation ripe with future harvests. (… You must know that we loved each other too much to get married … truly, Maurice was too respectful of the, the … in me … and the ties that bound us … yes, he … yes, deeply … his difficult relationship to the *corps propre* … a relationship, he said, that he deeply questioned and …)

"Crap and that recital tomorrow."

Essential to write the article tonight, final deadline: or else it wouldn't come out before ten days and the pianist, daughter of the old assistant-prefect, would be furious, and would pull some strings.

Laure Boitard thought about Maurice again. A genius. Authentic. Different. Above everything, above all. But how to stop him from drinking, from emptying himself of his substance, from filling himself with alcohol? Otherwise he'd never accomplish his cyclopean oeuvre. It was up to her to help him. (… Yes, it's true, after all … alcohol … a double-edged poison … That's what's wrong … a drug … It's a drug after all … A drug. Alcohol. Me. Save him. Him. Fast. Succeed. That's the price to pay for the work. His. Ours. I must. Protect. Inspire. Procreate. The one whom. To be the one. Laura, *laurus*, laurels. *Lugdunum*. Lyon. *Populus*, poultry. Laura de Noves. *Il Canzoniere*. Laurel. Laurent, gril (grill?), laurel-thyme (laurustinus?), laurel-sauce, died hair: L'Oreal. Did Dante really like women. Truly. That's what's the matter. Lauds, laureate, Lawry, Laurel, Hardy; Lauraceous: sassafras. Loan Load Lode Liar Law Lain. Leach. Leech. Me … to be me.)

A soft door sound (opening, closing?) ruptured her chain of thoughts. It seemed that Maurice Glairat was coming home. (… Such a soft sound … happy, perhaps … happiness … How… marvelous …)

She prepared a warm voice, a face full of emotion, leach leech; she got up.

"Darling," she called out. "Maurice?"

No, there was no one there. Actually yes. A movement she felt behind her, in the darkness of the recess, towards the children's room.

(Is it Maurice …? Him, taking shelter there? Fallen so low? The kids, when the both of us … We … No. Madness. Let me check.)

She opened Amélie-Lyane's door first, the fourteen year-old. The adolescent, with a ravishing crook of the elbow and her head resting upon it, was snoring. All flowers, all pimples, all shadow, all vapor, centenary laces, rose shrimp, black nails, liliaceous. Laure Boitard admired her in the light of the corridor (… I'm a bit of a lesbian … like all women).

She closed the door, felt a passing vertigo (so little alcohol?…), and moved to the living room to get her glass of vodka. Then she went and opened François-Gérard's door. No light, but she heard a loud sound of box springs.

"François-Gérard?"

"… Yes," said the boy.

"Oh, honey, aren't you asleep? Can I turn on the light?"

"Oh, please, no, Laure, it'll hurt my eyes!"

"Sure honey, I understand. Did you make that noise?"

"What noise?" asked François, feigning surprise.

"I mean … the door! That door sound!"

"Oh yeah, when I hmm, when I had a piss!"

"A piss, honey?" said Laure Boitard. "Really. But … you forgot to flush the toilet, didn't you?"

"Oh yeah. Right. 'Cause I couldn't. Laure you know."

"What do you mean *couldn't*, honey? Is it broken?"

"Hmmmm, no, I mean, couldn't piss." (François's voice took on a distressed tempo.) "I don't know what's wrong with me tonight, I just can't sleep, aw fuck, I don't know what's up. Sheeesh! What a bummer."

"There, there, honey," said Laure Boitard. "Don't worry. I think I understand. Yes, I understand! ... Girls have sensitive issues at your age too, you know ... The relationship to the *corps propre* stops being, in you ... Hmm ... you know ..."

She took a sip. She scanned the penumbra for her son. He had his blankets pulled up to his neck. "*Too* high," she thought. "What is he hiding? ... That? ..."

"How about I talk to you about me!" Laure Boitard continued. "Yes, me, your mother, there's no need to look farther than that! But ... honey, I hear what you're telling me, what you're expressing. More than you even think. My son ... I'm sure that—one day—you'll make someone very, very profoundly *happy*. I know it. Really ... There's no need to be worried. Just relax."

"Hey, Laure, do I still have to go to school tomorrow?" asked François, who excelled at taking advantage of the worst situations.

"Honey, I know ... You know the importance of ... That's really not what this is about, but still ... Wouldn't you rather go to sleep quickly, and tomorrow, I assure you ... You'd be sad not to have gone. That bloody school. It's idiotic, yes. But we all need those kinds of ... regulations. Would you like to take a pill to help, nothing over the counter of course, just some herbs?"

François accepted school, refused the pill. Laure sighed and closed the door.

(... Where is Maurice ... I'm worried. How stupid. About an ... an ... infidelity. Ludicrous.)

She wrote her music review for the next day.

Once François heard the typewriter, he turned on his bedside lamp, and threw back his blankets. He was still fully dressed. He got up, put on his pajamas, and looked for the shoes he'd quickly thrown under the bed when he came in. They were muddy.

He got back into bed, this time for good. That was a close call with the nutcase.

He blushed and laughed at his audacity. This was his first nocturnal escapade. He'd never imagined such a thing was possible. He couldn't believe he'd dared, and succeeded. He'd taken the service stair of the small building, wearing socks, his heart beating, and his spirit awake as never before.

Now he felt he understood everything. A huge weight had been lifted. He considered another bold move that he'd been itching to do. On all fours, he'd go see his sister sleeping, that numbskull. He'd touch her all over, with his flashlight; he'd snoop, ogle, and steal. Sniff. Cling to her. Shove the finger in, the dick. In the butt, in the middle of the hole, on the nose. Eww, lick the pussy. Nibble the ears. Bite, pinch, bone.

Shake. He was masturbating. He almost interrupted himself to put his reverie into action. He came. He patted around with an index finger to see if there had been sperm. Nothing, a droplet of ooze. It didn't smell like anything. Still, it should happen soon. And …

Laure Boitard was typing. She was exhausted from having already imagined so many compliments. How could you be critical when you were yourself a critic? It could backfire on you, you never know. Even strangers whom you thought were powerless sometimes had connections, occult support. And to butcher a book you had to read it. No time for that. She promised herself to type out a table of appreciative formulae, in all styles. Like an essay writing handbook, chapter *Learn How To Develop Your Argument.* Two or three afternoons of intelligent work and her columns would be written for her entire life. Get to it.

On her desk, she had squarely set the big jar of orange juice, the vodka, and the ice cubes in a Duralex bowl.

She would have been a poet, a novelist, someone.

"… The audience, who will have been struck as I was by Maïté Ducuq-Lepousseur's talent, will be unanimous to recognize that, neither Chopin nor, Beethoven, nor P. Petit, nor H. Limpuisset (author of a brilliant *Toccata* so, modern!) could find anything to criticize in this player. For indeed her energetic interpretations with striking nuance each touched, each time, it must be said, the heart of the matter. Music-wise. For the piano, even. This is why the large attentive but respectful audience acclaimed that endurance with which Maïté Ducuq-Lepousseur dominated and imposed the night's program, impressive and for which we all …"

This was a local artist, an old family, farms, property, administration, and alliances. The very best of Saint-Rémi (which was the county seat). She liked to give recitals twice a year, in the fifteenth-century armory of the celebrated citadel. She taught advanced piano at the municipal conservatory.

The noise of a door again.

Really the front door. Him.

Boitarda came running, Laure feet, to Maurice Glairat. Her vodka in hand, tintinnabulating voice (… tinabule?). Mischievous little Laurette. Sassafras, camphor, cinnamon.

"Darling."

"Shit … Beeeeeeeeeeeeeeeeeeeh …"

Maurice. And what a state he was in. (… Admirable return, admirable scene. This admirable book: us. Simply.)

Meanwhile, a second little transparent drop dripped from François-Gérard. He was sleeping flat on his stomach; he had fallen in love with the mattress. A cannon would not have woken him.

2

"Oh," moaned Mrs. Lescot, soft and doleful, "they've murdered an unfortunate old woman for fifty francs! …"

She was leafing through the morning paper.

"How much is fifty francs?" asked Joachim Lescot. He only understood sums in cents. He was clean, ravishing, freshly combed. He was eating buttered toast with hot chocolate.

"5000 cents, my little chicken," said Yvonne Lescot. "They're dreadful. A poor old woman from around here. Just like that!"

"5000 cents! … Wow, she was so rich!"

Joachim widened his eyes in admiration.

"No, kiddo, it's ain't nothing!" Hervé corrected. "They stash their dough in their savings account. There's nothing left to steal. It's totally dumb to fleece 'em!"

He always took his breakfast at Mrs. Lescot's café, in the kitchen. Then he would take Joachim to school. He went to tech school himself; there, he'd meet up with Guillard, Cormaillon, and the others.

Joachim, in fact, did not need to be chaperoned: he went everywhere else by himself. Hervé took care of him mostly for pleasure.

"That's a lot of dough," Joachim insisted, amazed.

"Where was it?" Hervé asked. "Where did it happen, auntie?"

"I don't know sweetheart," said Mrs. Lescot in a desolate voice. "It's just too much, all this drama … It might just be that some kids did it, little eighteen or twenty year olds … Stupid kids! They didn't even do it on purpose; the paper said that she had a heart condition. She took a fright when she saw them, of course, at her age … and that was that. It's terrible."

"Hmm, must be kinda … kinda scary!" agreed young Lescot. "What if there was one here, in the kitchen! Who just popped up like that!" he added with enthusiasm.

He laughed. Hervé laughed as well.

"You have no heart," Yvonne Lescot reproached tenderly. "That poor woman, to end up like that …"

Hervé had picked up the paper. He found the article.

"She had sixty-five francs. Not fifty," he exclaimed. "Sixty-five. In her pocketbook."

Joachim rolled up his eyes in consideration, and fluttered his hand as if his thumb was burning:

"That's a lot of dough! … Hervé, read it to me?"

Hervé read the article in a lively voice. Mrs. Lescot sighed at each sentence, heavy-lidded, her beautiful face thickly blurred with commiseration. She glanced at the pendulum clock.

"You still have time for a toast, children," she offered.

Joachim shook his head no. Hervé said he was going to toast himself a bit of bread, just like that, over the gas flame, poking it with a fork. The smell peaked Joachim's interest. Together they nibbled the burnt bread, toasted with melted butter. Mrs. Lescot, who had a sweet tooth, accepted a very buttery mouthful, which she dipped into her son's hot chocolate.

"Still," she said with a sad smile, "you're not being kind to that poor woman."

"It's 'cause she got scared, momma. Otherwise she wouldn't be dead. It's her fault!" Joachim affirmed.

"Cannibal!" Mrs. Lescot said to him, laughing. "You're two little cannibals!"

She thought she would go and reheat herself a little coffee, and she started clearing the table to peel the vegetables. Hervé wanted to help her. She declined.

She sent the lot off to school. She reread the article: the victim was an old lady Mrs. Lescot didn't know, someone from the village in the vicinity of Saint-Rémi. They raised sheep, down there in the valley.

In that neck of the woods there were always good vegetables to be picked. Lovely early greens. She was in bed, she heard a noise, she went to her kitchen, she saw them, and she died.

How do they know all this, thought Mrs. Lescot. The male-factors had left no trace, despite the rainy weather.

I would have stayed in bed; let 'em take it all! … Old timers, they're a bit crazy, she thought again.

She admired her vegetables, imagining the wholesome cuisine she would make. A soup, first. Then, sheep breast and scrag end stew, with carrots, turnips, potatoes, onions. Yvonne Lescot salivated and cut herself a little piece of cheese.

She never opened before nine, and she didn't close before midnight. She'd explain it to people: she was a night owl. The café was beginning to be successful. There had been two difficult years after the death of her husband. It had been a bad crowd. She almost sold. But what to do, and where?

Little by little, her tasty dishes, her plump and motherly youth, her cleanliness, and her kindness had attracted a new kind of clientele. Single ladies at noon, honest workers. Thrifty employees. Some bon vivants. Less bawling and drinking, more eating, more chatting, and there was no shame in bringing the kids. One day she would move on from simple bar food to a restaurant with set prices. But she didn't enjoy waking early; going to bed early, that was the obstacle.

Oh, what about making some tasty snails for lunch.

Hervé was helping out like an angel. He would have been better suited in front of an oven than at school; these laws are idiotic. Whenever Mrs. Lescot rewarded her nephew, the latter would use the money to buy Joachim a toy or candies. That was one beloved little boy, and he didn't even realize it! Mrs. Lescot's eyes teared up a bit with tenderness. She cut herself a sliver of bacon.

He thinks sixty-five francs is a lot! She smiled. Joachim wouldn't hurt a fly. He was sad that steaks came from animals. Yet everyone has to eat, Yvonne sighed to herself. The poor beasts, the poor things, the little rabbits, the little calves, the little sausages, oh yes. All the little beasts. We're so mean …

She lifted and extended her arms in front of her to peel the onions without stinging her eyes. She rinsed her hands. She drank her coffee. Time to open soon. It was slow 'till eleven o'clock, but that wasn't a good reason. Everyone needs a routine.

She preferred her coffee black. Nonetheless, she prepared a real *café au lait* for the clients: the very finely brewed coffee would infuse in the milk, sugared beforehand. Clients drank bowls of it, gave her compliments, believed it was made with cream, had milk moustaches. What a delight. It was quite a bargain. A blue and white enameled coffee maker that could hold almost three liters. She needed someone with strong arms!

Hervé's parents both worked in a factory, at the fish cannery. She dressed the sardines; he maintained the machinery. He earned a good salary. They were never around, though they only lived a hundred meters away. The factory was in the back of the old port. Mrs. Pellisson would have liked a position at the cookie factory. She was being patient.

It wasn't surprising that Hervé took refuge at his aunt's, in the café. Actually it was convenient, it relieved Mrs. Pellisson from having to make breakfast, dinner (Hervé took his lunch at the cafeteria). At the end of the month, they'd figure out the money part; there were never any issues. And it was an opportunity to catch up, to see each other a bit.

The only time Hervé would get in trouble was when he came home too late at night. Oh, they didn't hit him; that wasn't the Pellisson style. They weren't soft, but the idea of beating a kid would have made them take a step back. Why not insult a door, put a plant in the corner, and slap a drippy faucet?

A veal foot, a spicy sauce. Mrs. Lescot salivated. She almost ate again. She reprimanded herself; she bit into a sugar cube. Now the windows.

It used to be an old grocery; she'd kept the iron roll-down shutters.

On the threshold, Yvonne Lescot contemplated the long empty streets, the factory walls, the flat horizon, and the old geometrical neighborhood with single-story houses. It was still cool. May was coming up. She would buy a cotton shirt and blue velvet knee-pants for Joachim. She'd lose weight for an embroidered blouse, or she'd take out a seam here and there. And on Sundays, Joachim's laughing neck in a bowtie, and she'd also tie a ribbon on herself.

Besides, for the first of May, they'd all meet, with the Pellissons; they'd take the ferry, go to the continent. The cows weren't as handsome there, but the landscape was less flat. The children saw a lot of cars and you couldn't smell the sea at all, which was strange. Tasteless odor of the interior.

Sheep tripe with red beans. If Pussort had cooked any, that is. But the beans were pretty old. Joachim, that'd be easy: two small knobs of veal or a small sole, a little bit of raw butter, no parsley, he spat it out. A handful of delicate vegetables, just barely cooked, so that they still had all their good vitamins and that they crunched, crunched, under his pretty teeth. Then a Laughing Cow, and a chocolate ice cream popsicle. He liked ice cream so much. It was fatty, sugary; it made his little belly all soft, all sugar.

Mrs. Lescot's eyes moistened a little with tenderness. No, it was not that hot. She poured herself a tear of old marc.

Maybe roasting a pretty young chicken, if there were any at Beauregard's. Joachim would be happy. He'd yum yum that little chick; he'd munch munch those thighs; he would be covered in shiny sauce. Yvonne Lescot, seduced by these images, decided on poultry.

She was still flabbergasted to have a son. Incredulous, even. This had been going on since Joachim's birth. If she glanced away, he would vanish in smoke, because it was impossible that he really existed.

Too short a marriage, widowhood, then motherhood: what had happened? Yvonne Lescot no longer knew. Once the little boy started to walk, the days were sectioned by long moments of not seeing him. He had disappeared forever. She had been dreaming. Now, a ghost-child would be forever paying her incorporeal visits.

Then she feared he'd die, far away from her; when he'd go to bed, cozy, winsome, in his room, he escaped her: he was about to stop breathing, his heart would stop beating, his flesh would turn cold and green. For the first few years, Yvonne Lescot woke up several times a night to make sure Joachim wasn't dead. Then she reasoned with herself. She now forbade herself these inquiries: but she had thoughts, painful twinges.

Every morning, she trembled at the thought of discovering a corpse in the little bed. Or of finding it empty. It was possible. Her husband had already been erased in that way.

No, there was no way to know people actually existed. You couldn't even be certain you yourself did. Take this poor woman in the paper; she couldn't have predicted that she'd be dead. If she had, she wouldn't have budged from her bed.

Clients came in; they drank beer. As for Joachim, he preferred shandy, mostly lemonade, of course, with three drops of beer to tint it. It had the color of his pee; it foamed just like it. Gone astray, Mrs. Lescot hugged the fat turnips she was peeling. Then she laughed at herself.

"You'd better get married again, my little lady!" she said aloud.

She stopped laughing. She did not really miss her husband. She had no desire for a man.

The Roquins sold produce. Julien was their last child, and they'd had him late. Now, the others were in the army, and there was only this one left to raise. A nasty kid, a sullen nature. Still, he was a good-looking boy, solid, not at all stupid for his ten years. But he'd skip school, hang around who knows where, and frown when they asked him to help a little with the business.

Last night, it rained: the vegetable gardens were muddy today. You'd have to wait till the land mopped itself dry, but the weather was still humid, with a yellowish sun and without heat. Simone Roquin had uncovered some raised beds; she was working in big boots, bent over them. Her husband spent the morning in Saint-Rémi, using the excuse of tools, engines.

Simone Roquin was no dupe. The guy would hear from her when he got back. If he had the slightest injury, and said one word that didn't mesh with the rest, she'd make a scene.

All of a sudden, Mrs. Roquin noticed footprints, barely visible, spaced widely apart, crossing part of the garden.

Now who's the bastard who's been walking 'round here?

She went to have a look. The prints were little, but clear enough to be followed, purposeful.

A kid? … The hell was he doing here? …

With her special flair, she smelled an occasion to be furious, to yell, perhaps to give a beating. She studied the tracks.

They lead to Julien's window! … That little fool, why would he enter his bedroom through the window? He's nuts! That kid is nuts! …

She got a hold of the situation, outraged herself, analyzed.

No, he didn't just go in! … He went out. Out, out! … And when was that? Little bastard. "What were you up to? What the fuck did that little piece of trash do …"

She inspected the surroundings again, went into the house, took her boots off, and examined Julien's room.

"You, my little fellow!" she growled. "Just wait until you get home, we're gonna set a few things straight. Oh this'll be the day. Yeah, have it out, with both of them. Those two, shit. Shit … Bastards! … Bastards."

She meant the child and the father.

She felt sure that the tracks were from the previous night. So Julien had gone prowling during the night? That took the cake. Hope he made sure his back was ready. She let loose a fair amount of imprecations at the walls, threats, insults, turned her tone up a notch, enraged by the fact that she was alone:

"The beating's gonna get good and bloody! The little shit!"

She was clenching her teeth; she could have beaten herself she was so impatient. She put her boots back on.

She had to plant a bed of March seeds that had already sprouted and wouldn't wait any longer: tomatoes, zucchinis, cucumbers, and an attempt at melons. But it was an almost delicate work, and she was too upset. She went to the kitchen in her boots, and screamed at herself:

"Shit, fuck the mud! And I gotta clean up! Right! I'm the one who wipes their shit off the ground! Mine smell too bad for 'em maybe? … What a bunch of bastards. Bastards! Go ahead, take it easy, you bastards! You're not the ones who gotta clean it up!"

She took a swig of weak wine directly from the bottle, with a violent suction. She was tempted to smash the bottle. She resisted. One time she'd indulged herself this way, and she'd regretted it: the smell of rotgut, too much splintered glass. What a mess, enough to dynamite the whole shack.

"Little bastard … And that old cunt! … With his whore again. His slut! That's just what he needs. Old cunt. Old c-cunt! So what the hell was he doing last night that little bastard? Oh, but I'm gonna find out. I'm gonna find out! Oh, I'm gonna find out! Dirty shithead. Fuck, those bastards pissed me off. I'm really pissed off. Grr, they're gonna hear me alright. Argh, those bastards, sons of bitches, sons of bitches! Might as well die, they'd be dancing on my dead body! Oh, the sons of bitches! I've had my fill of those two! …"

She put back the bottle, slammed the fridge shut; it trembled. She was starting to get hungry. She went for a piss.

Julien hadn't said no; he'd somewhat understood. Still, he hesitated. He didn't really know Marc Guillard. He was wary.

"Hey come on Roquin, let's do it!" Guillard insisted.

Julien had a strange little smirk:

"And what if someone comes in?"

"You're a dope, I already told you my dad's at Grandieu's."

"Yeah, but what if he forgot something?"

"He didn't forget nothing, why? And if he did forget, we'd hear him. Besides, he doesn't just walk into my room like that. Come on! …"

"Since he won't come in, why don't you lock it," said Julien.

Young Roquin eyeballed the furniture for weight. He was wondering if they could use something to barricade the door. There was money here, at Guillard's; you wouldn't've guessed it. Everything nicely polished, a bedside rug, a steel desk with the office lamp and the chair that went with, the well-ordered notebooks, and the books. Even a stack of detective novels, the expensive kind. He did pretty well for himself, Guillard. He got by. And not just a tad.

"You don't even have the key?" Julien Roquin asked.

Marc told him to drop it, and grabbed his leg, between the thighs, with a hand that wasn't looking for a leg. Julien shifted his ass, freed himself, and knotted his brows.

"Hey we ain't supposed to do that, I told you!"

"You dope, it's normal, people do it all the time," Guillard said for the thirtieth time. "You're not a baby anymore are you? Ain't my fault if people do it. So you a baby or what?"

"No," Julien said quietly. Guillard's hand was back, becoming precise, dexterous. Julien's strict, rustic and naïve face took on an embarrassed smile:

"Hey, don't touch that, you're a jerk! … If you touch that."

But Guillard was acting weird. He wasn't just trying to provoke Julien: he looked almost attracted by the kid. Or maybe he was taking him as fodder for an over-amorous dream.

"Why don't you get yourself some girls," whispered Julien, as he was being masturbated. "It's easy for you. It's gotta be easy! But I ain't one of 'em!"

His embarrassed smile widened as if he'd just discovered, through his own words, that he was a boy. He'd probably never told himself that. He laughed, shrugged his shoulders. Guillard got up from the bed and grabbed Julien by the neck and waist, like a dancer.

"So what about getting married, then!" Julien said thickly, making a comic, recalcitrant, satisfied, and self-important grimace as he received the kiss that Marc Guillard plastered on his cheek, near his mouth. "You … you get married! Go for it! Do it. Go for it! … Come on, stop."

"This is where we get married," Guillard answered.

He took out his penis with a flick of the wrist and pushed it, gooey, against Julien.

"Touch," he said.

Julien hesitated, then, continuing to shake his head no, he clumsily stroked Guillard's fat dick with two fingers. The latter grabbed his hand, and shifted it around.

The touch of it disturbed Julien. He didn't like it: you had a sensation; you felt something. It was disgusting.

Guillard squeezed the boy's butt cheeks with his hand. Julien wriggled and chuckled, and eventually let himself be unbuckled. The ass was dumb, it did no evil, but careful not to touch the pucker.

Julien looked himself over, his pants at his thighs. He smelled a bit of a smell. He took a glance at his underpants, what if they were dirty. Not much. Guillard kneeled before Julien and growled:

"I'll lunch on that."

He did so. His pubic area prickled lightly; the child inquired:

"Hey Guillard, so you shave!"

Marc Guillard shook his head no. Even so, his lips prickled.

"Oh yeah, you do shave!" Julien said. He shrugged his shoulders. That Guillard was nuts. Guillard, that icky slob. Oh, what a son of a bitch! Guillard eats your ding-ding. Guillard fucks sluts (girls, in Julien's slang). Guillard gets on with his two hands. He's nuts. His father's king of the winos.

"Ouch! Hey, stop being a jerk!" said Julien, who was holding the other's guy's skull, and didn't dare push it away, scared of being bitten. "Don't use it all up!"

Later on, Guillard fell on the bed with Roquin. He pulled him against him, came between his thighs, from the front, groping him messily from head to toe.

"Come on, hurry up!" Julien repeated, imprisoned, embarrassed that Marc was kissing him on the mouth and trying to force his tongue into it. People, up close, they were disgusting. It shouldn't be this way. Bastards.

Marc Guillard pulled out, rose to his feet. Julien wanted to get up.

"Wait, don't move!" said Guillard. He felt around for a handkerchief, and wiped the boy's crotch with it.

Julien dumped his penis back in his pants. So that's what it's like then. He made conversation:

"So, tell me, Guillard, will there be chicks at Roche-Notre-Dame?"

"Chicks? There? Don't be a dope buddy. Fuck no."

"Théret told me there'd be some."

"No way. We don't even know if we'll go with 'em."

"… Hey, you can say it if there's gonna be sluts there, I won't tell. If you don't say it's 'cause they'll be there. That's proof."

Guillard sneered:

"So what, you wanna bone some of 'em maybe?"

"No. It depends. Why not?" said Julien Roquin. "Yeah, why not. Could be. Could be. I'm just askin' if they'll be there."

"Anyway, it's none of your business," Guillard said dryly. "And I told you already, no. Théret don't want 'em either. Not even the guys from over there. There'll be problems."

"What problems?"

"Fights, they're kinda thick. They're rednecks in Roche-Notre-Dame."

"Oh yeah, and what about the guys from Saint-Loup?" Julien said maliciously.

"What about Saint-Loup? What do you know about Saint-Loup?"

"Nothing, I know. I know!"

"You don't need to. Cut it out. I'm telling you it's none of your business. Leave us alone."

"Hell no, it *is* our business. And you've got no right to be bossy. We don't have bosses. We don't need you guys. You guys are a pain in the ass. You're the ones who stir shit up. We were cool before you guys."

Julien seemed to hold back a surge of anger.

"I'm by myself, you can beat me up if you like," he said toughly. "'Cause I'm by myself now."

"Where's this coming from? I don't wanna do nothing to you," said Guillard, bashful.

"Yeah, well you better not."

It was almost one. They left the room. They were upset. It wasn't because of what they'd said, thought Guillard. The kid didn't care. No, he shouldn't jerk off with him, that's all there was to it. Julien had too much of a bad temper, a brute, the spitting image of his parents. Same with the other snotnoses: nothing doing with them. They say they know, they know, they're fine with it, and then when someone cums they get upset.

Marc Guillard wasn't wrong. Roquin felt humiliated to have been used for that. He wouldn't fall for that trick again.

Anyway, they didn't want to squabble.

"Stuff like that's disgusting," Julien mumbled. "You must be kinda weird if you're into that. You should've told me, I wouldn't've said yes. Only scumbags do that. It's disgusting."

"So we're not in a fight, are we?" Guillard asked, as kindly as he could.

Julien shook his head no. Guillard's sheepish look satisfied. In the street they went back to speaking as if nothing had happened.

The Dumay Bakery was still open. They went in. The Dumay girl, a sixteen-year-old fat cow with big feet, fat-tits, with the cheeks of a pork butcher and the eyes of a pig, appeared behind the counter in a rosy blouse. The Dumay family was lunching in the back. Fried food vapors and shitty cauliflower.

She didn't know the boys, who weren't regulars. Julien asked for a raisin bun, paid for it, handed it back, asked for a chocolate croissant instead, handed it back, thought for a while, decided on a pudding, then turned it down. At last he chose an *éclair*. The Dumay girl blushed with stupidity: she'd have scolded the kid who was taking her for a ride, but she didn't dare because of the other boy, the tall, beautiful one. Guillard was smiling kindly, shy. At first he didn't buy anything, then he took a little pack of strawberry bubblegum. He unwrapped it immediately and offered a stick to Anne-Grace Dumay.

She gasped, scarlet, that she'd already started lunch.

"Cauliflower," Guillard said amiably.

"Uh-huh!" whispered Anne-Grace.

"That's alright, keep it for later," insisted Marc Guillard, with a vernal smile.

The Dumay girl grasped the stick of chewing gum with a subservient hand, redder than her ears. She pulled it away immediately. She glanced at the coins, got mixed up, gave them the wrong change. Guillard rectified it, formed his mouth into a gallant muzzle once again, picked up his coins, and adopted a photogenic pose.

It was a bad move. The Dumay girl found him childish and figured out that he was really much younger than she was.

She flung her forearms out in an over-the-windmill gesture, and then she got revenge:

"Shoo shoo shoo kiddies, go home your momma's waitin' for you."

She nasalized *go'ome, mummu, wei'ing*. She clucked the rest. Marc and Julien busted out, shushed.

When they had turned the corner, taken an alley, found shelter under a porch, and seen that they were alone, they showed one another what they'd snitched to Miss Dumay's face. It was the loot of seasoned conjurers; you'd have thought they had eight hands and twelve pockets. Candies, cookies, crepes, chocolates, sugared almonds, caramels, licorices, pastries, plastic toys, kazoos, and the red rubber porcupine on which you leave the change.

They laughed, they appraised one another, they told each other their tricks: Guillard while Julien was being helped, Julien when Marc was cajoling the girl. They shared the take. Julien pocketed most of it. They had made peace.

Grandieu was a retired police captain. He owned a posh suburban residence, a large rose garden, and an antique staircase that led to a peddle shore. Grandieu had a small jetty constructed there, behind which he sheltered a motorboat.

His wife, a pretentious widow whom he'd met through a marriage bureau a few years before, also liked to go down there during the summer. She'd read or knit under a thatched hut and watch her husband leave, come back. He had a habit of fishing dangerously near the reefs. A maid would bring tea, and port wine. Mrs. Grandieu appreciated hiking, strolls, but not the rowboat, which she called a speedboat. Hugo was still so young at heart, so dynamic, and so vigorous. A sportsman! She was a hundred years older than he was! A few centuries even!

They say Mrs. Grandieu was the purse: Hugo had nothing.

Old Guillard was repainting the long, street-side fence of their garden. It was made of a low-wall that came up to the level of the thighs, embedded with thick bars that held up a strong wire mesh fence. Repainting all this was a big job, a big investment.

Mr. Grandieu was glad to keep Guillard Sr. company. The sun wasn't too bad around four o'clock. Between old timers they gossiped about business, news, the future.

In fact, Mr. Guillard was maybe fifteen years younger than Grandieu. But fatigue, sorrows, the bottle, a petty constitution, and a wrinkled-up kind of figure erased the age difference. And indeed, Old Guillard felt he belonged to the camp of the aging, the elders; they reassured him.

The peasant woman's murder had caused a stir. The island, with its one hundred and thirty square kilometers and its seventy-two thousand inhabitants, wasn't a place where murders happened that often. A good half of the islanders lived in villages with only a few hundred people; the other half was spread between Saint-Rémi, Saint-Loup, Pierrenoire and a few large villages. It was every man for himself.

The murder brought to mind people from the continent. It smelled of thugs, of Saturday nights, rabble, and the city. Grandieu reckoned that the perpetrators had to live in Saint-Rémi or its vicinity. Didn't a dubious suburb surround the county seat these days? Saint-Rémi had really changed in the last couple of years.

"What if they were from the continent?" asked Old Guillard.

Hugo Grandieu made an ironic pout. To come all the way from France to steal sixty francs from a poor little old lady was pretty comic. But tourism, particularly in the springtime, was upscale, luxurious. And this, this was the kind of crime little thugs on motorbikes committed. A measly break-in, thoughtlessly improvised by young drunkards who'd taken a bad turn.

"Yeah, your out-of-town rascal," Mr. Grandieu insisted. Or, if Old Guillard preferred, it might have been a Parisian professor, a leftist intellectual who wanted to have a good time … "You often spot 'em around here, with their chauffeurs, their purposefully torn-up clothes, their naked babies, and their shabby help." But Hugo Grandieu didn't seriously believe that. That kind of game. It would be too puerile.

Mr. Guillard had difficulty following such subtleties. He asked:

"Are they going to search for them, at least?"

"That was another problem," Grandieu sighed. "The police forces, on the island … or maybe they'd call in some people from the continent? To investigate a … well a … Sad to say, there were different kinds of victims: and this didn't really seem like anything worth …"

"Which makes these assaults even more odious," concluded Grandieu.

He clearly didn't belong to those people whom society neglected to avenge, and whose victimization was thus all the more scandalous, according to him. As a matter of fact, the elegant portion of the coastline where he lived had never, as it were, known such back-page police blotter affairs.

Guillard Sr. spoke of a general unease, and affirmed he'd felt the sting of it.

Grandieu, who was no old fogey, smiled voluminously. He answered that the police would no doubt make a small ruckus, to lull the public conscience to sleep. They would patrol, they would disturb the suspicious looking inhabitants of the island, adolescents, the unemployed, and foreigners without a penny to their name, disreputable bachelors. Besides, it sometimes happened that they apprehended culprits with these kinds of investigations, which always intimidated the weak.

"People aren't really afraid of the youth around here," said Old Guillard. He was from here, whereas Grandieu was continental. "What would be frightening," he continued, "is if it were the work of a professional … a crook, an assassin you understand: an assassin."

Grandieu soothed him. "There there, gangsters go hand in glove with the state, they don't commit such trifles. Kids are the ones who …" The idea that a machine-gun-toting crook could have invaded the kitchen of the old woman, between her cat and her slippers, put him in a good mood.

"No, Guillard. These are kids. Kids. Maybe even minors! And that," Hugo Grandieu abruptly added, "that, that makes me puke. The responsibility of the … People no longer care for their …"

Old Guillard asked some questions about juvenile delinquency. Grandieu, in fact, didn't know anything about it, and he confessed as much. He himself had an engineering background, he had worked in offices; he was a scientist, a serviceman: but not a cop.

They both had acquaintances who were cops. They exchanged opinions on this subject. They'd have information on the case. Mr. Guillard naively remarked that the burglars had been skillful, for amateurs. Leaving neither prints nor tracks, despite the mud the other night …

Grandieu shrugged. "They were wearing gloves; all the bikers have them. You can smudge footprints with the heel. There was cement outside, some gravel, a field, and an asphalted state road that the downpour had splattered and washed ten times over. At least, you could safely assume that there had been more than one of them; the kitchen tiles were a real pigsty. No, no mess here …"

"They didn't lose their cool, you know, with that dead woman on their hands."

Mr. Grandieu asked Guillard why he didn't just burn the old paint with a blowtorch. It would have gone much faster. Old Guillard pretended the fencing was too delicate. It was only holding together thanks to the paint that was there: it was all rotten on the inside.

"In that case," suggested Grandieu, "wasn't it preferable not to sand at all?"

Old Guillard furnished some arguments, offered forth a happy middle ground.

Towards the end of the afternoon, they hoped for beautiful dry weather. At least when Guillard would apply the first coat. The painter said it was a matter of patience. Hugo Grandieu, petulant, was of another opinion. The scraped fence tortured his sight.

"Yes, white, as usual. Slightly off, pale eggshell." It was most elegant, with the hedge, the honeysuckle, and the prodigious rose bushes.

The dark green, too, looked distinguished. But everything depended on the desired effect, no doubt about it. The style you preferred. Pure white did this, off white did that; the dark green did something else entirely. As for black, it would have looked dark: at least, that was Mrs. Grandieu's conviction. "She's fresh as a daisy, thank you very much."

"White is indeed the clearest tone," admitted Old Guillard. He didn't take any wine before the hour school let out, you could hear the bell ring from the elegant neighborhood school: three pretty houses covered in tiles, dollhouse windows in an immense, delightful garden. The kids were also cute and decent. "No riffraff among them," pointed out Mr. Grandieu, before adding:

"Yes, we're among our own kind … Oh, I know, it's not charitable, but you have to be realistic. The children of … of the help, for example, would be unhappy if they had to go to school here, and then return to their … What I mean is, you, you're well off, Guillard: the old Saint-Rémi, God knows … It's becoming a luxury. And by the time everything is actually renovated …"

"I'll be dead before we get kicked out," Old Guillard predicted.

Hugo Grandieu protested, solicited news about Marc. So, he wasn't going to come and help his father today? Oh right, too much work: school, it really takes up all of the kids' time. At least, he'd be trained. In short, he'd have a diploma. Mr. Grandieu chuckled at the word diploma. Old Guillard did too. They toasted to their health.

They had points of view on manhood, manual labor, the army, real estate and its con artists, corrupted civil servants, the end of all things, this strange century. Hugo Grandieu casually finished the bottle with his painter: a local wine, nothing really, a mere seven or eight percent, that hit the spot. He forcefully reiterated that the island lacked vineyards. It used to have such a palatable vintage. But the old timers were dying off and the vines were being pulled up by the roots. Soon they'd be drinking wine prepared without grapes, rotgut that would gnaw at their bowels and whose plastic bottles would litter the coastline. What a shame it was, with such an admirable climate, so suitable for crops. Grandieu believed it. Real summers. Real winters. Heavenly springs, heartwarming autumns. Yes, a climate. But this year: there was no explaining it but you had the feeling things were off to a bad start. You could feel it: you could feel these things. Mankind had unacknowledged powers, innate certainties.

Jean Roquin didn't get back home before two o'clock that afternoon. He'd found his wife in a state that was close to a nervous breakdown.

Tall, vigorous, hotheaded, he was as violent as she was but he didn't enjoy making scenes, or screaming.

He sat in the kitchen, and lunched on some rillettes, looking disillusioned, when Simone Roquin started to scream all of a sudden. He didn't answer, didn't even look at her. Standing up, embarrassed by her arms, she turned, stamped, harangued, and ran her trap. Roquin assumed she had her period: now rare, it remained volcanic, acerbic, deadly.

"It's Claire Fouilloux isn't it? She's the one you went to see! That skank. She's the one. That Fouilloux! Isn't that right!" accused Simone Roquin, more brutal than upset. Her husband didn't even bother to deny it.

What's more, she was right. Claire Fouilloux, a sixteen-and-a-half-year-old brat, relieved five or six family men including Jean Roquin. She was an employee at the Baron shoe factory; her job there consisted in sewing uppers. But she was often absent, and always late. She'd be fired soon. But she joked she'd soon find other uppers. Oh, her parents would beat it into her? Let 'em try and blame her. If her old man hadn't fondled and half-raped her as a kid—yeah, he should just shut up. As for her bitch of a mother ... there too, she could give you an earful.

Mr. and Mrs. Fouilloux, in short, weren't reacting. Claire would soon grab her stuff and hit the road; she'd make a life for herself on the continent. She already had the means.

In truth, the aging men whom she ransomed (invariably during their lunch hour) would cough up around a hundred francs. She'd scrounge for more, or for gifts, some kindness ... They rudely claimed that the room alone was ruinously expensive.

And they weren't lying. In Saint-Rémi, it was pretty hard to find somewhere to have sex with a minor, if you wanted a bed, a toilet seat, running water, a bidet. Flophouses couldn't be trusted, and each and all the families knew themselves all too well. You had to upgrade your station, rent a room at the Sphynx-Club.

It was a weekend inn for well-to-do continentals. They would go there for quick gourmet adultery, luxurious, unconventional, which they charged to their expense accounts.

The staff of the Sphynx-Club was starting to figure Claire Fouilloux out. She smiled at them, good girl. They would look her up and down, purse their lips, bow ironically before the spineless john who tipped excessively and accepted the worst room at the worst price. The incongruous couple pretended they were going upstairs to freshen up, then proceeded to lunch. The sham never varied. The daddies escaped by one o'clock, a hirsute Claire clinging to their forearms. She needed an escort; she would never have dared go down the stairs on her own after them.

Claire Fouilloux was meager and short-limbed. Breastless, almost without butt or face, she corresponded to male tastes. She had a recessed chin, drab features, protruding ears that stuck out through her hair, clenched fists, voided eyes filled to the brim with large, obtuse play-acting, as if she'd been batting false lashes that were a bit too long and had been glued crooked.

If she'd been less small, you might have mistook her for an adult, if she'd dressed her face up and got a false ID card. Though her ID gave her age at sixteen, her face was ageless; her large bony belly evoked a dead woman. The aficionados were excited by her civil status and ignored the rest.

As a matter of fact, she was likeable, she was good humored; she thought poorly only of herself, bastards, and other people.

"Yes!" Simone Roquin cried, snarling, "it's Fouilloux! Claire Fouilloux! Your bone bag! She's nothing but a corpse! Oh, you love it. You're so full of it! So you're into little girls now! Isn't that right. You're going to park yourself at the school gates. What're you waiting for? Go ahead. Do it! Why don't you just pull out your cock for the girls! Pull it out for them! If only that could get you hard for once! You impotent! Fouilloux! …"

She jumped at his face, but with a half-heartedness they both felt. He fended her off with one hand, without hitting her. And she didn't sink in the nails that she'd brandished to tear apart his cheek.

She retreated back to the stove and started shouting again.

"Oh yeah, little girls! Uh huh. Schoolgirls. That's what you need! Schoolgirls! Why not just rape one of 'em, you old fuck? Say it: you'd like to rape 'em! … You old sadist. And why not little boys while you're at it? … Why not get fucked in the ass? You piece of trash! … But all you've got's the Fouilloux, eh! That spider! That's all you got! That grasshopper! That's all you got, eh! All you got! … Oh, you think I'm disgusting don't you! Ohh. Ooohhh! …"

She jumped on her husband again. She had seized the lid of a cast-iron pot.

He rose abruptly, and disarmed her. He sat down again, feigning an air of calm, and went on eating.

For an instant, she was paralyzed. She was panting. Then she started up again, growling, with a rattle that swelled in increments until it peaked into a shriek as her cadence rushed onward:

"… And how much did you dish out to dip your wick in that whore? Oh you just dish it out for ass don't you? You don't give a shit. You don't keep count. No negotiations. You just lay it down. End of discussion. She can make you eat her shit, that Fouilloux, you just dish it out. You like that, don't you, dishing it out for ass. She has you eating her shit on all fours that Fouilloux. And then you ask for more! You need your shit don't you, and expensive, you need it. You could give a fuck. You piece of trash. You bastard. Bastard. Bastard. Well … well why don'tcha go back and gobble her turds, that Fouilloux! Why don'tcha go back and suck that spider's ass! Oh yeah! You'll have all the time in the world for that. All the time you want! I won't keep you up! Oh no, why don't you just go ahead and dish out your dough, for all we see of it! I ain't gonna stop you! What're you waiting for?

Why don't you just bring her over? It's your place. What are you waiting for? You old bastard! You piece of trash. You trash. Trash. Trash. Trash. Trash. Why don'tcha just go back there!"

She vented the usual threats of divorce, of immediate departure. She recited an old litany of insults against their line of work, their land, their shitty digs (the farm belonged to Roquin), their marriage, the past, the present, the past, the future, the past. She expressed the desire to kill others and to commit suicide: she believed in God, at least she would be given justice in the afterlife. She felt that too much was too much. She had a right to tranquility, to sacred peace. She'd worked and was still working like a dog: she deserved, if not respect (she wasn't asking for that much) or affection (she wasn't that far gone), at least a little calm, rest, rest. But her husband refused her even that. So where? Who? When? …

She continued on with these grand visions, chaffing her throat, forgetting the adultery. It's true that she rarely extracted a fecund oratory motif from it. As a puritan, she hated sleeping with her husband. She hated anything that was physical, except for grub and blows. She was intimately satisfied that Jean Roquin was discharging outside of her. Sometimes, in acute crises of insanity, she even dared to bawl that at him: she'd pay a whore to be permanently released from that filth. The Fouilloux or another. From her own pocket.

"From my own pocket! From my own pocket!" she shrieked. The disgust and spite inspired her to bare the mucous membranes of her lips. Jean Roquin was familiar with that menacing she-monkey grimace: it announced the climax of the scene. He was on his guard.

She threw herself at him a third time. She had grabbed a knife.

He towered before her, flung his whole arm against her ear, with enormous momentum. She fell. He bent over, seized the knife. She screamed, clawed herself to the point of tearing her skirt apart. She sobbed.

"You're a pain in the ass," he muttered heavily, in a low voice.

She stood back up. She was licking her tears. She sucked up the frothy saliva that was running from her mouth.

"I've had enough! Enough! Enough! Enough!" she shrieked. "Enough! Go find your whores! Enough! Enough! Enough! My God! ... Enough!"

She was wobbling; she was about to collapse, to knock herself out, to destroy herself completely.

Jean Roquin slapped her, seized her by the wrists, and shook her. She seemed to unravel. He touched her, hesitated to kiss her, and gave up.

A little later, they were more tender, calmed. She sat next to him at dinner. She even accepted, from the tip of a knife, a dab of rillettes, a pickle, hiccupping.

She sometimes ended it there; sometimes the scene included a second act; Roquin sensed that this would be the case. She reinvigorated herself. Her cheeks remained pale, but her eyes were growing feverish again, ferocious.

She went on again about the children, the ritual theme of this phase of the crisis. She enjoyed reconciling with her husband to the detriment of one of their sons, who'd remember it for a long while to come.

Their children. Oh! ... Those who were in the army, of course, never wrote. Except to ask for money, to request packages. Sweets! They needed sweets! And they never bothered to answer; they went on leave God knows where, after you'd tortured yourself for them, they didn't care one bit. As for Julien ...

Mrs. Roquin suddenly remembered what she had discovered. She blew up. Julien! She'd almost forgotten about that!

Oh, right! Jean Roquin hadn't heard the news of the day! Oh right! He wasn't in the loop yet! He didn't know! He didn't know! What that little scumbag Julien had just done! ...

She cackled, laughed, sparkled. She built up intrigues, took on airs. She loved staging her denunciations, her auto-da-fés.

She dragged Jean Roquin into the garden. With vehemence, alacrity, she showed him the footsteps crossing the soggy ground. She asked him five or six times what it meant.

Roquin said the tracks were spaced far apart. Mrs. Roquin put on an indignant face, as if she'd been insulted. That little scumbag had been running, that was all. But it was him alright! It was him!

Jean Roquin played along, won over by his wife's anger. He was brutal, obtuse, and formalistic: the evidence against Julien was obvious, indisputable. Nonetheless, he doubted that the child had dared leave during the night: perhaps the tracks were only from this morning? Still, the whole thing was very serious, in any case, very serious.

Simone Roquin was scandalized all over again. No, no, it was last night. Not this morning. Last night! She brilliantly unloaded her deductions. She even took the risk of establishing a link between Julien's skipping out and the infamous murdered old lady in today's paper. Roquin hadn't read it? … An old lady! She'd gotten her throat slit, right there, in her house. A village two or three kilometers from here. The walls daubed in blood. Oh he hadn't read about it? Too bad, she no longer had the paper. Yes, a woman who was still handsome, perhaps fifty-five years old, disemboweled from her neck to her genitals, all her guts hanging out. A sadistic crime, and they didn't waste a second: she had six million. Under her mattress, the fool. Six million!

Jean Roquin shrugged his shoulders. His wife was exaggerating. A ten-year-old brat. No way, but incidentally, Julien's crime was far more serious. A kid murderer, that at least you can under-stand; he's nuts, and that's that. He needs treatment. But Julien, he wasn't nuts in the slightest. He had disobeyed. He was hiding something. He had another life.

"Not nuts, oh no! Not nuts, oh not that, no. No, no, no," psalmodized Simone Roquin, as if to suggest that the child possessed a subtle mischief, monstrousness, and an intelligence that hadn't even been suspected.

Husband and wife agreed. They decided to take strong measures against the little brat. Tonight, when he came home, Julien would have to explain himself. The problem had to be nipped in the bud before it was too late.

The Roquins went to see their crops. The season would be bad. They vaguely contemplated remedies, some work, and purchases. They were acting out the theater of being deliberate, sensible, and masters of themselves. They spoke in harsh tones, without looking at each another. Their tension was rising. Their only thought was for tonight.

Julien came back at eight o'clock, which he was allowed to do.

He wasn't worried. He had emptied his pockets.

No one was outside. No light, except at the kitchen window. Nothing out of the ordinary. Julien went through the front door and neglected to turn on the ceiling lamp in the corridor.

He was two meters from the kitchen when he was pounced on. They gripped him by the arm, screamed.

His mother had heard him and had been lying in wait for him. From her corner in the hallway, she'd been waiting in the recess of a doorway, she'd been lurking and studying his shadow, vaguely silhouetted on the windowpane of the front door. She had already spotted the part of him that she would be able to grasp.

With a flick towards the light switch, she made light. Julien wobbled on his legs. Then he scowled, contracted inward, and almost closed his eyes. These sessions could happen anytime; he was always ready.

At first, he felt some curiosity about the pretext she might have. Then, shaken by abnormal brutality, he no longer thought anything.

Simone Roquin questioned and beat Julien there on the poorly lit tiled floor of the hallway, marked with muddy footprints. The bulb had a low voltage. This yellowish, sinister, miserable twilight was well suited to punishment, and the Roquins liked it. A smell of soup, leaks, turnips, carrots, drifted from the kitchen. On the island, it was said that a pot on the burner smiled. At the Roquin's house it would spit, hiss, rattle itself with the clattering of its own lid. For Simone Roquin had a passion for doing everything to the max. That was her word, her judgment, and her principle. You washed to the max, swept to the max, cooked to the max, talked to the max, inspected to the max, learnt to the max: and whatever wasn't done to the max, wasn't done at all. This rule placed a grimace of virtue on her perpetual hatred for people and things.

The questions she asked Julien didn't call for an answer: they simply added color to the shaking and the slapping. The child had no trouble staying mute; his mother was yelling so hard.

Then, all of a sudden, she let go of him as if he had become slimy.

Now he had to answer, explain himself, narrate, confess, or else. Julien denied everything, even the footprints. He knew nothing, had done nothing.

This was his tactic against those who were stronger than he was: to resist in full. Argue, imagine up sentences, keep pace, scheme, lie in front of the grown-ups? No. No more than if an elephant was charging at you.

His father had followed the questioning. Julien's thickheadedness had exasperated him. He had had enough. He suddenly burst onto the scene. Drowned in an ocean of blows and cries, the child didn't see him right away.

"Move over. Go to the kitchen," ordered Jean Roquin to his wife. "And you, take your shirt off."

Julien, startled, looked at his father. Roquin, sleeves rolled-up, had a dog chain hanging off his arm. A mutt of theirs, dead for some years now.

As the child seemed hesitant to take off his pullover, Simone Roquin, who was back, threw herself at him, and tore it off him screaming. He shook his head, and unbuttoned his shirt with more submission.

Solemnly, in a toneless voice, Jean Roquin asked Julien to explain why he had gone out the previous night. The boy lowered his head, denied everything. Roquin stayed calm, serious, and slowly repeated his question. Julien said nothing. Roquin took his time, rooted his eyes onto the kid, huffed through the nostrils, and waited some more, like a bad actor who knows how to impress a crowd of fools. He asked his question one last time.

Julien didn't answer; his lips trembled; a tear pearled up shamefully, quickly, in each eye. His father grabbed his skull to turn it around, held him by an arm and struck.

Simone Roquin assisted from the sidelines:

"The bastard! The little bastard! That piece of trash!" she shrieked. She was digging her nails into her palms; she looked at the dog chain, the arm, and the victim. She was so red she could have popped.

"The little bastard," she shrieked. "You brat! You brat! You've earned this one, that's for sure! That's right, you've earned this one! But what the fuck was he doing last night? What the fuck did he do? What the fuck could he have done? Well, he's going to talk! He's going to talk, holy cow! I swear to you he's going to talk! We'll work him to the bone! You'll talk! You'll talk! Oh I swear you'll talk! Little bastard! You little piece of trash! What did he get into this time? What is he up to now? Aren't we up shit creek enough as it is? Don't you think we're up shit creek enough as it is? Don't you think we've had it up to here with you? You think it's still not enough? It's not enough for you? Still not enough for you? You think we haven't already suffered enough because of you? You wanna kill us? That's isn't enough for you? You gotta do more? Gotta do more? Oh, you gotta do more! Yes we'll do more, we will! Oh it's over now! It's over! Over! We're not gonna let you walk all over us, lemme tell you! We won't be taken for no fools! You ain't gonna fuck us over! Oh no you're not, you ain't gonna fuck us over! If you think you can fuck us over like that! Well you won't! … He'd kill us! He'd kill us? This has gotta stop! It's gotta stop! This kid is torture! I won't take it any more! I won't take it! We can't take it anymore! No one could! What a cross to bear! …"

She screamed the word *cross* so coarsely that she hurt herself. She curled up, coughed, spat out a bloody loogie that stuck to her lip.

"He's gonna kill me, he will! He's gonna kill me!" she moaned as she went to get a drink of water in the kitchen.

At the same moment, Jean Roquin stopped hitting: he'd felt that the dog chain was falling against thin air. On the ground at his feet he noticed a red thing, soft, wet, without any decipherable shape. Jean Roquin contemplated his son.

3

Alain Viaud stretched out his left arm and showed Marie-Antoine
Péréfixe a circle of boys, seated in the grass a few meters away.

The gang hadn't been so large since Easter vacation. Some
were missing, there were some new guys, and you could see a
group of unknown boys who weren't the usual type. They were
in fact chatting with the older boys right now.

The boys associated at their whim. Nonetheless, they were
sensitive to identities of age, class, school, and proximity of
residence. As for Joachim Lescot's group—Viaud and Marie-
Antoine—they were kept somewhat apart. They were too
little: it was better not to tell them anything, for fear they'd
tattle. They were considered absent-minded, imprudent, and
almost dangerous.

They babbled on in their corner of the prairie, indifferent
to what the others were planning. The sun was delightful; they
felt good.

Péréfixe, a slightly dim-witted, very coquettish young boy,
was Joachim Lescot's best friend. He was a few months older.
That meant Viaud was the eldest. Péréfixe's parents ran a news-
stand near the school where the three of them would go.

"Them over there?" asked Marie-Antoine.

"No, not them," said Alain Viaud. "Him! … And him too! …"

"Them over there? What's wrong with 'em?"

Viaud lowered his arms. Nobody in the world had noticed
yet that he was left-handed. The little ones didn't take notice, the
big boys were not even aware of Viaud's existence and, at school,
he messed everything with his right hand. The only thing they'd

notice was that he was cross-eyed, because they had to make fun of him about it.

"There's nothing wrong with' em," chirped Viaud, who had forgotten what he wanted to say.

"Ok nothing," admitted Marie-Antoine, conciliatory.

He adopted a kind, interested face. He loved the dead calm. This corner of the meadow was very pretty. It wasn't boring at all, no.

"Oh yeah, I know what's with 'em," Alain Viaud said after a while. "'Cause he, wait a sec … Oh yeah, that's it. He put his dingdong in his chocolate turbine, so he's got a chocolate dingdong. See."

He was pointing at boys he'd never seen before. Marie-Antoine had no notion of turbines, he inquired about that.

"So," Alain Viaud repeated peacefully, "he put his dingdong in his chocolate turbine, and then his is chocolate."

"Who's he?" said Marie-Antoine.

"… Him over there! 'Cause I know it's him! He put his dingdong in his chocolate turbine, and then, after that, he's got a chocolate dingdong!"

Viaud flapped his arms open to prove the evidence of his claim.

Joachim Lescot was chewing on some clover, and didn't listen.

This time, Marie-Antoine got a little puff of a thought that might have a connection with what Viaud was saying. He smiled, cheekily:

"His noodle?"

Alain Viaud sighed. He didn't know that word, which was used in the part of the island where Péréfixe was born.

"You know," he explained placidly, "it's simple! … He has a chocolate dingdong because he, he put his dingdong in his chocolate turbine. You get it? 'Cause it's chocolate!"

"What is it I do?" said a laughing voice behind them.

It was Hervé Pellisson paying them a visit.

"Here comes Doormat, his dingdong is chocolate," said Viaud.

"Cut it out, Millipede!" said Hervé, mildly. "Don't use that kind of language around my cousin!"

He kissed Joachim hello, then Marie-Antoine. He shook hands with Viaud. He sat down next to them. He craved the company of the three kids, despite the height difference between them, and his voice that was starting to break. It grew clear and joyful again when he spoke with them.

He stretched his legs and spread them at a right angle. He invited his cousin to sit there. He leaned him against his torso and had his hair in his nose.

Joachim enjoyed being caressed. He also enjoyed hearing Hervé's belly echo in his back, because of the words, the laughter, the exclamations. The belly deflated, puffed out again, vibrated. The belt buckle bothered him a little: he shifted aside and didn't feel it anymore.

"Hey, you lost something," Viaud said quickly to Hervé, pointing to a tuft of grass, behind.

Hervé took a look: he hadn't lost anything. He understood and laughed. Alain Viaud played this trick on everybody. Gets you every time.

"I knew it but you got me again lamo!" said Pellisson.

"No I got this," Viaud answered.

He dug in his underpants. He pulled out an elegant dog collar made of flexible leather, fine, luxurious, and new. Wow that dog! They tie rich stuff to their dogs! They weren't broke for nothing!

"Where did you get it, in a store?" asked Hervé, interested.

"I got it on the dog!" said Viaud.

"You got a dog?" asked Marie-Antoine.

"The collar," said Viaud.

"That's the thing," said Marie-Antoine, "us neither, my mom, she don't have a dog like that. You can get gold ones too."

"Golden dogs," said Pellisson, "Holy Mary!"

"It's the collar isn't it," said Marie-Antoine.

"Hey, how'd ya get it," said Joachim, enthusiastic.

"On the dog," said Viaud. "The geezer, a geezer, it was her dog you get it? With a leash. You take away the dog, you you take away the leash, and then you get the collar."

"Yeah, if it don't bite," said Marie-Antoine.

"What she was doing?" said Joachim Lescot.

"I was downstairs," said Viaud, "a bench with the dog, you know."

"It didn't bite?"

"Dogs don't bite me," said Viaud, "we had a good laugh under the bench. And then he took off, then I did."

"I didn't get anything," said Péréfixe.

"I got something," cried Lescot.

He pushed Pellisson's belly away slightly, and rummaged in his pocket.

"I'm giving it to Marie-Antoine," said Joachim, showing the object.

There were whistles of admiration. Péréfixe accepted but he said:

"I can't keep it, my mother's gonna see it, she's gonna to think I took it. That's too bad!"

"Me neither," said Lescot.

"I can," said Alain Viaud. "Will you give it to me?"

"Okay," said Marie-Antoine. "I'll give it to you after my turn, okay, later? …"

Hervé was slowly smoothing the inner thighs of Joachim who was propped up against him. He asked him to narrate all he remembered about the theft. A stroke of luck, according to Lescot.

His mother had sent him to the Vasseur bar-tabac to buy two cartons of cigarettes for her clients. He'd stored the cartons inside his grocery bag, and then he'd taken a look at the comics rack. They were at the edge of a table where someone was having a drink.

"So you pinched that from the table?" said Hervé, fascinated.

"Yeah."

Whistles again. Lescot had a soft touch for his age.

But what about the client, then? He was there. Joachim answered, euphoric, with a racing, garish voice:

"That's when he stood up. Mrs. Vasseur was calling him to the bar for the phone. She said, 'Mister, your call!' I saw the pen, so I looked around if anyone could see me and then bam! He'd even left his wallet!"

"Hmm, he'd have bawled, you did good," said Hervé Pellisson.

His right hand had reached Joachim's crotch and he was absently wobbling the genitals.

"Well, I'm gonna piss," said Lescot.

He got up, took two steps, turned his back, looked over his shoulder towards the boys and continued his story:

"He said but where the heck is my pen you seen it by any chance Mrs. Vasseur? A 4-color pen!"

"Some are gold," noted Marie-Antoine Péréfixe, "my mom sells 'em, some even have six colors!"

"The ones with four cost thirty francs!" announced Hervé.

He had no idea of the price; he simply wanted to flatter his cousin.

"Wait?" Lescot cried. "How much? How much is it?"

"No, two thousand," corrected Marie-Antoine, tickled in his family pride. Joachim seemed to find two thousand just fine. He never would have imagined that he'd steal something so valuable one day. Two thousand francs!

"That's a shitload o' dough! …"

"You got that right," upped Hervé, indulgent. He'd settled the kid the way he was before, but he was waiting a bit before putting his hand back.

This time Péréfixe got up and went to take a piss.

"Hey you lost something!" Alain Viaud said quickly.

Marie-Antoine turned around, searched the ground with his eyes, then he shook his head and called Viaud a jerk.

"Why don't you do it? To me! Go ahead, do it to me! You'll see!" Alain Viaud protested.

"And he didn't suspect you?" asked Hervé.

"Yeah, but not him!" said Joachim. "Mrs. Vasseur said to the man, 'Mister, mister! If there's a thief around here it's Lescot junior! There in the corner! But that's impossible, isn't it mister, it couldn't be him could it!'"

"She said that?"

"Yeah, and then he said no no I wouldn't go that far, I'm not gonna accuse you kiddo, don't worry, no I …"

"Kiddo!" Alain Viaud sniggered.

Joachim punched him laughing:

"Hold on, the thing is, Mrs. Vasseur she told me, 'Hey, Lescot you haven't seen that mister's pen have you, a 4-color one?'"

"And you hadn't seen it?" asked Péréfixe, who wasn't following.

"Yeah, but I said no 'cause I said I was gonna look around on the ground for it! 'Cause if ever he became suspicious, see, I'd say, 'Oh I see it there on the ground under that stuff,' then I pretend to find it see!"

They all admired Joachim Lescot's cunning, dexterity, and audacity. The story was hardly believable. But the pen was there.

Joachim started telling his whole story again from the beginning. Hervé was kissing the back of his hair and his ears. Alain Viaud was writing on his hands with the pen.

Mrs. Théret, seated at the register, called in for René. She waited a moment, called a second time, and shrugged her shoulders. Wednesdays it was impossible to keep a hold on that one. He had an itch for gallivanting about. And God knows where he went. What could he be interested in around here? Made you wonder what kind of mischief they could get into. Mrs. Théret tried to imagine. No, really. Except for pranks. She sighed.

She squirmed on her seat, called for her husband:

"Edmond? …"

Long silence. Could he have gone out, as well? That wasn't his style. A husband as tranquil as a wall. Not only would he never cheat on his wife, but he also forgot a little too often to make use of her. Louise Théret doesn't complain. She was no prude, but those kinds of obscenities …

She went to the back of the shop, called out again. A feeble response rose from the basement. Well. Edmond was doing the inventory of the bottles. A man who never drank. A gem. Mrs. Théret sighed. He didn't even smoke. He worked. He obeyed. He took control. Mrs. Théret told herself that she has gotten married to a night bonnet. She swore she no longer remembered how they ended up making their three kids. The poor man must also have forgotten. What had possessed them? Well, so much the better.

A client came in. It was Mrs. Bintch and her granddaughter. The little Bintch, thought Louise Théret, who was caustic in her spare time. The child was five or six. The Bintches were very well known on the island, a very old family, top of the heap.

Mrs. Théret was not in the least jealous of women of that milieu, although superior in all ways to her own. She only envied continental women. If ever a chic tourist in pants, tanned, slender, sunglasses perched on top of her forehead, overpriced costume jewelry, as skinny as a goat with a voice like an airport, entered the boutique, Mrs. Théret would capsize from rage. She who was deemed elegant, beautiful, just full-figured enough, there she was, back to being a little barrel, a gossip, a housekeeper with a low ass, a poorly put-together and poorly-dressed house-maid in front of those pretentious cows from Paris. Women who had a habit of entering the shop demanding the most impossible products, with a motherly tone, smiling as if they were in front of a retard and hardly ever buying anything. And it didn't stop them from poisoning you for an hour, with their airs, sucking on their sunglasses to better spit on you in the end.

On the contrary, Mrs. Théret remained beautiful and elegant in front of the Bintches and their kind on the island, whom she always greeted politely.

Mrs. Bintch lowered her eyes toward her granddaughter:

"Yolande, come on! Don't put your fingers on the counter, you're going to get dirty dear!"

Yeah that's it shove 'em up your ass it'll be cleaner, thought Mrs. Théret, in an ironic vein.

The child preferred to pick her nose. Mrs. Bintch acted the client with talent. She didn't skimp. Louise Théret responded well to her cues. Unfortunately, no, she did not have mango vinegar. Not even raspberry vinegar? Not even raspberries. That's something you make at home, Madam. Certainly, Madam, but I was hoping, hmmm. I am sorry, Madam.

Yolande has dreamily besieged one of her nostrils and she occupied it with a thumb, gaping at the dusty darkened oak shelves. So many colored boxes! So many bottles! So many can'ts, no, cans! So many things, so many things. The nostril, well scratched, grew moist, little by little.

"I told you not to do that, Yolande, dear! At your age, you know better than that!"

The little girl furrowed her eyebrows: what rule was it, again? Oh yes, the nose. Shucks for the nose! Indolently, she let the guilty finger be wiped. Mrs. Théret, from up high behind her counter, frowned a smile at her. No daughter of hers would be so ugly and crass. Treasures, they were, the Thérets girls.

"And how are your treasures," said Mrs. Bintch. "I don't see them anymore. Oh, we live so far away!"

"They're doing well, thank you," Mrs. Théret said coquettishly. "They're a bit bigger than this little cutie here, of course, nine and ten."

"Of course, right, right, oh! Right! They grow so fast don't they, so fast, that's right!

"Oh yes, yes! They certainly grow fast! What a pace! …"

"Oh, yes, what a pace! That's the word! You don't see them grow! They seem to be getting married just as soon as they're born!"

"Oh yes, absolutely! Just as soon," approved Louise Théret.

"I don't know how it was in your days, but in my days, we didn't grow up so fast!" said Mrs. Bintch. "Little girl stayed little girls for longer, it seemed to me! Take your son; he looks like a big boy already, wouldn't you say? Huh! And yet he's only …"

"Thirteen years old," completed Mrs. Théret. "Oh yes, they grow, they grow. No sooner are they here than they disappear."

"Yes, yes, oh! Don't I know it …! What a pace!"

"Oh, don't I know it, it's scary! Well … This little cutie will still be around for a few more years, don't you think!"

"Yes, yes, yes! Of course! This little angel! She doesn't grow as fast as that!"

"Yes, yes, yes. Oh no! Let's not exaggerate! They don't grow that fast, no! … We still have time to see the years go by!"

"Oh! Yes, we have time! Oh yes, unfortunately! It just goes on by! …"

They emitted protective, nostalgic, tender sighs.

Mrs. Bintch bought ginger, bergamot, lemon preserves, a jar of marjoram, five grams of saffron threads, and two ounces of *Mao Feng Cha* tea.

"Oh, absolutely! It's so succulent, so fine, so light, and so delicate! You can't find it anywhere else! I'd come here just for that! But your whole store is … Oh! What an aroma!"

I'm sure my shop smells better than yours, thought Mrs. Théret, sarcastically. Surreptitiously, she threw carnivorous glances at old Bintch, lowered her eyes modestly, whispered "a very special tea, it's very special," would have killed a cat with a kick of the heel if there were one available under the counter.

Yolande had switched fingers and nostrils, and, just as the grandmother and granddaughter were about to leave, René Théret breezed in through the door. He was holding his sweater rolled-up in a ball against the side of his face as if he were keeping a gum inflammation warm; he quickly cut across the store.

Mrs. Théret didn't like her children to come in through the front of the shop. Especially René, who was always scruffy, in such a state, a tramp. What had happened today? A fight, for sure. He was hiding another bruise under his sweater. He must have learned how to box by now, judging by the number of bruises he'd come home with since he'd learned how to walk.

The door chimed, the Bintches were gone.

"René?" Mrs. Théret called.

It was Edmond who came running, and he said in a low voice:

"Come quickly, it's serious."

Mrs. Théret put on a *let's go* face; she skipped in front of her husband and entered the apartment. René was in front of the sink, he was washing his cheek, and he had stripped his top off.

"Let me see!" Louise Théret said dryly. She flicked her chin forward.

"That's a knife cut my little friend, am I wrong?"

René bobbed his head no.

His father, completely pallid, had just joined them.

"René, this is terrible!" he murmured.

Edmond Théret, a timid father and muffled husband, was terrorized by his son and his wife's violence. He comforted himself with the two little girls, who were gentle like him.

Blood was bubbling up from René's wound. It was long, a little curved, the sides neat. It spread out on the right cheek, began under the eye socket, extended down the mandible. It would have required several stitches.

"Should I call Dr. Gorin?" suggested Mr. Théret.

"Phooey," said Mrs. Théret, "that old monkey! He'll send him to the hospital; he's good for nothing. If he aims for one butt cheek he pricks the other. No."

She was in brilliant form, decidedly. But no one laughed.

"Let's see if it's really deep."

René, passive, inched his cheek closer to her. His mother, squinting her eyelids, acted the expert, muttered "hmmm, hmmm," her mouth tight, and said that it could have been worse.

"Call Ambreuse," she concluded. "At least she's not the chatty kind, and she won't be poking around asking for explanations."

René was patting his cheek and neck with a rag, which was already scarlet. The clothes he'd taken off were saturated with blood as well.

"Now I'm not asking you anything," said Mrs. Théret, "but were there other casualties? ..."

René said no.

"If you start fighting with a knife, guess what my friend, you'd better be ready for anything. It's either him or you!" Louise-Théret affirmed, heroic, as if she'd led a hundred dagger skirmishes.

"I didn't have a knife," murmured René. He told an exaggerated story in a single burst, exaggerated, half-false. He wanted to play the man, the tough guy, he wanted to boast, and protect himself from his mother by wrapping himself in a great adventure.

"I didn't," he said, "I was just having a normal fight with a guy, guys who aren't from around here, they're, hmm ... buddies from Saint-Loup … We were fighting normally, and then one of 'em tried to get me from behind … He's the one who had the knife, luckily I felt it, so I got the cut here 'cause he missed me … otherwise it would've been here, I don't know, he was crazy."

René had just slit his throat with an index finger. Mrs. Théret suddenly grew shocked and afraid. The boy's story disgusted her, woke up her fears in the form of hostility and anger. She imagined her son in a vacant lot or a dead-end surrounded with brick walls, under a full-moon, alone against the Black Wolves or the Blue Tigers, a terrible band of hoodlums, the sons of workers, of whores, each one of them brandishing butcher knives, razors, jagged bottles.

"You'll tell me your life story later," she said. "For now, I don't want you going out. You're not allowed. You hear? You hear? You can spend the day here, with me. And you've not allowed to see anyone. And you're lucky you got … this, or I'd show you what kind of a brat you are. Knife fights, at thirteen! … Or at any age, for that matter!"

Dr. Ambreuse would come by after dinner. On the phone, she explained what they should do in the meantime. Mr. Théret went out to buy the first-aid products. Mrs. Théret was fuming.

"… Here! With me! All day long! And when you go back to school it'll be the same thing! I want … you hear me … I want proof that you went! We'll have a special notebook that you'll have them sign! Stamped by the headmaster! Every day! You hear! And the rest of the time you're gonna stay here! With us! And those friends of yours, they can stay out! And at night you'll be locked in! Locked in!"

She made the gesture of turning a key in a lock. Then René finally had the right to go and lay down. He had lost too much blood, he was white, he was having vertigo, he was about to black out, Louise Théret could see it coming. Let him get on with it! She went with him, left the bedroom open and had to take leave of the boy: clients had come in. But she had her eye on him.

As was often the case when she had nothing else to do, Amélie-Lyane was asking herself what the better name would be: Amélie-Lyane Glairat, Amélie-Lyane Boitard, Amélie-Lyane Boitard-Glairat, Amélie-Lyane Glairat-Boitard. So far, because of some whim on the part of her parents, the girl had her father's name, and the boy that of his mother. Despite Glairat's reputation, Amélie-Lyane wasn't satisfied with this allotment. As a matter of fact, all things considered, she would have preferred her paternal grandmother's maiden name, Maurice's mother and grandpa Gaston Glairat's wife. Her maiden name was Constance Pinon. That was nice, 'Pinon.' The dream would have been *Amélie-Lyane Constance*. When her father would become deputy, she ... Oh that kid! François-Gérard was walking around again with his business erect.

"Go ahead why don't you, parade your dingding in the air," protested Amélie-Lyane, "it doe-sn't-in-te-rest-me-in-the-least!"

François-Gérard sneered. His sister sneered too.

Since their childhood, Laure and Maurice's progeny had maintained certain nudist, if not indecent habits. Laure Boitard considered it so graceful, so otherworldly. Despite this, since puberty, Amélie actively hid her body. François, on the other hand, took advantage of being the youngest, and of his twelve-years of age—provided he was alone with his sister. On the pretext of a bath he would undress, hang around naked, pestering her.

Amélie-Lyane was used to this ritual. She made sure to act disdainful and exasperated every time, as was required for the game.

"Another bath you're running for nothing, I guess ..." she commented with irony.

"No! I'm gonna take one!" said François-Gérard.

You could hear the bathtub filling up. François hated to wash, but when he was done with his display, he had to go through the motions he'd initiated. He would close the door, shake a foot in the water, grumble "glub, glub," wet his hair a bit, and stir the bath water a little bit more with his other foot. Then he'd slip on papa's large robe and douse his head and toes in eau de Cologne. He would drain the bathtub. As it was emptying, he would admire himself in the mirror, flattered to be himself, and pretending to be a clown or his mother. You're so handsome, so beautiful, Françoa-Géraaard. He'd scrunch his face into a rabbit pout. You're very rabbit, very, very, Françoa! What about the noodle, huh? … Hum, not bad. Not bad, my boy. He'd finish himself off in three tugs of the wrist, listening to the last burp of the drain. He would sample the smell of his dick with one or two fingers, which he would sniff, finding it delectable, as he left the bathroom. He loved that aroma, sometimes lessened by bathing, as he did take a shower once in a while. François had a disposition for pleasure, and, since the spring, a new taste for insolence, pranks, bad words, jokes, and imitations. He was nearing the difficult years.

"By the way it's not dingding, it's ding-a-ling," he said to his sister.

"Call it what you want, the poor thing, it doesn't make a difference!" said Amélie-Lyane.

They'd willingly jab at each other for an entire afternoon, an entire evening, exchanging conventional nasty remarks, laughing sourly, getting annoyed.

Between the four of them, the Glairat parents and kids, everything always sounded off. It was like the phoniness of vaudeville, staging bourgeois families the way they imagined themselves to be. Modern, nonconformist, wildly breezy: everyone was very funny and had a lot of personality, they adored each other, they shone. In the Glairat home, this tonality reigned to the point of nauseating the most complicit of visitors. You'd leave sickened. The Glairats would feel entranced by themselves and the show they'd provided: weren't they ideal?

"Oh the poor thing, it's sad enough that twelve years have passed and that he's still the same … if I were you I'd hide it," said Amélie.

Defeated, François, who now had an erection so intense that it pained his anus, cried:

"Yeah, well your pussy's as big as a cow's!"

"I don't see the connection, first of all, and don't you think you might be exaggerating just a teeny bit? Don't lay it on so thick …"

"Fine," François cut in, "not like a cow, let's say, like, uhh, an ass, uhh, a she-ass!"

"… You're dense, François-Gérard," said Amélie. "What about that bath? … Let me point out that your feet don't smell like roses! And the color doesn't look good either."

"My feet, my ass," yelped François. "You suck balls!"

Amélie-Lyane contortioned her face into an appropriate grimace and sighed through her nostrils.

"They're not dirty," her brother went on. "Here, look!"

He had come nearer, and under the pretext of lifting his foot up towards Amélie (she slouched in the style of Mrs. Récamier on the arm of an easy chair), he whacked her in the face with his little curved penis.

Amélie-Lyane was outraged, and pushed him away with a slap that lashed against the boy's member. He bawled:

"Ow! Hey, take it easy! Why don't you just go ahead! You're a jerk!"

"Shhh! … You don't even know what that means" … she said mysteriously, her nose lifted all the way up into the air.

She pinched the air so that her brother would stop hollering. He was tiring, he couldn't control himself, and he was becoming hysterical.

Unfortunately, François had just learned the obscene sense of the word. And he explained it with a gesture, eyes rolling up in his head, hand waving in front of his penis, salivating as he mumbled "mmmmhhhhhh." He looked at her with eyes that were particularly comical and shiny. "Mmmmhhhhhh."

Amélie-Lyane turned her face away and repressed a laugh, squeezing and stretching her lips, shrugging her shoulders, crossing her eyes over her wide, upturned nose, as if to say what a little idiot if he thinks he'll make me laugh how pitiful. She was only interested in mature men. In twenty-five year olds. By the way she wasn't a virgin: just a ditz.

"Naked again, François-Gérard!" Laure-Boitard exclaimed, gaily, as she entered the living room.

On the spot, the boy spun around on his heels and left the room.

"What a pretty little butt your brother has!" she added for Amélie-Lyane.

She threw her purse on the sofa. She moaned:

"What an exhausting day, sweetheart! I think I even prefer teaching, at least you're sitting down!"

"His butt is the only good thing about him!" said Amélie. "Sometimes I wonder whom you actually conceived that monkey with … By the way, have you seen Guillard Senior, I'm sorry, *Mister* Guillard?

"Don't be so hard on him, sweetheart! François-Gérard is still a child … he is natural, spontaneous … You're not jealous are you? … No, I haven't seen Guillard. I left a note, I asked him to bring samples tonight or tomorrow. Will you be here tomorrow?"

"You think I'm jealous of a monkey! He's a joker, that's what he is, that little boy of yours who you think is so spontaneous, what a ham! … Tomorrow, let me see, it depends what time," Amélie added in a tone that meant "this is my life, mind your own business."

Laure Boitard didn't appreciate that pose. For several months now, she'd promised to give her daughter contraceptives, under the simple condition that the girl would report back on how she used them. But Amélie hadn't asked for anything, and hadn't said a thing about it to this day. Why did she pretend to have a private life? It was ridiculous. And what a mark of defiance. Laure Boitard shrugged her shoulders:

"I suppose you could be here around seven or eight, right?"

"I could … yes of course I could, and for good reason I can!" creaked Amélie-Lyane, vexed.

"But sweetheart, you're the one who asked that we redo your room! I don't care! You're unbelievable! I feel like I'm torturing you. If you changed your mind, just say so, calmly, and …"

"With this rickety furniture, anyway, even reupholstered …" Amélie sighed.

"You're terrible, sweetheart … I know that you don't like your furniture, even though it's absolutely charming. Well, so be it! … All I'm asking for is a little patience, I hope you can understand that … But no! You always need it all right away …"

"What needle?" inquired François-Gérard with wit.

He'd already taken his bath, or what he labeled as such.

"… Oh no, something stinks!" moaned Amélie-Lyane, plugging her nose.

"What! It's daddy's cologne!"

"He wears less of it you know, sweetheart, he wears less of it," said Boitard.

"In any case, fine, I'll be here tomorrow. Well, that is, if he doesn't come by tonight," Amélie said. "But are you sure these adhesive fabrics …"

"You know I'm not sure sweetheart! Of course I'm not sure! We've never used them before, we'll see! Please don't be so … so … you are so … aggressive with me! You should know that …"

"Kitty, kitty, kitty," François taunted. "Meeooow! Meeeooooow! …"

There was a calm jangling of keys.

"Here comes Maurice. Not wetting the whistle *hoy dia*?" François said.

"You're too … too high-spirited today, sweetheart, you're becoming impolite!" admonished Laure Boitard.

She turned towards the threshold to the living room with concern.

Maurice Glairat entered. He didn't seem to have had a drink.

"Good evening, everyone. Good evening," he said, with a serious, sweet smile.

"So is it true that you're not plastered today?" François cried in falsetto. "Mommy doesn't want me to say it!"

"It's true, sweetheart," said Glairat mellifluously. "But don't say *mommy*, it's ugly. It's dumb. It stinks. It's passé. Don't say it. Okay?"

"Well, uh, *Laure* doesn't want me to."

"Yes, she doesn't. You've just said that. Right. She doesn't. Yes. But as a matter of fact, she may be wrong, since as a matter of fact in the end …"

He interrupted himself to suck Laure Boitard's mouth theatrically. He didn't remove his important glasses. As for Lady Boitard, she only wore them at school, or for writing. She was far-sighted; her lover was near-sighted.

Laure realized that he was reeking of … Vodka maybe, but with a touch of anise, or juniper, or …

"Akvavit," Glairat whispered in her ear, when he'd withdrawn his lips. "But just a little! 100 proof, I think … A delight that … Well, you know, Humières, the one who spent three years in Jutland …"

Humières was an old bachelor, an old teacher who had political connections somewhere, acerbic, contemptuous manners, and the vocation of a gray eminence. Parisians paid him visits. He hated Glairat. It was astounding that he would have invited him for a drink.

"At his house?" Laure whispered, prudent, her pupils sparkling with hope.

"Yes. Yes. Absolutely. At his house I have to say. At his house. Indeed. What a sinister place," said Maurice. "Sinister. And that old virgin ... Well."

"Honey! Is it true! I'm beaming!" yelped Laure Boitard.

"Maurice, you got a twenty?" François was saying, tangled in his endless robe.

Two or three times a week, he'd ransack his father's pockets. This privilege was official, mocked, ritually contested.

"Dopey! Look, dopey!" nasalized Amélie-Lyane. "You know, like the one in Snow White, the cartoon, the dwarf!"

"You got some yesterday, sweetheart," protested Boitard, almost stiffly.

"Sweetheart," said Maurice Glairat as he turned towards François, "I've got ... hmm ... 'twenty' indeed ... though I am not sure if you mean francs or cents ... well, *basta!* ... Hmm ... but ... do you feel it's absolutely essential that you search me? ... . Hmm ... Hmm ... Do I ever rummage through pockets, your ... um ... pockets, yours? ..."

"Only 'cause I don't keep wine bottles there, otherwise you would!" François-Gérard retorted. He'd unearthed and snatched a ten-franc note crumpled in a ball.

Maurice Glairat appealed to the ceiling with his eyes, shrugged his shoulders and smiled, spreading his arms a little apart, like a penguin putting on airs. He venerated his son. He would have placed him on a Pythian stool and draped him in vapors, as long as the child remained a statue of Liberty, only easy and better.

Yet François-Gérard had always been an obedient child, passive, hard working, well behaved, indolent, almost bland. A larva that the sap and juice of puberty (thought Glairat) were henceforth in the process of metamorphosing. The monster was going to blossom, to justify, to testify, to accomplish, to reincarnate, to transfigure, to be.

"You know that I'm in love with you," Glairat indulged, viscous, pointing a slightly trembling, slightly limp index finger towards his son's nose. "But don't you think you're going a bit too far … hmm … just a bit? …"

"Gee, that's just what your daughter says, exactly, that I'm going too far!" François cried.

"That's right, absolutely," said Amélie-Lyane, like a prude who couldn't tolerate a pinch. She emitted a long, irritated cackle.

Maurice Glairat, ear tugged by the new sound, fluttered his eyelashes under his glasses and slowly, pompously turned his face towards Amélie.

"Yes … My marvelous daughter … Marvelous … And what does she say?"

He dedicated a smile to her that was so alcoholic that even Laure Boitard had to face the facts. Glairat had come home earlier because he'd gotten hammered faster than usual. That was it. He would, in a minute, totter, purr, get his legs tangled up in imaginary obstacles: his legs, for instance. He was holding himself up too carefully.

"Dad you know I clobbered an old woman!" cried Francois-Gérard all of a sudden.

He was making it up. His sister shrugged her shoulders and shook her head. His mother didn't pay attention. His father reacted.

Maurice Glairat, indeed, reoriented his mask, lowered it with difficulty, saw François, spread his lips with difficulty, stretched them with difficulty into the smile of an indulgent patriarch who understood everything and contemplated, disillusioned, the generation of generations.

"… Death, François-Gérard, death … hmm … indeed … a kid's joke … A kid's joke … Yes … Hmm. Hmmm … Hmm …"

He shut his mouth again. Everyone understood that this was the final word. He would then exit the stage, remove his tie, fling down his vest, and vacillate to his room while he jostled about the furniture.

François-Gérard, dissatisfied, looked at his mother and twisted his nose in his fist.

Laure ignored the message. Maurice needed, so needed her. (… No, I wasn't neglecting my son … but it's clear that Maurice has such a great need for me … and that child's attachment to me … almost a sickness … pathological … psychoanalytical … for his mother … me … I shouldn't encourage it, I … me …)

She had to save Maurice, his immense brain, and his massive oeuvre. The alcohol. A terrible drug. The thing that was the matter. In short, adult problems. (Certainly, privileged adults, but nonetheless …) It was about time François-Gérard understood this, and gave their couple some breathing room. His sick attachment, pathological, almost psychoanalytical, to his mother, a dubious ambiguity in his relationship to his father … Jealousy? Be that as it may, it would be necessary from now on to compel the boy to detach from them, to project himself differently, to … This crazy love was so …

Laure Boitard followed Glairat. Their children looked at one another with satisfaction and dashed to pillage the fridge. They carried the TV into Amélie's room and, slouched on the bed side by side, gorged on cold leftovers and empty spiel while cracking jokes.

They adored these evenings when their father came home early enough so that Laure, monopolized by the drunkard, left them in peace. They almost reverted to their natural state.

The one they called Cormaillon the Elder, who came from a farming family—his mother had become a cleaning woman and his father a police officer—had given Jean-Baptiste Seignelet an obscene card game when they'd parted ways.

It all started because of tampons. Cormaillon had explained to Seignelet what the things that sporadically clogged the crappers at their place were used for. Jean-Baptiste had been stunned: he wouldn't have believed that hole could be so large, so long, and so vast. He'd been tricked by the swelling of the tampon in the water of the toilet bowl. Cormaillon, ignorant despite his fourteen or fifteen years, didn't counter it. An immense red cave gaped open all around them.

Afterwards, Cormaillon's cheekbones had become speckled with blood. His face had widened into an excessive smile that revealed a lot of his teeth, lemon yellow, short, and rotting. He'd also squinted his eyes into little rat's eyes, and his pimply forehead had shone bright.

He'd then invited Seignelet into a shrubby thicket on the edge of the meadow where the boys had assembled. He'd wanted them to touch, and had partially tossed off his clothes. At the time, he'd looked so crazy that pimples seemed to be growing in the middle of his eyes.

Jean-Baptiste refused, but did not dare leave. He'd turned away from the nutcase. His attention had wandered. Turds, toilet paper, candy wrappers, encrusted newspapers. Nettles. Not a single bird.

As he was orgasming, Cormaillon the Elder had nudged Jean-Baptiste in the ribs, and had panted or stuttered:

"Look! Look! Look!"

In his other hand, he was holding a bunch of fanned-out cards that Seignelet had looked at at first, politely. Hearts, diamonds, the frizzy heads of buck-naked housewives. Large wet nurse tits, arched and creamy horsewomen, chubby pear-shaped mothers. Women.

These pictures (the game was probably from the fifties or thereabouts: maybe Cormaillon had stolen it from his father, or a young uncle) were in color, with a decor of potted plants. The thighs were squeezed tight. Some legs had clothes, boots. Club, spade, jack, queen, king, mommy.

Penis fat red shaken frothy red fat polished. Slosh, slosh, white of slosh, slosh, a slosh of … A few. Sleazy white slosh. Daddy.

The juice nauseated Jean-Baptiste even more than the pictures. He was definitely not in a hurry to be like Cormaillon. It made your stomach turn.

Cormaillon had plucked some leaves from the shrub to clean himself off. They prickled a little, according to him.

Jean-Baptiste had hidden the pack of obscene cards in the tube of his sock, near the ankle, and carefully rolled back the leg of his pants. He wanted to toss it all away, to keep it, he didn't know.

When the Seignelet children went to bed, Jean-Baptiste stopped Dominique in the hallway, in front of their rooms. Philippe, the youngest, was already in bed. Bertrand was speaking with their parents; you could hear his raucous, ungainly voice twist around itself, moving from cavernous to shrill and back again. He was probably emitting convictions, promises; the tone was sincere, gay, and elephantine. That also turned Jean-Baptiste's stomach a bit: a communicative Bertrand. Bertrand confiding to mom and dad, expressing himself in their language, stepping into their view. Quick nausea.

Jean-Baptiste held out the pack, which was made of rigid and transparent plastic:

"Here! Cromagnon gave this to me! If you want it. They're old ladies."

Dominique smiled:

"Who?"

"A guy you don't know called Cormaillon. We say Cromagnon, 'cause he's …"

Jean-Baptiste mimed what Cormaillon was. Like Bertrand, pretty much, more or less. It must be age. Or not: Dominique was in the same boat too, with his thirteen or fourteen years. And he didn't look like them at all. He was well behaved, intelligent, and affable. He was kind even to Philippe, whom he liked a lot—without thinking about it, incidentally; a kid is just a kid, you don't need them to be anything else.

The funny thing was that only a thin wall separated these two kind souls, Dominique and Philippe, from the master bedroom where Mr. and Mrs. Seignelet rarely but lumberingly engaged in their labored lovemaking. Luckily, Philippe neither heard nor understood a thing. He was listening to something else, which mesmerized him at night and woke him in the morning: a, round, gentle, lunar clock as calm as the heart, which was the pulse of his blood in his ears crushed against his pillowcase. A nocturnal or morning bell; the strange central square of a village under the snow. For there was a sound of winter when Philippe curled up into a fetal position in bed: in the summertime he slept flat on his back, there was no more blood resonating, no more bells, or any imaginary country.

Dominique, on the other hand, heard the conjugal duties. He knew. It made him sick. He didn't speak about it to anyone. But he feared Mrs. Seignelet's strange whining, her answer to the swollen alcoholic stomach crushing her own puffy belly:

"Hip, hip, hip, hip. Hip, hip, hip, hip."

It was a chirped hiccup, sequenced, regular, as if someone were pinching Raymonde Seignelet according to the ticking of a clock, and she were mechanically answering the kazoo-sounding note of a swinging baby:

"Hip, hip, hip, hip. Heee … Hm. Hip, hip, hip, hip, hip. Hk! Hk! Hk! Hk! Huh, huh, huh, huh. Hm! Hm! Hm! Hm! Hm! Hip! Hip, hip, hip, hip. Hppp."

The rattling wooden bedframe accompanied this yelping, this tick-tock.

As for Bertrand and Jean-Baptiste, they shared a room sheltered from this scourge, although they'd have handled it better.

"Naked women?" said Dominique Seignelet. "No, I don't want it. Thanks for asking though."

Through the case, he'd caught a glimpse of the first photo: a forty-year-old standing in front of a jungle background with such thick pubic hair that it looked as if she was wearing a large knitted G-string, with black and brown flecks. Her hair was worn à la Colette, parted on the side, coarse and pudgy frizzes, disheveled. She was made up, and bared her teeth. Her hands, covered in knotted veins and furrowed with scale-like wrinkles, were stained from washing dishes and laundry in the sink.

Dominique laughed:

"This is what the guy's jerkin' off to? Crazy."

"Cromagnon? Seriously! It makes his ears smoke!" affirmed Jean-Baptiste. "What the hell should I do with 'em? Give 'em back?"

"No," said Dominique. "Put 'em in Bertrand's stuff, that'll be funny."

They were delighted. Jean-Baptiste pocketed the pack with satisfaction.

Dominique showed much self-restraint. He rarely masturbated. But recently, he sometimes stained his sheets in his sleep. Raymonde Seignelet had discovered it. She had been furious, outraged. Her eldest son had never been this filthy! Never!

And in fact, Bertrand knew how to plan ahead. His mother thought he was pure. Maybe she imagined that it evaporated in schoolwork, suddenly distilled into equations, frog dissections, geographical maps, Latin or German conjugations, into pole-vaulting, into pursed lips and crossed arms.

Dominique, on the other hand, didn't distill or transubstantiate anything, the little slut. All you needed to do was look at his clear face, with no pimples, to get it. Wasn't his perversity threatening the innocent Philippe? She should talk about it to Mr. Seignelet, bring Dominique to a doctor. Till then, she'd mention it tacitly, or give him a good spanking next time. The hypocrite. Oh, he liked to pretend to be holier than thou, did he! He was an infection, a sick kid.

Dominique was entering his room, but Jean-Baptiste held him back:

"No, wait … There's something … Wait. You … I can tell you, come. It's something that has … Come into the bathroom."

They took asylum there. Dominique, docile, watched his younger brother as he spaced out. He didn't like brushing his teeth in the evening. The taste of toothpaste in bed. The brush that was too stiff. He should have forced himself: you lose your teeth, you begin to decay, you smell bad, you … Dominique forgot the rest. He often thought about ideas, and forgot them at the same time. Yes, the body decays, decomposes, as soon as you stop scouring it, forcing it, it decays, it decays, you become a living carcass, you decay even more quickly than a corpse. Scour, brush, discipline, train, cut, slap the decaying machine, the vile thing: oneself. Dominique wrote poems without rhymes, which he hid for fear that someone might read them. He didn't trust anyone, and he had no friends. He would read his poems with something close to disgust. They were full of mistakes; they were dirty, dirty, decaying. Train, control, correct, sanction, punish. Dirty, dirty texts. Decomposed alive. Keep watch, slap, tear apart, slap, stop himself from doing that. Dirty, dirty, dirty. Worse than a body. What if his parents discovered this double of Dominique, nauseating, rotten, contorted, harmless and naked. Throw it in the fire! In the toilet, quick! Purify.

"I just clobbered an old woman," murmured Jean-Baptiste.

4

The Roquins put Julien to bed and treated him. They didn't speak to him, didn't look at him. They brought him food, changed his dressings. He lived flat on his stomach or on his side. He didn't read anything, slept a lot, didn't say a word, and ate almost nothing.

The open wounds healed rather quickly. He was able to prop himself up against his pillow. He'd have long scars across his shoulder blades. The pain that took the longest to heal ran along his spine, from the neck down to the waist. It hurt the most when he stood up.

Julien waited, stubborn and mute, to be back on his feet, to be able to run again, to bend over, to steal, to strike. Then he fled, around ten o'clock one morning, through the door.

His parents weren't far: they were working on the other side of the house. At noon, they discovered their son's disappearance, when Simone called him for lunch.

They didn't understand immediately. Then they got worried, visited Julien's room, the toilet, and the bathroom. They called out. They walked around the garden. No. There was no one there.

He hadn't necessarily run away. With his hot head, Julien had gone out without telling them that he was feeling better. So the beating hasn't amended him, that low-life?

Nonetheless, Simone Roquin rummaged here and there, with suspicion, and soon the truth was out. Julien had taken his clothes, some food; he had emptied a cigar box where they kept the money from what they sold (vegetables, fruits, seeds) to clients, to neighbors. About one hundred francs.

To go where?

This provided Simone Roquin with a lovely opportunity for a crisis, a chance to make a scene with her husband. There were broken dishes, a bleeding nose, shouts that the neighbors heard despite the sound of the radios. They weren't concerned; every one's got a right to his turn, isn't that so. It's them today, us tomorrow. What a temper, that Roquin: what endurance! What a voice! No one in the neighborhood knew how to last as long as she did: not even Mrs. Vitard when she whipped the dog that she kept chained up in the basement. Even though the poor thing howled as loudly as she did: it was stimulating. Mrs. Vitard, widow without children, was high strung. Viduity is so difficult. She got her dogs from the pound. They didn't last a year.

The Roquins had a lot of trouble agreeing on what was to be done about Julien. Simone wanted to inform the police. A child of ten can't survive alone. Julien wasn't far away: and the cops, if they hurried, would soon find him. Jean Roquin had another opinion. He preferred to investigate on his own. It would be more discreet, because the child's back was a problem. If Julien spoke, lifted his shirt, there would be a fuss. Of course, the police would understand, there was nothing to worry about: but people talk. All in all, when you were in business like they were, you had to watch your reputation.

Simone Roquin conceded to these arguments. She wailed against the general hypocrisy: who in the world didn't beat their kids? There weren't that many ways to civilize them, and everyone did it, sooner or later. They'd make sweet faces, they'd fondle their sweethearts in your face to better pummel them from behind, and then they pointed the finger at you if you were frank. Bastards. Scum. It was disgusting. Did it make her vegetables less tasty if her kid's ass was a bit red? Slaps don't bruise pears. The little shithead, if they'd spanked him like his brothers, he'd have stayed in line. Now it was too late. Roquin would see, she was sure of it: Julien would turn out dead, or a murderer.

Jean Roquin made a round of the bakeries, the groceries out-lying the town. His questions were indirect, astute, so he thought. He didn't want to reveal Julien's disappearance.

Nobody had seen the child. There were no leads on the gro-cers' end. Julien hadn't stocked up here. As for the stores where they didn't know the Roquins, closer to the country or in town, there were so many children running errands …

Question his friends. But who did he hang out with? Jean Roquin didn't know a thing. He stopped by the school thinking that the teachers could tell him something, give him some names.

A surprise awaited him there: Julien, that same afternoon, had in fact been in class. He had explained to the teacher that he'd been ill. She had asked him to bring proof the next day: he was absent too often; he was too much of a liar. Julien had promised a note from his father, a letter from the doctor, what-ever was necessary. He'd seemed worried, distracted, tired: maybe it was a real convalescence, after all. But he had such a gloomy nature. Jean Roquin wanted to pay a visit to the little boy's locker. The teacher showed it to him. It was empty. It didn't even have a lock anymore. She was surprised.

So that's what Julien had come for. What was he hiding in that locker that was so essential? What compromising stash?

His son's audacity worried Jean Roquin even more than his running away. He decided to confide in the teacher. She didn't think there was anything serious in what he told her. According to her, Julien would probably come back home to eat, to sleep. They should welcome him calmly, make him understand that he was excessive, that he was being a nuisance to himself.

"What if he doesn't come back?" asked Roquin. He had not dared mention the beating.

The teacher recommended informing the police if Julien didn't sleep at home tonight. But she didn't think that would happen; there was no need to exaggerate, the child was very … too independent, certainly, and if they'd exerted a more watchful control in the past, even some strictness, without going as far as corporal punishment of course, that might perhaps have averted the way things were now …

She emptied her load of platitudes; Roquin wasn't listening. He retained the idea of waiting until tomorrow to notify the cops. Only he, Jean Roquin, knew why the child wouldn't come home this evening, or tomorrow, or maybe ever. But other people weren't going to take his running away seriously after just a few hours. Tomorrow, the incident would have swelled, it would be evaluated, it would be reckoned with; another day and it would be presentable, credible. Roquin would no longer have to confess the cumbersome detail.

Yet the locker in the locker room was a problem. Was it a kid's mystery, one of those meaningless pranks that childhood feeds on, or a real secret? Jean Roquin could easily imagine his son associating with thugs, led into wrongdoing by older boys of the same bad seed.

Mrs. Roquin made another scene at dinner. What her husband had told her was monstrous. The empty place setting at the table was monstrous. This disgusting life was a monstrosity. Julien had been right to run away. She would eventually do the same. Enough was enough: she'd worked like a dog, she'd raised three thankless kids, three bastards, and she had been faithful, faithful! … To an impotent, a scumbag. She had the right, if not to some respect (she wasn't asking for that much) or some affection (she wasn't that nuts), but to rest, simply, to a holy peace, my God, to some rest.

Roquin received a slight injury on the forearm. His wife had trampled their dinner. He mopped the floor and improvised an onion soup for himself. Anxiety, anger, and resentment always made him hungry. He finished nearly an entire loaf of bread with his soup, soup that he ate straight out of the pan. He slept in his older sons' bedroom. He had resolved never to share a bed with his wife again: it was highly unlikely that this would disturb her, after all. She'd yell.

The following day, he went to the police station around noon. The officers were polite, indifferent. Would they find Julien? Hard to say. Searching the island was not conceivable. In short, no one would lift a finger. They'd wait for more information. Say, wasn't the Roquin boy friends with a boy from old Saint-Rémi, a certain Théret, René? Grocers. No? Too bad. That kid had also disappeared since, hmm, a few days. The coincidence was strange. They really didn't know one another? Sometimes parents don't know everything.

Well, Mr. Roquin should keep himself abreast. Yes, call. This time, that time. Put an announcement in the paper, a picture, and a description. A kid that young, how intriguing. No, the other kid, from the old town, thirteen years old. Yes. Nowadays, at that age they think they're men, the influence of television and what not. They want to live their life, the idiots. Do we have a life, I ask you? … It's no surprise they turn out badly. Nonetheless, Mr. Roquin shouldn't torment himself too soon. Then again … Unfortunately, yes, in these cases it's usually now or never. Fishy. By the thousands. Hot and bothered, hot under the collar. Heavy heart. Heavy thingamajig, really. No, not at ten … No, in this case it's … Hmm. In a way, yes. Not to mention the worst, of course. But those crimes happen more rarely than unfortunate parents think, rightly so. Oh yes. Oh, never again, no, no. Fishy. You don't seriously believe … America? God knows. Networks of … you never know. Yes, in the end, we don't know that much. If we knew all that was to be known we would know a lot. And how surprised we'd be.

His weight, his height, what clothes he was wearing, the color of his hair, of his eyes, etc. You've forgotten? His schoolteacher will tell us. The medical record. Background, parents, juvenile delinquency, opinions, perversions? Sure, sure, go ask his school. Mr. Roquin found everyone at the police precinct very kind. He thanked them warmly, he left satisfied.

No one had heard of Julien at the hospital, at the morgue, and at the port, no one had seen a small boy sailing off alone. Neither dead, nor injured, nor gone. Excellent news. Would it last? … Roquin thought about his wife again.

René and Julien's disappearance didn't make a big impression: they were nobodies. Announcements were published, republished, forgotten. The families suffered. Everyone understood. The month of May was rich in current affairs: spring was in the air. Deadly accidents, muggings, snatched purses, burglaries, the sap was gushing forth. Just like every year, indignation coming from the residential neighborhoods was expressed with firmness; feature articles echoed this in local publications. Maurice Glairat had produced a piece with an anarchist title: *Those With Nothing Fear Nothing*. He affirmed that only the rich got robbed; the one who goes around naked has no fear of being mugged. He cited the Gospels and skillfully won over the town elites in a well-handled last paragraph. This audacious sermon was a big step for his career. He saw himself as a sort of agnostic Saint Paul. And sensual as well.

One night, some vandals broke a few shop windows. This was new and serious: it had been years since the town had known such excesses. People pointed to the article in *The Reunited Republican*, to its brilliant paradoxes, to its panegyric to Attila's hordes and to the saints of God. This is what it led to.

The vandals, the police remarked, had committed strange thefts. All the stores (there were three or four of them) were petit bourgeois, useful businesses; all the objects stolen from the display windows were banal, stupid, bargain buys. It was as if some young, modest couples had wanted to set themselves up for free without overstepping their social status. They must have had children who were already old, tallish; and with abnormally large appetites for hammers and nails. Was it to each nail its hammer? … A crew of drunkards, probably.

But the brutality of the procedure was outrageous. So far, on the island, they'd been sheltered from modern violence. And they didn't want any of it. Why didn't they do those kinds of things in the communist suburbs, and leave the distinguished and whole-some coastal inhabitants in peace. There would be an increase in the number of police; they'd create militias of good citizens; the violence would be drowned in blood if need be, but they would stay among honest people.

The weather was beautiful. Despite themselves, people succumbed to serenity, to torpor. All was gentle in the world. Gardens dazzled, embalmed, captivated. There was neither the time nor the inclination for unhappiness. It was impossible to imagine that there had been thieves here. In our times, don't we have it all? What was missing in this springtime?

Aimé Bataillon was suffering in bed: he'd had a sudden desire for sweets that, like an incipient toothache, had progressively upset his old man's comatose insomnia. Nothing was more painful than these throbbing, patient, ignobly skillful urges once they settled in, titillated you, probed you, visited you, prickle you—and all of a sudden, bit you to the bone, ignited you from the heart to the toes and had you salivating and drooling foam like a baby who spoke. Isn't that what it was to be possessed by the devil, to be tortured by Temptation, by desire—the worst sort of desire: the one that pinched the stomach.

Too bad, Bataillon could not resist. He was never able to. There was no reason to force himself, except for the atrocious constraint that he was about to inflict upon himself, which was to get up. The necessary, abominable effort was kind enough to be brief, external. Mr. Bataillon shifted his butt cheeks beneath himself, and, crawling flat on his back, staking his elbows and his heels, he sat up in the middle of the bed. Then he wriggled his behind, which was very bony, to reach the edge of the bed where he dangled his legs. An immense heave stiffened all of his bones. That was it, he was on his feet.

His bedroom was in the basement of the house, where they'd set up the kitchen and the laundry room. Air circulated through these rooms via basement windows, spacious and without bars.

This tiny house belonged to Aimé Bataillon's children, his son-in-law and his daughter, who had agreed to host the old man after he'd become a widower, on the condition that he pay a monthly rent. He gave them the whole of his small pension. A bit of pocket money was returned to him, which he saved. He was treated like a difficult child, whose whims must not be indulged. He was fed properly, carelessly and without cutting corners. His room in the basement was dark, but safe and dry, nearly empty, but clean. Better to die here than at the hospice. That would be his privilege, on the condition that he not become infirm or incontinent: his children wouldn't tolerate it.

He also had two grandchildren, whom he sometimes caught a glimpse of. The parents didn't like to have the kids hang about the old man. There was something unwholesome about it, questionable.

Aimé Bataillon loved Arquebuse. The liqueur was too expensive: his son-in-law locked it up in the dining room cupboard, and he made a mark on the bottle to keep track of the level of the liquid. Some nights, Bataillon managed to steal a few drops. The back and forth trek from the basement took nearly an hour. The cupboard lock was easy to pick, but excessively difficult to close, especially without making a clanking noise, and readjusting the level of the liqueur was a delicate task. Mr. Bataillon used a little rubbing alcohol in which he melted a sugar cube. The effect was just adequate: in any case, his son-in-law was yet to discover the trick. Bataillon groped around the tile floor with his bare feet, found his slippers, felt his way along to the light switch: he didn't have a bedside lamp.

Like a kid terrorized by his parents, he crept around furtively, keeping an ear out for the smallest noise. He dreamt of dipping a piece of bread in apple jelly. In the kitchen, grab the bread, the sugar, the rubbing alcohol (the first-aid kit was stored above the sink), a glass, and the little red plastic funnel. He checked that he had his safety pin. He had a craving for a butter cookie. He didn't know if his daughter had bought any.

He crossed the hallway, entered the kitchen without turning on the light: the glow coming from the street through the big basement window was enough, and he was afraid of calling attention to himself. What if a neighbor, awoken by accident, or coming back from a dinner, noticed a light coming through the basement window and mentioned it to his daughter the next day, without meaning any harm? What then? Probably nothing, but two precautionary measures, ten precautionary measures, etc., especially when one was a thief. Grandpa Burglar, rather. No laughing matter.

He looked for the basket where they kept the old crusts of bread: he enjoyed sucking on them all with whatever sugar or jam he could get his hands on. There was only one very big and very stale piece. He took a knife from the drawer in the kitchen table.

A ring of white light abruptly shone on him:

"Grandpa, shut your trap and put down your knife. There you go! ... Nice and slow!" whispered a rapid voice behind him. He felt a point prick his back.

Burglars. Murderers. Youngsters. Aimé Bataillon obeyed and started to shake violently. A second electric flashlight lit up, a second voice said, in a laughing tone:

"Hey grandpa, got your underpants with springs on? Don't be scared! We're not mean!"

"Shhhh," cut in the first.

They forbade him to turn around. They made Bataillon explain how the house was set up, the layout of the rooms and of the sleepers. They had the old man do penance in a corner of the kitchen, and, on the condition that he behave, they poured him some wine and, upon his stunned request, brought him a chair.

From that point on, Aimé could imagine that there were at least nine or ten robbers. They seemed to have formed a human chain to bring out whatever interested them. A garland that, from the little garden or from the street, descended through the basement window, rummaged among the basement, climbed to explore the whole house and, like the trunk of a drinking elephant, sucked up its contents. Objects circulated without a sound, without a bump: but the old man perceived whispers, furtive steps, guidance, strangled laughter, a path of nearly immaterial whispers.

"Here you go grandpa, if you get bored we found this!" said the laughing voice from behind Bataillon.

He fingered the object that had been placed on his knees: it was the bottle of Arquebuse.

He was bold enough to open it; he drank his fill. Such solitude.

"We're off now. Don't move an inch and keep it shut. You wouldn't want us to tie you up? Not keen on a gag? Right, you got it."

It was no longer the comforting voice that was saying this.

And, in a breath, the house was deserted: no one, nothing. Stupefied, tingling, lips and fingers sticky with liqueur, the old man retreated fearfully into his bedroom. He wouldn't alert his children. He would pretend to have slept deeply. They would blame him for this, but less than his cowardice. Cowardice? No, he would never explain: once you understood, it was all or nothing. With them—with his children—it was nothing. He left the bottle of Arquebuse on a step of the stairs.

His room hadn't been burglarized. And with good reason. All the same he checked to see if some small articles were still there. He hadn't even bothered to glance into the kitchen.

Why had such organized malefactors, such expert robbers robbed such humble people? Who could be so poor that a Bataillon house, in comparison, would seem like a treasure chest?

Later, when he was snug in bed, the old man thought his children would probably put him away in a home, because of all these things they'd have to buy again. What an expense, this theft! He cried and fell asleep, knocked out by alcohol.

Claire Fouilloux asked herself if one day she'd be happy. She imagined herself married with children. It happens. No, that wasn't ideal. She'd rather be a widow, with grandchildren. She played back her preferred clichés. Be an old lady, that's what Fouilloux would do in life. An exquisite old town house, maybe in the Saint-Huy neighborhood, or in Chemins-tors. The house didn't have a view on the sea, even though the other rich people enjoyed that (but she would be original). She'd tell her old and faithful maid named Faithful sentences such as, "Faithful, my kind Mary, would you kindly make us some fries with cream" (she would eat everything with cream). The maid would be poor but honest, although devoted, crying, "My God, my good mistress, and the codfish that has gone up again! My God if the price of codfish goes up like this what are we gonna do, sweet Jesus, what are we gonna do!" (No, Fouilloux would never again eat fish.) "Mary mother of God!" Her grandchildren would be exquisite little girls, the poor dears. Above all, no boys, they're dirty, they only have one thing in mind, and they mess everything up. "The poor dears, the poor dears, how fast they grow!" the brave and honest Faithful would lament. Claire Fouilloux asked herself how much money this happiness would cost. She would manage; she would marry a dirty old man; she would blow him till his heart gave out, or something happened in his brain; she would inherit his immense fortune and would no sooner be an exquisite old grandmother, fat pink cockleshell ribbons in her dolls' ringlets, the poor dears.

Old age was the only thing worth living. It was a sign of the times. But it would be a long wait: when Fouilloux counted the years she had left before then, she felt a vertigo of despondency, of despair. She almost felt like dying long before she could become a happy old lady. A long time before.

President Gassé would have made a good husband for her. He belonged to the category of old creeps to be stopped dead by heart attack. Part of the rich and powerful on the island, head of the Fishermen's Union, of the Chamber of Commerce, etc. But he was already married. In his fifties, he had followed a whim. He had bought himself a twenty-year old tart, a midget who looked like she was twelve. He had given her two kids, God knows how. Now, the dwarf had lost her charm and Gassé cheated on her with other illusions. He had caught wind of Fouilloux. He had activated his shady connections to get to her.

Fouilloux, impressed, has accepted it all. Silly, grotesque things, nothing too dirty. That egghead President Gassé was amusing. He wasn't brutal. He talked to you as if you were somebody, even if you were naked. Nice weather this morning, don't you see fiddlededee! Tourist season is off to an astounding start. What hard work you do my little Claire. Oh no, Mr. Gassé, I'm not too bored with you. Oh what a silly girl, I meant at the Baron factory. Oh Mr. Gassé, I'm so sorry. Yeah the factory, of course the factory, right.

Henri Gassé's obsession was to come to the rendezvous with a briefcase containing a little girl's outfit, its size adapted to the floozies whom he'd dress up. Claire hadn't been warned: she was shocked when he began his masquerade. It was revolting that he would take it out on childhood. He begged Fouilloux to dress up. She looked her nose down at him, set conditions. He had to order champagne (a bottle! demanded Claire), caviar, pickles, hard-boiled eggs, in short all that she desired. She got five hundred francs in advance, in hundred franc bills. She drank, disguised; she smashed the flute with a lofty gesture.

Excited, stunned, President Gassé surrendered. The minx suggested that the septuagenarian don her outfit: Claire was a poor little girl all alone with a dangerous sadist; she was about to cry, to scream for her mommy. Quick, Mr. Gassé needed to dress up as a mother, quick! And he had to protect her, comfort her, and defend her from the nasty man.

"Will you dyke me, girly?" cried the President. He took the skimpy underpants, the sunken bra, the chintzy stockings, and curled his plump feet up in the silly Mary Janes. He played mommy as he imagined it. He sent for more champagne, he called to cancel his first meeting of the afternoon. He kept humping the so-called maternal underpants; he felt that if Fouilloux kept up her inanities he'd get an erection.

She was charming as a little girl. She looked like a big cardboard doll, somewhat flattened by use. Henri Gassé squeezed her like a spring chicken: it felt good. He recommended she trim her bush: not everyone was keen on young hairs, dear Claire. He also wanted her not to wash before they met. Fouilloux went "Eew! Potty! Assbreath!" pinching her nose and yelling. But she gathered that the president wanted to develop a habit with her. At five hundred francs a session, she had better obey. But still, to smell down there … Phooey, fine, she'd stink.

She squealed, unleashed, threw her leg up standing on a table. President Gassé ate her out, wet her underwear, tore things, bit some sensitive and private areas a little too hard, and went suddenly cold.

Claire was delighted he didn't slip it in. Decidedly, sadists were quite a find. That would teach her to get her cunt slammed by hicks who were too normal. She got it: she was done being a doormat; she'd play the prepubescent for gentlemen with means.

She looked younger than her age, Mr. Gassé had said it. Then, as planned, she'd become a happy old lady, and, in the meantime, she'd get tongues stuck up her butt. The champagne was strong; the bubbles stung a little. The caviar smelled like fish, what trash, and there wasn't even that much of it. She should have ordered fries and sausage with a lot of strong mustard. She whined:

"Fries and sausage! Fries and Sausage!"

She was drunk. All this was disgusting, in the end. Yes, it was nauseating to have a body; she preferred Nature; it was cleaner, and prettier. The beasts.

President Gassé said he didn't have time to take her out to the country. He had a flash of nausea: the kid was annoyingly idiotic, a borderline case. What a plague to like minors. Otherwise he'd have had superb women, fascinating, beaming, enthralling. Women. Intelligences, souls, unheard-of-curves.

"At least Nature's clean!" whined Fouilloux.

He felt like slapping her: he acted impolite. Claire, treated like a poor girl, like a kid, calmed down.

President Gassé let her pull herself together, gathered the little girl frocks, and left without setting up another rendezvous. Keep them in their place. Never drag them out.

It sobered Fouilloux to be turned loose. She cried. She couldn't find her stockings or her underwear. She'd been wounded in her dignity as a woman. The rich were worse than anything else. She didn't want their dirty dough, grazed from upon the sweat of the poor world: he was lucky to have left, Gassé, she would have thrown the bills in his face. Five shitty bills! And he dared, for that little money (think about the price of genuine leather boots!) to wound her, and to soil Childhood. It was enough to make you sick. Hicks, at least, were normal, and faithful, and they had a heart. They didn't shut you out like that; they knew how to enjoy life. They didn't try to impress you with caviar and champagne to hide their dirty habits.

That old sadist. He should have been in jail, with such bad vices. But no, Mr. was president of this, president of that, president, president, president. And what if she spilled it all, huh? Who was stopping her? ... Oh, he hadn't thought of that, the lousy smut. Oh, the look on that prick's face when the police ... Yes, the police. Immediately!

What? They'd try to silence her, Fouilloux? She, a future mother? No, she'd be able to say the truth. Her example, at least, would serve others. And, if ever she had a daughter one day, the poor dear, she would know how to spare her this. Even if she had to whip her day and night, chain her up to the bed, strangle her if need be. The essential thing was virtue. To be pure, clean, untouched, like the white ermine who'd do without rather than ... What, her daughter was rebelling, she was addicted to vice, wanted to live her life? Fouilloux would throw her in the water, a millstone around her neck, rather than tolerate such an abomination. Oh, if her own mother, that carrion, had been, hmm. Claire knew what. She lost it for a second. She quickly recovered the logic that suited her.

The scum, the scum! Finally, she left the room, sheepish, and went on her way. She was ashamed to be alone and to feel her own flesh touching her—since she no longer had underwear or stockings to separate herself from herself.

The personnel of the Sphynx-Club didn't spare her. They found ways to hold her up at the front desk, to make her pay for something that had been forgotten on the bill the president had signed. Gratuity included, yes, Mademoiselle.

Philippe Seignelet returned from school around 3 o'clock. The teacher had felt faint; there was no one to watch that many brats, and they were a nuisance. Everyone with a mommy at home had to go there quick quick without loitering in the streets and playing and chatting and looking everywhere, understood? As for the others, they would try to distribute them among the other classes, so that they didn't weigh too much on the teachers, overworked as they already were, all of them mommies as well, or soon to be.

They would explain to their moms why they were sent home, okay, Philippe heard with terror. They knew what to say right? Did she have to say it again? So pay attention: of course, if their moms wanted to confirm the lie, they could call the school: the children were going to copy the number down without any mistakes, they could do that much, couldn't they? But the moms shouldn't all call at the same time! They would remember to tell them that? Yes? Was that perfectly clear? They hadn't made a mistake? No mistake, no mistake? No? Yes? Good? So let them quickly quickly go back to their moms, quickly.

They made them go. Philippe immediately found himself alone. He went quickly on his way.

Mrs. Seignelet was unpleasantly surprised. Sunken into her easy chair like a kid on a potty, she was admiring her own habits via women's magazines and was polishing off the garlicky dry sausage that she wolfed down each afternoon because she pretended she was never hungry at lunch, to appear scrawny and shame her voracious children (Jean-Baptiste and Philippe; the two others ate at school). It was her way to perform, from dawn to dusk, the role of the victim.

In her own intimacy, she only enjoyed the most processed foods, bizarre chemistries, poisons, dubious and stinky delicacies. The very same which she would denigrate, rat-nosed, before her own family.

She bought, borrowed, and perused many magazines. She would explore them avidly, masticating her fats, her baguette, her margarine spread under cured pork shoulder, cracklings, and dried sausage. She avoided only the pages that she had to read, the ones with no images. She criticized the styles and recipes aloud, by herself (she would speak and squeal to herself all the time, even when there were people around). She could only be flattered or wounded; she only knew these two emotional or intellectual categories; her feminine readings alternated between them so strongly that she'd emerge hysterical, amplified, furious, shaken, and unsatiated.

No one would ever *see* her being idle. She had tamed her world so well that if ever anyone caught her doing nothing, they would feel guilty, ashamed of themselves. Mrs. Seignelet had established for all time, through continual shouting, complaining, commanding, sighing, and slapping, that she was constantly being tortured. No one would have dared to doubt it, not even her husband. She was sacrificing herself, killing herself, giving away her life: if you didn't believe it, you got a beating. All the children of the house dragged behind them, like a menace or a destiny, the long and interminable rancor that Mrs. Seignelet heaped upon whomever seemed to underestimate her martyrdom. This designated five guilty parties for her just prosecution. Bowed ears, sunken noses, anxious gazes, the children waited for the mother to alight on them. You didn't go home to be safe. When you entered mom's lair you entered the cage at your own risk, and you'd better watch out if the beast hadn't nodded off.

"You're not going to say hi to me?" hooted or whinnied Raymonde Seignelet, incensed, wrathful by system and by taste.

She had quickly hidden her sandwich between the back of the armchair and her own body. She wiped her greasy fingers mechanically on one of her knees. The stockings screeched.

"What's with the long face? You want to get your ears boxed? Or would you rather I do it twice? ... You better change that face quick!"

Philippe shook his head no, yes. Mrs. Seignelet let out an exasperated, dangerous, satisfied sigh. She flung her magazine away, slamming it to the ground like a launderess pounding a washboard. She left the bottom of the easy chair, perched at the edge of the seat on the tip of her buttcheeks, and shrunk, coiled up like a spider about to leap, a cackling mummy stuffed like a fœtus in a coffer. She went on:

"What the hell are you doing out of school this early? … They threw you out? You still sick? … You take that face off right now or I'm gonna give you a good reason for it! … So they sent you home? You must have made a fuss again; it's always like that with you! Your brothers never did this to me! Never! You hear me, Philippe? If they'd even dared at your age they'd have gotten such a whipping! Such a whipping! Such a whipping! They never did a hundredth of what you're doing! … Philippe, I warned you, you change that face or I promise you're gonna get it! You want it? You want it? … Tell me you want it? Do you? …"

Philippe shook his head. Sometimes, Mrs. Seignelet would go on with this game until the kid cried. She'd slap him for crying. Oh, so he hated his mother, huh. Oh, not even a smile, huh, not a single little smile! This was when she was at her best. Other times she started slapping right away, before Philippe had been brought to tears: at least then he would have something to cry about. There were also the days when Mrs. Seignelet was in a good mood—which incited her instead towards sarcasm. She would terrorize the child to make fun of him, jeer at his fear of shouts and blows, bring him to the edge of tears, stopping just before they gushed out. She'd immediately make him appreciate how fair she had been, how magnanimous. She'd clearly warn that she was putting the beating aside for next time, and that there'd be no shortage of next times.

Yet she gave very few punishments. She preferred to relieve herself blow by blow. Thrashings in due form were generally Mr. Seignelet's privilege. He had a protocol, and did not improvise. For Mrs. Seignelet, on the contrary, slapping was like sneezing: it built up, you did it, you blew your nose, and you didn't think about it anymore. She thought about it so little, she was so idiotic, so unconscious in her shrewish nastiness that she'd have been revolted if someone pointed them out. What slander. What lies.

"So what did you do? Go on say it! … They didn't send you home at this hour for nothing did they? I'm waiting. I'm waiting, Philippe! … What did you do?"

Philippe tried to repeat what the teacher had said they should tell the moms. He showed such disarray, such weakness, that Raymonde Seignelet felt insulted, provoked. What was he seemingly daring to accuse her? What was he insinuating with that sniveling muzzle, those idiotic jitters in the eyes? Would she tolerate a seven-year-old brat admonishing her like this? As a matter of fact, it was her right—absolutely—to be childish, touching, and weak. Those little bastards, they wanted to take it all away from you, didn't they, even that, even that!

"What do you mean, your teacher's sick? Oh so this is the new fib? I'm warning you, you're not a good liar, Philippe. You know how this is gonna end, right? You know? Answer me, yes or no? How is this gonna end? Philippe I'm all ears. Are you gonna answer me, yes or no or what? Oh, I'm so tired of this! … So what's it gonna be?"

The kid shook his head, burst into tears. Mrs. Seignelet felt a little let down. She hadn't wanted it to end this way. She was gay, benign, and comfortable today. Her stomach was well greased, her limbs were well softened, her brains cowardly, thrilled by the prospect of a great photo-romance and of her garlicky sausage. She just wanted to play a little with Philippe, she had no hidden agenda, and now that little twat made a fuss. What a nitwit. He couldn't compare with his older siblings. Bertrand, especially, had been an exceptional partner. You could torment him like a slave, a deportee, or a dog. He resisted, bounced back, and was a perfect match for the dumbness, the ferocity of others. He had become a fat moron who weighed a hundred tons, a stocky, squat, and grateful adolescent. He would become a technician some day, maybe an engineer, maybe he'd work in nuclear power if they slapped him around enough. What a promotion for his father that would be, his father the GED bureaucrat, the career loser. Bertrand was the hope of the Seignelets. He loved the natural sciences. Of all the forms of knowledge, they alone were able to force open and imprint his brute neurons cretinized by blows, orders, duties, narrow-minded mores, and right ideas.

In contrast, Philippe, the youngest, wasn't promising. At the slightest put-down, he would turn the other cheek. He would end up asking to be scolded, or beaten, before he'd even confessed why he deserved it.

In any case, he deserved it, sure thing, like all children. Cutting class at his age! Good thing he was crying, now that the deed was done. Mrs. Seignelet threatened him: if he blubbered a minute longer, she'd go to the post office and call to find out the truth. If ever he'd lied, he'd get a good spanking, tonight, after dinner, from his father. So? … Should she call? …

The threat had a strange effect. Philippe's sobs subsided; he seemed relieved all of a sudden; his white, domed young child forehead grew smooth.

His mother saw this, understood her failure and changed tactics. Really! The little liar thought that she'd go out of her way, as if she didn't have enough to do this afternoon already! As if she cared about all this school bullshit! Abracadabra! He commanded and everyone had to obey, was that it! The world was turned on its head. He should get a spanking for that phone business.

Philippe did have the face of a culprit. He was waiting patiently, painfully, for his mother to be done. Later, his brothers would come home. Jean-Baptiste, who was nice, would come first; then Dominique, who was really nice; then Bertrand, whom the others didn't like but who had almost managed to seduce their parents. After that, everything would be alright. And after that, dad would come home, and the other black moment would begin. They would eat dinner. After that, they'd be allowed to go to sleep and everything would be alright again. After that, it would be tomorrow, and all the black moments would start over again. After that ...

"Tears, nice try!" jeered Mrs. Seignelet. "You think you look good? Oh, you look good, alright! And why is it that you're crying? What did I do to you again? Oh, the poor martyr! Oh, poor kid who's being tortured! What a laugh! ... What a laugh! I wouldn't miss this for the world!"

Philippe heard "waddalaf" and didn't understand the word. In any case, things that were very funny or very laughable invariably "waddalaffed" the Seignelet couple. It was their great judgment, the apex of a hierarchy of hilarious facts, of ridiculous people, of astounding, priceless spectacles.

"It's really hilarious! It's hilarious! Waddalaf!"

Making fun of the tears was the only method Raymonde Seignelet knew of to make them stop, and if that didn't do it she reviled, vituperated the child.

"So? ... You're not even happy you're out of school? You don't like holidays? You're really set on pulling a heck of a face. Oh, I never get a holiday! But you, you don't care, everyone caters to you. And you're acting unhappy. Everyone gets what's comin' to 'em! Go on, cry! You little brat! If you think you look good! Hheehahh! ..."

She was happy: to accompany the sound of vomit, she stuck an enormous tongue out at him like a little girl making faces at a stupid boy. Philippe caught a whiff of garlic in the face; he could see deep down into Mrs. Seignelet's mouth. There were lumps of chewed-up bread at the back of a pale, grayish tongue, with no other saliva than glairy sinews, on the sides, that extended down to the bottom teeth.

"Okay! I've had enough of your drama for now!" squealed Seignelet. She was in a hurry to end the session; it was boring.

The gleam of mockery had suddenly died out: she was furrowing her eyebrows and forcing her eyelids open to reveal the sclera, groaning:

"Philippe, will you stop? Will you take that look off your face? … Oh my goodness, what a gang, what a gang! Don't you think I've got enough on my plate having to sit across your asshole brothers all night? And your dad, your drunkard of a dad, don't you think it's hard enough that I have to deal with him too? … You better not act like them Philippe! I've had enough of you kids, and of your dad! You better not start acting like them I'm telling you! You better start acting normal or things are gonna turn sour! Are you done? Are you done? Tell me are you done?"

Philippe whispered yes. Mrs. Seignelet sent him to the kitchen; he should sit at the table and be quiet. She was intuitive: she never let a child go before she'd tormented him enough that he'd feel guilty for having provoked the scene. She was responding to her sons' monstrosities, that was all. Philippe was especially abominable, whatever he did or didn't do. This was because he was more often at home, and longer than the others; he was a pain; you had him on hand every time you wanted to release some bitterness, a bad mood.

Philippe was thus guilty by principle, by definition, by opportunity. But only in the eyes of his mother. Others treated him well. His father more or less neglected him. Teachers terrorized him, because of the physical analogy between them and his mother, but they didn't inspire any aversion in him. Far from it, he adored them. They were calm, patient, moderate, and loyal. You generally understood what faults they accused you of. They didn't perpetually upset the order of things, contrary to Mrs. Seignelet, and if, on Monday, they declared that the trees were red they didn't slap you on Tuesday when you obediently answered, "They are red!" to the question "What is the color of the trees?" Yes, teachers were really kind.

Other boys found them mean, apprehensive, annoying, dumb, dingy, devious, prissy, and impossible. They were scoundrels, to be sure. Philippe was very scared of these boys. And when the best students made fun of the teachers or criticized them like this, Philippe couldn't believe his ears and felt the universe tremble, collapse in the same way that everything always collapsed at home—except for the stiffness of the protocols, the punctilious soul of the parental gods and the harshness of the punishments. It was exhausting to be so scared all the time; school at least should reassure him. But no, nasty schoolmates prevented even that.

Mrs. Seignelet joined Philippe in the kitchen: she wanted a glass of wine. To mask this desire (for it was a well-known fact that, austere and agonizing as she was, she never felt any desire, drank only when she was *dying* of thirst, ate only when she was *dying* of hunger, renewed her wardrobe only when she only had *rags* that she had fixed a hundred times, went to bed only when she was *dead* tired, and by the way, didn't catch a wink *all night*; she would have bared her teeth if someone had dared to insinuate that food, wine, clothing, and sleep were pleasant things. No, she had never even heard of the word *pleasure*, and she suffered hellish tortures while her husband and kids feasted on drink and food, lounged in bed, and played the fashionistas in impeccably *patched-up* garments) she attacked the child:

"And don't think you're going to spend the day reading. You think your back isn't hunched over enough already? You better find something else, and make it snappy!"

She emptied her wine with a sneer, as if she was being tortured with vile purgatives, foul medication.

"Why don't you go clean your room and leave the book here? What do you wanna read for? For all the use it is to you at school, when the teacher can't even get a word out of you. This room is a real pigsty. And don't go tell me Dominique is the one who leaves toys lying around under your bed, okay? Besides he's gonna hear from me too. I've had enough of you both. More than enough even. Get, scat."

She said this nearly every day to everyone, without any particular motive. This was how she nurtured her climate, her infuriated aura, and her dying woman's anger.

Dominique and Philippe, less unkempt than the other two brothers, and as neat as children can possibly be, generally kept their room very clean. As to the tidiness that reigned there, it depended on their courage and their pastimes—as was the case all around the world and at all ages. But Mrs. Seignelet, an especially lazy, dissipated, soft, almost dirty woman, stood watch and tracked down the shortcomings of others with a vigilance and a brutality worthy of her invariably sour humor.

Philippe, who was delighted to have been dismissed, disappeared into his bedroom. There was nothing worse than having to spend the afternoon under his mother's gaze, or even near her. The bedroom was his refuge; he felt less vulnerable there, he believed he was less exposed to the arbitrariness, the spitefulness, the crises; he could breathe.

Mrs. Seignelet slammed the living room door and shut herself in with her magazine and her sandwich again. She felt as if she'd done some housework, as if she'd tidied things up. She enjoyed this security, this well-being. She got up almost without a sigh once she'd finished the dry sausage and felt thirsty again. She even forgot to go and see what her brat was up to.

During those long stretches of laziness, in the afternoon, Raymonde Seignelet had her rites, which were invariable, and which her less impressionable children, Bertrand and mostly Jean-Baptiste, had discovered little by little: they would snigger about it at leisure, and would quench or feed their hatred for the Seignelet couple by snooping about and collecting their fatuities, their filthiness, their stupidities. Even Bertrand regained some good cheer through these hygienic exercises.

What was strange was that Mrs. Seignelet hardly concealed a thing. There wasn't much there to uncover, and she even displayed her dubious gluttonies or her discreet tendency to drunkenness (or rather to sucking at the bottle: she liked to down wine, sugary aperitifs, muscats, and vermouths by the isolated mouthful, as medicine, but she would never get drunk, that greedy mug and icy mind). She would announce with a stupid whiny squeal the reason why she inflicted this or that thing on herself, things which anyone else would have considered treats but which for her were additional sufferings, constraints, ordeals. Thus, when Jean-Baptiste or Bertrand "discovered" one of Mrs. Seignelet's vices, it was simply that, suddenly, their mother's accusations no longer fooled them; they plugged their ears, they saw what there was to see, they yellowed with revolt and spite. What! This old, nauseating, lying, wrathful, infantile and unclean cow had bullied them, and was still browbeating them? Incredible! And they would sketch out for one another Mrs. Seignelet's flaws, and would parody, suspect, speculate and invent other defects, like schoolboys taking revenge on an obnoxious supervisor at school or an Ubuesque teacher.

Dominique and Philippe didn't have that kind of good health. They took their father and their mother at their word. They wouldn't have allowed themselves a criminal glare as Jean-Baptiste did, or an ironic statement or a two-way mien during dinner, or let themselves doubt the veracity of the parental discourse, the perfection of Seignelesque usage and customs, the legitimacy of the tongue-lashings, the respectability of the crabby moods, the profound humanity of being slapped, the serious nobility of adult pettiness, dad's sublime sacrifice, mom's heartrending abnegation. So when Philippe would walk toward a window, look outside, and his mother would immediately drone out a shouted prohibition, like: "Don't touch the tiles you're gonna get everything dirty again! Obviously you're not the one who has to clean up! You don't give a damn about how hard your mom has to work, do you! Well, I do! And what do you need to look at through the window, huh, with your dirty hands that you're gonna smear everywhere?" he sincerely believed that he was infuriating and that his mother was being persecuted constantly.

That poor soul wore her life out, in fact, to repair all the nasty things everyone did their best to do. Each object, each centimeter of the house was sacred, almost taboo. It was mom's labor. To use it, or to simply be there, was to destroy her work. Raymonde Seignelet excelled in the art of making you guilty for your very existence. Your breath, even that came at a price. Wouldn't she have to get up to open the windows and air out the room? If ever the children cleaned something, Mrs. Seignelet, as her only acknowledgement, would squeal that they'd soiled the broom or the sponge, poorly emptied the vacuum cleaner, badly arranged the dishes, left a disgusting sink. She would summon the culprit, who'd be astonished:

"But where is it dirty?"

"What do you mean? Where is it dirty? Can't you see! There, there, and there! ..."

And with a finger Mrs. Seignelet would condemn some invisible imperfections, or an infinitesimal oversight. She would be furious. You'd lower your nose, defeated. Yet she didn't play this game in order to have the criticized work executed a second time, but instead to finish it herself and act the victim. Of course, yes! They'd wanted to clean this, and this! To lend a hand! Sure! But everything had to be done all over again, that went without saying! ... There was more to do when they helped her, as they said, than when she did everything by herself!

Actually, this tactic allowed her to unload a large part of the household chores on her children, whom she hired as laborers at any instant, and whom she rewarded with reproaches, sighs, annoyance, threats. Once the task was completed, you were as much at fault as if you had refused to do it; you weighed heavier still among Mrs. Seignelet's thousand torments. Whatever you did, she would endlessly remain a panting victim—and a mountain of acrimony.

Nevertheless, the days were endless, exhausting and nerve-racking for the four Seignelet children, as they went from home to school and from school to home, from father to mother and from mother to father, from imperfect report cards to holey socks, from shameful appetites for one kind of food to scandalous aversions for another, from whines to cries, from hateful faces to dormant persecutions, from spankings to slaps, from prohibitions to yelled orders, from tormentless hours to appalling holidays.

Raymonde Seignelet's intimate festival, the perhaps unique occurrence when this ordinary woman experienced some pure delights were these lazy afternoons she defended so savagely against intruders—as Philippe had just discovered. There, gulping down her hideous picnics with a dog's maw, lying across her fat easy chair as if she were on a hammock, she would stuff herself with tales of fitness, diet, elegance, beauty, castles, dissecting the advertisements, throwing an evil eye on the silly children-for-rich-ladies who illustrated the advertisement for socks or underwear, and, when this warm-up came to an end, she would dive into her photo-romance, her detective magazine. She read flabbily, like an old fart dozing in a chair, and combed her hair with five fingers, pulling and flattening till it lost its wave, scraping her greasy scalp with her nails. She would gather an ooze of sebum and dandruff that formed a crescent moon of grayish, sticky lard beneath each of her nails, which she would then sniff before extracting with her thumbnail, finger after finger. Once this flushing was accomplished, she'd resume shoveling her skull; and this activity would go on till dinner announced the beginning of another round of lard and slapping.

5

Julien shook his head:

"No, she wasn't dead when we left."

René Théret agreed. They hadn't killed anyone. Marc Guillard didn't seem to agree. Two old bags in a couple weeks, that was too much. The first one was understandable, the heart case. But the one yesterday evening shouldn't have croaked. Marc hadn't been part of the expedition, despite his knowledge of the layout of the place, since the Grandieu's might have been able to identify him. He had prepared, timed, and explained everything, like in the detective novels he read. And then he'd waited for the boys to return. They hadn't mentioned Mrs. Grandieu's death. Marc had found out about it in the paper, this morning.

"They say it's you. Grandieu told 'em it was you."

"He said that on purpose," protested René. "I'll betcha he took advantage of it, that's all."

Julien gave big nods of approval:

"Yeah, that's what he did. Me too, I'll betcha that's what it is. She wasn't dead. We'd have told you."

"But what do you mean took advantage?"

"Old Grandieu? That's it! That's the thing!" said Julien mysteriously. He preferred letting Théret explain: he'd be better at it.

"That's the thing, yeah! That's the thing!" René confirmed, with a strange tired and cheerless smile, which bared his canines and furrowed his lower eyelids.

"… What? You think that he …"

René and Julien shrugged their shoulders together.

"Obviously, it had to be him," continued Théret. "He took advantage of it, like I said. He knew we'd get blamed for the whole thing, you bet he saw his chance! It was his lucky day!"

He seemed to judge it perfectly natural that a husband would milk a burglary to strangle his wife.

"That old fart, think about it, she must have been at least eighty or something!"

"That's right, more like a hundred, the old geezer!" giggled Julien Roquin. "Fuck what a stink bomb, she probably went in her pants when we tied her up! That old geezer! He made out pretty well that old bastard, didn't he!"

"They say it's the gag that suffocated her, so she wasn't strangled. So that means it's not your fault, if you think of it. Not more than last time!" said Marc Guillard.

"No way, that's impossible" said Théret. "No way! We barely stuck it into her mouth halfway; we didn't even tighten it. Come on, this is no joke."

"Ewww that didn't stop her from farting with her ass!" Julien cackled. "Wow what an old bag! ..."

"It wasn't that, it was the dentures," said Guillard.

"Dentures? What dentures?" said René Théret.

"Dentures. All old geezers have dentures. When you gag 'em they swallow 'em and that chokes them and they croak. Everybody knows that!"

"Who mentioned dentures? The paper?"

"No. Me. I'm telling you. She ate it, man."

"Shit," whispered Théret.

"Yeah, that must be it," said Julien. "The stupid bitch. You sure that she had one, Marc?"

"You bet, with all those teeth. Didn't you see she had a whole load of 'em right there in the front part of her mouth?" said Marc.

"I dunno. I didn't notice. I wasn't ogling her in the mouth or anything," said Théret. "What about you Julien?"

Julien hadn't noticed the state of Mrs. Grandieu's teeth either. But it didn't change anything. Codgers and old bags have false teeth and rich ones even more so. Yeah, oh yeah. What a drag.

"You, you sure it strangles 'em?" suggested Julien.

"Not strangles, chokes. Yeah, has to."

"… You tried it?" insisted the child.

Marc Guillard snickered. Kids'll tell you the most incredible things. You gotta spell it all out for 'em …

"When do you think I coulda tried it out, huh Dracula? Where the fuck do you think I could keep one of 'em dentures? In my butthole? If you got teeth you can't use 'em dopey!"

"Hey, I didn't mean you," said Roquin. He didn't like people to make fun of him. He didn't like it when someone took advantage of his age. No one would ever again have the right to be stronger than he was. Never again.

"I'm just sayin', maybe you tried it on someone … I dunno!"

"Right," said Guillard. "I just walk around and when I see an old bag I tell her, 'Hey Mrs., could you swallow your teeth so I can see the effect?' 'Cause there's a buddy of mine who'd like to know?'"

"… There's something else, by the way," interrupted René Théret. "François, you know, the teacher's kid, apparently he lost his mask there. Not his gloves, just the mask."

During their night raids, the boys took a set of precautions that were intended to dissimulate their identity and their age. The older boys attacked, after they'd turned off the light and blinded the residents with their lamps. Then the other children entered the scene, faces masked. These masks were either Mardi Gras masks, or the grotesque or serious products of their own artistry.

Besides, as yet, they'd only committed very few burglaries. It was especially difficult to set up. The risks, though, seemed slighter to them than those less ambitious operations that took place during the daytime and with their faces uncovered, shoplifting, for example. The supermarket on National Square was the younger kids' favorite hunting ground. They were cunning enough never to take what might interest thieves their own age. Once a boy had come out with a bag full of bad chocolates. The others had called him crazy, and an idiot.

No, the pleasure of the robberies resided in their uselessness, their incongruity, the pleasure of fooling adults, thwarting their surveillance, and being the strongest. They had immensely admired a kid from the North Side, Puymorin, who was ten or eleven. He'd stolen two pairs of lady's underwear almost in front of the saleswoman. He had let one stick out of his pocket ostensibly and had dragged it around the store until they noticed, then questioned and searched him. The underwear discovered, Puymorin had cried, wailed, pretended that his mother had forced him to steal the garment, under threat of an even worse punishment. And in one breath he'd recited a shopping list of the same order, stockings, tights, etc., that his mother had ordered him to steal. He confessed that finding the right size had been a challenge. He monkeyed around, made everyone laugh with his innocence, uttered a cascade of another thousand lies, was threatened, reprimanded, feared for an instant that they'd take him home, managed to move some saleswomen to pity at the last minute, was supported, absolved, and released. As for his nasty mom, it was a long time since she'd run off, the abject creature.

Puymorin's daring surpassed the outer limit of what the kids from the gang would have dared to undertake. And he wasn't that clever, since he would no longer be allowed to set foot in that supermarket chain and even ran the risk of being identified anywhere by the store employees or by some client who had witnessed the scene. But the boy had shifted to small, self-service groceries. He'd drop by during peak hours, choosing the busiest stores. There, he'd lavish the clerks with polished, polite looks, would zigzag between clients, stuff his socks with food, buy some milk or a cheap bottle of wine or a salad, and, decent and kind, he would leave unsuspected. As much as they all discredited useful thefts, these aroused a little envy. They were very dangerous.

"The article doesn't mention a mask. Is he sure he lost it at their house?"

"He told me he had set it down in the kitchen because he drank some beer, just before leaving. When we left."

"Boitard's such a moron! Can you guess what kind of mask he had? … The top part is a mask of Zorro; the bottom is a fake beard, totally red! With, like, a fake baldhead made of cardboard. I'm telling you he's loopy."

Julien simply wore a ski mask. The other boys' whims seemed unworthy of their group and of their actions.

According to Marc Guillard, forgetting the mask in the Grandieus' kitchen wasn't a big deal, if François hadn't … He suddenly cried out:

"Shit! What about fingerprints! In the mask! They're going to see it's a kid! … I mean, there are guys who wear masks for heists. The police could have thought the guy just didn't have a big head. But now …"

"A guy has the right to have little fingers without being a kid," René Théret noted. "My art teacher, his hands aren't even as big as Julien's. And François isn't really that small. It's not sure they'll get it, the cops I mean."

Nonetheless, they all felt this whole mask business was very worrisome. And why had the papers chosen to hide that particular detail?

On the other hand, the boys were surprised that the case had been described as a major burglary: silverware and jewelry worth a few million old French francs. In principle, each boy took what he wanted, and they didn't have to answer to one another. But they showed themselves the loot, and everyone talked about what had happened, traded, and destroyed together. Yet no one remembered having stolen what was listed in the press.

Still, that was secondary. They took stock of the case of the two fugitives. They contemplated a new spot for the hideout: it was still uncertain how secure it really was. They discussed the evolution of operations at length. The little Guillard kernel was still fairly quiet, but you could tell that there was too much pressure against it from all directions. They were all slightly scared. Anything could happen, and no one really knew what they were doing anymore, or why. The two boys who had left their families were a dead weight, heavier than the two old ladies who'd been wiped out, in fact—they'd been killed without anyone touching them, from old age, in short. A feeling of guilt hung about; they'd reached a point of no return; yes, they were scared.

Except for Julien Roquin, maybe, and some of the smaller kids. They were determined ... But to do what? Julien seemed to blame the big boys for their unease. They should take care of themselves! They could do and think whatever they wanted! Julien repeated that he didn't need them. First of all, too many boys knew about their hiding place, and some had even already caught wind of the next one. It was stupid. And it was stupid to be so many when they did the heists. Now that they had almost all the useful things they needed, it was time to lay low. To make themselves scarce. And get rid of those gossipy idiots like Boitard and the rest.

Julien could perfectly picture himself moving into adulthood and even beyond, as a wild man, in a deserted corner of their island. He couldn't yet do without accomplices, but the time would come. After that, he would travel the world. He didn't tell them this. It was his secret, the key to his fierce patience, to his self-control. It was what he lived for. And although he was only ten years old, all the others seemed like nothing more than babies at play. Things would probably turn sour for them because of this.

Julien, on the other hand, would pull through. He'd live through this murky adventure. It made him sweat, and made his heart beat, if he thought about it for too long. He was on another ocean, on another planet, and already among other men. He no longer had anything to do with his friends; from so far away, he didn't hear them, didn't even perceive them. From as far away as time, the immense future that he'd dived into after leaving his family forever.

Mrs. Lescot asked herself why Joachim hasn't come to kiss her goodnight. He was usually in bed at this hour. Could it be that he stayed up past eleven! That little rascal! Or maybe he'd been reading his stack of comic books all over again! What a reader! He read so fast he sometimes skipped over the entire text, only following the images and not understanding anything about the story. So he'd bring the comic book to his mom so that she could explain it to him.

"Hey sweet pea, cutie pie, don't you know how to read anymore sweetheart?" Mrs. Lescot would chide him. "Have you already forgotten how to read? … Look at this cute little monkey who doesn't knows how to read a thing, not a thing, not a thing, not even his comics, the little, little monkey! … I just have to give him a big hug, this little sweetheart!"

"Ooh, ah, ooh, ah …" went Joachim, obligingly.

Mrs. Lescot was opening mussels on the stove. A client was leaning on the other side of the bar, guzzling down rums and telling her about seafood pies. How could he like that kind of junk? wondered Yvonne Lescot. She didn't dare make any comments about it. Drinkers get hung up on an idea and then never let it go. It was no use answering him, or talking about it.

"And, I mean, not just any kind of dumpling! No way! That's not what I want! I won't fall for things like that! If I gotta eat flour might as well be bread! No way! It's just too much …"

"Right, right, yes, right, bread," Mrs. Lescot said, mechanically. She couldn't leave her mussels unattended; people around here ate them barely cooked, but very hot; you had to keep a close watch. She would then go and see if Joachim was in bed. And one plain crêpe for Mrs. Bignon—a boozer, by the way, but a decent woman nonetheless, and not badly off with the annuity from her pension. It was more like she was bored, really—wait, or did she want jam. Well, now, Yvonne Lescot didn't remember.

"What kind of crêpe was that, Mrs. Bignon?" she cried toward a smoky corner of the room.

"Whatever kind you like, sweetheart!" Mrs. Bignon answered. She had a fishmonger's tone but a fluted, cooing voice, with very round notes. She must have learned how to sing, at church, in the old days, and belted out sentimental songs at weddings, where her large shrill organ, her vibrato, was a shock. Those kinds of grannies who were filled with romance, their enormous breasts puffed-up like the chests of doves, stirred up filial affection in Mrs. Lescot.

She was thinking she might put up a television for the evening clients. It'd be nice, if all of them were cooing, motherly and solid like this old Mrs. Bignon. And perhaps they'd lower their voices a little. Mrs. Lescot wasn't against a little noise, nonetheless. She never felt more pleasure in her café than when it was really busy, when you could hear the blend of conversations, calls, laughter, the clinking of glasses, alcoholic effluvia, the squeaking of chairs being pulled and of tables being brought together. And that hubbub mingled with the blue smoke of cigarettes stretched long supple threads through the room, knotted nets, hammocks, and strange suspended bridges where Mrs. Lescot floated, affable and pendulating, amidst the vapors.

"And they stuff 'em for you with white mushrooms!" said the dumpling drunk. "No, seriously, tell me, do mushrooms grow in the sea? In the sea, what a joke!"

"No, no, you said it!" whispered Mrs. Lescot, who answered Mrs. Bignon in a louder voice.

"If you could wait just a second. I'm a little worried, I need to go check on my sweetheart!"

But first, she served her mussels, and she was uncorking a high-quality white when Joachim appeared in the room. He was dressed in his new blue velvet short pants and his geranium red jumper with little canary yellow stars shaped like snow crystals. The scholarly Mrs. Lescot would knit those jacquards when business was slow. For the most part, she did this so as to not eat too much, since idleness gave her hunger pangs. She already felt a little chubby, and since she wasn't averse to a little glass of wine either … so yes, knitting, little stars.

"Oh, cutie pie!" moaned Yvonne Lescot as if the child were wounded, "isn't it time for beddy-bye? Oh, sweetheart!"

Joachim Lescot didn't seem the least bit tired; wide-eyed with his giggling mouth and sharp cheekbones, he was a real little angel, as fresh as the morning, thought Mrs. Lescot. She was wondering what made her son so pretty when the latter began to tell a prolific story that had to with do with fights, scamps, mischievous kids, and dough.

Alarmed, Mrs. Lescot nonetheless understood that Joachim had spent the evening playing cards with his cousin, Hervé Pellisson, and that they had brought in a wealthy party. Joachim claimed to have won five thousand francs. And in one fell swoop.

His mother smiled. He was mixing up francs and cents again. No, no, swore the child, five thousand! It was five thousand! He even had them in his pocket.

"At the *Imperial Hotel, Royal and for Travelers!* Yes Madam! Just six years ago! Unforgettable! No one alive has ever eaten the likes of these! You have to believe me!"

"Come on, sweet pea, Hervé doesn't have five thousand francs, you know that! … Another one, Sir! No, no fries tonight! Casserole! Yes! Two beauties, yes!"

"No, no, it's true, five hundred thousand francs!"

"Five hundred francs, cutie pie. Come, will you show me?"

"Honey, you aren't napping on my crêpe are ya?" inquired a jovial Mrs. Bignon.

"Coming right up Madam, coming right up," cried Yvonne Lescot. "See what did I tell you my little rabbit, this is a five-franc coin! ... Five hundred old francs see?"

In fact, Joachim was lying about the origin of the money, but he had given the exact amount at the beginning. Hervé had given him fifty francs (five thousand, as the kids counted), which was his part of the loot from some business that had taken place that evening, with the sole complicity of Alain Viaud. And Joachim, although he'd been enthusiastic, had to return the money straight away since he wouldn't have been able to keep it. Hervé would serve as a banker; the sum would be crumbled into small change and sweets. Joachim would have preferred to save it up for his Mother's Day gift, but it was impossible to use it for that, of course. They had invented the story of the card games.

"Also, your cousin isn't being reasonable! First of all, to deprive himself of five francs as if he had too much, the poor thing! And then to keep you up till midnight or eleven! And you're not even yawning, you little rascal huh, you had yourself a good time didn't you! ... Did he leave without saying goodbye?"

Mrs. Lescot wasn't surprised that her little boy was a night owl, like she was. It only bothered her on account of school schedules. Joachim always slept his ten hours. Nothing in the world could have made his mother cut his sleep short, especially not class.

"Hervé's the boss now! He's our boss!" exclaimed Joachim, unable to keep quiet.

But he had an accurate idea of the degree of attention his mother gave him, and he took advantage of it to confess nearly anything that was weighing on his heart at that moment with impunity. If he had told Mrs. Lescot crimes, the latter, amused, would have kindly lectured him about confusing his books with reality. You know it's naughty, Joachim, to kill and steal from everybody like that, my favorite munchkin.

"He poops, that's why, that's the big sausage, there, there, that's coming out of him there! … He … He farts sausage! Ew! Ew!"

"My little sugar plum, that's horrible, you little monster you, what are your talking about with Hervé and his sausage! And here I was wondering why no one came to kiss me goodnight! What strange questions you have! Hush now, hush!"

Mrs. Lescot wasn't prudish, and her son's bad words or scatological pleasantries—he loved silly jokes—didn't shock her. Sausage! She laughed as she imagined her nephew Hervé, crouching on a squat toilet, with a gigantic chocolate-colored spiral suspended from his rear end.

"Oh! What a munchkin! And who didn't go beddy-bye yet! … What's Hervé the boss of now? … You? … You little cutie pie!"

"No one knows how to make 'em anymore! Two, three mussels, two, three clams, two chunks of fish, a frozen shrimp, some fish bone broth … and they call that a dumpling! A timbale! And this is the seaside! What am I saying! The sea! In the sea we are! We're sitting in it! The Ocean! …"

"You know what, you know what, I wouldn't mind a little bit of that!" said Joachim, in front of a ham omelet his mother had just brought up to the Singlin brothers, two single workers. They worked shifts at the SaViCo factories, and sold *l'Humanité* on Sunday mornings. They went to the earliest mass to be out on time. Everyone loved them. They were big and hairy, ate a lot, worked hard, and had fluted voices so similar they appeared to have only a single one to share. It was funny to see them at dinner exchanging lines, as polite as a young couple who had just been engaged and barely dared to take each other by the hand. People said they were bachelors by necessity rather than by choice.

Mrs. Lescot swiped a piece of ham and presented it to Joachim's lips, so he could nibble at it. The child rubbed his belly jubilantly and followed his mother to the Singlin brothers' table. He confided in them that he'd eaten a piece of ham from their plate. It was delicious! It tasted like butter! The Singlin brothers laughed, delighted. In a single voice, they told Joachim to take another piece of ham from their plate, and since the little imp was so adorable you could eat him up, they each gave him an amicable tap on the tooshie. Joachim dodged them, burned his fingers and mouth, explained that, "No, tomorrow morning he wasn't going to school. Because … Oh right, because … Yipppeee!"

He rushed back to the bar. Hervé was with Mrs. Lescot. Oh, he was eating something?

The dumpling drunk had found someone to talk to. The man was also a gourmet, and had decided to depict the most enormous crayfish he had ever encountered in this world. There was his sister's wedding, his son's communion, so-and-so's retirement party, so-and-so's biggest win at the races: life seemed to be merely a series of opportunities to offer oneself crayfish, and, sprinkled with crayfish from baptism on, it led infallibly to a few dying breath crayfish, which were the most gigantic, without a doubt, if not the most digestible. The seafood man was humbled to silence. Where could he fit his shrimp in, his clams, his scallops, among such a heap of crustaceans?

"… We were a dozen gorging on it sir! A dozen! And the portions, Lord have mercy! The portions! Humongous! The antennae …"

The cafe was slowly emptying out and the voices hushed imperceptibly as the air outside grew cooler. The atmosphere, however, was growing homier. The benign regulars came closer to the bar, changed tables as they carried their drinks, as if there was soon to be a single light and a single fire where Mrs. Lescot sat cackling with the two children, stuffing them with sweets, scolding them for still being up, delighted.

"So you've been playing war? Oh, what a dummy I am, I should have come see you in the bedroom! It's really not that far! … And my honey bunny who wasn't even gonna say goodnight to me! I could have easily thought you were lost to me, my little cutie pie!"

She was doing the cleaning, washing glasses, and formulating an idea of tomorrow's shopping list. Joachim was staring wide-eyed at the drunks on the bar. He loved these kinds of people. He was standing as tall as he could, but he could barely get his nose past the edge of the bar. His eyes were growing red from fatigue and began to sting a little.

He'd look at the characters, every evening. The more ridiculous they were, the more he would smile in ecstasy. Veneration of the drunks. He would have given them all the bottles to make them happy. They were ragged husbands shunning their wives, shunning the TV, the endless routine, and the con jobs they had built for themselves. Joachim relished these swindled, duped men, these bastards. He himself didn't have a daddy. They were all bright and shiny. The boozers were really a fascinating crowd, much more than other people you might know. As a matter of fact, Joachim thought it was normal to be thirsty. He was only disconcerted by those things in the really tiny glasses.

"Yes, mommy! A shandy for the both of us, first Hervé and then we'll go to bed!"

Joachim was the only child that Mrs. Lescot had ever heard say *mo-mmy*, the way it was spelled. Although she must have taught him this. Did she pronounce it that way? Impossible to say. You'd have to talk without listening to yourself, so that it would be spontaneous; otherwise it was cheating. It was as if you wanted to look at yourself in a mirror while you were looking up. But Yvonne Lescot loved Joachim's *mo-mmy*; she perceived a privilege in it that she could cherish; a piece of the kid that was hers alone, hers, and forever.

"Toots," cried Pellisson, "you're just a lush! I'd rather have milk, auntie, if you have any left."

"Of course, of course, kiddo. What about you Joachim, wouldn't you rather have milk too? It isn't good to drink shandy before you go to bed, aren't you ashamed of yourself?"

Joachim accepted the milk, if she poured some banana syrup in it. "Why bananas?" asked Pellisson. Mrs. Lescot obeyed and laughed, "May as well wonder why one day it rains, and another day it's nice out." Joachim passed around his banana milk: everyone thought it was delicious.

"Hervé, my boy, your parents are gonna be upset, did you see what time it is! Oh my goodness! ... You haven't gotten home so late for more than a month! I kind of feel like going with you, my little Hervé, yes, I'm gonna come with you!"

Hervé refused sluggishly. Yvonne Lescot insisted. She was afraid of her brother and sister-in-law's strictness. It wouldn't take more than two minutes or so. She would bring the boy back and would be a little delayed herself. Busy night at the café, wouldn't Hervé do the same?

The boy accepted. He said that there was no need to hurry, now. Mrs. Lescot said that she hadn't suggested this for him to take advantage of it and dilly-dally. Hervé answered that she wouldn't be able to leave before having closed the café, there were still clients, and she wasn't going to toss them out.

"You betcha I will! Five past midnight! ... Gentlemen, we're closing!"

She repeated this two or three times, and shut off the lights in two or three increments. A few minutes later, the drinkers were in the street and Joachim in bed, drifting off into a heavy sleep, smeared with kisses, sugared with bananas, gorged with milk, as happy as the way they tried to be through him.

The closed café smelled good; Mrs. Lescot was airing it out thoroughly from the back because of the tobacco, and a denser, more turbulent freshness than the one outside penetrated the darkened room through which Hervé and his aunt were walking.

Since the burglary, Hugo Grandieu had been doing a lot of thinking. He found the whole business so extravagant that he was having trouble convincing himself of its reality. And what he'd discovered about himself startled him even more.

He wasn't really surprised to have killed his wife. The crime had been almost abstract. No, what Mr. Grandieu didn't understand was that he'd actually improvised the murder, something he had never even thought of before. And moreover, that he so intensely hated the one he called the *old bag* since the ambulance had carried off her corpse. Strange youth serum this voluntary widowhood.

Grandieu had freed himself with great difficulty after the thieves' departure. They'd tied his hands with metallic thread that was thin but braided like the halyard of a sail, or a flag. Aching, his blood flow cut off, Hugo Grandieu had finally managed to break the tie at his wrists by twisting them one against the other, his hands behind his back. He thought highly of himself because of his success, it had taken him at least an hour of effort. The overheating thread had burnt him quite a lot.

He had rushed straight away to rescue his wife, who was rather loosely tied to a chair. He'd realized that she had passed out, and just as he was untying her gag, he …

But why that inspiration? His plans had been quite decided, he had imagined every detail as he was busy setting himself free: he'd free Mrs. Grandieu, would call a doctor, then the police. These actions were simple, concrete, and reasonable. He would reestablish the natural order of things. In short, they would negate the burglary and the strange chasms that it had opened in the composed and smooth universe of the villa.

Yet, instead of accomplishing what he had imagined, Mr. Grandieu had suddenly pulled away from his wife and left the room.

It was a little after midnight. Mr. Grandieu had decided to wait until two in the morning before calling the police. If Mrs. Grandieu was still alive, he would set her free, tend to her. And, if she was dead, it would have been the work of destiny.

Grandieu had gone through the villa room by room. The thefts made no sense. He had picked out traces of vandalism, broken objects, urine, and turds. Lastly, in the kitchen, this strange mask, this child's disguise. That had been a shock. Mr. Grandieu had suddenly remembered a thousand little things he had noticed during the assault, strange things, anomalies in the voices, the steps, and the silhouettes, and later, when he had been blinded and shackled, in the tumult. At that very moment, he had thought that children were helping the thieves: maybe it was a family of gypsies. There were some campsites on the western coast.

But the incoherence of the burglary, the piggishness, the mask (and even the dimensions of the turds, of the traces of piss), all pointed to the true identity of his thieves: a band of brats, without God or master.

Grandieu reminded himself that such a thing existed. You read about these kinds of occurrences in the national dailies. The affliction might very well have invaded the island. Mr. Grandieu pondered this thought a while longer, toured the villa one more time. His suspicion became a certainty. A handful of children, maybe a half-dozen. Yes. The dwarves with falsified voices who had assailed and overpowered the Grandieus, akin to a horde of trained monkeys, were kids. If Grandieu talked, the police would inevitably reach the same conclusion.

But this version of the events did not suit him at all. Not if Mrs. Grandieu succumbed to the abominable aggression.

Regardless of who the rascals who'd sacked the villa were, Hugo Grandieu was absolutely loath to make them shoulder a homicide. He decided to improve upon the burglary, to give it a more serious turn, a more adult one. The assassins would be grown-ups. Besides, Mrs. Grandieu's death would only become more credible, more banal.

"Let's at least hope they didn't leave fingerprints those little imbeciles," thought Grandieu. He had a vague, visual, and tactile memory that he plumbed. Yes, those who held torches and those who had bound him wore lukewarm pink rubber dishwashing gloves, with the pulp of the finger bristling with nubs. Such light, swift, mean and soft hands. Dumb cat paws.

But he too, in fact, should wear gloves. Now he was his own thief, he had to be careful.

Go check on his wife. He asked himself if the gag was sufficiently tight. If not, this gamble, this heads or tails was lost in advance. And Mr. Grandieu had resolved not to tighten it further, and to let destiny take its course. He went back to the room, which was on the first floor. Mrs. Grandieu hadn't regained consciousness. At least there was that. She rattled. What was visible of her face was rather engorged. Hugo Grandieu imagined himself, for a fraction of a second, flipping his wife head over heels so as to accelerate what was to come. But wouldn't that be cheating with his resolution?

He treated himself as a Jesuit, and gave himself until three o'clock in the morning. Furthermore, he had discovered that the kids, not satisfied with having cut the telephone line, had also carried the headset off with them. Retards. But that would force him, an excellent thing, to go cry at a neighbor's door for help.

Mr. Grandieu inspected the villa one last time, sweeping away the traces that might have appeared too puerile (among other things he gathered the turds, widened the puddles of urine, wiped down objects, doorknobs, light switches). Then he ransacked himself by the book, adroitly, that is to say aggra-vating what had already been done. He even sacrificed the beautiful things, the books, and the china. Mrs. Grandieu's jewelry was more of a problem, since its total value amounted to a very high price. He decided that the malefactors would have stolen what his wife had left on her vanity, and of which he would provide a precise description—like a good soldier gifted with a flair for observation. The rest of the jewels would be pro-tected in his safe, which the burglars wouldn't have known how to open. Barbaric brutes, amateurs. And Grandieu was deter-mined to dispose of all the jewels supposedly stolen, as he had done with the whole of the loot he had pulled together so far. For what would betray him if not half-measure, greediness, and pet-tiness? Certainly, there was no better lie than a lie that clung onto true facts.

This pillaging of his own house aggrieved Mr. Grandieu. So the sea was going to engulf all these beautiful things. Grandieu calculated that the death of his wife was costing him around seventy thousand francs. A ruinous verisimilitude. The "stolen" objects belonged almost exclusively to Mrs. Grandieu, admittedly, but it would mean that much less to inherit.

And why had these idiots taken his old rubber tobacco pouch?

He assembled the booty in a duffle bag, added the ridiculous mask to it, and discreetly went out to throw the lot in the water. Not just anywhere, he knew his inlet. And the bag contained too many non-perishable objects. It was therefore necessary that Mr. Grandieu recover it, given a few days, to destroy its contents completely and definitely. The whole business of human molars which were found twenty years later, while someone was turning and digging in the soil of a garden, tormented him quite a bit now: this was almost his own story—except that his would end well. He pondered the ways of making the silverware vanish.

Returning from his expedition, he checked the mise-en-scène of the burglary. He could contemplate it, study it with fresh eyes. It was perfect. He had admirably known how to compose, around the authentic traces that he'd subtly enhanced, the physiognomy of important and brutal labor. The whole, thanks to the relics left by the little bastards, had a kind of vulgarity that was impossible to invent, especially when one was the retired captain of the police force.

Mrs. Grandieu finally died at three-twenty. Mr. Grandieu had been surprised to experience neither compassion nor disgust in front of the dying woman. Was it because the gag concealed the bottom part of Mrs. Grandieu's face, and a big cloth napkin covered the top? For Hugo Grandieu, the old bag no longer had anything human about her, or even animal. Her agony was a material event, like the landslide of a cliffside path, the slow rupture of a telephone pole, the flow of dirty water in a bath. Mr. Grandieu felt sure he'd never know remorse. Never any nightmares: how could he identify with *that?* Thus Mrs. Grandieu did not die—for lack of a witness to believe she had ever been alive to begin with.

The formalities that followed did not present any difficulties for Captain Grandieu. The papers duly stated that the poor old lady, etc. The police—dear companions, dear colleagues, and dear comrades—had discovered nothing nor had they looked for a suspect; they'd glared at a subaltern who had found that the B&E smacked of the baby bottle and kids. Grandieu was respected. His wife was canonical. By principle they waited for her to die. She had died of this, well, well. No mystery. You can die of a fart, in old age. Oh, the filthy thugs.

But now Mr. Grandieu no longer understood his act, which he recounted to himself over and over from dawn till dusk, and even as he was asleep. No doubt about it, he understood why it was pleasant, opportune, that his wife be dead; besides he would follow her soon enough … You think you are in perfect health, you are only sixty-nine, you are slim, with a full head of hair, you run, you get it up, you have balls, and you can really knock it back, and *wham*. It's even sadder than to die young. No, the difficulty didn't lie in that, he thought. The real question was this: what good was it to have killed someone who was already on her deathbed?

For old lady Grandieu was not in the least cumbersome. She'd treated herself to a superb, mature gentleman for the conversation, the bearing, the style, to cocksuck him, and to sometimes be screwed by him. She used to love doing it on all fours. Certainly, Grandieu'd rather be fishing, and he wouldn't have said no to a schoolgirl, except you-know-where. But what about honor. In the end, he missed her now. He was bored. His habits seemed hollow to him; he no longer had anyone to show off in front of and for whom he needed to be disciplined.

This spike of emotion succeeded in erasing any remaining trace of anguish in him. He hadn't killed his wife! She wouldn't have survived anyway. And those little imps. This was what they called killing for loose change. Get a new maid. Take one who … But what about widowhood? Perhaps a tour to … And what if he brought back a little negress from South Africa, around eleven or fourteen. Same thing as a houseboy, but for the police. Yes, yes. A … umm. He was daydreaming, picturing himself on a cruise.

Leon Bloom Square was the square that Alain Viaud liked best. First of all, the guardian was downright senile. If someone stole his wooden leg, he would shout out loud how fed up he was with people walking on his feet. He was an old, old vet. He never moved from his green sentry box, as if, once and for all, he had understood that it was under these kinds of shelters that you could be the best guard. The entrance of barracks, atomic factories and ministries were proof. But the sentry box of Leon Bloom Square was not at all strategic. In the summer, it opened onto an ice cream vendor, in the winter, onto a chestnut vendor. The rest of the time, you had to look far into the distance in order to see anything, particularly if you were a bit deaf. The hard of hearing had the same astonished eyes as myopic people who would have given up reading. The guardian of Bloom Square bothered no one; he was treated very well. Who better than he could achieve this miraculous balance so involuntarily: to be at once neither grumpy nor amiable? The guardian of Bloom Square was part of the seasons, the alleyways and chairs. He was lame. To consider that he actually controlled the garden was as far-fetched as considering that a chair refused to be sat upon, an alleyway to be walked through, or a season to be named and loved.

On the other hand, Alain Viaud went to Bloom Square because many people and many things passed through there. In particular, tourists went there to see the statue of *The Doomed Whaler*, a vengeful piece that the municipality had ordered from Paris a while ago, when that city was Wagnerian. The *Whaler* was a bearded harpooner, some nude-calved Nick Land, and the miracle was his hand at his eyebrows. For it was placed in such a way that you couldn't tell if he was hiding his eyes or searching for prey. And that is how this Parisian art of a day could become provincial forever. There was so much to reflect upon!

But instead, the tourists cackled. You know how tourists are: they always have this nasty laugh in front of the things you love. They'd spit on you for not liking what you need to be rich to like. Oh, Viaud had diligently spied on the tourists. They made wishy-washy faces, they gave the impression that they were above the world, but in reality their dirty little eyes whirled ceaselessly surveying all presences in their surroundings. The rich feared for their own life the moment a single tree leaf stirred, then would say, "Oh-la-la, the delicious breeze, and what kind of tree is that, hmmm, is it, isn't it, pff." It was impossible to steal anything from them, with those squinty eyes that would not spare anything or anyone, as if they had their own part to suck in everything that lived, and that passed by, and that was there. There for them, obviously.

Nonetheless, tourists interested Alain Viaud. He wouldn't go see them where they lived (old poor neighborhoods, rich neighborhoods today); and he knew that the rich wouldn't set foot in the faceless places where real people lived. But some intermediary regions existed, indigenous enough for Viaud to pay them a visit and feel at home, singular enough for the foreigners to frequent them. Pine beach. The Pottery, Painted Seashells & Parasol Festival. The pedestrian street downtown, with its chains you could swing on and its retail stores that were too expensive for shopping, and too monitored to steal anything. Beautiful people strolled along there, in pairs, caring about nothing else but showing each other with their hands and eyes how beautiful they found each other, and how beyond all of this non-sense (that it to say, the merchandise) they stood. It made you wonder why they all came together, and during the same hours, to demonstrate—with a veiled smile on a glassy eye, a languid eye on a soft smile—on the only merchant street in town that they were way beyond these things and only had passion for the love of themselves.

Viaud got it, really. It was quite luxurious to be indifferent to luxury: but where could you show it, except on those two hundred meters of ruinous shops? The things which lay behind the shop windows and the people who walked outside of them resembled each other almost to perfection: you no longer knew which one was here to buy, and which one was for sale. Everything was on display. It only took being invisible, like young Viaud, to bring to light the role and raison d'être of the exquisite old working-class street. Still Viaud didn't know that the intelligentsia from both sides of the spectrum loved his island and actually came from Paris, from Bordeaux, from Lyon or from

Marseille to exhibit their tan belly buttons, their disinterest, and their faded vainglories in the street that was off limits to those who had less than so many millions. Otherwise, he'd have figured out that, whenever he ventured out there, with his slightly cross-eyed gaze, his strange stubborn and insolent face, his poorly-fitting clothes that didn't at all drape the curves of his body and were instead a collection of sacks, satchels, sheaths, curtains, rags and armors beneath which, fresh and swift, he went everywhere without even considering for a moment that he might be seen by others—his moronic native style was exactly what gave the luxury street its touch of perfection. Those hundreds of mongrels and bitches spent fortunes and made themselves up into laid back models, in the style of a Monoprix, Uniprix, or a Mammoth shop window so that a Viaud could admire them, approve of them, feel that they were, at heart, close to him—mankind, mankind, in the end, honey, you know, Humanity, sure Man is dead, but what about Humanity—and so that they could likewise be sanctified by others than themselves.

As a matter of fact, this was exactly what Viaud came here for: the models and puppets. They were shiny and they moved as if it were Christmas. How lucky to live on a tourist island, you got it all year long. What striking faces.

Bloom Square was better, however. There was sand, something that Viaud, who lived two or three hundred meters away from a shoreline of pebbles, oil slicks, and sewer waste, took for a kind of powdered gold. It was the precious little pit in the central square, squeezed in between its planks—in there, four children would get in each other's way. And it was the immense carpet of the paying beaches on the well-to-do coastline, down there, on the other side of town. On the beaches, those beaches, it wasn't humid and granular as it was in Bloom Square: it was all dry, light, it slid like water between the toes, it smelled of sunscreen and peanuts. The problem, with so many wonders, was that you couldn't do anything. You'd have to own balloons, children, parents, and styles. And Viaud had no desire whatsoever to burn in the sun. When he saw some tourist children laying conscientiously on these beaches on very pretty towels, black sunglasses on their nose, flowery cloth over their wee-wee, and who tanned themselves in the sun as they offered their foreheads—interminably—for someone to dab arnica on a booboo, Viaud felt like biting their fingers, to see if they moved.

But, of course, he didn't touch these luxurious children who'd been destined to beauty treatments on high-end beaches.

The Potteries, Painted Seashells & Parasols Festival was very different from Pine Beach, and from the pedestrian street. Grade-schoolers were allowed to exhibit their works, the things they were taught to copy from their teachers. It was very interesting. Alain Viaud liked plaster of Paris a lot. He modeled everything, everything, all those very original things they asked him to make, and afterwards, he would undo it all. At school, they'd gotten used to that fact: Viaud didn't have parents; he was emotionally disturbed. He needed love, that was all, hmm … hmm … pff.

He really enjoyed visiting all the pieces that hadn't been broken (it was free). He thought they were really pretty. He said so. And the teacher went, "and, and …?" Viaud cackled. It titillated him. He'd like to walk along the shelves sliding his hand as if pushing a little car. To make them all fall down. It would really be even prettier. He was as fascinated in front of these rows of objects that were ready to be broken (well, after all, what else could you do with them) as he was before the aisles of stealable things in the stores. It didn't say so on them, that was true, but Alain Viaud got it all the same.

The other beauty of the festival was its emptiness. People went around noon because none of the restaurants in the area were open yet. They went again at five because the sun was still in the sky, already … ooh yes, well, it was better off to be in the shade. That was it. An edible silence reigned in those large rooms, a labyrinth of ugly, damp hallways where the piteous products of local and school art crumbled at night and crackled during the day. Blissful, thick, compact, more frozen than the silence of museums, more timid than church silence during service, it was a silence that was like still water. Viaud was crazy about it. He'd hide to be able to stay inside longer. But the teachers kept a close watch. The ones who knew him wanted to socialize him, heal him; the ones who didn't didn't stand on ceremony and chased him off straight away. During off-peak hours, there were only a few of them to guard this treasure trove of humble works in which everyone, old and young, woman and man, the pottery master and the poignant toddler has poured their hearts. All, all their hearts. So scat, or stay right here in front of me Viaud, stop making a scene my friend respect the work of others if you don't want to … You are in society here.

It was very hard to escape the young girls or altruistic and respectful women of the Festival of pots. Too bad for Viaud, who sensed the only beauty in those corridors that was to be felt: absence, inanity, and blankness. He would never be educated. And he didn't want to be either.

Thus of all privileged places the best was Leon Bloom Square. It had the sole inconvenience of being a bit dangerous. Well, a bit strange rather, at times.

It had taken Alain Viaud a while to notice it. It had taken a few coincidences. For example, last month, this is what happened to Viaud. He was sitting on a wood-plank bench, busy undoing all the knots of a hairy and wet packaging string that he'd found on the ground. On the bench opposite from him, a man was reading a book.

Viaud was soon done and got up to go have fun with something else. Then the man also got up and showed his penis to the little boy.

Alain Viaud planted his crossed-eyed gaze on that thingama-jig and examined it minutely, with an air of suspicion. Then he snickered with contempt and took his own out. I mean, really. Then he left, buttoning up his fly and shouting:

"Hey, go get dressed at Buttnaked's! What's your problem! ..."

The man, terrorized, fled in the other direction.

At the public urinal, Viaud patiently waited for the younger children. When he saw one in short pants who'd come to take a piss, he'd approach him sneakily, casually, preparing his trick, and suddenly he would plunge a finger straight into the kid's ass through his underwear. The little one would step aside, complain. Viaud would sniff his finger and shrug his shoulders:

"It smells like doodoo," he'd remark. "It smells very much like doodoo. Or like shit."

And he'd move away nonchalantly, this finger to his nose. Sometimes a kid, instead of protesting, found it funny, thought he was invited to a game. Viaud wouldn't change anything in his response, wouldn't smile, would sniff and move away just the same. He found that, decidedly, people's anuses smell rather bad. But only in Bloom Square could one document this important truth. Formerly, Viaud, on all fours in the sand, or in elementary school, would put the finger into anyone who presented himself or herself to him, by chance, in a propitious posture. Generally speaking, girls' anuses were easier: that is, if they were wearing a dress. He would sink his finger in, stiff as a crayon, and would forage with violence with his nail. It was very mean to the other little ones. He'd make them cry. Everyone distrusted the cross-eyed boy, denounced him, he'd be punished; he'd sniff his finger, indifferent to the rest.

Now, if his victims complained to their mommies or their guardians, Viaud would leave the square and think no more about it. He accorded no real importance to his humble mania and wasn't even aware that he was suffering from it. Nevertheless, the idea of Bloom Square, the finger in the rear, the special odor you could extract from it were intimately associated in his mind and imposed themselves on him, at intervals, much more vividly than the temptation to steal. Alain Viaud was a loner. He knew himself because he listened to himself and only ever did what he wanted. And was likely to remain that way forever, since he already knew all there was to know.

Mrs. Thérèse Ambreuse raised her hand a little and protested:

"Oh God no, I have no idea where your father is, my dear! Don't you imagine one second that he tells me anything! Oh he hasn't changed! It'll be like this till the day he dies. Or I do, that is."

Dr. Ambreuse looked politely scandalized. She had taken advantage of a lull in her schedule to accomplish a family chore: let them know she wouldn't be free on Mother's Day, and offer her gift in advance. Her relationship with Mrs. Ambreuse was the most neutral, the most non-existent there could be. The least word or gesture that didn't express this total insignificance would have shocked the two women, struck them as indecent. The gift was the very image of this pact of platitude. Every year, Pauline Ambreuse brought her mother a copper object for Mother's Day, a pewter object for her birthday, a sandstone one for the day celebrating Sainte Thérèse, chestnuts for Christmas, and flowers for the New Year, and this would invariably happen at a slight interval, either early or late, from the appointed date. Her work was her alibi: a plebeian medical practice, service at the hospital. In truth, if Pauline Ambreuse studiously avoided being there on holidays, it was because such accuracy would have been too much as well. What was there to celebrate? Obviously nothing. Nothing at all. No circumstance, no event, no human being.

"Don't you worry, he'll notice all right that you're not here. It's already too good of you to disturb yourself to come and let us know. I'd understand if you just called, you know. And you know, these so-called holidays …"

Mrs. Ambreuse wasn't saying this to hurt her daughter or to insinuate that she thought precisely the contrary: such custodial subtleties were foreign to her. All she tried to do, and this according to an unvarying protocol, was to cancel her daughter's visit, to annul the offered gift, and the absence to come. To appear to give them any importance would have been worse than incest. And the entire length of the visit was devoted to a series of rituals, each of which meant: do not touch each other; do not speak to one another.

Did a secret of coldness or hatred lie beneath these precautions? Dr. Ambreuse didn't like to ponder the question too much. A useless effort—and one that was slightly unsavory. Why not evoke family memories, while they were at it? It seemed pornographic to think that Mrs. Thérèse Ambreuse and her daughter had ever been another age, or had ever had another way about them or another countenance than those which they expressed today, in this banal living room, saying empty things with empty gestures and an empty gaze, as if to respect or outline that vast grayish void between them, and within each of them.

Pauline Ambreuse had little humor, but appreciated it in others. She was one of those people who are exactly as alive and as intelligent as the people around them or their company of the moment, and reflect with an unflagging fidelity their character traits and even their soul-searching. She let herself be filled up and emptied out in turn, would have committed suicide near someone who'd just done it, would have had a formidable personality near a genius, and there, beside her mother, she grew insipid, stagnant, and exhausted.

"I bought an electric rotisserie, by the way," she said.

"That was a good idea," replied Mrs. Ambreuse. "I don't really remember how your kitchen is, but I ..."

No, no conviction. Maybe slightly piqued?

"Uhh, eight or nine hundred francs," said Dr. Ambreuse.

"Oh no, Mrs. d'Alost paid seven hundred and fifty for hers; or at least that's what she told me."

"They come in a lot of different prices."

"I'm sure. But seven hundred and fifty francs, that's not really a bargain. Nine hundred francs isn't either," said Thérèse Ambreuse, the mother.

"Yes, there are cheaper ones," said Pauline Ambreuse.

"They're smaller, that's all. Mrs. d'Alost can easily fit a chicken in hers, even a pretty big one I think."

"It must be quite large."

"Oh no, you can still fit one even in the smaller ones. Otherwise what would be the point?"

Pauline Ambreuse smiled weakly. The conversation stopped. It had seemed a bit tenser than was customary. Mrs. Ambreuse was hiding something, holding something back. Something to confide? Unthinkable. A dissatisfaction, rather. Mr. Ambreuse? …

"You did get it as a dual-voltage, right?" Mrs. Ambreuse went on. She didn't appreciate the drawn out silences. The protocol of inanity necessarily included a certain production of words, phrases, agreed upon intonations.

"Yeah, yeah. You never know. Dual-voltage has two options," her daughter answered. "If ever you have to move …"

"Oh no, Mrs. d'Alost got hers in 220 V. There's no chance she'd move you know. That might explain the price difference."

"Yes, that's it. It could practically be the same."

"Yes, that is, a smaller model, but the same kind," said Mrs. Ambreuse, almost warmly. "Keep in mind that she's all alone … And she never hosts. Or she can make something else just in case she has someone over."

"Yes. She doesn't have to …"

"No. And also, with one chicken, I'm telling you, she says she makes enough for four servings. Four meals. So I mean, if she's got guests, she could … But that's really the exception. Yeah, there's enough for four. That's for sure!"

Mrs. d'Alost was an aged neighbor whom Dr. Ambreuse had never seen, but with whom her mother swapped magazines sometimes. Neither would host the other, however, at least not for drinking or eating.

"What about her oven?" asked Pauline Ambreuse, vaguely satisfied that, with this whole rotisserie thing, she'd succeeded in launching a subject that was so rich in sentences that could be uttered without worrying that any of them would have any content.

"Naturally," said her mother. "In theory, all she's gotta do is put another chicken in the oven, if she needs two."

"One of them spit roasted, and the other in the oven. It's just as good. They must practically be done at the same time."

"If that was the case, I know, of course. But at her age … That was the reason, mostly. She just sets the rotisserie in front of her and …"

"Yes, and also the upkeep," said Pauline Ambreuse. "An oven …"

"You have to consider that. She has to do everything herself at her house. That doesn't make you want to … And the oven is a gas oven. I swear, I myself, sometimes … when it comes time to turn it on."

Mrs. Ambreuse gave a hint of a pleasant laugh. She was kindly making fun of her fear of explosions.

"No, the risks are really … well …" said Pauline Ambreuse.

"I mean, no, it's not that I think everything is gonna blow up, but! … Oh no, no way, I just ask your father. Besides, you never know."

This time, it was Dr. Ambreuse's turn to breathe out a pleasant laugh, and her mother, once she'd understood, accompanied her. What she'd just said was such a joke! No, of course, she wasn't implying that she'd preferred that her husband be the victim of a potential explosion! There was no such risk. It was … a superstition, a phobia that he helped her to ward off. In any case, if the range exploded, the whole house would explode along with it. So, if you were bent over it or waiting off to the side, it wouldn't make much of a difference. No, it was a phobia.

"… And it's been like this ever since I was a little girl!" Mrs. Ambreuse confided.

She was now more than sixty and, she'd taken to evoking her childhood—her three or four first years, no later. And only memories entirely deprived of substance, of personality. She would remember a flower, a pendulum clock, a habit, a stereotypical individual of the time, a custom that she hadn't experienced first hand but that someone had described to her, and that could be as singular as taking a fresh drink in the summer or opening an umbrella when it rained.

"… I don't know what happened with ovens, if anything," she continued. "Something that was done to me—or maybe just fear—well the fact is that ever since then … At any rate …"

"Kids, sometimes … You never know what goes on in their heads, well, all for nothing in the end," approved Dr. Ambreuse.

"Yes, it must be something like that, I think, it must be, because otherwise what else could it be?" said Mrs. Ambreuse. She offered tea, coffee, an alcoholic beverage, or a fruit juice. Her daughter refused half-heartedly. This was also part of their habit. Pauline Ambreuse would conclude:

"No, really, I'm not thirsty, thank you."

"I know your principles, I know, I wasn't forcing you," Mrs. Ambreuse would invariably answer.

As any young female doctor should, she had strict principles relating to anything that could enter her body. Beginning, of course, with food, remedies, beverages, tobacco, etc. As for Mrs. Ambreuse, she was less disciplined. For example, a cup of hot milk or even chicken broth, around five o'clock, with her drops … The piercing pain that sometimes drilled through her just right there, one of those psychosomatic illnesses that everyone catches nowadays, even in the best climates. After this courtesy Mrs. Ambreuse had paid to medicine, it was time for her daughter to leave. Mrs. Ambreuse would slip the words "medical vocation" in a sentence; it was like a discreet allusion to her daughter's stubborn celibacy, and the only vaguely personal item of the entire conversation. Dr. Ambreuse would not answer. She would take her leave. The car would be make a sound as it drove off. "Another twenty or thirty years and I'll be like her," thought Pauline Ambreuse. "But I'll *pull my plug* before that."

6

Through the glass display with large draped window shades, Mrs. Seignelet examined the main room of the restaurant.

"Hey, check out those flowers on the table! I mean, what a waste! That's money flushed down the drain right there. Cause they don't give 'em to you! Don't you go thinkin' that! But they'll be on the bill all right! They ain't losing a thing, don't you worry! They ain't losing a thing! …"

Mr. Seignelet and the children were standing a little behind—for fear perhaps, that the clientele of the restaurant might be observing them—and they waited for Raymonde Seignelet's verdict. She was being celebrated today along with all the mommies.

She pulled her head back. She wasn't at ease. She was feeling scruffy in her ugly spring coat, unsteady on the high heels that made her walk like a duck, like a little girl trying on women's shoes. She usually wore laced up shoes that came up to the ankle, or, at home, reinforced slippers. Now she was forcing herself to have the composure of a lady, arching her back, holding her chin high, sensing that her mimicry, and her facial expressions patiently modeled to reign over a concentration camp suburban house stood out as pale, dry, sour, hollow and petty in the face of the peaceful splendors of the restaurant.

She clenched her handbag to her belly with her ten fingers, puffed out her chest, and gave a disgusted scowl.

"No, all this fuss, all these chichis … They try to show off and in the end you always get the worst grub in these kinda places. Did you see those prices? …"

Robert Seignelet was beginning to feel embarrassed and slightly irritated. Taking out the wife and children on this Mother's Day had been his initiative. It was a gentle Sunday, light and fresh, the way they are around here in June. The table for six was reserved. He courteously insisted and tried to offer his arm to the elegant Mrs. Seignelet, specially permed for the occasion.

But the latter brusquely disengaged herself, her features furious as if a cop were trying to apprehend her. She yelped in a middling voice, in her droning and aggressive tone.

"Uh uh! Uh uh! Please, let me go! Uh uh, I'm not goin' in! Uh uh, I'm not goin' in there! … You go ahead if you want! I'm not goin'! All these laadeedaas, these loudeedous, all this play-acting! You go on, Robert, take the children! You go on! Go! I'm goin' home! There are taxis, aren't there! There are taxis! I don't need you! Go on then if you like it! I ain't stoppin' you! I can get home by meeself! What do I care! Robert, take the kids, go on! …"

The Seignelets shuffled in place, sheepish. Philippe, who'd grown nauseous in the car (where Bertrand had him squeezed on his knees), was breathing in rapid jolts and going green. His morning *café au lait* was coming up, three hours later, intact but sour, full of bilious flavors: the taste of vomit. He also sensed the squarming and twingeing of liquid diarrhea in his butt. He didn't dare say anything. But if they didn't go into the restaurant very, very quickly … Once they were inside, he'd ask right away, and in front of people, or maybe because of Mother's Day, Mrs. Seignelet wouldn't yell.

The place was called *The Golden Vnycorn Etynge Howse, Tongres, Droole & Sons.* Those sirs cherished the noble type, *mediaeval hostelrye, seygeuryal, ymperyal, ynternatyonal,* etc. The restaurant was flanked by *The Admirals' Grill Room*, founded in 1805, the year of the battle of Trafalgar, as was explained on the banner of the menu. *The Golden Vnycorn* was very reputable, people came from far away to eat very good things that were very expensive and very refined, and cooked with talent by the brigade of Misters Droole & Sons. The local Rotary club had its banquets there. And on this holiday, families, and not necessarily the wealthiest one, had reserved all the lunch tables. It was quite the contrary. This lunchtime, the chic of the clients couldn't have offended Mrs. Seignelet.

"Go ahead, I'm tellin' you! … Uh uh, it's just not for me!"

On the edge of despair, Philippe had just confided his torment to Jean-Baptiste, who'd looked at him stunned, full of compassion, and had passed the information along to Dominique. The latter had whispered it into Bertrand's ear, who'd rapidly glanced at the kid's face as if to evaluate the imminence of the catastrophe. Another glance at their surroundings had horrified him. There was nothing, no café where you could enter without being embarrassed, no hidden nook, no alleyway, no construction site where Philippe could have dropped his trousers unbeknownst to passers-by and to his mother.

Finally, Bertrand laid it all on the line and, bothering Mr. Seignelet, put him in the loop.

Robert Seignelet looked at the kid, heaved a long exhausted sigh, took a quick scan of the horizon as Bertrand had done. There was no recourse. They had to enter *The Golden Vnycorn*. But how could he reconcile the mother's desires with those of the child? Mr. Seignelet felt as if he was sitting on a mule whose front and rear was trying to dart in opposite directions: quickly, hold this one by the bridle and that one by the tail. And stay calm.

He sent his four children as an advance guard into the restaurant: he felt confident, alone outside with Mrs. Seignelet, that he'd be able to convince her to follow them in. The fact that he too rarely invited her to a tête-a-tête flitted through his mind. But that was really not the custom around here. And meals in town seemed to arouse her touchiness as a spouse, a mother, and a cordon bleu with a strange intensity. Mr. Seignelet knew that in the end she'd agree to go in. As a punctilious domestic divinity, she simply required that a long ceremonial be accomplished, one which honored and confirmed her preeminence. Then, once she'd thrown her lightning bolt, uttered her cries, stamped her feet in a sacred uproar, and reduced her victims to smithereens, she'd haughtily consent to visit the temple of a rival goddess: *The Golden Vnycorn*, Misters Droole & Sons.

Bertrand, who was charged with representing the head of the family in the hall of said temple, discovered, aghast, that no placard indicated the toilets. He'd have to ask. In a pinch, he might have dared with the young lady at the reception, but it was too late: she'd called a maître d'. She'd delivered the four Seignelets over to him—all in their Sunday best, white shirts, ties, shoes a bit bulgy but very well polished. And now Bertrand was stammering—his face scarlet, pathetic squeaks interjecting through his hoarse voice—through his narrative of a table for six and of parents who were still outside.

In the meantime, Jean-Baptiste and Dominique roosted their eyes on the little Philippe, moldered by the heat of the hall. They were prisoners of the machinery of a sinking vessel. An engine, before them, was about to explode any moment now, or a water-way was going to let loose, a boiler spurt from all parts. What on earth was Bertrand waiting for?

Suddenly, Jean-Baptiste perceived in Philippe's cheeks and forehead a new change of color, the indicator that usually announced: *warning, imminent ejection*. He grasped Philippe abruptly and cried:

"Where are the bathrooms? Quick, he's sick!"

The maître d' evaluated the danger and, pinched but courteous, indicated the john. They had to cross through the enormous dining room. Bertrand finally came to his senses. He tore Philippe from the hands of Jean-Baptiste and carried him off, running and repeating in his ear, with the same menacing growl and the same wrathful eyebrow as his mother:

"Philippe, you're not throwing up! Philippe, you're not throwing up!"

The maître d', reassured once the plague had passed the backdoor without shoving or polluting anything, bent over the other two Seignelets boys and contemptuously invited the gentlemen to take a seat. Jean-Baptiste and Dominique looked at each other, embarrassed. How could they, alone, walk into the sumptuous dining room that was smothering with its costly objects and runners in full garb, dangerous and humiliating, nightmarish with luxury and with protocols? But how could they say no to the gentleman in a uniform, whose threads or kicks must have cost more than all of the four children's laborious harnessing? A dreadful flunky, with a mug like that of a schoolteacher who slapped kids around, or an undertaker who'd strike down an audience with a single glare to stop them from laughing in front of the bier. And if they obeyed, and reached the table without being insulted or bitten, what would they do there? What would they dare to touch, or not touch? And how would their brothers find them among the chaos of tables, tablecloths, sideboards, trolleys, and armchairs? And what if Mrs. Seignelet refused to enter in the end and they all had to decamp after being seated? And what if Mrs. Seignelet finally agreed to enter and she and Mr. Seignelet saw the boys comfortably settled at their table without their permission, reveling and nibbling—why not, at this point!—the rolls? And what if, as their parents came in, the kids respectfully rose from the table, and everyone found them ridiculous and smiled with derision as they pointed out the grotesque family to each other? And what if all went well but Philippe was too sick, as it sometimes happened, and they had to leave in order to put him to bed?

"I'll just stand here," Jean-Baptiste whispered eventually.

"Yeah, uhm, we'd rather wait for 'em here," said Dominique in turn. The undertaker bent over and disappeared.

"The asshole did it on purpose to fuck with us!" said Jean-Baptiste in a hollow voice.

"Shhhh!" counseled Dominique.

The receptionist had probably heard them.

"Here they are!" cried Dominique almost immediately, in a joyful tone.

It was the Seignelet parents. For the children to be happy to see them had required all the embarrassment they'd experienced in their absence. Mrs. Seignelet had miraculously calmed down. What on earth could her husband have said? They wished someone could tell them the recipe.

But, in truth, there wasn't any. Once she'd made a scene, and felt a pang of hunger and a sweet tooth for good cocktails, Raymonde Seignelet would tame herself. Moreover, she insisted in being classy in classy places, ymperial, royal, etc. She'd act as if she were infinitely above those people, those minions, sommeliers, gastronomists, gluttons, stuck-ups, lavallière-adorned broods, Empyre of the Indyes lobsters and other Gay rabbyts. All those chichis and laadeedaas, she saw right through them. She wouldn't be fooled. And if the aspic of crayfish was simply monkfish, she'd detect it. She had an inkling that it was going to be monkfish. Maybe it was because of the maître d's imperceptibly snide obsequiousness; maybe it was the mind-blowing luxury of the tables and the splendor of the bouquets. Yes, she knew (obliged to leave her fake greige silk coat in the cloakroom) that Misters Droole & Sons, if they had money enough to throw flowers out the window, could have at least christened a somewhat fresh piece of monkfish as *crayfish*, and not this kind of dried, half-rotten codling that they'd tried to redeem with drubbings of spices and had drowned in industrial gelatins. At least she'd have a bellyache for something, this time.

She imagined what her attitude would be as she'd look at the menu, and how she'd demystify the dishes one by one for her hayseed of a husband and her birdbrain kids, they who mistook a velvet swimming crab for a toothbrush, or who thought that "veal sweetbreads" were veal and sweets. And those intolerable flowers! They even smelled a little. How dare they put flowers that smelled in the middle of a restaurant table. She creaked, her voice atonal.

"Yes Robert, I'm telling you they smell. I can smell 'em, yes. I can smell 'em. I'm telling you, have them taken away, or at least push them to the side … Look, I'm telling you they smell! It's the kind that smells! They're … Well, mmmh, I'm telling you! … Anyway, I don't want those disgusting things next to me! … For what they cost, first of all, they'd be better off not smoking us out with them, but trust me, this is as humdrum as it gets! As humdrum as it gets! …"

The maître d', who was distributing the menus, overheard this remark; he made a slight motion towards the table to grab hold of the vase.

"Are the flowers inconveniencing you, Madam?"

"Oh no, let 'em be, oh dear! … Pff! … It's all right!" Mrs. Seignelet moaned politely, as if to insinuate that she'd been mistreated and tortured for so long that she no longer heeded such minor details. She had used her "dining out voice."

Mr. Seignelet, firmly resolved to remain gallant come what may, said to the maître d':

"My wife finds their scent, hmm! … too strong."

Under the table, Mrs. Seignelet sent him a kick to shut him up. But she missed him, since he was seated to her right and she had to reach out at him with her heel. Gosh, what a cretin. Naturally the minion was triumphant.

"These are chrysanthemums, which have no smell, Madam," he said, urbane, as he had the vase taken away. In its place, they set a silver candelabra.

"… Chrysanthemums in June! He's insane!" whispered Mrs. Seignelet. "As if I didn't know what a chrysanthemum was, that rubbish, that laadeedaa has nothing to do with chrysanthemums, nothing to do with 'em! Anyway, he's wrong, there are some that smell, there are some. And those were the kind that smells! Yeah they were! Come off it! You think it's pleasant to be spied on like that … Is that kid insane or what?" she cried louder. She tossed a circular glance around the room, guessed that she'd been over-heard, and continued on, whispering and shooting the child a death stare:

"Philippe, come on, you better stop with the bread, got it? You were throwing up not even five minutes ago and now you're eating bread? Completely insane, that's what you are! … And you think that … (she let out a false laugh that sounded like the cry of a frightened nanny-goat.) You drag this kid to a restaurant, I don't even know how many stars it has, and he fills up on bread! What a loon! … And did you go poo earlier by the way with Bertrand? Did he go poo? I'm warning you, you're not gonna start your whole shenanigans all over again while we're eating! It's not gonna end well!"

Philippe shook his head no. Mrs. Seignelet launched some additional thunderbolts at the little boy, and then she reckoned she'd given him enough of the stink eye and she plunged into her cocktail. Like a circus target, Philippe had received his collection of daggers. Nailed to his place, he would keep quiet for a good while.

He was feeling good. For the ease of the wait-staff, and because he was the youngest, they'd seated him at the worst spot at the table, at the farthest end, his back turned to the path of the waiters. He was delighted. The room was air-conditioned; you could breathe easily. His elastic bowtie didn't constrict his throat. His belly, now completely empty, was no longer suffering—other than from hunger. The soft manners they had here were delicious:

the moderate voices, the restrained gestures, the faces that didn't grimace. He was safe here. All in all, the beautiful shiny table service, the starched tablecloth, the napkin that was so thick he'd surely not be able to knot it around his neck all by himself, the armchair he was nestled in, feet dangling, well protected by the back and the armrests, inspired a disproportionate feeling of affection and confidence in him. Shy and fearful anywhere else, Philippe was the only Seignelets who felt at ease in this affluent restaurant. He would truly regret a place that was so benevolent and so peaceful. It also amused him to see all these people left and right eating lots of dishes with strange noises and which resembled the lids of soup tureens or the windows of a pork butcher shop at Christmas. It was the greatest beauty in existence! The children seated at the other tables, immersed in these oceans of white linens, were like little invalids in bed, leaning against immense pillows so they could drink a bowl of broth: but here, among all this whiteness, you could see salivating muzzles and great silver forks poking out.

Also, Philippe was very far from Mrs. Seignelet. His stomach, his body, and his brain suddenly discharged from that weight, were becoming small animals, surprised to be unbuckled and let loose to run in a prairie without a collar. And these playful, surprised and ingenuous animals, and this joy, and even this prairie, all this was Philippe, now, immobile and mute in his seat, calm as a saint, almost evaporated into paradise.

It had been a close call. Indeed, at first, Raymonde Seignelet had ordered that he be seated next to her, so that she could watch him and stop him from being picky and making himself sick again. But it was inconvenient, and Robert Seignelet, who could already see how the meal would unravel if Mrs. Seignelet could satiate her whim, had protested with a conjugal purring and a pleasant tone that he wanted his wife to himself for a while, and that they should let the children take care of themselves.

"Oh that's easy to say! ..." had squealed lady Seignelet, as if her husband had dared suggest that the kids didn't need her. But he had repaired this diplomatic blunder. The cherry kirsch, thinned with soda, that Mrs. Seignelet was savoring made her indulgent; and she, also, ended up wanting to be a spouse rather than a mommy that afternoon. "Wasn't that," Mr. Seignelet commented as he listened to himself, "the true meaning of this Mother's Day, in the end?" Then, stimulated by the aperitif, he brainstormed: it was (Mother's Day) a day to be a woman, to be only a woman (and what a woman!), in the same way that Labor Day was a day on which you didn't work.

There was laughter, then Mrs. Seignelet, although she was won over, adopted a grumpy tone with a significant face, eyes sidelong, a shake of the head, an irritated pinch at the corners of the lips but in an exaggerated, thus congenial way, and said:

"Yeah, well, for me, whether it's a holiday or not, every day's a working day. All that's just talk, talk is real pretty but as for work, well, I'm the one who's gotta do it. Talk is cheap alright! Cheap! Talk! Nothing but talk, huh."

"Honey ..." began Mr. Seignelet, his vast lip in a heart-shaped pout, his eye veiled with fluffy love. And he said god knows what about the sanctity of his wife. So Philippe was allowed to skedaddle to the end of the table. Anyway, his brothers were old enough to keep an eye on him couldn't they, short of doing something better, they could at least do this for a bit couldn't they? And wasn't he gonna decide to lay low for an hour, wouldn't he, and leave his brothers in peace?

It wasn't until a bit later that Philippe, stunned by his well being, had started to munch ecstatically on the little piece of bread that had enabled him to torment Mrs. Seignelet one more time. But then she'd forgiven.

This morning at home things had started off rather well. At 9 o'clock, the boys had filed into the kitchen one after the other to offer the decided upon gifts. Because he had no pocket money, Philippe was the only one who didn't offer anything. By convention, he was being morally associated to his eldest brother and it was for the latter's gift that Mrs. Seignelet had pecked Philippe on the cheek like the others, even though he'd come empty-handed.

The gifts were three potted plants: a *Pandanus*, an *Aucuba* and a *Croton*. The Seignelets always offered pots to their mother. This represented the savings of several weeks. They plotted their purchases terrified at displeasing her, provoking a yellow face and small eyes squinting with disappointment, instead of the peaceful, absent mask that Mrs. Seignelet wore when her notion of what was suitable was duly respected, and incarnated before her eyes.

These particular pots, reasonable, prudent, totally ugly but recommended by the florists, had, as a matter of fact, satisfied her. She'd blown into the four children's noses her fetid breath of *café au lait*; she'd chucked the kisses that the pairs of cheeks had deserved; she'd let herself be dispossessed of the dishes and the housework, according to the local tradition. Idle, she'd dragged around in her bathrobe, her feet naked in her slippers, and had feigned to start some substantial chores (who knew what those were) since she had the time and it was Sunday for everyone except for her, holiday or no holiday. In short, everything had gone marvelously till Mr. Seignelet had entered the scene.

"What, you just got one nut?" asked François Boitard as he fingered the sac.

"No I got both of 'em!" said Camille Gassé, who looked at himself. "Which one's not out? … Oh yeah, this one."

With two fingers, Camille pressed a bulge on one side of his groin, near the penis, in the pearlized whiteness of his pubis. The testicle was immediately propelled into the ball sack, next to its twin brother.

François-Gérard, blown-away, wished that Camille would do it again. Rather proud now, the little Gassé (he was eleven) confirmed that he could pull both of them in and out at will, and proved it. He pinched them like cherry pits, the ball sack emptied out and two protuberances filled up his pubis. He pressed down on it, and the ball sack filled up again. It was indubitably funny, albeit somewhat repugnant, especially in that moment when the skin was empty.

Now it was François' turn to try to push his own balls inside. All he was able to do was to hurt himself. What hole did Camille use to slip 'em back in?

"So you've got a hole then? Like girls do? …"

"No, I've got two holes," explained the little Gassé, amiably. "One for each!"

"Camille, that's also a girl's name! You're not a guy, you're a girl!" said François.

"No, it's also a boy's name. Mine aren't real holes anyway, they don't open!"

He started his experiment of instructive and amusing anatomy once again. He even thrust his index finger into the inguinal canal to prove what he was claiming.

And so the two boys were quietly busying themselves in François' room. In the other room, Amélie-Lyane was reading, and, in the living room, Laure Boitard was preparing an article.

She usually didn't do this. But she'd recently received some critiques from her readership, which the editorial board of *The Reunited Republican* had imparted to her. She was deeply offended. She found it unfair.

The whole business was idiotic. A young local composer, Loys-Aymar Pion, forty-nine-years old, professor at the municipal conservatory, had staged an opera of his own making at the theater in a worldwide premiere and finale. Text, music, and *mise en scène* by the author, who also directed the orchestra. The piece, for two actors, had received a lukewarm reception. Additionally, the regional radio technicians (the composer had the ear of power) had dozed off during the presentation, which they were supposed to record in view of a later broadcast. Whence some singularities on the tape, and even a long pause in the tape. The author was desperate, if not defeated.

After having been fiercely appealed to, Laure Boitard had written a committed, enthusiastic review, whose historical importance had struck her greatly. She had seen herself as a prophet; she was the one who would be quoted in a hundred years—the sole lucid listener of the great, misunderstood man. She could decipher the future. Certainly (her article conceded) this was a debut opera, and coming from a quite young author. But why was youth so systematically ostracized? Why such an obstinately cultivated divide between the generations, such racism? Talent—it had to be acknowledged—was not limited by age or borders. Had they forgotten, for example, that the illustrious author of *The William Tell Overture* had started writing his celebrated *The Singing Magpie* at the age of twenty-five? Yes, indeed, twenty-five!?

That little slip of the tongue and that beginning, which had escaped from Laure Boitard's excessively agile fingers and her too-swift thoughts, had been noticed. Several readers (some of those fanatics who always signed "a longtime subscriber" or something like "Anselme Ledoyen, retired schoolteacher, forty-eight years of grammar school instruction") had ironized, in the style proper to old farts who were bored and devoted an entire day to polishing three sentences they found witty, French, and well constructed. The old morons. Did they think Boitard had so little culture that she'd confuse a brand of candy with the title of an opera, etc.? Couldn't they at least do her justice and suppose that she, etc.? Did they never consider the fact that, etc.? No, the old morons, enthralled to be able stick it to her, had had their opportunity to write a letter to the editors, it had them cuming in their trousers, pissing from their prostates. Misogynists, once again.

Furious, Laure Boitard was nevertheless quite flattered. Till then, she had been convinced that no one ever read her. Her article on Pion had shown the contrary. (… A new step … at bottom, this is it … I am being read. Read. I am a … a true journalist. Authentic. Different. No one else at *The Republican* is … They are all anonymous. Insignificant. Interchangeable. Losers. Except for Maurice and I. I. He. I know it. Today. Those old morons. The next step. To despise them. To exist. To leave. This island. Illusion. To become … national. Us. A destiny. That's it: we have to acknowledge it. We have. A. Destiny.)

The conclusion was obvious: from now on, she would care for her articles more (and would neglect her classes a bit). She'd dare to express her ideas. Shake up that conformist and blabbermouth audience. Those provincials, those ninnies who only knew about Rossini candy—Yes sir! Candy indeed! There are slips of the tongue that are in fact truer than …—but deaf to contemporary genius. Incapable of understanding the Pions, the Glairats. Incapable of leaving behind their primitive culture and their old tics. The other night, she'd accomplished something huge at last. For her. For them. For mankind. Henceforth she would affirm herself, struggle in the open. She'd work like a dog but damn it, she wouldn't end up a teacher in Saint-Rémi. Success. That was the thing. That was it.

She dreamt of a new Saint-Germain-des-Prés. She and Glairat would be its heroes. They would write far-reaching articles, she'd do it the feminine way, and he'd do it the virile way. They would push everyone aside and would change everything everywhere. She could just see the apartment where she'd live, with a view on … on … that cafe where … She had a sudden craving to reread Beauvoir. She leafed through *The Republican*, pensive. Well now, Mother's Day. Today? Thank God for the newspapers. How romantic! She didn't care for such popular inanities. Spelling. Flowers. Mommies. No, she needed to reread Beauvoir. To vomit. To succeed. Quick.

François-Gérard set about explaining to Gassé what he had supposedly done to his sister. Camille, naive, fully believed in his spiel. He asked for more details. The questions were so singular that François perceived an ingenuity in him that boded well for a certain project he had trotting around through his body. Camille Gassé had very large ears, very detached and very pretty, and short hair, nearly buzzed, that was a dull blond. His father, President Gassé, was hosting Mr. Glairat. Mr. Gassé was the president of the parent teacher association, of course. He was passionate about education. The lofty, audacious, and competent views of the most brilliant teacher on the island "*mattered him*, Gassé." (The expression was his.) Glairat, trying to please the luminary—a non-conformist who was so charming you'd have thought he was single—mumbled, or trumpeted like a duck a variety of improvised ideas that sounded flashy. The subject of girls' education especially inspired him. He quoted Fourier, dared Sade. President Gassé was in seventh heaven. "What about your big girl Amélie-Lyane?"

"There! I stick it in there! … No, not there. There! Yep. Right there!"

François-Gérard was demonstrating on Camille's naked body with his finger. The latter, candid, let him do everything. Stiff as rabbits, they couldn't stand it any longer. François-Gérard was using the most extraordinary cusswords to describe his sister's body and the kind of relations he had with her. The Gassé kid commented, "Hhhmm! You're so lucky to have a sister!" and he was on the verge of letting himself be laid out on his stomach. François was absolutely stuck on demonstrating what you do to sisters. So they don't get fertilized, duh! The little Gassé would experience the effect, and then he'd let François know if it was good.

"Yes, I'll let you know!" Camille promised energetically.

And satyr François had him spread his butt cheeks. Small white pink.

This was the first attempt of their entire lives in matters of coitus. Camille's derriere was funny. Prettier than he was. So was behind his ears. François-Gérard was coïtusing without leaning too much on Gassé. The little butt cheeks, the hemispheres, and the pipe of the hole down there, they were awesome. It fitted down to the millimeter. It was more than pleasant, thought François, unleashed, his ass flapping like a young dog, who was getting more and more excited in addition to his pleasure because, before he'd even finished, he told himself he would immediately do it again. The thought of this second time doubled his appetite for the first.

"We'll do it again, after!" he announced to Gassé's ears.

"After what?" Camille asked.

"After now," said the other.

Camille Gassé sighed, but said kindly:

"How long does it last? …"

François-Gérard didn't answer. Docile, Camille added:

"I'll tell you what it's like, after … Like we said."

"Oh yeah, uh," panted the young Boitard absent-mindedly.

On Sundays, Mr. Seignelet didn't appear before his family until ten o'clock: shaved, combed, with a tie. He placed a high price on this care. His dignity and his personhood would have been gravely compromised by slackness. But this morning protocol only governed his entrance on the scene. During lunch, he'd slough the vest, unknot the tie or at least loosen it. After the meal, during which he'd methodically wine himself, he would stop playing dress up. In the summer, he'd wear a wife-beater. His bulging belly, his short, spindly and hirsute arms, his chest swollen with the limp, watery, grayish and satiny fat of alcoholics prompted a sort of nauseated terror in the children.

Fortunately, Mr. Seignelet only ever touched to hit, and never hit unkempt.

Fortunately as well, his exposures were brief. But they were sufficient enough for the boys, when they considered it, to appreciate almost to the point of affection the spectacle of their father well dressed—his sickly, heavy body of white worm flesh, hideous from the disproportion between the massive trunk and the scraggly paws, and between those and the elephantine violence of the blows, this nightmare body cramped in a costume that simultaneously erased and reconstructed its material horror and brutality. He smelled of brown tobacco, of the office.

Amiable, peaceful, sure of his own household, Robert Seignelet had wished a happy Mother's Day to his wife. Raymonde Seignelet, in her housewife duds, disheveled, with no make up, her asscheeks sagging in her crumpled bathrobe, and her feet yellow in her reinforced slippers, contrasted ludicrously with her husband disguised as a dominical bourgeois. She had sensed this, and felt the laboriousness of the verbose congenialities and of the bow and scrape that Mr. Seignelet was putting on for her. His hands, before he'd drunk his first apéritif, trembled, clumsy, incapable of the slightest precise gesture. His lips also trembled, and, sipping his coffee, he seemed to look for and fear the rim of the cup, as if it were blurry and sharp at the same time.

But the cup trembled in his hand. Or else it was the one fixed object, strangely fixed, between a *motioned* mouth and inconsistent and phantasmal fingers.

There lay the other motive for the suit and the early-morning attentions. Mr. Seignelet, rolling from bed, suffered from an intolerable need. During the week, he could knock back his first glass very early, before going to the office. But on Sundays, he had no alibi for going downtown as soon as he awoke; and he wouldn't have dared drink at home at an improper hour. His cravings would smolder in his attention to his toilet and dress.

He'd eventually come have his coffee and immediately have the pretext of the shopping to do for lunch. He'd flee.

Wife and children would feel relieved. He'd return in excellent humor, never late, often with small gifts, sweets, a little bouquet. He would settle down in the living room, in front of daytime television, in the company of his wife and progeny who were summoned to assist in the paternal rite: it was a duty. This marked the beginning of the second cycle of alcoholization, which was quite long.

Towards two o'clock or thereabouts, the Seignelets finally sat down to eat. Mr. Seignelet inaugurated his third cycle, composed of fine wines of the lowest rank; he was a connoisseur.

After the meal was the fourth cycle, a composite one, and the only one that was dangerous for Mr. Seignelet's family. Mediocre eau-de-vie and liquors preceded a return to ordinary wine. At that moment, it often happened that Mr. Seignelet's mood would veer to black. He was wary of his tides of choler. He turned them instead into a will to police, a will for justice and execution. Not exactly eager to arouse the furious lunacies of his spouse, he hassled her only rarely. This implied a perilous audacity, inspired perhaps by certain mixtures or dosages of particular liquors. His children served as his sole victims most of the time. As detective, Mr. Seignelet would search his son's lives, schooling, affairs, manners, answers, readings, and their rooms for the clues to a crime. As an examining magistrate, he'd question, evaluate, and construct the accusation. As prosecutor, he petitioned. As judge supreme, he condemned. As hangman, he executed the sentence. All that was lacking in this parody of justice (which would end in cold abuse or moral tortures lasting for as long as the ethylic tribunal had determined: a week, a month, a season, a school year) was a defense lawyer—and the guilty party. The children were not meant to answer: they were serving their sentence. In sum, this submissiveness amounted to proof.

The fifth cycle of drinks was the pre-dinner drinks. Mr. Seignelet would link this to the preceding cycle without a pause. Groggy and—if such was the case—satiated, he would immure himself within himself or, on the contrary, become too expansive, with a powerful, frightening cheerfulness. The sixth cycle was the dinner wine. It led to the seventh cycle: the wine after the meal. This last cycle would last till lights out, in a torpor. His face red, Mr. Seignelet would shake again, spill his drink, and go to bed comatose, prideful, and full of meaning.

He drank less during the week. He would rarely move beyond, or rather, he would often reach the fourth cycle, that of the policing mood. This is why the Sunday sentencing, if it had a prolonged effect, was rigorously followed. If he drank only little, they'd escape. The criminal record would be wiped clean, the crimes that had been most exactingly alleged the day before had never taken place. Mr. Seignelet, however, wouldn't stray from his seriousness and rigor, and his principles maintained all of their expanse, their vigilance, and their rectitude. This is why his children (even if, little by little, the older ones were growing conscious of their father's excess) didn't see themselves as victims of a delirium, or of a sick man. They had a father as fathers shall be: a chief. They respected him extraordinarily—or rather, feared him, and his infernal trials even more than his punishments. They feared his presence, and feared to think about him, to imagine or even to know anything at all about him, and to be in his thoughts.

The only moment when Mr. Seignelet appeared vulnerable was thus during these Sunday mornings, just before he left to do the shopping for his wife, and to do the rounds of the cafés. Then, wan, feeble, mute, he evoked a tall, post-operative patient emptied of all his blood and who'd been forced to rise, to dress himself, and to leave. He was as frightening as a dead man. It took at least one delicious prospect, a spring picnic, a holiday, or a banquet awaiting him, for a little rosiness, despite the fast, to appear in his face and for him to become garrulous without having had a drink.

But Mrs. Seignelet hated this disarmed baby more than anything, whether he was pink or greenish, aphasic or chatty. A long time ago, she had grasped the link that existed between how sloshed Mr. Seignelet was and his sociability. She knew him to be unbearable sober, companionable during his second cycle, and impossible after that. When she wished to attack him, to ask for money, or to settle something, she would survey his state attentively. She wouldn't even count the glasses. His face, hands, eyes, voice, postures, and reactions informed her right off the bat, along with a glance at the level of the bottles.

In any case, as long as he remained sober, he wasn't anything but a sort of detritus that she felt like pushing into the trash with a push of the broom.

She welcomed the holiday compliments woodenly. All this monkeying around, these laadeedaas. Then Mr. Seignelet revealed the surprise he had organized: the outing to a fancy restaurant. That day, his wife would thus be relieved of her culinary duties.

Mrs. Seignelet had exploded with rage. What was the point of these stupid, last minute surprises? Lunch was already set; she'd ordered a roast veal, ice cream. And now? When would they eat them? During the week? She didn't have the means—let him figure it out!—to buy *them* a roast veal on a weekday! And what about the ice cream? It would melt. It wouldn't stay cold until tonight in this old freezer, who knows how old that thing was! Besides, no one ever ate anything in the evening after those goddamn binges at the restaurant that spoil your appetite more than anything else. So?

Mr. Seignelet, who felt intimidated to have to confront his wife without a drop of alcohol in his belly, reasoned:

"Listen, honey, this was supposed to make you happy! There's no need to get worked up like this … especially since this is … about …"

All this playacting was so annoying! thought Raymonde Seignelet. Make her happy! What was he doing sticking his nose in it, what and whose happiness was he talking, that old souse? His alright. His. Definitely not hers. It was his alright. His. 'Cause she didn't give a fuck!

She wanted to know the name of restaurant. Mr. Seignelet claimed to want to surprise her. She hollered again. She still needed to know how to dress the kids, didn't she? As for her, on the other hand, that was easy: it would be what she had in her closet or nothing.

Robert Seignelet had suggested that everyone dress to the nines. Mrs. Seignelet announced sourly that her best dress was at the cleaners. No need to get decked out for these holidays. They were among family. What about him, Robert, he wasn't really going to go out in that suit, was he?

"You and your ideas!" she sighed. "Lucky I went to the hair-dresser's on Friday! And at least I got your newer one."

He thought she'd softened. So he presented his gift, a silver brooch like those worn by the poor grandmothers of the region. Raymonde Seignelet pounced:

"You gotta be crazy! What ever made you get that nasty thing? That's for grannies! You find it in a pile of sawdust or what!"

She was referring to the ugly trinkets and trashy jewelry they sold at the fairgrounds. She dipped into that herself, by the way, but as for tolerating a gift from that place … Her husband protested. She was exaggerating. She was getting fired up for nothing. The brooch was made of pure silver; he'd picked it out at Roze Jewelry.

"That thing! …" moaned Seignelet, nauseated with pity. "That! … And anyway, why are you givin' me a present? Since

when did you become a son of mine? So you're my son now? …
He's insane! He's cracked! That's it! He's insane."

She absolutely needed to know the price. Stunned, she yelled
that he'd been ripped off. That hideous thingy, at that price!

"Wow, that old man Roze really conned you! Totally
scammed you! He musta seen a sucker coming! … Ripped you
off he did! You musta been loaded, ain't no other way."

"Please," Mr. Seignelet cut in harshly. Indeed, any allusion to
his vice was a declaration of war to which he reacted with
indignation worthy of Jupiter. The worst offense. The one
absolute crime. No, Robert Seignelet didn't drink. He would not
allow himself to be so accused. What! To be considered a … Certainly, he did appreciate good wines, fortifying spirits. But he had
a good build; he could hold alcohol like no other. Could someone boast of having ever seen him drunk? Never! Never. And
never would he forgive an insult so immense, so unheard of, if
one of his own, or anyone dared, against all odds, to profess it.
On the spot. He would execute the culprit on the spot. There
was no clemency for such crimes. Parricide. Blasphemy.

Mrs. Seignelet had no desire to provoke a scene, least of all so
early in the day. There'd be no getting out of it. With a "fine, fine
… fine. But in any case, it's awful," she erased the defamatory
adjective that she'd pronounced. Mr. Seignelet, calm, mollified
but still ruffled, responded as a pedant:

"Say that you don't like it, sure. But don't say it's ugly. You
have every right not to like it. You don't like it, so be it. That's
normal, normal. You have every right to. I'm not discussing your
right. I'm not discussing it? Hmmm."

He affirmed that the brooch was an authentic copy of an
antique, according to Roze, and had been chiseled by hand.

"A copy of an antique!" his wife cackled. "Well, the model
must have been a sight! Oh it must been a sight! Oh my! A
copy! …"

Later on, Robert Seignelet had suggested that the brooch could be returned to Roze's. He'd exchange it for another.

Mrs. Seignelet declined:

"No way! He'll give you one that's even worse! I'd rather keep this one! You know what you got; you never know what you could get! But come on now, be honest won't you? It's just awful!"

The skirmish ended on that note. The rest of the morning, Mrs. Seignelet had settled for henpecking the four children, without much conviction, they should at least try to be somewhat neat, and not too scruffy. Mr. Seignelet remarked that maybe they needed bread, etc., for dinner, and he disappeared from the house till almost noon. He returned ceremonious, affable, amorous and patient, as if he had learned manners in the vermouths, the *blanc limés* and the anises. He had successfully called off the ice cream and the roast.

"What do you mean Mother's Day?" François screeched boorishly.

"Sweetheart, no yelling!" exclaimed Laure Boitard. "Isn't it amusing?"

"Mother's Day, my ass!" repeated the boy, knackered. He looked at the Gassé kid scornfully:

"Gassé, you celebrate smothered gays do you?"

"Puhlease," intervened Amélie-Lyane. "That's not really funny ..." (She had come to read in the living room.)

"Mommy, yeah noon yeah," said Camille, "a party, yeah."

"And you got 'er a flower pot did ya? Your feasted mother? ... Oh, hey! ... Listen up, Amélie, your fea-sted mother! Hey! Get it? (He enunciated.) *Your-fisted-Mother!*"

Camille Gassé laughed blissfully. Laure Boitard furrowed an indulgent eyebrow. "Disrespect, fine, but vulgarity, François-Gérard ... And in front of the Gassé kid ... That's wrong. The president's family has its traditions, its convictions, they have to ..."

"Camille got his balls jammed in the car door!" retorted François-Gérard. He was a little afraid that the boy, who was too innocent, would let something slip about what they'd done in the bedroom. This hint would intimidate him.

And indeed, Camille Gassé's face turned red. But he didn't think François was being mean. Because François really was a true friend. Until now no one had explained and shown Camille so many things about existence.

Amélie-Lyane, snide, hummed the camp song about balls, a coachman, and a car door. (But how did she know? thought Camille, whose cheeks were veering toward burgundy.)

"Oh that's funny!" Amélie suddenly said to her mother. "Can you imagine that a second ago, just now, I was looking at you, and I had the impression that you were ironing! Can you believe it? How weird! We're a bit crazy, aren't we! …"

Laure Boitard was proofreading standing up, her palms pressing against her worktable. She had an abstracted smile.

"… For indeed, one might wonder if, on that 5th of May 1818, Karl (Charles) Marx suspected that, 99 years later, famous if not wealthy, his work would provoke the renowned Russian revolution. Clearly, born very young into an unknown family, nothing disposed the young Charles to one day discover Marxism. And yet nonetheless …"

She crossed out *disposed*, weighed *predisposed*, wrote *destined*. This article wouldn't go unnoticed. It was a hefty morsel. There were one or two right-wing communists on the editorial board of *The Reunited Republican*; they would dissect her text. She'd be denigrated. They would wonder: "Why is she sticking her nose where it doesn't belong?" But she'd no longer be ignored. They would expect her next articles. She would become powerful.

"My poor Amélie-Lyane! … Thinking about all those Suzy Homemakers they're celebrating today makes me depressed. Ironing Day, as you say …"

"It's 'cause she's jealous!" cried François Gérard, on edge. "It's 'cause all of Amélie's miscarriages can't celebrate her mother's day! You know the little fœtuses who cry in the dumpsters! Boo-hoo!"

"Oh, come on, François you're mental!" said Amélie-Lyane, repressing a laugh. This is what she had come for.

The joke about the bawling fetuses had its origin in the campaigns that certain groups had led against abortion. In Saint-Rémi, the issue reemerged at least once a year. The doctors who refused to perform the operation had had their names published at the bottom of a manifesto. They were all luminaries with upscale clienteles, fat revenues, property, and faith in God. According to them, the ill-killed fetuses with their heart-rending cries disturbed the chaste dawns of Saint-Rémi.

"… But in order to envision Marx as a child, you must forget the large-bearded doctrinaire brandishing *The Internationale*. Better to evoke his brothers and sisters who'd died of tuberculosis, or his family, composed of children and parents who never knew the prestigious destiny of their second-born son and brother. For Charles was so wise, so hard working at the beginning! This must be kept in mind to understand that …"

She wondered if she was right not to mention Marx's parents' conversion to Protestantism. As a matter of fact, these questions were always frowned upon, and there was a risk that her colleagues in the party would accuse her of god knows what. Anti-Sovietism? She crossed out the entire sentence. She felt that she was really making progress: she was working for others, now. She beamed.

"… *The Internationale*. Better to evoke his brother and sisters who'd died of tuberculosis (four of the eight Marx children). But, fortunately or not, young Charles was to survive this terrible plague that …"

She needed to search for details on tuberculosis (what did they call it? Phtisis? Phthisis?) in Glairat's *The Universal Encyclopedia*.

"What, François? … Well, no sweetheart, the pool is closed on Sundays, where do you want to go?"

"Hey Laure, your house is fucking boring," François said plaintively.

He wanted to impress young Gassé, in whose house they didn't use swear words among family. The Gassé parents—the old gentleman, the itty-bitty wife—were very gentle, and really delicious with their children. But out of gentleness precisely, they avoided swear words, an informal register, and any kind of tangible vocabulary. President Gassé's two little boys were thus bland and good children, decent without even intending to be.

"Pine Beach perhaps?" suggested Boitarda.

"Brrrr! Hell no! That's where you catch those …"

He no longer knew what. He'd contemplated an abusively laborious pun about head colds, brain-freeze, and main sleaze, something of the sort. He'd immediately imagined his sister whining:

"That's weak, François-Gérard … Weak, weak …"

So instead he said:

"… Those … Hey, your beach is full of fags, Laure! So you wanna send me to the batty-boys! Well you don't say! Tsk-tsk! …"

"What are you going on about François-Gérard? That's enough!" said Laure Boitard. "You know I might eventually have to ask myself some questions about your education. Really, I mean it. You lack a kind of … of elegance."

"We can call to see if it's open," said Camille Gassé. "The beach! … I'd go to the beach. If we all go."

"Hey whoa," said François. "Only if Amélie comes with us. You know what I think of faggots … Hey Amélie?"

"You think you're so handsome they're gonna come runnin' after you," said Amélie-Lyane. She kind of wanted to go out with the brats.

"No, it ain't me! It's Camille's ears! They are so awesomely tent-pitchin'!" cried François-Gérard. "Hey, Gassé's ears are what season my kebab! That's what's got me jonesin'! …"

This had gone too far. So this was the awkward age, then? It was going to be fun. "And it wasn't nice for Camille. That child had the patience of a saint," surmised Laure Boitard. "Strange way of having friends," added Amélie-Lyane. "Someone as nice as he was."

She added, however, that François-Gérard was right about one thing: they were bored-as-fuck today. "Let's check the sun at the window. If it was hot enough, why not … Might as well call. It was more than a kilometer to the beach; they weren't gonna go all the way there for zilch."

"For what?" said François in a falsetto voice.

Young Gassé was in seventh heaven. The only thing was, Amélie-Lyane made him a little sad. Twice as big and tall as he was, this wasn't a girl whose panties he'd ever be able to pull off. For François, it was easy: he was so cheeky. And older, taller. And anyway, she was his sister. Camille's cheeks went all melancholy and shiny because he wanted to kiss her. He laughed.

Amélie-Lyane looked at him and thought he was cute, for a kid, with his ears that were fit for an intellectual, or for a village idiot. His physique reminded her of … oh … who was it … Jean-Paul Sartre as a kid? No. In his case, it was the eyes. Jean-Paul Beauvoir … No, that one wasn't Jean-Paul. Oh shoot! Right, the ears. They were nice though. They probably checked out each other's pecker, thought Amélie-Lyane. No idiot, it wasn't Sartre and de Beauvoir, it was Camille with her bro. Kids, all those little phallos, they gotta explore 'em, compare 'em. Amélie-Lyane went through a series of images of François' pelvis in her mind. She swallowed some saliva. Is that kid for real. She also recalled the smell in her nose.

"So, whose gonna call the beach?" she said, vaguely getting up from the sofa where she was stretched out.

Camille Gassé volunteered. They accepted. The beach was open.

"… Yet his father died as early as twenty, at fifty-six years to be precise. It was a blow to the young Karl, who was only twenty years old and whose relation with his father hadn't always been easy. Hadn't he left the good city of his birth, Trier, for Bonn? That irreversible death, clearly, could be considered an undeniable family event in the end. But fortunately, however, Charles Marx was to wed the future Jenny Marx five years later—Jenny Marx who, as a young woman, sported the von Westphalen name without hesitation, her family name, in spite of which she and her husband had remained engaged for nearly eight years. A perseverance attested by the fine, steady handwriting in the notebooks (20,000 pages, they say) that Marx was to fill during so many years of readings and studies. For indeed …"

"No, actually, I'm not hot. I'm not going. Did you see what the weather's like François?" Amélie said, flabby.

Camille Gassé was extraordinarily disappointed. As for François, he thought about his pal's butt cheeks. Gassé, what an asshole! You could fuck him in the ass as you swore to him that he was eating a custard pie. What a weirdo. You bet he'd make a beeline right for his ass, at Pine's Beach.

"Mom, will ya give us some dough for a cab …? Oh, sorry, Laure! So, will ya?"

"François-Gérard! Is it too much for you to, hmm, to ask a bit less … callously? And do you know where my …?

"Oh, look at them, goin' off in a cab!" said Amélie-Lyane.

Camille glanced at her with the amorous glance of a dressmaker: he was putting her in a bathing suit. A two-piece, with red spirals printed all over.

All of a sudden, he imagined himself face down between the beautiful thighs of François's big sister. His cock poked a nose in the air. He felt like crying. How was it …? When would it happen? … She didn't look like the kind, of course. But who else then? …

"Pffff, never mind, he's a pain in my ass," said Amélie-Lyane. "Sorry Camille, it's nothing against you. He's the king of the jerks."

"It's not the king of the jerks, it's jerking off," replied François-Gérard in an antistrophe. Camille suppressed a melancholy air. He was no longer interested in the beach. All shoulders were shrugged.

"We'll do it again!" suggested, François Boitard saucily when they were together in the taxi.

Gassé didn't answer. He felt too much sadness, too much solemn love, without ideas. It would be so long before he could be happy. When were you a grown-up?

"How old's your sister?" Camille asked gently.

"No, wait! Not here! Dude!" thundered François.

The beach was nearly empty. It was gonna be totally boring. There were some boys like them, some little girls, some moms. Camille Gassé guessed that François was about to do that thing again in the beach cabin. His good little nose perked up again. It was shitty not to be able to … Besides he was too shy to masturbate with the guy. First, the door lock.

"Hey, Ca-camilla! Hey, vanilla? You ever knocked off any old farts?" François-Gérard cried out as he lowered his briefs. He had a sports bag with some towels and two swimming suits, one for him and one from last year for Gassé because he was smaller.

"Do you mean kill?" asked the child.

"Obviously! I'm at two already. I'd bet you're still at zero."

Camille Gassé thought he looked handsome in the swimsuit. He was glad that François forgot to show him again what they did to sisters. He pulled open the lock, went out. No, it wasn't cold. Amélie-Lyane should have come. They were even gonna go swimming. What had François Boitard said again? … Oh. Right. He'd killed two old farts! He was funny, that's for sure. What a guy.

"You mean real old or—let's say, uhmm, like your sister?"

"Hey, you're totally ass-backwards!" answered François, particularly delighted to trample the shy, rich kid. "Not my sister! Real old farts! Grannies! We crapped on 'em, schlaakk and slurp, those piggybanks! Get it, Chamomile?"

No, Camille didn't really get it, but François told him everything.

Besides there were lots of … and we, we, we. Gassé had to be part of the gang. He'd get all the girls' dickholes. Yeah. Floozies were dumb but you needed 'em. And their *corn holes*!

It was getting scary. In the swimming trunks, Camille's little nose desperately strained, quivered, twisted in misery. Boitard talked too much. Camille craved touching so much, he would have eaten sand. But who, where?

"Hey, look, he's got a boner, look at that!" hooted Boitard, who hadn't missed a crumb of his victim's emotions. On the spot, he made up the fact that there were extraordinary trials to be carried out to join this gang where they all fornicated. And it so happened that François had the right to let in whomever he wanted, and to administer the tests. If Gassé wanted to be admitted …

He'd get all the dickholes, cross his heart. But first the test.

"Right now?" asked Camille.

"Obviously!" said François, astounded by the boy's trust. "You just gotta smoke someone now."

Camille Gassé didn't even answer.

"We all smoked one!" added François. "And I killed two!"

They were up to their ankles in the gray water of the beach. Foam, and white lather danced around their feet and calves; the drying water pulled at their skin, prickling, leaving a layer of salt. The horizon was a cold blue. François Boitard had a nasty scar on his left forearm, as if he'd been tattooed or encrusted with a fat, reddish millipede. He had, so he said, picked it up in Meribel-Les-Allues, when he was six or seven, and was already going down the deadly black diamond. "Breakin' an arm skiin', what a whackadoodle!" he boasted. And he explained the accident, making gestures. He acted the part of the tree, and then boom.

A long boat was passing in the distance. A white ocean liner, almost blue or pink as if the twilight, over there on the curved horizon, had come down too soon. It seemed as if you could see time zones, school schedules, or the patterns of planes in flight. An optical phenomenon projected this otherworldly vessel onto a backdrop of gold and pale blue where it was already night. They made music, there must have been dancing, displayed fineries, the shaking of cocktails.

But here, on the beach, it was still full sunlight. Camille Gassé had a strong desire to travel on the enormous boat, white, blue and pink, that they'd soon no longer see. But he truly had no desire to kill someone. Surely not today.

"Do I have to?" he moaned. The water wasn't cold. Camille caught François Boitard's sarcastic answer. So he ran to drown himself. He could swim really well. François, who was sensitive to the cold, didn't join him right away. The water, in the sea, when you are in it, keeps you from talking: François was in no hurry to fall into that noise. He watched the young Gassé cleave the wavelets and approach the golden sun. The minuscule boat had disappeared beyond the sphere of flickering water that resembled the entire world. Camille turned back, shook his face and laughed. He was far off in the oily water. François wasn't coming. Gasse's kindness humiliated him.

Mrs. Seignelet had denigrated the special menu that Droole & Sons had envisioned for mommied families on Mother's Day:

"It's the cheapest, that's for sure! … Honey. That's for sure. The week's scraps they're fiddling with to palm off on people!"

She exulted:

"You're damn right, this is their dream day, everyone's popping up, damn right, it's like this everywhere! Six months since they started gathering scraps, that's what they're sellin' you, and for three times the price mind you!"

Mr. Seignelet had asserted that the crayfish roasted in white butter of this "Mother's Day" menu was fished with a net from that great seawater tank—as you must *sea*, sweetheart.

Mrs. Seignelet regurgitated a squeal that was shrill enough to shatter the crystal:

"You must be joking! But that's worth ten! That's worthtenned! It's sidesplitting how you get taken in every time! You're worthtenned! You're so funny! Oh my, Robert, it's staggering! It's a joke! Just look at yerself! Look at yerself! And you believe it! You believe it! … Did you see what they're chargin'? No. Whatever. Jeez …!"

Mr. Seignelet repeated half-heartedly that really, the seawater tanks … (And in fact, he'd let aside a large budget for the occasion, for it was in his eyes the biggest celebration of the year, with Christmas.)

"The seawater tanks!" triumphed his wife. "The sea-wa-ter-tanks! You are worthtenned honey! You're really worth ten! You and your seawater tanks!"

She hadn't planned to tear apart the seawater tanks. In the meantime, she was searching, squealing, like a bad boxer clinging to the arms of his opponent, with the knotty arms of a monkey and the movements of a praying mantis. And sometimes the opponent, who received this tedious bouquet of arms with fat, inflated palms, made it last, so that nothing happened. Likewise, Robert Seignelet awaited his wife's broken down argument. She took a sip; she stuck out her tongue to suck in the cocktail, holding it in while she set down the glass, and finally announced that she would speak:

"Slllllllh … Let me tell you they put plain sham kirsch in this nasty thing. You bet a Sunday like this is their only chance. 'Cause hear me out, we're all supposed to be in a good mood, right? So no one's gonna chew anyone out and they exploit that, they pawn off on you whatever they want. 'Cause no one's gonna chew 'em out on a day like this. The sons of bitches!"

And yet Mr. Seignelet once again insisted on getting the crayfish that they'd eat almost, so to speak, alive—in the special-mommy day menu. The set meal was one hundred and twenty francs a head, including a live crayfish for four people. You could get a half-portion and a 15 % discount for ages ten and under.

Besides, everyone wanted this menu.

Mrs. Seignelet finally settled on her argument, the consonants of which she whistlingly whispered between her teeth:

"You wanna know about the seawater tanks? You wanna know? Well I'm gonna tell ya. They fish em' out in front of you alright! That always gets the suckers! Then they take 'em to the kitchen! You won't see 'em anymore. And you, smart alec, you think they bring the same ones back in. Right! Yeah right! Back there, they plop 'em in a bucket and you get the frozen kind! You betcha! … And it works! People get snookered all the time! They get snookered all the time! Frozen crayfish!"

However, she ended up accepting the menu: but without the crayfish. It was for four anyway. The children could eat her portion. No, she didn't want anything instead. The whole thing was a racket, no need to saddle oneself with an extra charge. A lovely hoax they were, family holidays. What a shame.

During the meal, she continued her imprecations, her denigrations. But she ate a lot, in her greedy, vomiting dog manner. She tasted her husband's crayfish, figured that it had not only been frozen, but that it wasn't even fresh and was even somewhat undercooked. As for the famous Droole gentlemen's *beurre blanc*, it was nothing but pickle vinegar whisked in margarine, and with added cornstarch for it to look so thick. The meal was all for show, wasn't it … At least, the roast—they'd microwaved it—was copious. Mr. Seignelet, who had seated Bertrand in front of him, dispensed lessons in oenology in a low voice, recited the name of estates, climates, vintages, emitted judgments, pronounced vocabulary. He then wished to instruct his eldest son in the solemn rite of tasting, made him masticate, tastickle, gargargle, lift an absent but concentrated gaze, smack his glottis, his tongue, and his lips. Redder than the wine, Bertrand had to obey. Besides, the bottles were terribly bad, for Mr. Seignelet's erudition in this area was as pompous as it was illusory, and his palate was dead.

Lunch was very long, very tiring, and very abundant. Mrs. Seignelet, strongly addled and wounded to death by such glitz, had a hard time containing her voice. She shot her family red looks. You would have thought that she was ripping out hearts, eviscerating, chopping off heads. Her children had behaved monstrously, had liked everything, eaten everything, had shown pleasure, hadn't committed any noticeable blunder (Jean-Baptiste stole two pieces of silverware).

Philippe didn't get sick. He had fallen asleep on his little tummy, which had been pacified at last. They woke him up for dessert.

That day left Mrs. Seignelet with an entire month's worth of rancor and sour humor. Come evening, she resumed her government and her customs.

7

They didn't know how to talk to each other.

"Lucky for us, it's summer," said René Théret, somber.

"What's good is this soap," Julien Roquin answered. "'Cause it has a smell that don't smell like nothing."

Julien washed himself more often than René. And he stole or spoke much less. He had no trust at all in Théret. And, for Théret, Julien was just a kid, which is to say a nobody.

What Julien loved was the early morning. Leaving the basement, you could see the gray stones of this house that was nearly without a roof and walls, and out front stretched the long since abandoned salt works. It was no longer worth the effort. The inhabitants of the island, in spite of their poverty, had come to disdain these little thingies where a few old-timers continued evaporating, raking, exploiting the beautiful gray salt of the sea. It was a job for beggars, for imbeciles. The strange, idiotic and solemn agriculture of crystals. Now, it was dying.

What remained were these overgrown salt fields which Julien, his gaze flowing down to the sea in this golden dawn, venerated because they made his heart beat. Long rectangles formed of somewhat frothy blue water or blue sky, and of skinny dykes scattered with equivocal grasses. That water mounded into mirrors flustered the child. To live there, just in front of the sea, and that remnant of shanty that resembled the Roquin house in so many ways, but demolished, and without either furniture or rage.

In early July, the island was sickening. Too much blue black in the water, too much reddish gold and yellowish on the rocks, the earth. Too many sun-stricken birds coming from Africa, from

Oceania?, settling ponderously down upon these cubes of rock with the belly and important mien of lunching vicars. Slowly, Julien had started to feel that he, himself, existed here in a similar fashion.

Théret was the one who bothered him the most. Julien wished he would go away. That rich kid. With his rich kid scar on the cheek. As for Julien, he wouldn't confess, he'd never show the long grainy and torn-up gashes crisscrossing his back. He couldn't even follow them over the length of his skin, as he turned over his arm. There was a missing portion he had never successfully touched.

In any case, he would never let that jerk of a Théret see them. And he needn't boast of having gotten into fights with the jerks from Saint-Loup. They were brutes. They would have cut up anybody like that. You shouldn't be getting into fights in the first place. And if you're fighting you shouldn't go for the face. It's nasty. It's cowardice. Théret had been slumming it with some moth bitten, brutish, smutty goons. No one had anything to do with these bastards.

Through his hatred for Théret, Julien was expressing his fear of the kids from the countryside. Who owned the island, after all? Surely not people like Roquin. No, the island belonged to these boys who could pull out a knife against their friends. These boys, at the second cry, the first look, the slightest threat of correction, would have been able to escape their parents. Or return it a hundredfold. Of course, no child from Saint-Loup had Julien's back. And their crimes didn't even make the papers. And they could peacefully return home to eat and sleep. And they were more likely Théret's age than Julien's.

Théret was one too many, yes, really. And he should have stayed home. Had his parents condemned him to bread and water, chained him in a basement, and whipped him to death? He had left out of vanity. Besides, since then, it was easy to see that Théret wasn't holding up. Julien told himself: "He's gonna crack, he's gonna go to the cops. I gotta go someplace else first."

At the beginning, Julien had quite liked Théret. Maybe he was the vaguely Catholic sort who gave a pleasant impression. Now, he imagined him a coward and a traitor. The cohabitation weighed upon them.

Théret got up. The boys each had a bed composed of a great jumble of blankets, quilts, pillows, sheets and tablecloths that came, like everything in the basement, from burglaries in which they hadn't participated. During the day, they pulled the piles under a hole from where a large light fell, and they read. Julien went out often, rambling the moors and the shore the way he used to when he lived at his parents and skipped school. As for René, he spent his time wallowing and reading, ravaged with anxiety. He masturbated a lot, as soon as the child was gone. He used stimulating scenes from crime novels.

He drew nearer to Julien Roquin and flung to the ground, onto the pile, the book he had just finished. He looked around:

"This one was good. Ain't there another one like it? …"

It was a series that Marc Guillard had brought. The hero fucked, fought, he was rich and strong, and he had everything. The killing occurred with moderation. The victims deserved their fate, or they were nobodies. The illustrated covers overflowed with tits and thighs. It wasn't a bad distraction. Julien examined the novel with a glance and recognized the image. No, he hadn't much liked that woman, in the black slip.

"Yeah, they're good," he said. "But I think that's all of 'em."

"So I read them all," said Théret.

He yawned, stretched his legs; reading put you into a stupor. It wasn't at all like TV, or the movies.

"I'll be off soon, I think. What are you reading?"

Julien showed the book, which was called *Pirates and Captains*. It was a buccaneer novel, a book for kids, thought Théret.

"Guillard's?" asked Julien.

"Yeah."

Théret sighed. He couldn't stand the imperceptibly spiteful frostiness that the kid displayed. A true savage, Roquin; Marc Guillard had warned him.

"This can't go on," said Théret. "We're not really gonna hole up in a basement forever. Huh."

Julien shrugged his shoulders:

"Why don't you go? You, you can go back to your parents. You can try. They're not gonna kill you are they. They don't know 'bout what we do. What we do has nothing to do you."

Hurtful, but true. Théret had already thought about it a hundred times. He could go home. His parents would probably forgive him. And what if he wrote a letter first? They would answer him, uhm, in …"

"What if I wrote to 'em, to my folks?" he said. "The things is, where could they answer? That's the snag."

Roquin sat up in his cluster of blankets and rags, like a barbarian nomad.

"You tell 'em to get yes, or something like that, and their names, printed in the paper, if they agree. That's what I'd do."

René reflected:

"Yeah, but they'll obviously say yes so that I come back. And then what if they wanna demolish me afterwards. Or lock me up, you know …"

"Do they hit you, your parents?" said Julien, suddenly interested.

"No, not exactly no," René confessed honestly. "My mother, she does a little, just like that. But they aren't real swine. No."

Julien fell back into his cushions:

"You can talk about that with Guillard."

"Yeah, I'm gonna talk to him. Well, I'm off. Hey, is there anything we need?"

"There's no more bread, no more mustard," said Julien, conjugal. "And also, we need paper to wipe our ass."

"But we still have some! A whole four pack!"

"Where is it?"

"Hmm, wait, right, in the kitchen. It's pink. Just look for it. See ya."

"See ya. Don't forget the water, when you come back."

What they called the kitchen was a little basement room with a vent, which might have been a boiler room. There, they stored or threw away whatever would have bothered them in the "bedroom," a vast room that was partly filled with rubble and partly open to the outside, and to the rain. There was a risk of waking up dead, or of being buried alive one of these days. Otherwise, the hideout was fine; nobody ever went through there, not even once a year.

What's more, fetching the drinkable water wasn't complicated; you'd take a water bladder and climb to the old semaphore, a short kilometer towards Saint-Rémi. There was a rivulet that was slightly brackish but plentiful enough. They'd mix this water with a bit of wine or some Pernod.

Down towards Roche-Notre-Dame, they also had a nameless river, with long deserted curves. Julien would go there to wash his laundry, for the child was tough and serious like a kind of unmarried laborer who relentlessly took care of herself, her do, her cubby, her togs, rageful with virtue. Julien didn't put that much energy or assiduity into it; nevertheless, he had the cold cleanliness of an animal that was repelled by mud, excrement, and foul odors. Washing and bathing at the river happened at a good clip.

Likewise, Julien would wander far from the lair to take a dump. He'd follow the shore and seek a sanctuary, eyes anxious, ass heavy, as if he intended to lay eggs. Incidentally, he'd use the expression "to lay eggs" to designate the action of taking a dump, spoke of eggs instead of turds, and would say: "I'm going to the henhouse."

One or two minutes after Théret's departure, he got up as well. He was hungry.

He explored the nonperishables in the kitchen. He also found toilet paper, blocks of padded white paper printed with flowers that were pink like a grandma's nightshirt, and perfumed with lily of the valley. He didn't smile. That sort of thing left him uncomprehending, without a thought.

A few tough guys that Julien and René had never seen before had delivered the latest supplies. Guillard wasn't being smart; he was going overboard. Did he want to create an army or what? Decidedly, Julien was tired of them all. Really tired. Tired of the little kids who were dumb, and of the big kids who were bastards.

They'd stolen the nonperishables on a grand scale in a super-market up north. Another stupid carelessness. They had the money; why didn't they just do their shopping discreetly, without taking the risk of being caught, or of talking. Why such provocations, especially dangerous for the two fugitives? Julien trusted no one; he was certain he'd be denounced on the first occasion. Things were going too far, they weren't up to it any longer. No. No. Just leave.

Julien picked up a jar, intrigued. It looked as if there were black animals inside of it, aquarium animals with an orange belly, as irregular as jellyfish, compressed, and nauseating. He deciphered the label: *Tri-cho-lo-ma Portentosum*. The disgusting black animals. He pronounced tricho like *tree show*. And some people actually ate that. It was worse than the pink asswipes. Another jar was stuffed with white filiform worms, about the length of a little finger, and which seemed to have fat yellow balls. It was hard to believe. Julien didn't even want to know what it was. Those kids really stole for kicks.

And naturally, René had eaten all of the tomato ravioli. Julien fell back on a can of meatballs that had the word "tomato" on it too. He ate it cold. It was mushy. Yes, it did have a tomato sauce. He promised himself he'd soon go slowly—it was a bit early—pull his lines in by the boulders.

Before that, though, he peered into a hole in the ruins for something that he'd hidden there for himself: a flask of acetone. He poured some on his sleeve, and bringing it to his nostrils, he got violently drunk off the vapors. Just one puff, never two. Then he went off to fish, his eyesight spotted with billions of gray suns. He sucked in the sea air. He regained his sight.

"Well, why don't we go in there, dear!" said old Mrs. Bintch. "They'll probably have some!"

Yolande Bintch followed her grandmother into the stationer's. Mrs. Bintch immediately emitted a stunned whine:

"Mariette! … Could it be, my god? Is that you?"

"Mrs. Bintch! What a surprise! My goodness! We'll, I'll be …!"

"My goodness! It really is you! My god! So I'm not mistaken!"

"My goodness! … You know I wouldn't have recognized you, with this little girl!" Mariette Péréfixe exclaimed.

"Oh well, I would have, I would have, Mariette!" exclaimed Mrs. Bintch, "of course! Of course. How could I possibly be mistaken! My God!"

"Yes, oh yes," said Mrs. Péréfixe. "But what brings you to this neighborhood Madam? It's not really a neighborhood, hmm, I mean, let's admit it! With all these factories! Well I'll be!"

"Come, come now," scolded Mrs. Bintch, "your factories are great! Great! … But you haven't explained why you're here, oh dear, a stationer's, if I may say so! And all this, these … office supplies? Oh, it's very good. Very very good! Very good!"

"But you still haven't explained to me why you are here, Mrs. Bintch, in our dreadful neighborhood, huh? If I may ask?"

"Well, you see, as a matter of fact we've come for a factory! You see! For this darling!"

"How about that!" said Mrs. Péréfixe. "My goodness! At her age! How old is she, anyway? She's already a big girl, isn't she! Is she your granddaughter then?"

"For the last eight years!" exclaimed Mrs. Bintch in a tone of moved indulgence. "Eight years, my God!"

"Oh, she's eight years old. Oh, very good. Oh, but she isn't too big for eight, is she. Oh, well, well, well."

Mrs. Bintch made a sign of negation while bringing a handkerchief to her mouth as if she was about to cough. She was, in truth, breathless from astonishment. She asked for a chair:

"Oh! ... Oh! ... My God! ... Oh! ... Phew ... Oh! ... Thank you, Mariette, thank you! ... Oh! ... If I'd known! ... No, not eight ... Oh! ... And we were just passing by like this, by chance if you will! ... Oh! ..."

Mrs. Péréfixe offered her a glass of water.

"No, no, my dear! ... It'll pass! ... Not eight years ... You ... Eight years. You! You! ... Not her!"

"Well, you're right, my God, now that you mention it, eight years! At least! It must be! Well, well, well! ..."

In a few sentences Mrs. Péréfixe narrated the tribulations that had led her from Mrs. Bintch's office to the noble profession of stationer. A marriage, yes. She had a child.

Mrs. Bintch wished to see the child. She held a sincere affection for her people, and couldn't understand how eight years could have gone by without any news from Mariette. However, a slight chill set in when she the age of the kid was revealed— nine years and some. So Mariette had had it when she was in her service? Really. But how? ... Mrs. Bintch refrained from bringing up this detail.

"No, wait!" exclaimed Mrs. Péréfixe suddenly. "If my boy is nine! Mrs. Bintch!"

"Well, what of it? What do you mean?" cautiously answered the old lady.

"Well, it's proof that I left more than nine years ago, oh dear! At least!"

"Well yes, of course!" Mrs. Bintch swiftly approved.

"Nine years ago, oh dear! At least! Well, well, well!"

"Oh but what-what-what-what a treasure! But whaaat a treasure!" stammered Mrs. Bintch, giving up on the complicated arithmetic of maids' pregnancies. She'd had, oh, so many.

Marie-Antoine had just appeared, a pretty boy, and was graciously playing the simpleton. His mother inspected him, admired him and approved of herself all at once, and sighed tenderly:

"My, my!"

"What a treasure!" repeated Mrs. Bintch. She couldn't believe that a menial's brat could be so nice, so nice. The husband had to be very, very nice. Certainly. Certainly.

"And what is your name, my dear?" said Mrs. Bintch as she drew the child in with both hands towards the chair where she was seated. He smelled so good, so smooth!

"Marie-Antoine!" twittered Marie-Antoine, with a good little air of one who was very interested by the occupation of telling the old Madam his name!

He smiled. Very pretty teeth. Very nice. Very nice. Delicious smile. Of the highest order. Very pretty manners. The father, of course.

"Marie-Antoine! That is a very pretty name, my dear!"

"Yes!" said Marie-Antoine, beatific. It was also his opinion.

"Well, well, well! …" sighed Mrs. Péréfixe in admiration. Yolande Bintch had come closer, her finger in her nose, to be able to see the big nine-year-old boy. He didn't really look like he was nine years old, to start with. And also (Yolande inexorably foresaw this) he must have been a first-rate oaf. She felt like pinching his thighs. Marie-Antoine had them bare up to the middle, white, blond, chubby and shiny, just the kind you pinch to create big black and blue marks (thought Yolande).

"And what's this little girl's name? If I may ask! ..." said Mrs. Péréfixe mischievously.

"Of course!" said a magnanimous Mrs. Bintch. She was gobbling up all of Marie-Antoine's nude parts with her eyes, and dying from a desire to roll up his sleeves. The exquisite little hands. Nine years old! My God! He still looks like a baby! So pretty! So chubby! So lithesome! Maybe a bit dopey, but nobody's perfect, my God, unfortunately! Besides, when you think about what we owe to intelligent people, bombs, birth control, hormone-injected meat ... my God, yes, such unhinged times, eventually you think ... (Mrs. Bintch didn't venture these ideas aloud.) "Darling, will you tell Mariette your name?"

"Marie-Antoine!" said Marie-Antoine coquettishly, docile. But he hadn't been following so well. Mrs. Bintch laughed, swinging his hands:

"Go on now! Not you, dear! ... You, dear! You, Yolande!"

"Aren't they such darlings!" said Mrs. Péréfixe.

"No!" Yolande answered.

"Go on darling, don't be a sourpuss, Yolande, darling! That's not polite, you know! Mariette is allowed to know your name!"

"No," Yolande repeated.

"Yolande, darling? You know it's very bad to say no? Come one, tell them your name! Don't you already know the little boy's name?"

"No!" Yolande reiterated. Mrs. Bintch scolded:

"Oh well, then, we won't know it, that's all. And we'll know that you're a very rude little girl, and Marie-Antoine a very nice little boy. Do you hear me? Don't be naughty! It's really naughty to be stubborn!"

"No!" said Yolande.

"Leave it be, it's alright!" begged Mrs. Péréfixe, a bit offended.

"What's her name?" a curious Marie-Antoine inquired with the old lady who'd suddenly released his hands—finding him, after reflection, a much bigger boy than she had predicted.

"See Yolande, the little boy who's so nice he also wants to know your name! … You won't tell him either?"

Yolande, disconcerted by the reasoning, hesitated.

"Oh! Yolande, see! You will tell the little boy your name!" said Mrs. Bintch.

"Oh! Yes! Yolande's gonna tell us! Yes, the dearie! Oh good!" said Mrs. Péréfixe, moved, humiliated.

"Oh? She's called Yolande?" asked Marie-Antoine.

"Yolande!" said Mrs. Bintch. "Do you hear that? The little boy wants to know if you're called Yolande! So you're going to tell him? Huh? Darling? Just finish my sentence: you are call-ed …"

"I dunno," said Yolande, who pulled her finger out of her nose.

"Come now don't play the fool here, come come! You know very well what you're called. Come come. Just repeat after me: I-am-call-ed …"

"Granny!" Yolande declared, mopey. When would she be allowed to pinch the dumb boy?

Mrs. Bintch announced:

"There you have it! … Education today! Even when they are past six you can't get them to say their name! It used to be two! Two years old! But nowadays everything happens late."

"Oh yes! Let's face it. What they call progress …" sighed Mrs. Péréfixe.

"I agree with you Mariette. Let's face it. With their progress, my God! …"

"They talk your ears off with it! My my my!"

Marie-Antoine looked at his mother's ears. No, no. They were in their usual place. She must have put them back, quick, quick, to listen to Mrs. Bintch. He imitated her.

"Go ahead now and pick a coloring book my dear. Do you have coloring books, Mariette?"

"Of course …" protested Mrs. Péréfixe.

She sent her son to show the pile in the back. Yolande's eyes lit up.

"I wouldn't swear, but we do have factories around here, you know," added Mariette Péréfixe. "Around here people are… Oh, it's a hard job you know. If the school wasn't so near and all. If you know what I mean!"

"A factory! Am I silly, my God! Oh, how silly one can be sometimes, wouldn't you say!" exclaimed Mrs. Bintch.

"Truth be told," said Mrs. Péréfixe politely, "it's the same with animals, no matter how much we love them, the truth is, there are some days… It's the way we are. It's just the way we are."

"That's the truth. And even the children," said Mrs. Bintch, lowering her voice. "It's a fact, Mariette. Oh yes, even the children!"

"Even the children, that's the truth, it's a fact, oh yes!" said Mariette Péréfixe. "Even he'll get a little smack from time to time, it's a fact!"

"Oh, but of course, of course: what can you do? But what was I saying, oh … Yes! The factory. The factory! We didn't come for a coloring book, ho, ho, of course not! How silly we are sometimes!"

"It's a fact, Madam, it's a fact. So it wasn't a factory? Oh, you see, I was thinking that …"

"Yes, see, sometimes people believe that … But no! A factory."

"Let's face it. A factory. Why of course!" said Mariette.

"Of course, there you have it. Would you believe that her uncle, my son, her father's brother, my son, this little girl's uncle …"

"Yolande?"

"Exactly! But you must remember them, of course."

"Of course! I remember them. Certainly! …"

"And as a matter of fact …"

Yolande was being shown the coloring books as she was scoping out the spot she would pinch. Finally, biting her lips, she attacked.

"Ow!" went Marie-Antoine, very surprised. He rubbed his skin.

"Dumbass," said Yolande.

"… Oh but of course! But how can one be so silly, truly."

"There you are! … His uncle's factory. All those great big thingamajigs …"

"That your son bought from Hermant."

"That's right. That's right. Oh, what a bargain! Oh! Yes!"

"That's right. And you wanted to show her. Her uncle's."

"Dumbass."

"Ouch. Ouch."

"Are you finding a coloring book sweetheart?"

"Marie-Antoine are you finding a coloring book for Mademoiselle Bintch?"

"No dear, really, you can say Yolande, Yolande! She's just a child …"

"That's true, she's a child. But I wouldn't permit myself …"

"Shhh, that's my ding-a-ling. Don't touch it! You're little!"

"Show me."

"No, you can't touch it. I'll show you but you don't touch it."

"Dumbass."

"So the little dearie isn't sulking anymore. Oh but how darling your darling is Mariette, when I think about it. Oh! My God! He is—exquisite!"

"I was wondering about the Hermant factory. So your son …"

"Absolutely first rate, oh! Yes. I told her uncle, my son, 'Let me tell you my son,' I told him, 'your brother, my son, told me he envied you furiously.' You wouldn't believe it. What a good deal!"

"That's a fact. Let me tell you. I was wondering about the Hermant factory. You understand, in a factory neighborhood."

"Surely! That's right! That's it. You know better than all of them. When you live …"

"That's the truth, when you live… It's the whole picture."

"That's what I say to myself, I'll tell you, better than them all."

"It's a snail. You fail," Yolande said. She pinched.

"Ouch! Not there, not there! Ouch! Ouch! …"

"It was so good to see you, my little Mariette! Finally …"

"Of course! Absolutely! What a surprise!"

Mrs. Bintch was about to fetch her granddaughter when she suddenly noticed through the window a silhouette on foot that she thought she recognized. But who was it? The son of … of … oh … that boy, who ran away from … from his … Why it was René, René Théret! Absolutely. How staggering. That must mean he'd come home, the prodigal son, back to his parents? What a scandal, what a …?

Mrs. Bintch promised herself to go to the Théret grocery at once. She would use her son's car; an employee would drive it. She called Yolande.

"Dumbass."

"Sweetheart, come on! Yolande? Did you find what you wanted?"

"Ding-a-ling."

"Ouch! Ouch!"

Marie-Antoine vanished into the back of the shop, running. There was another one who didn't know how to say goodbye, thought Mrs. Bintch. He was cute, well, almost, but he had no education. That was his menial side cropping up. You can take the boy out of the country but … Like father like s …

"Come, Yolande, come, my dear. We have to leave!"

"Turd. Dumbass. Ding-a-ling."

"Yolande! Oh! What naughty little words sweetheart. Oh! Be nice, now come. Bring your coloring book to the lady."

Guillard showed Théret that everything was alright and took him up to his room:

"And how's Dracula?"

"Fuck, what a pain in the ass," said René Théret.

"What, he tryin' to get some?" said Guillard who drank from everybody's milk dish and hadn't yet taken advantage of Théret's disarray.

"Don't be such a dick!" said René. He aped a bitter movie star smile that he'd picked up watching vintage TV and identifying himself with it, in spite of his thirteen years.

"What … you don't jerk off. Faggot! With Julien?"

"Man, you're nuts!"

Théret loathed it when people talked to him about things like that. Whatever was "sexual" seemed to him either a stain, like the yellow crust in his underpants, or a future duty like one day having to go to the army. Marc Guillard's jocular gourmet air shamed him to shivers that reached all the way to the very interior of his bones. His cold, gray, red marrow, like at the butcher's.

"What. He jerks off with everyone, I know it!" Guillard affirmed.

His humanity was to bestow vices.

Théret, looking terribly weary, shook his head. No.

"D'you miss it?" said Marc. "Wanna have a go?"

"So even you …" whispered Théret, funereal. "So, you think that … And with all the risks I took to come here …"

He donned a big mask embattled with the sins of the world. He had a horrible fear that this bastard of a Guillard would try and cop a feel. And he felt even more horribly ashamed of his utterly small cock. For he would have liked to be superior.

"It's getting better," said Guillard tenderly, flicking his chin toward René's gash. He smiled like a groper.

"Yeah … Yeah … Pfff … Yeah …" Théret grumbled or huffed like an old, scarred hero who, in the end, understood that maybe the war … (Still, we were brave.)

Cloaked with a *human dimension*, he said weightily:

"See, Guillard … See. Really, in the end … I think we fucked up. Why'd we do all this?"

Marc Guillard, too happy to be honest, was bothered by the question; this mania they had of taking themselves seriously.

"Aren't you a bit preachy? What's up with you?"

Théret understood that he was being clumsy. Guillard liked to kid around; you had to get to him through other means. He was harebrained.

"Come on, it can't go on like this Marc, really," he said.

"Okay, fine," said Guillard. "When we're cooked we'll just go somewhere else. It's not like we're short on places to go. You wanna go back to your mommy, baby doll? … Hey, sorry. I wasn't calling you a girl."

Guillard was a bastard; he made up arguments to fit the objections as they arose. Until then, he'd never mentioned leaving, exile, or the future.

"You never said anything about leaving did you. When?"

"Well I am now," said Guillard. "No one had said anything about the two old farts either … I mean, all that bullshit!"

"But go where?"

"Oh that's not the issue. We can stay here. I'll stay."

René Théret felt like an adult, a father. Guillard was too annoying. Théret said, in a harsh voice:

"Since when did you start playing boss? After our bullshit, like you said. There wasn't any before. It was good for you, seems like …"

"Do I look like a boss? Shit!" said Guillard kindly. "We've been working like dogs for weeks for you and Roquin, and you tell me that we're pissing you off? Fuck you man."

"I ain't into it anymore. I got it. I had to see you. But that's it. Got it. That's that, see ya. I'm done."

Guillard rose, feigned astonishment:

"Listen René. What're you gonna do? … You gonna go back there?"

Théret smiled like a bitter old hero:

"Don't worry, I won't rat on you guys."

He left.

He was very embarrassed. He hadn't come to see Guillard to break up with all of them. It was the … the role which had seized him all of a sudden. It had to be done, had to be played. It took hold of you and there was nothing to do but obey. Now he couldn't go back to the hideout—could never see any of them again. He was alone. He wasn't attached to that solitude. He had played a part: but where was the audience, the approval, and the reward? No. Nothing. No one. You don't play alone. You need enemies at least: Théret decided to go home. He would go back to his skin, his soul. His parents.

Jean Roquin pulled himself up from the Fouilloux. She'd felt old, all of a sudden, when he came. He felt repulsion. He enjoyed young girls because they never seemed to come. A moan of pain, or even of irritation, aroused him: but a look of satisfaction made him want to give a coldcock. Yes, Claire Fouilloux, orgasming like a satiated granny, had aged: now, she was guzzling her little sugar boy, her lolly.

Once she stood up she turned back into a little girl. Jean Roquin told himself he'd gladly fuck her in the ass. So she could keep the child look. Would she do it? Ponderously, he told her:

"You know, it'd be better in here. Just to make sure we don't have any problems."

He withdrew his finger before she protested. He hated shit. He'd touched an ass that was as gooey as a cow pie, and a fatty, large, doughy anus.

"Hey what's your problem, isn't this enough for you or what?" rasped Fouilloux.

"No, it's not enough," said Roquin, aroused by this wavering resistance.

"Fuck off! Fuck off! Won't you fuck off already daddy?"

"What. What. Hey, what?"

"Oh shit! That's enough!"

Her cry reminded Roquin of his wife's hysterics. He made a theatrical gesture:

"Well, fuck you too. Shit! And guess what, I've had it with you too! I've seen you enough! Fuck. And all this bullshit now is 'cause of you. I don't need you. I don't need you." (His finger must have smelled.)

Discombobulated, Claire hesitated. Roquin hadn't yet given her the money. She was better off holding her tongue; otherwise she might not get anything. When you're doing business, you don't tell off the clients, or you choose the time and the person. She said:

"What did I do to you?"

"You said shit, you'd had enough," said Roquin.

"It happens, give it a break! You all think that we're always … You know …"

"Okay, I get it. But you could still speak correctly, decently, you know—I'm paying, damn it—decently, well, you know, if you're into it or not."

"No, not that," said Fouilloux. "The lil' one, no way. Not that."

"Why didn't you say it like that right away," said Roquin. "You're totally in your right, now. Now it's fine. Now I'm not criticizing you."

"… So when should we see each other again?" said Fouilloux, tired.

"Oh …" said Jean-Roquin, who was surprised by the question and immediately saw what advantage Claire Fouilloux had given him. "Oh … My little girl, that depends on you … How much … You know."

"I don't do the lil' one, like I said."

"Oh well, fuck it, you can get screwed by whoever you want."

Fouilloux didn't have the heart to respond. Besides, she had a rendezvous of an unusual sort, in town, in a private residence. It was the first time she'd make a house call. An old widower, a Mr. …Vuillard or Couillard or Fouillard or … something. Always the same type, of course. She had gotten him by way of old Magnin, a fat, impotent cheat of a plumber who sucked. He loved Aunt Flow, Mr. Magnin. He made enough for it, with all that plumbers rake in, especially renovations. Old Gouillard, or Fuyard or Bouillard was one of his colleagues, a house painter.

"Sure you don't want a little something right now?" whispered Jean Roquin as he tapped his cock against Fouilloux's ass.

She almost screamed, clawed, reflected abruptly, found the fat rubbery glans soft like the sea, asked three hundred francs for this specialty, obtained them, standing up, arched her back.

Mrs. Théret stood up behind the counter, stunned:

"René? Is it you? … Are you coming to kill us or to sleep over?"

This tone brought tears to René Théret's eyes. His mother having joined him in the middle of the empty store, he fell into her arms. Lachrymose, but tough, she insisted:

"You comin' home or you just passin' through? …"

"I'm comin' home," said René. "I'm comin' home, momma."

He wasn't sure he'd get off that easily. Parents are resentful, inquisitorial. Maybe coming back was free, but what about the rest? He nearly imagined himself remanded to the police—all confessions made—by this dragon of virtue.

"I won't say we were waiting for you," affirmed Mrs. Théret. "Your father isn't even here. Your sisters are at school. I just opened. I'm going to close up for a little bit. You got something to say to me, maybe? Probably not of course."

In a drawer, she searched for the placard "Closed for illnesses" that her husband had calligraphed in Chinese ink on a Bristol card in that curious English. They attached it to the window of the door with a little scotch tape. It wasn't awfully clever, for food vendors.

"You no longer play the shiv?" asked Mrs. Théret in her dated slang, once she'd closed shop.

"The what? ..." said René, sheepishly. He really didn't understand. Only the roguish, almost indecent tone touched him.

"Don't play the altar boy," said Louise Théret. "Come, we'll be better off in the kitchen. I'm thirsty. There is some beer. You want some?"

A sad, bland, flat family beer, sold by the liter.

"The shank, if you prefer," Mrs. Théret went on.

René still didn't understand. His mother drank:

"Oh ... Oh ... What, shank doesn't ring any bells? Oh well, you don't read much, for a crook. I know, high school isn't really ..."

"The chourineur!" said René suddenly, who remembered the book.

"Oh yeah, you're right!" conceded Mrs. Théret, dry and satisfied. "The chourineur. Of course. I botched it. Well anyway, chourin or shank, is it over? ... No more drama?"

"Yes," whispered René. "I never had one, y'know."

"You swear?" said Mrs. Théret. "Can you swear at least?"

"Yes," said René.

"How many bodies? ... There must be bodies. Go on."

This question, which was merely theatrical, cut Rene's legs out from under him. He grew livid. His mother noticed all this. She faced René but without touching him:

"What, there are? There are? It was too perfect, there are? ..."

"Two," said René.

However he had answered in a very low voice and as if in a cough. Mrs. Théret heard "who," furrowed her eyebrows, and repeated, in a shriller, tenser voice:

"What's who? … Yes? Or no? … You're scaring me René. Answer me."

René Théret caught himself in the nick of time:

"No, of course. No. Why are you asking that?"

Mrs. Théret, relieved, put on a scandalized face:

"Oh well, that would have been the last straw! That really would have been the last straw! Still living in the movies, after all."

"You know," she added, "that this is too serious for a smack and you're too young for what it actually deserves. You know that?"

René pitifully recognized his guilt, the indulgence of the maternal judge, the nobility of the Théretesque soul. He was allowed to go hide his shame in his bedroom. There he felt more humiliated than a dog pushed away with buckets of water. Self-obsessed, he hadn't noticed his mother's bitchiness (she had *played it* to perfection) and only blamed his own cowardice. He was in deep shit now. He felt like running away again. He cried, strapped in, lost. His bedroom was tidy, even the books; his bed made.

"Hey!" said Marc Guillard gaily. "Well what a day! Come in, hurry up! Oh I'm feeling good! So? …"

He flipped the lock and showed the boys up to his bedroom. They had never come here before.

"This is your bedroom?" asked Pellisson, stunned.

"Hey, you lost something!" stated Viaud, pointing to a step on the staircase behind them.

Marc didn't fall for it. He seized him voluptuously by a butt cheek.

"When we gonna get married, Millipede? You've got a beautiful ass you know?"

Viaud dodged.

"Didn't you," he said, "invent the dynamite to cut the mustard, no, the knife that makes you sneeze? Yeah, it's him! He …"

Guillard wished to offer some refreshments. He went down to the kitchen. There, he bumped into his dad, very disheveled, in briefs, socks, and a shirt.

"Hey, sorry dad!" said Marc. "What're you doin' here?"

Mr. Guillard was awkward.

"Yes, I just came back from, hmm, Magnin's. I gotta give myself a scouring, see. A good shower. But first the White Spirit."

Marc sensed that his father was lying. What's more, he showed no trace of paint. He had probably gotten a haircut that very day. And why would he have worked at Magnin's? He kept Marc abreast of all his jobsites.

"Sounds like you've got visitors?" said Mr. Guillard.

"Yeah. Buddies, you know. At this hour."

"So I heard. I can take it easy down here I hope? You won't need anything?"

"In the kitchen, dad?" asked Marc, intrigued.

"Yes, or the dining room, well, down here."

Mr. Guillard's bedroom was on the ground floor, behind the dining room as a matter of fact.

You got yourself a whore, thought Marc.

This happened very rarely, and never during the day.

"I'm bringing up the beer and some glasses, okay?" said Marc.

"Yes yes, of course … I'm tired you know."

"Yeah dad. Well, I'll grab something to eat while I'm at it."

Mr. Guillard, sheepish, patient, waited passively for his son to finish.

"He must have come to get *her* some ice cubes." Marc, in the stairwell, heard the noise of the ice being broken and tinkling.

"My dad's downstairs tucking into a blood sausage!" he announced to the boys as he entered the room.

Viaud sniffed.

"He's eating it raw?"

"If you cook that sausage I promise ya it's gonna whoop!" said Guillard. "It ain't no pork sausage!"

Neither Viaud nor Pellisson had gotten it. Guillard explained himself more clearly after they shut the door and he'd indicated to the boys that they should speak in a whisper.

But Marc's visitors weren't interested in Guillard Sr.'s love life. He offered bread, butter, pâté, a garlicky sausage, and made the beer froth in the big mustard glasses shaped like steins. Pellisson said that he would have preferred milk. Guillard thought it would be imprudent to go back down.

"We'll find him with his dick in the butter, the bastard!"

"The butter is right here," said Viaud.

The boys explained why they'd come. Hervé Pellisson claimed that he felt remorse for having enlisted the three little ones, Viaud, Péréfixe and Lescot. Things, here and there, were turning too sour. The papers spoke of a wave of petty crime that was without precedent. No one had yet understood that they were dealing with children so young. But now the police were beginning to investigate for real, the reporters were showing interest, and, if this went on, so would the TV.

"We won't be able to hide if there's the TV," affirmed Alain Viaud, as if he were speaking of the eye of God. They laughed.

Even so, it was certain that if the television took notice, the cops would turn up the heat.

Moreover, according to Pellisson, the relations that Guillard had built with various thugs compromised them all. It had already become impossible to disentangle, among the crimes that scandalized the island, what belonged to whom. The time had come for the little kids to pull out.

"And you with?" said Guillard.

"At first it was fun. Now it's not funny anymore," said Pellisson. "Those who don't stop this time will never see the end of it. Oh yeah, what about Julien Roquin?"

Guillard told them what he knew. He didn't narrate Théret's flaking out. Roquin's isolation down there at the hideout was polluting him. He couldn't imagine the boy lurking in that hole without a companion, without an elder. Not even one night. Marc should have gone to check on him immediately, and come up with another solution. Bring him back here?

"Didn't those guys from Saint-Loup steal a jalopy in front of the cathedral?" asked Hervé Pellisson. "You shouldn't run with 'em."

"It might be them, yeah. But I don't know 'em anymore."

"They are bastards. They are fucking things up. So are the ones from Roche-Notre-Dame!"

"No they're not. Not them. Not at all," said Guillard. "They're cool."

"That's your business. I'm just telling you that we're done, and so are the little ones. It was ugly, really. Kinda sick!"

Hervé Pellisson's repentance and his nauseated look were feigned. He loved stealing, adventure. What he was afraid of were brawls, tough guys, motorized vehicles. Violence. The police. From now on, his middle-class and puerile gang had to be completely dissociated from Marc Guillard.

The latter wasn't offended. Pellisson wasn't good for much; the brats, crafty but too chatty, were a permanent danger. And finally, Guillard was becoming ambitious. His projects were getting bigger in scope. He dreamt of a hold-up, with real arms—and with real millions to boot. He hesitated between a savings bank and a pawnshop almost next door to each other on Jonathan Swift Street (it was the luxurious pedestrian street). He was carefully ripening this project, didn't talk about it with any-one, and would recapitulate it on bits of paper that he would immediately burn. The more arduous problem: his troops. He shouldn't associate with boys older or more hardened than him, for fear of being squeezed out. He had realized that he would be making a mistake if he hooked up with "hard" thugs, but so too if he lugged brats along. He regretted René Théret's defection. If Pellisson and the Lescot gang left, on the other hand, that was rather an advantage.

"We haven't dusted anyone. We didn't do anything bad," he remarked. "You see something sick in that, Hervé?"

Hervé was never hard-pressed for a nice recitation of moral principles. He let it flow. It went with his face, his voice; he was the good son type.

"You're a total bigot!" Guillard criticized half-heartedly. "Oh the poor old ladies, you say! Did you bawl afterward?"

"Yes absolutely!" Hervé confirmed. "I can't help but replay it. Sometimes it wakes me up, I'm scared!"

"They come back to eat your ass out," said Guillard. "They're vicious, those old timers! You see, they were just waiting to croak to come give you hand jobs! Ghost pumpers!"

"And that other old guy! …" said Pellisson, scandalized. "We weren't nice with him!"

"We weren't nice with him!" Marc Guillard imitated. "We didn't even tie him! What more do you need! And he didn't kick the bucket did he?"

"No, but what a fright he got! … No, it's wrong. It's wrong. It's terrible to have dragged in the … children."

"Children!" cackled Alain Viaud.

"Yes," said Hervé, solemn. "You'll see when you grow up, Viaud. You'll see that I was right … Would you like someone to kill your grandmother, even if it was just 'cause they were afraid?"

"Yeah. I would," said Alain. "When? I'll scare her. Afterward we can kill her if we gotta, on top of that."

The two elders laughed at his cruelty.

"And then?" continued Pellisson, accusingly. "Where would you go? Where'd you go? To the Department of Social Services? You'll be all alone!"

"Yes," said Viaud. He furrowed his eyebrows and squinted even more, staring into space. They often mentioned the orphanage. He had it coming. He wouldn't mind killing Old Viaud, to punish her for exposing him to that. He sure as hell wouldn't let himself be put in prison.

"Yes. We need to kill her," he repeated. "I'll go stay with you, Doormat."

Guillard suddenly intercepted a door sound that he knew well. The Guillard pad, squeezed between two beautiful old houses, gave out on one side onto the street, and on the other onto a blind alley—which you could observe from a transom, next to Marc's bedroom, on the mansarded landing.

"Come over here!" he said. "Hurry! We're gonna see my dad's chick! He's letting her out through the back!"

He brought a chair and climbed up on it:

"Wait. No. It's just him leaving by himself. Maybe she's waiting for him to be the lookout. No ... He's taking off. He's in a suit. Shit. Hmm ... I feel like going downstairs see if she's there or if there was no one. Wow!"

Mr. Guillard, indeed, his pleasure taken, had had a problem with the treasury department: he didn't have enough money in cash. His companion was an unanticipated glutton. He was forced to go get some bills from the bank immediately.

Marc Guillard went down the old wooden stairs. He was prodigiously skilled in the art of not making the steps squeak. And this particular staircase should have been classified a blue ribbon, best-in-show staircase, so much did it cry and crack. Every day, the boy practiced his cat burglar scales wearing socks. He forbade Pellisson and Viaud from following him before he gave the signal: they weren't virtuosos enough.

Guillard got to the ground floor. He listened a moment. He leaned, peered into the keyhole of the dining room. He turned shrimp red.

He had caught a glimpse of Claire Fouilloux. She was finishing getting dressed. In that lighting, she looked like a barely pubescent young girl. Marc thought she was younger than he was. His father was banging that.

He climbed up the stairs with a silent and supple swiftness that astounded the other two. He shoved them into his bedroom.

"So?"

"She's a fat granny, as big as this!" said Guillard. "A real barrelhouse. A herd of cows in a padded bra."

Viaud was delighted. Guillard, now impatient to chase off his visitors, entertained them with additional untruths. He rapidly concluded the interview:

"Come back again, we'll chew the rag!" he said.

Pellisson promised vaguely. In fact, he was contemplating breaking it off completely. And the little ones would never go alone to Guillard's. This was goodbye.

"Seeing as she heard you when you came in, you go back down in a hubbub, you leave, and I'll come back quietly. That way she'll think there's no one here," Marc Guillard explained. He was dead aroused.

"Yeah, I know," cackled Viaud, "you wanna get a taste of it, of the sausage. It. The sausage in the cow's underpants. The sausage panties!"

"Shhh!" said Pellisson.

"He's gonna get a taste of it," Viaud insisted. "He's chucking us out."

They tumbled obstreperously down the stairs and left through the back door.

Marc Guillard slammed it very hard and came back silently to the front of the dining room door. His strategic spirit was abandoning him. His heart was beating too fast. Impulsively, he pulled out his member and leaned once more to the keyhole.

He didn't see a thing. The girl must have receded into the room. Gotten naked again. Marc, suffocated at this idea, lost control of himself. A little girl. A whore. Stark naked. Whom his father had just fucked. He was going to leap on her, insert himself inside her by force. Jizz and blood would splatter everywhere. He straightened up, his temples humming.

Claire Fouilloux opened the door: she was looking for the toilet. She came nose to nose with the adolescent and she saw his disorder. He was very cute but what a perv with his big gluey thingy. Little bastard. Who was it?

"Oh!" she cried, surprised. She closed the door brutally. She'd thought she was alone in the house. Did that Mr. Pouillard or Nouillard or Gouillard intend to have her spit-roasted by children? In front of him? Seeing youngsters be deflowered turned some sick bastards on. For one or two seconds Fouilloux imagined herself coupling with the boy she'd caught a glimpse of. She felt a brief, tired intimate pinch. Nasty little pig who takes out his big wee-wee in front of the damsels. Oh.

Marc had brusquely readjusted. He had mentally photographed Claire Fouilloux during her apparition at the door. He was disappointed that she was, all things considered, ugly, old, and flat, his father's kiddie. But he was enchanted that she had seen his. He lost all illusion of being able to fuck her. He was feeling bound to her by the exhibition he had made. He was feeling an unbearable frustration. A rut to be pacified without delay. Climb back up to his room, or try the dining room, in spite of everything? There was neither lock nor key. The girl didn't look that scared, or stuck-up. Simple, rather.

In Guillard's mind, the disappointing image of the door and the overwhelming image of the keyhole were superimposed— and recomposed as his dad's exquisite whore-child. He squeezed his member strongly. And if she didn't want to, he would blackmail the old man, to make him force her.

To push it in so hard that it came out between the shoulders, a dagger stab in reverse. Marc freed his member and called, while masturbating:

"Miss?"

He opened the door at the same time. The Fouilloux, hardly surprised, sighed with annoyance, and disdain. She played the grande dame, searched for a tone of voice:

"Well, are we not done here? Don't you know how to blow your nose all by yourself? You've got no shame for a kid. Gosh."

She was seated at the dining room table, a rustic, perfectly waxed, Brittany style Henri II.

"It's my dad!" said Guillard, coming closer. He found it extraordinarily pleasant to show off. He had intuitively sensed that he didn't displease her. Fouilloux looked like a variety of girls of sixteen, or thereabouts, that Marc Guillard rubbed elbows with, mocked, chatted up, young saleswomen, waitresses, etc. He was sure that this one, at least, would jerk him off.

"The old guy?" said Fouilloux. "Your father? … Oh. And why did your father call you? To give you a spanking?"

"Yeah right!" cried out Marc Guillard, delighted, and, with both hands, in a rapid kid movement, he pulled his pants down to his knees. Claire Fouilloux, who had never seen a beautiful boy naked before, felt her cheeks flush; a timidity took a hold of her; an unreasonable desire. Here! This! With a kid! …

"You're nuts sweetie!" she whispered maternally. She slipped her dry hand under the fat moist, hairless balls. Marc Guillard could no longer restrain himself.

"How 'bout going to see Julien?" suggested Alain Viaud. Hervé Pellisson nodded. It was a long walk. He didn't really feel like it. And there was always the risk of getting caught at Julien Roquin's lair.

"Getting caught?" asked Viaud. "Why?"

Hervé explained that too many boys knew about Julien's hideout. Any of them could be caught, inform the police.

"They'll unleash two roller pigs and that'll be that!"

(He meant: two bike cops.)

Alain Viaud objected. He imagined Julien's arrest instead with a big black car with a blue light, numerous cops armed to the teeth, spotlights on the dilapidated house, sirens, a grand spectacle. It would be broadcast live, obviously.

"You're nuts!" laughed Pellisson. "Roquin's no gangster! He hasn't done anything wrong! They'll bring him back home that's all. No, I'm telling you. But if we're there with him it's another story. They'll think … what, what … a gang. I mean, Théret's already down there."

"Ass Théret," said Viaud, sibylline.

"Butt cheeks Théret," said Hervé after an interval of meditation. Viaud's declarations were always so abrupt; he was the kind of guy who talked to himself.

"Théretballs," added Hervé.

"No. Ass Théret," said Alain Viaud, obstinate. "By the way, hey, Pellisson, is it still on for Tuesday?"

"Yeah. Tuesday at six. Or else the one after. Depends on what she's doing. I'll let you know."

"We're gonna kill her."

"Hell no, we're not gonna kill her!" Hervé protested. "What an obsession! … We're not gonna hurt her. First of all, she won't be there. I chose the day on purpose."

"If she's not there why do you care if I want to kill her?" said Viaud with logic.

"'Cause we don't need to. You, one day, some other time, you …"

"No," Viaud cut in. "Your cousin'll go in first right, I'm too big."

"You big? … I think you should be able to get through too."

"No not everything," said Alain Viaud. "The butthole will stay out. Let's bet. My butthole."

"Yeah," said Hervé. "And the cops'll find it and they'll say, 'Oh, I know this one! Nothing new here!'"

"No they won't find it. They'll fall in. They'll trip on their own feet. And bam. Into the juice. No more cops."

"Want me to walk you home then?" offered Hervé.

"Yeah. You go that way and I'll go this way."

Viaud showed opposite directions. Hervé shrugged his shoulders. As the little boy pulled the jokes out with an invariably serious air, a cold tone, and a somewhat moronic style, it was hard to know if he was kidding around and how to respond. A guy who doesn't laugh, doesn't cry, never seems angry or content is seriously difficult to hang out with.

"I'll leave you then, if that's what you prefer."

"I didn't say that. See ya!" said Viaud.

He was already several meters away in a second. A bit wounded, Hervé Pellisson turned back on his path. It was no fun at all to go home so early; but he didn't like hanging out alone. Sometimes, the little ones also bored him. There are some days when the whole world was boring. Useless.

Or else it was the fact that Viaud had abruptly turned him loose that emptied everything of its interest, of its color. First the break with Guillard. And now Alain was running off.

Guillard hadn't been upset. On the contrary. He certainly had projects that would help. He had always had a grand vision. No, not really because of books. He wasn't nuts, he wasn't kidding himself. He didn't go that far. But he knew he was deft, shrewd, and bold. He understood everything quickly. He beat people to the punch, just in time. He'd become a smooth operator; he'd direct people, things. Except if, before that … Pellisson thought back to the ugly aspects of their different undertakings. He had lied a bit when he'd told Guillard that he had nightmares about it. However, there was an atmosphere of unshakeable worry. The feeling, at times, of a horrible, degenerate story, one that should have never begun. All they'd worried about was their impunity. They'd been barely surprised not to have been discovered, caught, or even suspected; they had the best reasons to think they were innocent, but something heavy and black, nauseating, enormous, was swelling underneath. It wasn't remorse, a feeling of wrongdoing, viciousness, or error. It was an irrational, disgusting, gigantic fear.

Hervé Pellisson felt it particularly when he was alone in the street, as he was now. The massive, unbearable thing awoke in him and—without insinuating, aching, or biting—would slowly, monstrously diffuse panic. Impossible to resist. It spread. It started with this impression of emptiness, of being let go, and it veered little by little into a viscous, bland, achromatic mud. You became this mud. It was worse than being beaten, abandoned, or punished. It was an insurmountable nudity, a bloodless solitude, as immense and flaccid as a humid day.

What relation was there between this and petty theft, some amateur burglaries, a few righteous and inoffensive games (as Hervé saw them)?

At least one: no sooner did you feel this enormous tide of disgust, distress and fear than a crazy, absurd desire for theft would appear. Simultaneously, Hervé decided he would renounce all crime from now on, and scanned around for an occasion to immediately commit one, the most violent, and the biggest possible.

He came close to snatching the handbag of a passer-by, judged the environment too unfavorable, and entered a Uniprix supermarket.

8

"No I can't fit!" whispered Joachim Lescot.

"Yeah you can!" said Hervé. "I'm sure you'll fit!"

"Yeah, it's working," said Viaud.

"He says he can't," said Marie-Antoine.

Hervé, kneeling by the window, examined Mrs. Arnauld's basement once again. He was annoyed. He'd neglected to arm himself with a torch, since they'd decided the expedition would take place at the end of the afternoon. But you could hardly see a thing in this goddamn cellar.

Fortunately, he had cased the place several times before. He would be able to describe it to Joachim.

"But why can't you? If your head fits, it all fits! You've fit through tighter bars than these!"

"No I can't!" little Lescot repeated.

They had broken the glass, opened the single-paneled window. The basement window was very well located. A garden wall, some bushes, a sort of lean-to, and the house itself, protected from prying eyes. The only thing was not to stand up. The neighboring houses were rather close. You could hear children playing in certain gardens.

"He's scared!" said Viaud.

"Come on, what's with you? ... You afraid of going to jail? They aren't gonna catch us! If we hurry!"

Joachim Lescot shook his head. He wasn't afraid of jail. He was quite calm! Nor the guillotine!

"If you're not going down the whole thing is ruined," said his cousin. "We might as well just blow. It's ruined then. Because of you it's ruined."

No, Joachim did not want it to be ruined. He finally decided to confess the motive for his refusal:

"That's it. Because of that, there," he said, pointing with his index finger into the depths of the basement.

"What, that?" said Pellisson. "There's nothing there. You can jump easy. It's not even high. There's nothing there!"

"Yes there is!" cried Joachim, disgruntled. "You don't see them? All the sp-spider b-beds?"

"There are spiders?" said Marie-Antoine, aghast.

"In the ceiling," said Viaud.

"You're a butthead!" said Pellisson to Joachim. "There aren't any, it's clean. We could see 'em if we saw 'em! The webs!"

"Now I can see 'em too, the spider heads," said Péréfixe, who had come closer. "They are big."

Hervé sighed:

"Joachim? Listen just go!"

"Marie should go," said young Lescot.

"I don't know," said Marie-Antoine. "It's scary."

"What time's the fossil comin' home?" asked Alain Viaud, who was beginning to grow impatient.

"She comes back for dinner," said Pellisson. "At eight. But it's not an old bag: it's Mrs. Arnauld."

"Are we gonna kill her?" offered Viaud.

Hervé, bothered by the bad start of this affair, wasn't in the mood to laugh. He couldn't keep his troops in hand. But he wouldn't admit defeat so quickly. The house made his mouth water, excited his sweet tooth. How could he force one of the two little ones to go down? What promise could he make? Or what threat invent?

"Joachim, listen …" he repeated.

The child really didn't want to. He said:

"No. Why don't we go in another way?"

At night, of course, they would have tried. The louvered shutters weren't closed. To climb to a window from down here, break a pane, open it, nothing was simpler. But now, it was impossible. Anybody could see them. And after nightfall, there would be too many obstacles: Mrs. Arnauld would be back, Mrs. Lescot would worry that Joachim wasn't back for dinner, the Péréfixe parents would be terrified, stunned, calling everywhere … It was now or never.

"What about you Alain, you sure you can't fit between those bars?" asked Pellisson in desperation.

"Pff, yeah, sure I'll fit," said Alain Viaud.

"Well then asshead, what are you waiting for?!"

"It's 'cause I didn't want to," explained Viaud.

"So you don't want to?" said Hervé. "What a ding-a-ling!"

"Oh. Sure, sure. Spiders don't bother me."

Makes you want to bang your head against the walls, thought Hervé Pellisson. A real bunch of nutbags. Brilliant idea he'd had, taking on the three little ones. Hervé looked at his watch. He hadn't stolen it; it was a brand new communion gift. The Pellisson parents hadn't skimped on their son. The watch was superb. Six twenty.

Viaud tried headfirst. The space between the bars was barely sufficient. The child started over, putting his feet first. He slid into the void the whole length of his legs, contorted himself, got his butt through, then was afraid he was stuck. Hervé kept hold of him as he completed his descent. They heard him drop. Lescot had been following the action with great interest. He wouldn't have thought Viaud was so crafty.

"Where do I go now?" asked Viaud, winded.

Hervé Pellisson described the operating procedure to him. The goal was to reach a door that, from the basement, gave out onto the garden by a ramp, and unlock it. As soon as this was done, Viaud would give a signal, and the three others, on all fours, would trickle down to this door.

The thing was accomplished swiftly. The Lescot gang was in.

Mrs. Arnauld, unwed, was an excellent woman who taught mathematics at the tech middle school. She was well acquainted with Hervé Pellisson, to whom she had given private lessons, which he came here to take. And, each Tuesday, if she didn't have class, she would offer herself an afternoon outing, either in Saint-Rémi (she lived in the northwest suburb), or on the continent. It was rare that she would stay at home on such a day, especially during the picnic season.

Her house, a rental, was remarkably arrayed, almost upscale. The children felt bashful. When you break into a place like everybody else, at night and with murderous intent, everything seems abnormal and you feel at ease: you perform a number of difficult and bizarre gestures which you've never even practiced, you have great presence of mind, you feel no fear of the darkness—you stay on the dark side of electric lamps. If you run into the people who live there, you terrorize them; anyway, surprised in those early hours, they always look ugly and dumb.

Whereas here, nothing of the sort. Outside, the end of a beautiful July day, a feeling of summer holidays, decent little gardens. Inside, an impression of bonhomie, of welcome. You might have thought that Mrs. Arnauld, hearing the kids pop out of her basement, was going to emerge from her living room, wish them welcome, offer them a cup of hot cocoa and an apple tart. Her hair would be neatly made up; she'd be wearing high-heels, with her nails lacquered. She would complain with a smile about not being on holiday yet, with exams to grade and a thousand other chores to finish. She would thank them for their visit and she would gently send them on their way, with the smell of vanilla, sugar and butter on their fingertips.

"What do we need to steal?" asked Joachim Lescot, intimidated. "I don't want anything!"

He saw that Alain Viaud, instead of pissing everywhere, was looking for the bathroom, a hand on his fly.

"The most interesting is the money," said Hervé. "I know that she keeps a lot of it, sometimes."

"Why?" said Joachim.

"'Cause I saw her," said Hervé Pellisson.

"So," said Viaud, "she's a pinchfist, a tight-ass, a cheapskate. She's setting herself up a stash."

"Huh, huh?" asked Péréfixe. "So, is she stealing?"

"A miser isn't someone who steals," said Pellisson. "It's someone who stashes everything on the side, Jeez!"

"Yeah, miserness, yeah," confirmed Alain Viaud.

"But still, where'd she get it, before having it?" insisted Joachim Lescot, staggered by this story of the lady teacher hoarding money at her house.

"She works," said Pellisson. "She gets paid!"

"Yeah, paid," cackled Alain Viaud. "A teacher, yeah!"

Meanwhile, Hervé Pellisson was touring the living room furniture. Nothing was locked. This living room abutted a minuscule dining room whose round table, very sculpted, was used as a desk by Mrs. Arnauld, who rarely had to remove these books, these notebooks, these writing utensils, so as to roll out the tablecloth and set the table.

Viaud was pilfering absent-mindedly, like someone who nibbles without appetite. He grumbled:

"It's no fun when it's not nighttime and when nobody's even here. It's not kickass. We're not havin' a kickass time. We see everything before it happens. It's like we're at home. By ourselves."

"Well, not for me!" said Pellisson. "I hope she didn't put her dough in the bank. 'Cause I'm not finding nothing."

The old and modest villas of this suburb generally had a floor built under the eaves, a design that was rather uncommon on the island. The children went up to visit Mrs. Arnauld's room. They liked being there: it was dark, they were packed in, worried of getting trapped there if someone appeared downstairs.

The pillaging itself felt exciting again. However, they did not dare to spill open the drawers, or to break, or soil anything. Upset that he was not able to steal anything that he could have taken and kept at his house, Marie-Antoine Péréfixe looked at the others and felt a measured fear. He would have liked them to task him with a physical manoeuver: to bring down piles of sheets, the rug or the clock, to count handkerchiefs, or wads of money. Stealing was, all and all, a disappointing thing, idiotic, a pain in the ass. Marie-Antoine no longer understood why they were still playing at this. (It was a lot more interesting, for example, to leaf through some cutouts with a mean little girl, in a nice shadowy corner.)

Hervé wore a long face:

"Zilch, nothing," he repeated.

"What did ya wanna buy with it," asked Joachim Lescot, "with the money? Why'd you want it?"

"It was to have it, you know! Can you imagine what we coulda done with it!" said Pellisson.

"No," confessed Joachim. "What could we have done?"

"'Cause afterwards we do what we want!" said Pellisson.

"Yep, whatever we want!" Viaud ascertained. Joachim still didn't understand. He didn't experience the astronomical and mysterious desires that his cousin and Alain Viaud seemed to know and to value above everything. His wishes were granted from dawn to dusk. And, like Marie-Antoine, all he appreciated in the thefts was the amusement, the change of scenery, and the physical artistry. Not the ill-gotten gains. Nor could he harbor them. He took and gave back.

"With how much?" he asked without conviction.

"Oh yeah, how much by the way?" said Viaud.

"I dunno," said Hervé. "I know that she hid some, I wasn't able to count it! Obviously! ... No, for us money's the best. That's what's useful."

"And to bring to Roquin," said Alain Viaud.

Pellisson didn't answer.

Hugo Grandieu had had a terrible nightmare during his nap. Since his wife's death he often experienced ridiculous, solitary fears. He had a phobia of vampires. He expected uprisings, attacks from behind, giants with black lions' faces or scarlet tigers. He feared the shadows, the recesses, but also, even in broad daylight, the whole interior of his house. It sounded too empty.

But, until now, his sleep had been spared. He slept long and soundly, keeping a nightlight on to lessen the anguish of being alone. He had neither dreams nor startled awakenings.

After this dreadful nap, he asked himself if the phobias would from now on contaminate even his unconscious hours.

Still Mr. Grandieu had no remorse. He thought about his wife, but with pleasure. This furnished his dull days, reassured him, comforted him when he came home and when his idiotic phobias manifested. He missed old Mrs. Grandieu's company more and more. The starchy rituals, the petrified mirth, the insignificant habits, the conventional pleasures, the hollow chitchat, the insipid moods, the heartless good manners. After all, this automatic world was the most civilized of all; and one could only taste peace in these solid-color representations. It seemed empty? Precisely. Since Mr. Grandieu lived in the new emptiness that he'd created, he felt all the beauty of the previous one. He had hated the void of conformism? Now, all he had was the void of death.

Beyond these startling observations, Hugo Grandieu could not discover within himself the strength to reconstruct the state of things of which he has deprived himself. He wouldn't have much trouble finding himself an automaton, a parrot, a mummy, and to live one last time the imbecilic peace that he'd shattered. No material obstacles. There were more old bags of her sort than there were old guys like him. But he has lost the spring in his step. Something stopped responding. His nostalgia remained exactly in its fixed and stubborn nostalgic place. It did not see nor want the future. Nothing to be begun again. Nothing to be tried. Mr. Grandieu was simply sinking towards death, and his regret of the good days was the appropriate, decent occupation for these days that were not even bad. In truth, the only unpredicted, odious, uncalled-for things were these phobias, these panics—and now, these nightmares. They probably expressed that Mr. Grandieu was afraid of himself and of the abominable, certain, ineluctable and imminent event that was enclosed in his old body.

He had dismissed the maid shortly after his wife's funeral. People had appreciated this elegant gesture. Now, a well-groomed, ageless, idiotic and nearly mute shlepper tended his household. She barely knew how to cook, unfortunately, and it wouldn't be long before Grandieu would exchange her for a molly-coddling governess staying in town. Mr. Grandieu had a vision of rich, heavy flesh, glossy and white, like the flesh sometimes dissimulated by certain old ladies with wilted faces and spoiled voices. He supposed that such anonymous, almost abstract meat could interest him far more than the freshest of green fruit. Young people are so cumbersome! A biddy who would lend her fat ass exactly the same way she brought in the tureen, the roast, and the heavy cake, that was the ticket. Paid.

And perhaps that might be enough to bring back the quiet sleep, and to hurl the negro vampires with leonine faces back into their grotesque universe. Among the elderly, age was not a thing.

Mr. Grandieu often met with Captain Lorge, who was leading the investigation on the wave of juvenile delinquency that had besieged the whole southern region of the island. In their conversations, their hypotheses, there was the possibility of a double dealing which delighted Hugo Grandieu and which made him despise "the cops" more than ever.

Indeed, Grandieu—and he alone—knew that the attacks, the pilfering, the burglaries, the involuntary homicides were authored by very young children. The police, admittedly, had sensed and deduced, if not proven, that these were the doing of minors, but they were searching within an age bracket that was much too high, and where they could unearth more culprits daily than justice demanded. This relentlessness to find delinquents where they ought to be (thug rabble between fifteen and twenty years of age) was what most nauseated Grandieu about Captain Lorge and his acolytes' investigation.

No. It wasn't a motorcycle helmet, a flashy and mean piece of hoodlum armor that had been forgotten at Mr. Grandieu's. He felt like putting Captain Lorge on the right track. He pointed out the ludicrous, incoherent, and unmotorized petit-bourgeois aspect of some of the crimes. But the captain then countered with other crimes that were apparently more ferocious. Grandieu no longer detected "his" thieves in them. After a while, whenever there was a new hit, even if it was just mentioned in a few words in the papers, he knew if they were *his* or Captain Lorge's. Then he felt affection, a certain tenderness: "There … those are my scoundrels." Even if his own safety as a murderer hadn't been at issue, he would have forbidden himself from denouncing them all the same. Their business, objectively, was in no way more estimable than the crimes of the ruffians. Even the ribald and sloppy vibe wasn't easy to read, from the outside. Their excesses and blunders made them neither more nor less reprehensible than the others. Grandieu, to say the truth, tracked them down and loved them because they resembled him, him and his crime. Something non-violent, something not perpetrated, whatever the substance of the facts may be. And Mr. Grandieu supposed that these children were as uncatchable as he was because of this. Besides, if he swore to Captain Lorge that this, that, and that other thing had been committed by some kids, he wouldn't harm them and wouldn't help the cop. Where and how could they be found, except by a trap or red handed? When birds devastate a fruit tree, we say "it's the birds" and we fire at will. But as for designating the culprits ... Grandieu thought, and often repeated to himself:

"Let's hope *they* don't fuck up."

He lived with them now a little. And gave them too much credit. In truth, what was being done was merely ordinary and wasn't as colorful as he believed. The infamous wave of delinquency—no matter whom it involved, and from where it came—was surely nothing more than a gust of dusty air, a bucket of dirty water thrown across some less mobile debris. But for Mr. Grandieu, who was already afraid of vampires and dreams, what was one more illusion; and thus he recomposed a morality for himself. His age old values still held. The soul and the army.

Some arrests took place. Interrogations. Banalities, no more. Even the pettiest newspapers barely deigned to mention it. It was happening too often. Imagined things were more easily renewed, fatter and more digestible; delinquency bored people, they preferred detective series. The public had only woken up for a few days when the rape of a little girl near Roche-Notre-Dame was reported. Her age was mouthwatering enough, although already a bit commonplace: nine years old (at nine, in Peru or in Pakistan, a girl has already been a wife and a mother for a long time, affirmed the newspapers). But she'd been neither killed nor even really coerced. And she had denounced culprits who wouldn't be of much worth either once they'd been arrested and identified: among the twelve year olds, there was not a single drop of sperm or blood. Families turned their backs on the affair with contempt. Bucolic mores, country bumpkins giving it a go. You call that rape? Journalists making mountains out of molehills.

"Hey, I can make you eat shit on foot, on horseback and in a car!"

"I can fuck you sailing or driving!"

"I can fuck you with water, oil, or mustard!"

"Hey, stop it, we know 'em by heart," said Dominique Seignelet, rather embarrassed. He passed along the bottle of Martini.

"I'll do it with Clorox bleach and a toilet brush," said his brother Jean-Baptiste without even hearing him.

"And I'll make you eat shit in socks and under an umbrella!" said Benoît Gassé, ingeniously. His little brother laughed:

"I'll do it on one foot and with no hands!"

"Me, hmm, I'll fuck you in reverse!"

It was François Boitard, coming up a little short. The Gassé brothers' capacity for repartee had caught him off guard. Those bourgeois got down and dirty real fast.

"And I'll do in the oven, in the double-boiler, and on the spit!"

"Me, in black and in color!"

"And me, at sea, on a mountain and in a boat and on the moon!"

"What the hell am I doing with these kids," moaned Dominique Seignelet. He didn't know how, or didn't dare to improvise, to participate, for fear of falling flat, of not being the best, of looking stuck-up—as if that were at stake.

"What're you doin'?" squealed Boitard. "Easy, you're getting fucked by hand and at the factory, in a picture and at the movies, by the hour and by the minute, through the radio and … hmm."

"On TV!" Benoît Gassé tranquilly appended.

"Yeah and I'll fuck you by propeller and by jet propulsion! In a train bunk and on a fold-up seat!"

"On a ladder in a hammock!"

"On an old nag on a bike!"

"By letter and by postcard!"

"No, me, I'll fuck you with pills and suppositories!"

"And me, with fries!"

"And me, with garlic and onions!"

"And me, totally naked, totally dressed!"

"Huh?" said Jean-Baptiste. Up till now, he was the one who had drunk the most. He didn't have nausea, but a kind of very hard and very rapid marble swirled behind his forehead. However, a violent need to be quiet and to loosen his belt had taken hold of him without warning. Dominique detected at a glance that his brother felt bad; he was accustomed to deciphering the face of their youngest brother, Philippe. He moved closer to Jean-Baptiste and whispered:

"Is it the Martini?"

"What?" groaned the child. "'Cause I …"

"What about you, Dominique, make one up! You didn't say any!" François Boitard was shouting.

Dominique shrugged his shoulders. It was true that the kids annoyed him … they were … neither fish nor fowl, endless. If you gathered together a few that were the same age and of like character, it was like opening all the faucets in a house and not being able to shut them off.

François said:

"… And what if I told you that I make you eat shit from a bottle from a can in powder form and from a tube?"

"And me, in square in triangle in diamond in trapezoid?"

"And me, in Moscow in Paris in Peking and in Rome?"

"And that I can piss on your bus crack?"

"And that I can make you eat shit in a bury-toe?"

"And me, in a torna-toe?"

"And me in a toe-truck?"

"And me in Toronto-toe?"

"And I finger you in the bloop blap bloop?"

"And I finger your bim bim box?"

"And I finger your bum bum broom? And I …"

"Shhh! That's enough!" begged Dominique.

He glanced around for the bottle of aperitif. He took on an almost severe air:

"You're nuts to get drunk like this. No wonder there are screw-ups afterward."

The boys protested that they hadn't touched a thing. The bar of the villa, truth be told, was so well-garnished that they could have had enough to fall dead drunk in less than an hour. What they lacked was food. The villa was the residence of a Parisian family who came there two or three months a year. The whole neighborhood of the beaches was dotted with similar properties. A good half of them were, at this moment, unoccupied. The boys had tried one at random, not to burglarize, but simply to enjoy the comfort, to have fun, to meet up. The awkward and scrupulous presence of Dominique bothered them a little. There wouldn't be any damage. They weren't even wearing any gloves.

The Gassé brothers were enchanted by the invitation. François Boitard had charmed them. They had never said so many curse words in their entire lives, least of all, in front of each other. They had thus discovered that they knew the same ones, a rather unsurprising similitude, since they attended the same high school. François could only surpass and surprise them by forging words, by composing aphorisms. When you are the son of a famous philosophy teacher, it's the least you can do.

Dominique Seignelet, for his part, was meeting the children for the first time, and it was also his first crime. Since Jean-Baptiste had told him the story of the old lady with a heart condition, and rolled out the secrets of their gang, Dominique experienced confused and painful feelings. He had gathered that Jean-Baptiste was, perhaps, exaggerating his responsibility. The old woman hadn't exactly died when she saw him, Jean-Baptiste, specifically. But the child, who had at first sworn to his brother to break up with the gang and to renounce any felonious activity, hadn't kept his oath. On the contrary, he had little by little incited Dominique to accompany him on his strange outings. He had made him witness to certain exploits—shoplifting, for example. Dominique's morality was essentially composed of timidity, prudery, and fear of corporal or emotional punishments. Jean-Baptiste possessed none of those traits of character: it was natural (understood Dominique) for him to dare to commit any act he believed was innocent.

Jean-Baptiste, however, had so far not succeeded in dragging him in. As a matter of fact, the gang had splintered into a number of informal groups: meetings happened only by chance, they didn't organize or conspire together anymore, and there no longer existed an army in which to enlist Dominique or any new recruits.

There was nothing untoward in this debacle. Things had begun unpremeditated and without objective, they had continued by chance. It was obvious that the Glairat boy would have liked to create, if not to lead, a small commando unit composed the way it was today. Only Dominique didn't fit in. His age, the difference in height with the four others, etc., weren't essential inconveniences. But, despite his kindness, he displayed too deep an aversion for all of the things that excited and gratified the kids. He was like a five or six-year-old kid, simple, oafish, and would have been an encumbrance.

"And you were saying there'd be preserves!" politely complained Camille Gassé. Everyone was hungry.

Pantry items in the kitchen had turned out exactly null: some coarse salt, a heeltap of cloudy vinegar, some packets of Alsatian yeast, starch or flour dust sprinkled with mouse turds. Jean-Baptiste, who'd come back to his senses, rose all of a sudden and cried pompously:

"I know!"

They stared at him with outraged attention, observed a caricatural silence. The boy unveiled his thought slowly:

"In some houses … When people stockpile … They keep shit to eat …"

"Yeah! Yeah! Yeah!"

"Well, they keep it … in … the … basement."

The last word produced a disappointment. They'd never heard of such a thing. Vacationers and tourists who'd hide the snow peas, the hunter sauces, and the boxes of pasta they hadn't consumed in their basement from one season to the next? Inconceivable. He was drunk, pickled, plastered, blitzed. He was hammered, shit-housed, sloshed, loaded and over-loaded, Jean-Baptiste! The child protested:

"Not true! Some of 'em have whole collections!"

"Of camembert boxes, right."

But they got up and went to look for the basement.

"It would be good to try out all the houses like this."

"Yeah. And if we don't jizz it up too much, people won't even call the cops."

"Yeah, that's what we need! Not muck it up! No harm no foul! Like camping!"

"What for, no! No! We gotta bust it up!" François protested. "Break everything! Drink everything! Fuck it all up! Otherwise why do people's houses? I might as well stay at home, then."

The villa, strictly speaking, didn't have a basement. There was only a single room downstairs, made of raw concrete, where the boiler was, with a little workbench and several cases of champagne.

"Break 'em or drain 'em?"

This serious problem led to a prolonged discussion. Dominique was for not touching anything. The bottles were warm. The clock was ticking. The Gassé brothers would willingly have popped a few corks, but as a game, without any drinking, and without any glass shards. François and Jean-Baptiste campaigned for clamor, destruction. Dominique insisted: the more serious the damages, the higher the risk of having the police on their asses when the vacationers found out. If one single person from the neighborhood remembered having seen their gang prowling around here ...

"On our asses?" cried Boitard. "Us? The ass-lice on the pole? What, what? Never! Never! The police is ..."

He expressed his idea through a complex grimace, with sound effects. Nonetheless, the Gassé brothers fell in with Dominique's opinion, and Jean-Baptiste, attentive to the sole immediate danger—returning home late to the Seignelet homestead—saw his own enthusiasm grow tepid. Deprived of a public, François Boitard gave up in turn.

That evening, Maurice Glairat had to admit to himself that Humières wasn't as unpleasant as rumor had it. Laure and he had invited the old intellectual to their house for dinner, and against all expectation, Humières had accepted. Since summer vacation had begun, it was true that Saint-Rémi had been losing its most brilliant citizens, the prefecture, on the other side of the water, didn't fare better, and Paris was worse still. Humières must have been bored stiff, with his bearish character and sedentary habits. Despite everything, Glairat felt that the deference the old eccentric displayed was not unrelated to his, Maurice Glairat's, growing reputation. To host Humières at his house was to hold a concrete, dare one say palpable proof of social achievement. People would hear about it.

"At first, I considered ... hmm ... titling this piece ... hmm ... *The One-eyed Diva* ... you see ... the allusion, well ..."

"Darling!" said Laure Boitard. "What foolishness!

"A stupid idea, indeed," grumbled Humières. "And was the ... the text cast in the same mold? ... Plagiarism, pastiche, or charge?"

The evening would be extremely brilliant. All that stood in the way was the problem of the children. They had spent the day at the beach (excellent thing, that they'd seduced the little Gassés) but they'd be back any minute. Glairat didn't know whether Humières tolerated teenagers and young cretins. It was highly improbable, since he displayed a ferocious hatred for the senior boys and girls at the high school. Rumor had it that he only appreciated kids who were less than three. A nanny in the heart of every misanthrope. Pregnant women withered on the stalk.

"The text … my dear Humières … the text … Just imagine me at thirty, thirty five … a virgin, let's face it … a virgin … The text! Oh! … I only recall those first lines which …"

"… *that*. Not which. Recall those first lines *that*," cut in Humières.

"No no no!" cried Glairat, offended. "I insist on the *which* that scandalizes you! I insist! Is it not … Hmm. For …"

Maurice was marvelous, thought Laure Boitard. He was only drinking light kir royals. He was master of the game. The other old cunt. An out-and-out alcoholic. *Which. That. Which.* Which memories I recall. Which recalling I memorize. Moron. He disgorged it like a plughole. Dirty plughole. Gray. Skeleton.

"That? … Or …? H …"

"Yes," said Humières, grabbing "that," which is to say the champagne. He was wearing the ridiculous bowtie of a music teacher, a rather white shirt, a rather blue suit, black shoes that were extraordinarily thick, round-toed, and which made, even on the carpet, a strong boot noise.

(Slippers asylum. Assault. Pan fear. Of the worl. Him. Enormous boats … how … Barges. Say barges slang. Barf. No. Not. Cradles. Walk in the. Armored cradles. Shod. Blockhaus. De-shoed goes crying. Cribbing mama. Tumble accordion. He has. Fear.)

"And did you save your *Myopic Diva?*" said Humières, cackling. His amiability had something of the abject.

"Oh, certainly not! Certainly not! … Hmm … I don't even think I ever re-read it. I was piling up sheet after sheet…"

Maurice Glairat was lying. He had carefully pressed his first piece in a fat file with the others. He shamelessly re-read himself, relishing it, each time he felt the urge for absolute literary pleasure. None of the texts had been finished. Glairat didn't fancy himself a writer; it was rather a stage of his evolution … A …

"It was simply a … hmm … a stage, the writing … a step towards—please allow me to dare this disparaged word, my dear Humières—a step towards maturity. Literature …hmm… has an infantile side hmm … which …"

"Darling!" cried Laure Boitard. "I am not of the same opinion! Please understand, Humières, Maurice must *write*, absolutely."

"And after this story of the bald vagina or what have you?" asked the old teacher, politely.

"After, oh … Like all writers, I'm afraid," said Glairat in a negligent tone. He'd have liked to know whether Humières imagined himself a scribbler as well. A life so hollow. He wasn't spending all his time reading was he? Oh yes, the mysterious visitors. The obscure intrigues. The little Machiavellian plans minutely combined on blotter leaves that were immediately burned afterwards. The favors of this world's highest powers. Fibs. An old peon who makes believe. Residues of an honorable family, detritus protected by his name. Smoke and mirrors.

"He-llo. He-llo!" said François-Gérard, parodying his father as he walked in. "What? … Again with the champagne? What a day!"

He recognized Mr. Humières, whom he often spotted at the high school. The old man, seated very low, gave him a bony hand, curled up into a pinch, and let it be taken without shaking that of the child.

"Amélie-Lyane isn't with you, sweetheart?" said Laure.

"No! She's having a fuck downtown! I think with the two Gassés!"

"François-Gérard, my son …" said Glairat, "I will be … no, I wouldn't say happy, or desirous … well … a wish … a profound joy … very pure … that you display this evening … hmm … yes, for our guest, indeed … but also for our joy, I say it and I'll repeat it … if you, thus, showed us the … extraordinary refinement of your manners … your language … in short, could you be polite? Flood … hmm … us with delicacies?"

There was a certain tension in Glairat's monologue. François could sense it. Tough luck. He was frustrated by his escapade, his new crime. He would have liked to have sacked the villa. Instead he was condemned to playing the insipid child for a whole evening to help his father hit on an old cunt. Scutwork. Anyway, he'd obey.

"Uh, well, dad," he said in an exaggeratedly contrite, aggrieved, and comical tone. "I know I gotta make bank! … Well, anyway, Amélie-Lyane really is with the Gassés. I've got no idea why, but she's there. Poor kids! If it was me … I'd hide in my jeans."

As he spoke, he had insolently poured himself a raspberry champagne, and had slouched across an armchair.

"Sweetheart, did she at least indicate a time when … Don't tell me it's for Benoît and Camille that she … You do enjoy giving a paradoxical turn to your declarations, don't you?" questioned Laure Boitard. This evening, she predicted that she'd be a bit bestial, a bit authoritarian, and a bit motherly. François would certainly get it, in light of the tone. He had a sense for ambiances.

"Yeah," François began leisurely. "We'd all left Amélie at the beach …"

(Well. It's alright. He got it. What a stick in the mud. Humières squeak freaks. Serves him right. He hates them. Drunk look. Amé. fucks the little Ca. & the little Be. Pip pip pip. Take out. The. Salads. Not too icy. That old cu hasn't yet said a single intelligent thing. In fifteen years it'll be me. Same model. I'll have a Chanel style suit. Keep his wits for. Him. Pretends that he. Oh yes. Very well, Amélie very. President Gassé's dwarf. Cradle one under each arm. So Amélie got him. Gifted young girl. A real horse. Rings under his eyes. François onanizes himself. No Pill for the boys. It's true that.)

"… And if Mrs. Gassé wants to have her stay for dinner she'll call. I feel like I need an aspirin 'cause …"

A sybaritic migraine was beginning to grip the boy's skull. He also felt like masturbating before dinner. But headaches made this pleasure painful, shooting pain, needles. At least he could eat with a dick smell on his fingers, a way to spice up the food, the conversation. But no, not even that. He had gone swimming in the early afternoon. It couldn't regenerate that fast. And François didn't enjoy the smell of anuses. What a nasty, nasty evening. He got up.

"… And decided to confess to us that he freelanced for the Intelligence community! … And that's the mystery!"

Glairat brought his glass to his lips. Humières deigned to snicker. Intelligence. Right. People would make up anything.

"Thirty-sixth subaltern," added Laure Boitard. "Can you imagine, Humières, what there is to fish for on our poor island! Subversive! … They probably gave him a hundred francs a month! … Or a year …"

"How palatable," said Humières.

"Very palatable!" said Glairat. "From here, I can see the tenor … hmm … of his reports, hmm … The sub-prefect brought, hmm, an inflatable British-style doll, from Great-Britain … long toothed, no breasts, no ass, smile and measurements hmm, Duchess of Windsor … Ha, ha, ha. Came in yellow or tartan."

"Ha, ha. What you're saying here about British ladies is quite false, Maurice!" said Laure Boitard. "But anyway, yes, this poor

Knutysson's reports … The laughing stock, I suppose, of the … Because indeed …"

"I much appreciate it," said Humières. "Poor Knutysson, you said it."

In his room, François had flung himself on his bed and unbuttoned his pants. He was vaguely fiddling with himself not knowing what to think about. He was mostly waiting for the aspirin to kick in. The vermouth from the villa was refluxing in the form of multiple bitter vegetable tastes that hijacked him up to the nostrils. The prospect of having to sit down to dinner any minute horrified him. And having to speak. And to hear. And to answer. And to see. He didn't feel nauseated. Instead, the finger of champagne that he'd swallowed had calmed his stomach. His malaise was more abstract. He … he'd had enough of being a child. That was one way to say it. François was thinking bubbles.

Four or five times a year, Laure Boitard was an intrepid cook. In that case, she needed a difficult, unsettling, formidable audience. Then, instantaneously, the sardine salads with apricots, the rabbit with vanilla and the oysters with sweet chestnut cream hatched as if by magic under her inspired fingers. A creative warmth overpowered her. She would boldly sculpt her dishes, generally without tasting them—so as to be surprised at the end. She had "the gift," she progressed in confidence. Beware the innocent, farm-raised chicken when, after having fondled him dreamily as she enumerated the contents of the refrigerator to herself, she was suddenly struck by illumination. Beware the vegetables, the crustaceans, and the spices. The most inoffensive can could transform itself into a mortal weapon. Such were the perils and beauty of Art. The one who seeks finds, alas.

Tonight, however, she had bridled her talent. This grinch of a Humières surely had anachronistic culinary tastes; she did not wish to displease. She had prepared some cold dishes, then they would entertain themselves grilling skewers on a balcony barbecue. Insignificant, but neat, digestible.

The telephone rang. It was Amélie-Lyane, who announced that she would be dining with Mrs. Gassé. The latter exchanged some pleasantries with Laure Boitard. "And what will you eat?"

"Such courteous delightful people, those Gassés!" she said after she'd hung up. "Unfortunately we'll have to forego Amélie-Lyane."

"Gassé?" said Humières. "The fisheries, eh? Right, I believe you. Plump fortune. Black market, denunciations, racketeering. That's old history. A charming man, today. Excellent company, excellent. Family of the future. Tradition. Everything."

The comment cast a chill. What Humières had just said was well known. But why recall it, why resuscitate old hatreds, and besides, did he, Humières, socialize with more innocent people? A bigwig is a bigwig, it's take it or leave it, and let he who had never, etc., throw the, etc. For that matter … in the end.

"You frighten me, Humières," said Maurice Glairat at last. "Your way of … your desire for … such intransigence …"

"Laure, ahem, dad, I, I'm not feelin' good, not feelin' good at all," said François, who had reappeared. "I better go to bed. Can't eat. Everything's … spinning. Ow. Seasick. My head."

Permission to retire was granted. They were rather relieved; Humières had practically blanched at the kid's entry. (Such visceral hatred of. Of everything. Of everything. What does he like? Sterile. Dead. What's constructive about … Nothing. Nothing. Pure negation. Blindness. Mouth. Sweeps. Destroys. Bastard. The word. Bastard. I knew it. The word. We should, we shouldn't. Maurice leans on. No. Red herring. Only sure sign, love. To lean on lo. Secret success. No, a pack of hate. To make believe he is lucid. That if he spoke, he.)

"I like your son very much, what a pity!" said Humières suddenly. "Very pretty boy. Adorable. He must throw the pederasts into a frenzy. You haven't had any problems of the sort yet?"

Maurice Glairat, annoyed, smiled with a protective air.

"François-Gérard, my dear Humières, is at that age when … hmm … friendships, hmm … are certainly ardent but … highly pure …"

"No, no," cackled Humières, "I meant getting his butt cheeks pinched. Molested, that is. He is very … I confess that I …"

"It would be," said Glairat pompously, "a great intellectual enrichment for him, oh, how great, surely! But … the question, I mean, let's say, of reciprocity … Have you considered that? I believe he is … hmm, rather a tease: he's my son … Hmm."

Laughter. Humières admitted that at his age, his sense of humor and his love wouldn't go as far as having his butt pinched by a young boy. But even still, the boy was toothsome. He really understood those who, younger and more audacious … François came in again.

"I'm fucked. Fucked. I confess everything. I confess. I'll drop everything. This is my last hour. Oww. A wild tasting poison … Oh, hmm, can I go outside? To breaaaaaaa-tttthh-hhhe? Otherwise, it'll be flip flop flap flap. Thanks Maurice! … Bye sir."

He exited. Humières devoured him and said:

"What we should ask the connoisseurs, Glairat, is whether they prefer the mug or the derriere? At twelve the two are so … worthy of one another. Sublime passion."

That sarcasm didn't go over well. They refilled the glasses. Then they noticed that, since he'd arrived, Humières hadn't pronounced a single sentence that was directly disagreeable to his hosts. He seemed to particularly appreciate the house, the champagne, the sofa; and he let Glairat blather on without interrupting him, and he even egged him on.

"This July is very cool!" he said. "Will you be going on vacation soon? I never leave Saint-Rémi. Truly. What's the use of seeking out desert islands at the ends of the earth when we have all this? I stay home. Amongst ourselves."

In the street, François breathed deeply. It wasn't because of his pretend malaise, but from anxiety. Just a moment ago he'd decided to abandon his family, to stop being a monkey. To leave at once and without a thing. Besides, they wouldn't do anything to him if he came back one day. He'd write them a letter, tomorrow, so they wouldn't be scared. They'd have a bad night or two, that would shove a stick in their spokes.

But where to go? François didn't know about Julien's hideout. Who to ask? At this hour, difficult to go to a buddy's house without stumbling on their parents.

François resolved to wait until the next day. He would ask Guillard. He would spend the night outside.

Or no. Why not pay a visit to the Gassés? It would seem like a joke. He'd surprise his sister and the others during dinner. He'd snatch something to eat—and maybe some money. He'd incite Camille into following him, to run away as well. They'd go off peacefully and sleep in the villa they'd sacked this afternoon.

The plan was excellent. François absolutely had to convince one or the other of the Gassés, maybe both. As for the Gassé parents, they were too civilized for the unexpected apparition of Amélie-Lyane's little brother to embarrass them. But he had to hurry.

François crossed the bustling neighborhood. Despite his entertaining projects, he felt melancholic and alone. There were lots of tourists in town; the rich vacationers seemed happy. They were mostly couples. Used-up people who pretended to be phony youngsters, like François' parents, and who offered themselves the caricature of gentleness, cheekiness, and love once they'd passed fifty, when they'd finally acceded to the higher-up positions and the better money, after half a century of servility and gloom. All of a sudden, gerontocracy touched them with its grace. Those piteous, crumpled, moron-like and nearly dead doormats would invent a mask, a voice, convictions, and, with hairpieces, dentures, light clothing and slimness, mime the freedom and freshness that henceforth they would be contributing to strangle and destroy in those younger than themselves. In gerontocracy, a quinquagenarian was finally able to have an adolescence, and hop, chirp, "create," seduce, and make love. François, cleaving through the crowd of the well-to-do, recognized, suffered, and execrated this carnival of the old. It was like at home. He wasn't only a fetus. Instead, he was something invisible. A virtuality. In thirty years, perhaps, mysteriously, he would be granted permission to be born, to have the first inkling of an appearance and a hint of a voice. He felt a strange distress. He took the nearly deserted avenue that led to the Gassés.

"No, it is not hot! Start with the side of the plate!" squealed Raymonde Seignelet. She herself was avidly hoovering her soup, cooled by this sipping from the tip of a spoon.

Mr. Seignelet was turning his plate and sampling prudent spoonfuls from the periphery of the liquid. It was a delicious summer soup, a fish soup. They'd eat the fish later, with a white caper sauce.

"Well Philippe?" said Mrs. Seignelet. "What's with you? Isn't this soup good? … What do you mean mmmmmmm? Is it good or what. It isn't good?"

"It is," said Philippe.

"So eat. We're not gonna wait for you all night. We're almost done. Look at your brothers, they're done almost too."

"It's *too* hot," Philippe dared to say. He blushed very hard.

"What do you mean too hot? I told you to eat it from the edge."

"Succulent, my dear," asserted Robert Seignelet. "Your fish soups—no, dear, your fish *potages*—are authentic, I'd say, culinary success stories. Succulent. Mmm …"

"Tsk, tsk," said Mrs. Seignelet, "right, betcha it don't beat the soup in the can! Their Provençale soup, Provençale, did you hear that! But just ask those little brats if they don't like that better, the canned ones, ask 'em! They spit on everythin' you do for 'em and they don't even say thank you! … Took me two hours to make this soup! Two hours! You betcha they don't give a shit! A can, I'ma stick it up their ass! A can alright! Ain't worth a damn, this or shit!"

Raymonde Seignelet's tone wavered this evening. She seemed to possess some remnant of good humor and joviality, which inspired and nourished the only sort of volubility she knew to demonstrate, irascible, parasitic, on the edge of anger. You couldn't tell if she was going to stick to those rambling and amiable nasties, or pour on the fury, the cries, the true rages, and justice.

Philippe hated fish, capers, and soup. Tonight's menu would be a parade of tortures. Mrs. Seignelet cooked the lowest quality products with the most uncouth recipes. Foodstuff, in her hands, thus went from mediocre to foul, from insignificant to inedible, from dubious to pestilence. She didn't put in as much work as she pretended; she knew how to produce this kind of metamorphosis in the blink of an eye.

Mr. Seignelet, impatient for wine, scraped the bottom of his plate and, with a large movement of the tongue, licked the back of his spoon. He sincerely loved soup. And not to soil the tablecloth.

"Lemme point out that I even thought 'bout the white wine!" chittered Mrs. Seignelet, in a tone of significant reproach.

"I noticed," said her husband, as he pulled the liter of yellowish and icy liquid towards himself. "I noticed it's ice-cold. I really appreciate it. You can really appreciate something without saying a thing. I really appreciate it, dear. Thank you, dear. I know how to recognize what pains you …"

"I didn't take top shelf!" cried Mrs. Seignelet. "But for the price they're askin', it should come with a carwash! Anyway, it's all the same shit. They just switch up the bottle. Ain't nothin' but the bottle. Slap some flashy ass stickers on 'em, and there you go, you're payin' twice the price for window dressin'. Oh, they know their way around a wallet those bastards! … Careful tho', it's got eleven percent."

"Exactly … absolutely … absolutely right …" answered Mr. Seignelet in a low voice. But he was rather embarrassed, white wines violently upset his stomach. After one or two glasses, he'd have to maneuver adroitly to return to the usual red wine. Too bad for the bitterness caused by the fish. But he would eat so little of it.

"Come on, there's some left! You aren't gonna leave three poor spoonfuls in there, are you? Bertrand! Your plate! Dominique! … Ain't you done yet Philippe? What! You lookin' for a slap? That what yer waiting for? That what yer waiting for?"

Philippe said no. Besides, the soup was easier to handle once it had cooled off. The tomato taste stood out, the aroma of rusty iron softened, and a nice pissy effluvium timidly emerged like the smell of the front of the underwear on Saturdays (the Seignelets changed underwear every Sunday morning). He was more afraid of the fish. It was usually a big clump of cod, whose bones and stock, with a bunch of heads and parings from other critters that Mrs. Seignelet would claim "for her cats" at the fishmonger, were used to prepare the soup—which was the water of this dully colored, spiced, and floured gruel, more liquid than upholsterer's glue, and even more odiferous. The child would drag the strong tasting fish with the big fibrous fins interminably around his plate, and would often prefer a slap, squeals, and being put to bed violently. But the worst was the sauce: water, flour, grease, vinegar, and the abominable little verdigris-marbled greenish pimples also known as capers. Among all of the things that Philippe had witnessed being eaten but had never been able to find edible, this condiment ranked among the highest. On the contrary, his mother found them delectable and never hesitated to shoulder this expense, this gracious gift.

That day, to vary her recipe, she had stored fish, capers and sauce in a baking dish, had sprinkled smashed dried bread on the gluey surface and had put the whole thing in to brown. She was greedy for such treats. She had also vigorously boiled cut up potatoes that she christened steamed potatoes. You'd have to absorb, rake through it all, under the threat of thunderstorms, war and lamentations.

Gluttons, Bertrand and Jean-Baptiste were happy. Dominique, who was less voracious, would attempt to escape the chore of *seconds* and would probably be reprimanded, called scrawny. The unknown variable was Philippe's conduct, or his fate.

And yet, in summertime, meals were more serene than during the school year. Mrs. Seignelet grew negligent. The good weather, the beach, the little garden stole away her world. She had days that were less encumbered by presences, and, provided that her brood shouted as far away as possible, she could sufficiently contain her own yowling.

The Seignelets would go on vacation during the second half of the month of August. The expedition took place in an automobile and lasted two weeks. They'd probe the continent. Mr. Seignelet educated his family. Meadows, roads, fields, domestic animals, Michelin maps, snack bars housed on famous sites, old towns, dams (he had an obstinate and unexpected taste for reservoirs, and for the sources of rivers, waterfalls, lakes, glaciers and gorges), historical museums, great men's dwellings, folkloric and savory manifestations, wood crafts, regional costumes, country wines and farmstead marcs: these were all pretexts to load his family in the car and, over the course of interminable days of driving during which, badly seated, you had to look, listen and keep quiet, he dispensed to his ungrateful progeny the startling knowledge that he trawled from guides, automobile magazines, winery pamphlets, and the lyrical, endless and bombastic prose of the tourist offices.

These instructive holidays presented only one dark spot: Philippe's health and stomach, now and forever. With their repercussions on Mrs. Seignelet's mood. That was why, if they left the island satisfied, they rapidly reached a point of saturation with tourism and were relieved to come back.

"Hurry up, shit, I'm burning myself, shit!" cried Raymonde Seignelet. "The placemat, quick, here! Shit, they don't give a damn that I'm burning myself, huh, the little brats, they could give two shits!"

She put down the fish platter, squealed once more, and dropped the kitchen towels that had served to protect her hands, hands she examined as she blew on them. Her food had bitten her.

Her pleasant mood returned. Mr. Seignelet finished the white wine by pouring it for his eldest son. Bertrand winetasted the acid. He caught a smell of old Gruyère rising from his crotch: he hadn't gone to the beach today. He had been studying a nasty softcover book, entitled *Grammar of Love*, by a doctor. Among other things, the author disapproved of blowjobs, which he called *hideous oral sexes*. This expression greatly tormented Bertrand, capsized him, and would cost him several ferocious hand jobs. *Hideous* was just too successful.

Pauline Ambreuse prepared her syringe:

"Your grandson isn't here?"

"That rascal," said old Viaud, "that bandit? You bet he isn't!"

She sighed. She didn't kick up a fuss for the shot: she lifted her skirts to her waist, turned her behind, and lowered her ecru canvas pants and her cotton underwear. Dr. Ambreuse had to suppress a laugh every time. The old woman would bend forward, leaning onto the back of a chair. As someone who is accustomed to pain but who attaches to it neither prudery nor sense, she would give a good brutal "Hunh!" when the needle sank in, then she would forget about it.

"Won't Alain be coming back to eat?" asked Pauline Ambreuse as she slowly discharged the syringe.

"I can't hear anything from behind!" cried the old Viaud.

The doctor repeated, in a forced and didactic voice.

"Oh yeah, sure he comes home to eat!" said the old lady. "Oh yeah! You're right about that. Like a rat he does. Like a rat. And he makes a clean sweep, you bet your sweet patootie! A clean sweep, so long as he steals it! Sure thing! ..."

"That's good, he needs to eat ..." Ambreuse went on in the same voice. "And so do you! You have to eat well and shit well! It's important to shit well! Very good!"

"Oh that, that, my dear, oh no, I wouldn't say everything is peachy there! Oh, no no no. Some days are not good! Not good at all."

"You eat too many potatoes! Beans! Ham!"

"No," protested lady Viaud. "No! That's what would put me right in the trenches! The beans! No! Let me tell you, I do too hard! It gets blocked! You see! It gets stuck I don't know where, and then try and go and get it! Real rocks!"

She straightened up, let go of her skirts, and dusted herself off. Dr. Ambreuse liked to stay and chat, though, usually, she wouldn't come so late. It was the length of the day that determined her working hours.

The two women went back to the kitchen. Mrs. Viaud offered her an aperitif, an orange Ratafia that she topped off with a very fresh red wine. She served them half a mustard glass each. It had a vague taste of raw liver, of gland extract.

Alain Viaud appeared at that moment. The old lady insulted him, showed him her fist. The rascal! Viaud didn't even say hello to Dr. Ambreuse: he climbed up to his room, gripping single-handedly at the ladder. With the other hand, he was squeezing a chunky package under his turtleneck.

His room was the attic of the minuscule hovel. The old bag

couldn't climb up. There, Viaud hoarded an indescribable and varied booty, more abundant and brilliant than the treasures of the magpie's nest. But in fact he was indifferent to the collection.

"What are you hiding now, you bad monkey?" cried the old lady. She hadn't missed the bump under the turtleneck.

Suddenly Dr. Ambreuse had the singular desire to climb the ladder and visit his hideout. She asked for permission. To her surprise, Viaud accepted. The grandmother copiously approved what she thought would be an inspection, and she sat down.

Viaud had rapidly concealed the package he had just brought back under his mattress. Pellisson had finally discovered Mrs. Arnauld's nest egg, and Alain Viaud had immediately demanded his share. Hervé was to keep Joachim and Marie-Antoine's. Viaud had thus received nine thousand francs in one-hundred-franc bills—nine hundred thousand francs, as Joachim would have said. Come tomorrow, Viaud would give all of it to Julien Roquin, as a gift.

He talked long but little with Dr. Ambreuse. The latter saw detritus rather than treasures in the child's collection. She felt moved to have tamed him. She sincerely loved him. Viaud hardly opened up. He grew very unsettled, suspicious, proud. He felt a brutal pang of affection for the Doctor. He didn't show it. They parted startled.

That same evening, the corpse of Jean Roquin, the father, was discovered in a saltworks on the Eastern coast. He had been stabbed.

9

Following a very short investigation, they arrested Simone Roquin. The papers published Julien's story.

The father stabbed, the child missing, the mother (according to the neighbors) furious and insane: it was a throwback to another century.

The two eldest sons were called back from the barracks. They were handsome lads, brutal and wary. They furrowed their eyebrows, didn't badmouth anyone. You'd have thought they were moles.

All the assets belonged to the father.

Captain Lorge, since he was in charge of this new case, felt like linking it to the ones he'd been handling. He supposed that Jean Roquin was—as is often the case—an invert murdered by a thug. One evening, this Mr. Roquin must have tried to rape his young son, Julien, who had fled for that reason. Because normal fathers rape their daughters, according to the murmurings of the social workers who frequent this crowd and who complain that, among a thousand family rapes, a thousand legitimate incests, there aren't even ten that the high court judges agree to take into consideration. To pronounce the degeneracy of a man's fatherhood? It was abortion, only worse.

Yes, it's fortunate that the Roquin case is that of a pervert, thought Captain Lorge. It was easy to understand the unfortunate spouse. Making an effort not to harm tourism, Mr. Lorge had apprehended and questioned the few Saint-Rémi boys known to be snitches and sell-outs. He established a thousand reasons for tormenting them, but no grounds for indictment.

With rage in his heart, Captain Lorge had to relinquish the culprits that he would have liked to keep. At least he had made them sweat; that would teach them not to have murdered someone on time.

He had to make do with Simone Roquin. A virago, that was for sure. An adulteress? Decidedly, however solid, these leads weren't what they used to be. Druggies? Analysis of the Roquins' crops did not lead to the discovery of cannabis or poppy. Crazy? The psychiatrist described her as a spouse and a mother, *very impassioned* by these two duties. She had to be released.

Jean Roquin hadn't been dragged into the saltworks. The very readable tracks indicated he'd been on a walk. As for the murderer, it was clear he had walked in the grass and in the pools.

Unless the crime had been committed in an unusual way. The complex, erudite, almost shy autopsy report revealed everything early on. Everything, except the identity of the murderer.

The doctors had been surprised by the variety of the stabbing wounds. Dimensions, depth, placement, impact evoked the state of a cork target riddled with arrows of all shapes and sizes. A child's crime.

They concluded that Mr. Roquin had probably had a rendezvous at this saltworks: a note to be destroyed, which must have promised a mouthwatering meeting. His gay lover? His son? Who knows, a woman? A deal? Blackmail? Reasons for living.

As soon as he was done working, and before dinner, he had come here. On foot. It took fifteen to twenty minutes, at his age and from his house. He had found no one. All of a sudden, the arrows (penknives, kitchen knives, scout daggers …) had been loosed upon him. He had stumbled, turned, not seeing a thing. His lungs, filled with water, proved that the stabbing wounds, whether from thrusts or throws, had made him lose consciousness, but had not killed him. Jean Roquin had died by drowning, nose down in a pool of seawater. Then, the arrows had been pulled out.

The hypothesis of multiple assailants excited Captain Lorge. He didn't have time to think about it, someone was sent from Paris to investigate in his place. The rich had grown tired. They had solicited the central power. Jubilation. They looked forward to a spate of arrests just as, in times past, in the villages that convicts had to pass through, people awaited the passage of the galley crews, working sputum in their cheeks, stones in their palms, preparing their insults, indulging in all the violence and the shouts that they had denied themselves till that moment. And the people of Paris were going to root out and torture as they pleased all those whom the islanders wished to see *condemned*. Then they would go in droves to the other side of the water to check out the trial. They would yowl as was decent if ever the magistrate hesitated to confirm the guilt of having been arrested. In an inegalitarian regime, anybody the police touched was a scapegoat. Cops didn't take in just anyone. Being accessible to them meant you were already guilty. You were only innocent when the cop and the judge looked toward the horizon with vague eyes while you made what your fortune, your reputation, your relations, and your age allowed you to. Liberty and the law sold to the highest bidder.

However, on the island, the crime squad and their Parisian elite were treading water. It was all too country. The few local crooks—nightclubs, Sphynx-club, hashish, discreet pressures on the merchants, the exchange rate on fish and meats, invisible suggestions to the overly virtuous journalists, immaterial feed to the electoral coffers of the dominant class, candid infiltration of the factories and the syndicates—the crooks, real worker ants of the established order, weren't worried. And in relation to the Roquin case, those gentlemen from Paris found that the briefest and most just solution, the one that, in sum, would do the least harm to the designated culprit and appease tormented consciences, was that it was a crime of passion. Simone Roquin had to be consulted. To be assured that she'd murdered her husband (by hurling the fine—that word saved the day—*family* silver with no intention to kill: he had died by drowning, that was proven). And that she had committed this attempted murder, one that ended poorly but had a very pure intention, because Jean Roquin liked to hit on thugs. Such a husband, indeed, merited an acquittal.

Thugs? Simone Roquin foamed. She spoke of the Fouilloux. The cops, foregoing any forgeries since they'd finally been given facts, became intensely interested in Mrs. Roquin's jealousies. They had the girl followed for a few hours. She had a rendezvous with Old Guillard. They were arrested together. Consternation: Fouilloux wasn't alone at the old artisan's house. A certain Claudine Moraillon, thirteen and a half years old, her buddy, was also inside the pseudo Brittany-style dining room in oak-paneled particleboard. Red light ballets at a painter's house: the high-spirited journalists went all out. A palette, they said, that was a little too uniform: when would the blue period begin? It was the holidays after all; they had to sell *this*.

Old Guillard committed suicide in his cell the night following his arrest. Marc, his son of fourteen years or so who ran the risk of being taken in by the benevolent State, had fled and vanished. The two poor girls had been entrusted to a mix of doctors and nuns: they were reparable.

Julien smiled:

"So what, Guillard you're not into it any more? You won't touch it anymore?"

"No, no way. Why."

They were going to change hideouts. The dilapidated house was too dangerous. Too many people in there. Too many busybodies around. And the warm weather allowed for anything. This morning, they knew where to go. Julien radiated with an abrupt enthusiasm.

"'Cause you did it. It was for real! You remember!"

"Well, I don't do it anymore," said Guillard. He put on a funereal mien.

"Your father's dead. Mine too," Guillard said again.

"No," said Julien.

"What do you mean, no."

"No. I can't explain. But it's not the same."

"What. It is the same. We're fucked."

Julien ignored the remark:

"Your dad killed himself."

"Yeah. Well, yeah. Damn right he did. The bastards."

Marc Guillard made a face and shook his head in a way that meant that it was too hard to chitchat about that. "It is, it is."

"Well, my dad," Julien went on with a round, startled laughter that made his voice lisp, "it's not the same for me!"

He had an air, a calmness, the grace of wanting to take everybody in his arms and force solid clumsy kisses onto their cheeks:

"Mine got killed!"

He laughed abruptly.

"There you go. Mine got killed!"

Marc Guillard shook his head.

"Come on Dracula. Just say it's you who did 'em. Come on."

He sighed. The kids were a drag, with their imagination. A baby crying from hunger made more noise than a righteous man murdered. Pains in the ass, these kids, pains in the ass: you think you get life served on a silver platter. Well, thought Guillard, balls to them.

Julien smiled again, delicately; he wasn't offended.

"No it wasn't me. Anyway I don't know who it was. And anyway the cops don't either. They say he drowned. He got his schnozz all wet. That's what they say."

"Dracula, you're not scared?" groaned Marc Guillard.

Julien blushed and abruptly felt like showing Marc his tortured back. Now that there were so many inhabitants here, he was forced to go very far away to undress, bathe, or swim. The other boys pulled off their shirts under the sun (by hetero dressage, they had a vain prudery of their lower parts). Julien couldn't. He would have had to explain. The martyrized skin, under his fingers, mimicked an engraving of grapes in relief. He kept a shirt on, and bathing trunks.

"My mother's in prison," he added.

"Mine, she was dead," said Guillard.

This face-to-face made no sense. Marc wished to be stricken; Julien was happy. One of them had taken to hiding despite himself, the other by choice.

"Anyway, you remember you used to do it!" said Julien as he tapped the crotch on Marc's pants.

"Come on, I told you, fuck, stop it, fuck!" cried Guillard. He had stirred his penis in the Fouilloux's cunt. Could he, now, fall back on those errant ways, those virgin simulacra?

"If it's gnawing at you go see a whore!" he moaned.

Julien's expression turned to ice immediately. He felt offended. He spat on the ground without answering. He moved away.

He hadn't told anybody about the money Alain Viaud had brought him. The amount was incredible. So far he had never considered any project involving money. At best, you steal what you need: but you don't possess. Now, instead of inspiring dreams in him, this fortune prevented them. It seemed to say: Julien, make use of me. Nothing more, nothing less. What Julien wished for, he didn't know how to translate into money; and that which he knew how to calculate was nothing in the face of these nine wads.

Besides, decked out as he was, he wouldn't dare present a hundred franc note in a store. Only supermarket cashiers took the bill coldly, without worrying about the bearer. They'd seen too much, or not enough.

But, if Julien had gone anywhere to buy or pay for something, or for a pack of things that cost more than one bill, he'd have been immediately suspected, questioned, and seized. Alain Viaud's short million was only good to be frittered away: it was the same as a few hundred shoplifting excursions. It was nearly as difficult to get rid of, as these thefts would have been to carry out. The money was not really separable from those who had the right to possess it: they'd arranged it so that anyone else who spent the same sum would look like an imposter. Julien was poorer than ever.

He stopped against a fat rock and looked at the three new-bies. They were all older than he was except for the one with the big friendly ears, Camille, or it was very close. They were going for a swim.

Since the boys had arrived, Julien was feeling the weight of how much time had passed. He was the on-call brute. The austere old-timer, heavy, fraught; the one who was already in the cell when you got thrown in. The youngest among them avoided him. They feared him as they would a freak. And now, they even suspected that he'd killed his father, which flattered him but maintained an air of distrust around him. None of these children knew how to talk to one another. Who would have taught them? However, they each hoped for it, brooded on it, circled around it, dabbled in it, played a solitary role, suffered, was naked, and began to hate. Each of them had fled an infirm milieu, a family. They were among the maimed. They stammered, they limped, no word would ever be born, and no gesture would ever be invented. It was too late. Clashing crutches, prostheses, pains in phantom limbs, skull tops made of steel and screws, articulated hands, false teeth, leather noses, and glass eyes: shipwrecked children simulating seeing each other, touching each other, and speaking together. They were the survivors, the most nimble and the most combative of all. They all showed the others the one eye that hadn't been stabbed, the one arm that hadn't been chopped off, the sex organ that hadn't existed long enough to be pulverized, the ounce of brain no one had known how to extirpate and burn and which, by itself, tried to understand everything, to repair, to save, and almost to love and to imagine the world.

But among the gang no one else apart from Julien felt this. He felt the hollowness, the falseness, the mimicries, the effort, the fear, and the carrion. The boys, even Guillard, seemed to belong to the same species as the adults they had fled. They weren't mean, of course.

Julien decided to abandon them. He would pack up his stuff, his money, and would pretend he was going to the new hideout. But he would keep going far beyond it.

He would even leave this part of the island. It was too crowded. The risk of meeting the other boys, the enemies, was too great. Julien would go up north. Scattered villages, agriculture, no beaches, no ports, and no police. Forests, landscapes, numerous hamlets that were deserted forever. He would be like an adventurer who discovered an unknown land and took possession of it. In principle, he would give up spending his money. Stealing in-kind, from the houses and farms, would be more convenient for him, and almost less dangerous, since no one would see him. When you bought anything, on the other hand, you were forced to show yourself.

François Boitard reigned supreme over the two Gassé brothers. He had debauched them effortlessly: it was a farce. They'd take a wild vacation. They had the right. The parents would forgive them. They'd written to them.

The Gassé brothers weren't so sure that they'd be forgiven as willingly as François had assured them. The escapade delighted them but gave them much anguish. They still needed a few good reasons. Playing castaways made you unhappy when you didn't have permission from your parents.

François swept aside these fears. Benoît and Camille were mollusks. Let them drink a good draught, if they were afraid.

Weren't their days fun, lively, ideal? Wasn't it a thousand times better than anywhere else? They had never lived so large. They could completely do without adults. They ate what they wanted, when they wanted. They got sloshed. They lived three quarters in the buff. They were no longer ashamed of anything. They slept like pashas (from the villas, they had taken masses of bedding and household objects). Let the Gassés go home to their mommy, those brats, he, François, wouldn't do the same. They were free!

In reality, François would have suffered violently had Benoît and Camille abandoned the game. The three of them formed a little kernel of high school bourgeois kids very different from the other boys. Even those whom François had known for a while, like Guillard or Roquin, had changed character and ways. Of course: they had big troubles. They cohabitated by necessity. Their future was dark, sealed. If François had had to stay alone with them, he wouldn't have lasted long. As for the boys who would come visiting but didn't sleep in the lair, François had nothing to say to them. They were friends of Guillard, half-thugs in studded leather jackets, suburban morons. François was afraid of them, and even hated them. They ignored or mocked his gang of rich kids. They visibly restrained themselves from kicking their three asses. They chided Marc for having brought them in. The hatred was shared.

As for Guillard, he was in a tight spot. His big hold-up plans now embarrassed him. He found himself guilty, depraved. Danger, uncertain till then, had taken on a terrible hue after his father's arrest and suicide. Reality had taken a step further. The laws had confirmed their authority. What should he become? Would a big hit, several million, have improved the situation? Marc doubted it. Even if he were richer, where would he go, where would he live, where would he not be a suspect? For the next four years, the only place for Guillard would be the orphanage—or its tough equivalents. Otherwise he'd have to remain clandestine from here on out, solitary and vagrant. He didn't think he had the courage.

The boys from Roche-Notre-Dame had recently accomplished two very big jobs, the same night and on the same elegant street of Saint-Rémi. They had ransacked a pharmacy, then, having noticed a gunsmith and knife shop next door, they'd helped themselves lavishly. The theft of the medicines hadn't been their own initiative. Some older comrades had pushed them into doing it, giving them a list of products, labels. They would be resold as drugs. The profits would be considerable. The kids had gone for it. As for the weapons, that was for pleasure. Rifles, pistols, daggers. A delight. They had given Guillard a pretty Browning 6.35 with ammo. Marc had appreciated this kindness. To have a weapon and to keep it in his pocket gave him a profound sense of well being, as if the revolver was a world in miniature, possessed of a new geometry which one could open up at any moment to take refuge in. A spare planet, hard and dense, that Marc could join at the first big trouble. He had taken a long hike to practice shooting without the others hearing him.

Despite their bad boy style, their get-ups, their scary faces, and their voices that were already offensive and brutal like those of rookie cops, the kids from Roche-Notre-Dame were good guys, and courageous, thought Guillard. Too bad the bonds between him and them were still too loose.

"But why? Why? Aren't you going to tell me why?" Laure Boitard asked her daughter.

That was her constant theme, since François' disappearance in the company of the young Gassés. The two families, far from having chilled their relations, had strengthened them. They would discuss responsibilities later. For the time being, they had to find the children. And understand.

President Gassé was caught between the devil and the deep sea. The Fouilloux business was quite upsetting. There were those absurd deaths of the common folk. It could not be hushed up. And since the spring, the throng of news items solicited the attention of the entire island. There was talk of a plague. The good days were over.

Investigating the Fouilloux would reveal everything. The president needn't fear anything so excessive as a summons, an interrogation: he had obtained assurances on that score. But he could not prevent tongues from wagging. He already knew that he had been credited with having slept with Claire Fouilloux's friend, the one who was thirteen or so. Revolting calumny. People's malfeasance. How to refute it?

Thus he would see neither police nor judge, but hereafter his ways would be revealed to all. An essential part of his social facade, of his career, and of his ambitions would be ruined.

On the other front, there was the fugue of his two sons. Dragged in, obviously, by the young Glairat, the son of intellectuals. Even this influence seemed absurd to President Gassé. Few children on the island were better treated, more privileged, more satisfied with their lot. Calm, docile, even a bit dull. Mr. Gassé could not believe that this flat and well-raised passivity hid personalities rebellious and perverse, that one or two naughty escapades proposed by the son of an imbecile would have inflamed them. Benoît and Camille didn't flee. That was unthinkable. They had been kidnapped.

The idea of an abduction (in which young Boitard served as the worm) was the most satisfying. President Gassé developed it with his wife. He discovered on this occasion that Mrs. Gassé felt only a very hollow, very cold interest in their sons. While he neglected her, he had supposed her a good mother, making do with the consolations of her role. This was not the case. The boys' disappearance annoyed her prodigiously. She understood quite well why her husband hesitated to resort to extreme measures, to shake up the police, etc. She didn't believe it was an abduction:

the demand for ransom would have arrived by now. A sadistic kidnapping was ruled out: three children at the same time, two of whom, let's be honest, didn't really have what it took to awaken those kinds of passions … No, they were having fun, they'd return. Their letter didn't lie. Mrs. Gassé simply hoped they wouldn't have committed too many criminal acts, and that they would return soon enough for the trip she had planned: she wished to visit Indonesia. They made beautiful embroidery there.

President Gassé finally conceded to this dedramatized interpretation of the facts. And, seeing as his sons were indeed going to reappear docilely in no time, he merely engaged a private detective to sniff around the island a little, and he enquired about the harsh but elegant boarding schools that existed in Switzerland or in the Île-de-France. Mrs. Gassé agreed with this project of harsh internment. But let them come home, first!

Laure Boitard had taken a completely different stance. Her son wasn't, might never be, anyone's heir. She wouldn't think of considering an iron-fisted education. Recourse to the police, even to a private eye, repulsed her. But she absolutely had to understand. Digest. To reconstitute, writer-like, each step, each feeling, each second of the interior journey that her son had lived through, surely, to lead to this, this flight. She had never spoken so much, especially at home or without being paid.

Maurice Glairat, after the avalanche of cases surrounding the death of the produce vendor Roquin, has detected in himself the calling of a magus. His chronicles—the first about the two minor girls—were veering toward the prophetic. Their tone was biblical:

"… For indeed, this drama—and we must indeed affirm it—questions us. Implacably so. But no, oh! no! Infinitely much more so, it interrogates us! And I would even dare to think that, this being so, it speaks to us. It speaks to us, to each of us, to all. For it is terribly—Hideously? Oh! Let the pusillanimous among us hush! Your hour has passed! Enough!—terribly true. Isn't it what, fundamentally, caused our hasty indignation? In full good conscience—I'll risk, oh, the word!—one need answer yes. Yes—Yes but? … No. Time is running out. I must—we must, you must—utter our cry. For the heartbreaking, the mute little F***, she …"

The moral support given to the families was well appreciated, so too the discretion paid to the debauchees, and the heights of visions that were so profoundly lofty. So Glairat aggrandized day after day. His vehemence worthy of an agricultural expo was no laughing matter. It was said that he meant it as a kind of offbeat humor. Whoever denigrated Glairat was a bungler or was against the ideas defended by the columnist. What ideas? It would be indelicate to seek them out. They were, in short …

"I told you, he's a kid, he just wants to fuck around!" said Amélie-Lyane. "He'll be back here anytime now, he'll pull out a festoon of curse words, and basta. A baby. A dumb baby."

"But, Amélie-Lyane, if it was simply a matter of … puerility … no, no, that's impossible. He … can you imagine him returning here, and all of us starting over as if … no, no. He must have experienced something, you understand. Whatever that might be: something that was his own—and against us. Against us! But why? Why?"

"You're looking for explanations as if he was an adult," sighed Amélie-Lyane, as irritated as she was annoyed. "You're making up his psychology et cetera, you gotta be kidding! You're worse than dad! Frankly, much worse. Supposing that's even possible of course."

"Don't say that!" answered Laure Boitard. "Maurice, in my mind, has marvelously dealt with the whole thing. Marvelously! You don't realize. You call François a baby, but I find you … quite childish when you try to judge those who …"

"Fine, I get it," said Amélie. "The thing is, if you don't stop talking to me about François, simply because you're looking for someone to hen-peck, well then my good mother, I'm so sorry! You've lost me! Or else, maybe you want me to think that I'd be better off doing the same thing? 'Cause that's what I'm gonna end up thinking, if we go on with these little nicety-nice conversations! 'Cause if you just wanna shit on me, go right ahead, but why don't you just get to the point, that'd be more honest, instead of pretending you're worrying about your François. Whom you don't give two fucks about, by the way, and you know that better'n I do."

For an instant, this barrage from Amélie-Lyane petrified Laure Boitard. She denied any truth to it, mentally. It was out of the question that her daughter could say something true. Especially in that aggressive tone. Such violence! Such disorder! The poor kid.

"Sweetheart," said Laure Boitard at last, mollifying. "You're so completely wrong that I give up even … Can't you see at least up to what point you … That's also proof. That too. You speak of puerility, but have you felt—see?—have you felt what grave revolt, what heavy event in the end, he … . and you let yourself be dragged along into being crude, and ruining everything—it's unacceptable crudeness, sweetheart, because truly, I'd be happy if you would blame me for anything that flows through your mind—Anything! Anything! If that comforts you—but don't blame me by being crude, with youself, with both of you, I beg you. You're forming your personality … with difficulty, like all of us at your age … I understand, I know how much the maternal image can be mistreated at this time …"

"Oh fuck! Fuck!" yelled Amélie-Lyane all of sudden, getting up and giving a kick that flipped over the living room table and the drinks that were resting on it. "To hell with it! To hell with your salve! To hell with your psychology! To hell with your bullshit! Your bullshit! Shiiit! I've had enough of your shit!"

She left the room. Laure Boitard, cheeks on fire, hadn't moved. At that stage of identification-with-adults, such nervous fits were deeply troubling. And Amélie-Lyane really had no consideration for her, Laure, who was tortured by the boy's escape. It was the awkward age, so be it, but such egotism, such cruelty … Amélie hadn't gotten it from Maurice or from her, it was incredible. Grandmother Pinon?

Fruit juice stains, so difficult to lift from the woolen carpet. Laure sighed, her heart beat askew.

Julien Roquin followed a cliffside path with swift steps. The sun beat down upon him and flooded him with strength. The sea, around here, was long and round, more sparkling than elsewhere. You could see all of it. There were no boats.

His knapsack was full: it wasn't easy to steal things, and he liked his comfort. He had hijacked a marvel: a sleeping bag made for yachtsmen, big, cozy, waterproof, that the boys had unearthed from some villa or another. With this he'd be able to bivouac wherever, to be more discreet, more mobile than any animal. All his essentials, tested, sorted, reassembled ten times since he'd left the Roquin house, offered a similar convenience.

It must be this success that had caused his mood to change. And it had been such a long time that he'd wanted to break off from the others. A dream occasion. Here was his first true day of freedom. He walked past an overhanging, chalky coastline. He smelled the Ocean which stung him and enveloped him with millions of stars; he didn't have to hide any longer, to stop anywhere; knapsack on his shoulder, he was the king of this island. It wasn't the same island at all.

Summer was good for business at the Théret grocery. Pretty, the young girls were in the shop and served the clients. René lugged himself about, more or less naked. Mr. Théret counted, arranged, telephoned, calculated, made orders, read trade journals. Mrs. Théret prevailed over those chores and gave cutting smiles to the seasonal clientele.

The turnover was rather sizeable. So much the better, since the autumn would be worthless. They weren't getting rich; they were just getting by.

René was virtuous and unhappy. He knew all who had perpetrated those evil deeds reported by the papers. He had lost all penchant for revolt. He didn't even need to curb, here or there, a burst of anger, a disgust, or a retort that was a bit too sharp. His facial scar spread, grew tan, vaguely thick. He thought it granted him virility. Something he particularly needed. He found his penis really small. He had also learned, in a pocket medical dictionary, that difficulty in pulling back the foreskin was a formal defect that you ought to operate: it nurtured molds, unbeknownst to you. One day, a cluster of colorless worms with glossy undulations was going to come out of his tip. He wondered how to explain this to his parents so as to get an operation. Furthermore, the operation indicated by the dictionary was without nuance: circumcision. If there was something better it was more expensive, and probably wasn't covered by insurance (the dictionary, although " practical," didn't stoop to discuss money).

René Théret was aware of other bodily defects. He was told that he ran as if he wanted to bash his knees together at high speed. The image was hurtful. He also had a ridiculously long big toe on each foot, and it was becoming more pronounced with time. Thus his shoes either wounded his self-esteem or his toe. This embarrassment perhaps even contributed to his bizarre deportment when running, and to his more and more old-fashioned opinions on the subject of marriage.

For he would marry. He would be at least twenty-five years old. He would have grown a dirty blond, English tobacco, playboy-style moustache (he didn't yet know that these moustaches were chiefly the favorite appendage of virile queens). He would marry a very young and pretty virgin, who would have no opinion about toes or phimosis. They wouldn't have children. Or they would but only, of course, under such and such conditions. He wouldn't be a grocer. He liked to titillate the sciatic nerve of frogs and to activate the cog of a microscope. A white lab coat would be very becoming. Dr. Théret. Heads nodding.

He hadn't yet confessed this ambition to his parents. It would be, admittedly, a burden, a cross for them to bear. However, eventually, they would see him on television, operating live. It would be beautiful, moving, they would be well rewarded. He would smile very kindly to the little girl before her anesthesia, and this affectionate and noble smile would be particularly striking on screen. He would still be young.

He waited for autumn: he would give his all to the scientific subjects; he'd be an ace. The teacher—new to René, for he'd be passing on to what they called the high school—wouldn't believe that the junior high sent them such an exceptional recruit. René would understand it all. He always had the appropriate bearing for each teacher, according to his or her character. Besides, he was modest, solicitous, diligent, and thoughtful: he wished to rake in without delay all the knowledge that the master had strewn about. In a pinch, he would have him repeat:

"Mr. ... excuse me." (He'd moisten his lips; he'd be in the first row.) "I didn't hear everything."

In fact, none of the precious words would be lost upon him: but he wished to show that he loved and that he was loveable. He wished, supreme refinement, he, the first, the best, the undreamt of, the only, he wished to display a weakness! How beautiful the autumn would be!

"My little Théret, come come! ... Are you tired, my boy? ... Who'd like to repeat for Théret? Gentlemen?"

The teacher would be old. Another brown-noser, but less subtle, would read his notes (chemistry or biology: it would be too complicated or too risky to interrupt in mathematics). The teacher would say: "There you go. Is it clear, now, Théret? ..."

Théret would remoisten his lip avidly, but humbly. He (it was a little cavalier, but so charming! he knew that), he would shake his head respectfully, lovingly, to say yes, and would immediately lower his eyes. Knowingly, the teacher would pick back up, in a dryer tone. And there would be no risk of shifting off course after class: everything would happen during. That was what pleased René: to have it all while avoiding it all. He would not be the last of his kind the world would ever see. However, he had guessed that at this price, he'd only obtain simulacra: he would become a fake good pupil, a fake doctor, a fake husband, and a fake man. But, all things considered, this was what he actually preferred: the true was too impure. Too many anguishes, nasty things, doubts. Only imitation produced what a model never was: a gold standard, a rule, and implacable power. It was better to write grammar books than novels; to play the music of others than one's own; to support the opinions of the strongest over the rest. What was truth? Beauty? Justice? Conventions, if not manias. He may as well choose, then, those manias where the winds of the century blew, where the breath of fortune hovered. Dishonesty, baseness? Feeble words. All was beautiful that succeeded: René would never be fooled again. He has thus become very attentive to his parents, who (this had been a sore spot not so long ago) were well acquainted with this special art.

For Théret, this spirit of ambition and resignation marked the first stage of maturity. In a few months from now, he would know what the word balance meant. Not to mention the word adaptation.

"I am … so pleased with you," asserted Mrs. Théret, dryly, between two clients or halfway to the storeroom. "So pleased! I feel reassured. Alright. I'm not saying anything. But you'll see … you'll see, René, that between an older son and his mother, when everything gels, when there's mutual understanding … Well. I'm not saying anything." (She smiled as she frowned.)

Despite everything, René was still short of the age when he could hear this without his stomach turning. But that would pass.

The second hand news that he received of his old friends or accomplices also left him ill at ease. He didn't reproach himself, of course, for any cowardice. Yet, if the misdemeanors, and sometimes worse than that, which were the topic in the papers didn't inspire any jealousy, dreams, or hope in him, he still felt alone. He liked being with them, and thought endlessly of them. He was wrong, he shouldn't be unhappy. He was embellishing his memories. He was like an old veteran: he flattered himself for what he'd done because nobody was able to check on it, and he needn't fear ever having to do it again. It was much more beautiful like this. René remained a bit torn apart, but he had chosen his side. Another big summer of family warmth, tacit agreements, and wordless solicitations, and he would forget even his battle scars, or he would dream of aesthetic surgery for them as well.

Julien did not have a map and did not know where he was going. He had never wandered so far.

Sometimes, when he saw a gullied path that fell from the cliff onto a rocky beach, he felt like going down. But he thought that the boys, or anybody, might happen to come across his trail, and he wanted to be unkempt, to fish, to make fires, to have a good time.

He could imagine the depths with large fish and old crustaceans. No one ventured on these slippery, friable boulders from where you could fall into foamy, loud whirlpools full of clean water. It was the western coast; no more land till the Americas. Currents of contrasted temperatures, of different directions, brewed through this enormous space, and crazy winds, as drunk as chests, jostled above it. Julien knew it. He was resolved to be inside it, one day. He was not in a rush. He was afraid, and, crouching upon a lathery boulder, his nylon line in hand, he shivered slowly to the sound, to the movement, to the color of the water. But he'd go anyway. He'd take his time. He was built to resist, to keep patient. His day would come, for sure.

He was hungry. He had some bread, a can of Italian sauce, a can opener, and a knife. There was talk of pocketknives with eighteen blades and accessories, only Julien didn't yet know where they could be stolen. Nor what these retractable tools were.

He saw before him some trees, a stretch of broom, weeds. The wind made them rustle. He hid there. He ate. His cheeks were hot with light, because he'd left at the worst hour. The heat stunned him; it was pleasant. Julien felt like sleeping here perhaps. There was even water, and, in the metallic gourd swathed in a wet rag, it tasted good. He wasn't a thirster. After his meal, he snuffed a little acetone and fell asleep, eyes open on the branches that moved, the breeze luminous and pointy, all the blurry blue down there. He had screwed the cork back down in time. He softly felt his stomach under his crossed arms.

Sister Euthanase was no brute. As a matter of fact, a strict religious neutrality was observed in her establishment. However, the practicing Catholics could go to service. The others too, naturally.

The Moraillon and the Fouilloux had been separated. Sister Euthanase apologized for that. The mother superior, the captain, the doctor, the psychologist, the psychiatrist, the representative of family services, the delegate from the consumers' union, the delegate from the opposition party, the guest register, and what beds were available had decided it that way. But Sister Euthanase realized full well that the two adolescents, in this place that was new to them, were a bit sad. Displaced, in short. A tad lost, who knows? However, it wasn't possible to help them overcome together this difficult—quite certainly—although necessary ordeal (as they would later understand!). And Sister Euthanase ran from one cell to the other, and was so stuffed with consolations, with kind phrases to say, that she pronounced them to herself in the corridors, overcome with impatience because of the long journey.

She still had enough left for the kids, who weren't quite sensitive to such affectionate methods. They almost resembled the evil that people mentioned about their kind. But, being profoundly democratic, Sister Euthanase didn't let herself be taken in. She knew that the little ones had been fondled and deflowered by monopolist capitalists. Sex between the teeth or that kind of historical horror. It was enough to make you despair of God. The children were innocent. How could you make them feel this, and still keep them confined and subdued?

Fouilloux, to tell the truth, was rejoicing. She liked the nuns. It annoyed her horribly to be buckled in without company, but, since she had expected prison, this treatment comforted her (it was the refined initiative, although a tad dated, of the sub-prefect himself). Sister Thing was an unbelievable dumb-bell. The bed was small but fresh and immaculate. The barred window showed a garden of pines, boxwoods, and stiff flowers that evoked the most decent of all paradises. You had to ring to go to the toilet. At noon, they'd been served delicacies: raw red cabbage, raw carrots, potatoes in oil, a filet of smoked herring, then boiled red cabbage, boiled carrots, boiled potatoes, all of it slathered in butter or just about, and a piece of smoked pork breast. There had been enough mustard, enough convent bread, enough of the nearly red wine that they could drink to satiation. All you could eat as well of the convent's sheep's cheese, which was sold for a fortune to restaurants. And a seasonal apple. And this evening it would all begin again.

Claire Fouilloux was growing impatient. If only there had been a TV, or a least a radio, in the rooms. But there was nothing but tracts full of written phrases, professional journals for priests, few illustrations, not a single LP. For want of enjoying reading, Claire Fouilloux was reduced to thinking.

Yet, Sister Euthanase's visits didn't entertain her. According to Fouilloux, the nun was trying to worm something out of her. She knew how they were. They pretended to fuss over you. Their faces so white, so smooth, you'd believe they'd been washed with iced holy water. Fouilloux was suspicious. Too bad, she would have loved being a sister, having a sister for a friend, being between sisters. She envied the nun, but Sister Euthanase was by no means proposing that she become a sister. She probably judged her unworthy. It was more than likely (thought Claire Fouilloux) that Sister Euthanase had never sucked a dick. Not even the dick of a big fourteen-year-old child. And she pretended she came to comfort you.

Fouilloux often thought about Guillard, the son. When she'd heard about the death of his father, this had even been her only reaction: what will become of him? Of Marc?

"His cock smelled. It smelled good. He sucked me too."

She would have liked to say that to the voluble Sister Euthanase. Now that the priests and the priestesses didn't speak to you about their idols of choice anymore, from back in the day and all, there wasn't any romanticism left. Bacon and cabbage: it made you wonder. Didn't their good Lord, in fact, prohibit pork? Or was it the one after that? Well, one of them ate bacon, and not the others. Sister Euthanase thus worshipped a tolerant God, who loved the pig, the adolescent gone astray, the sisters. He had everything but speech.

For a moment, Claire had the eccentric idea of writing a note to Claudine Moraillon. She needed some … some paper and some … Right, a ballpoint pen, a marker, a … In novels, the jailor sister always refused to lend those devices, as if they cost money. Sister Euthanase, on the contrary, immediately pulled out a notebook and a pencil from her pocket and kindly offered them to the Fouilloux, who was a bit perplexed:

"I dunno what to say," she explained to the nun.

"My little Claire! What a child, Our Lord, what a child, Our Lady, what do you say? To your friend? Oh! Oh, Oh! "

"I won't know, 'specially if you're lookin'!" said Fouilloux, ruffled.

"Our very holy Trinity, such defiance!" whispered the sister.

"Whoa, I know there's a lotta pigs in here, come on," said Claire Fouilloux. The sister, strangely, understood the allusion. Fouilloux gave up on communicating with her little friend. According to Sister Euthanase, Claudine was doing wonderfully. Every instant, she expressed a thousand good thoughts, of affection, of repentance; she exhorted her comrade to have patience. Probably, she would soon suggest that they attend mass together or go to vespers, if the sister continued getting bolder.

"Do you know," said the sister, "that your patron founded a celebrated order and that her skull is revered in eight parishes of France? There are still," (Sister Euthanase had a frank, pretty laugh) "eleven other skulls of Saint Claire in Italy, four of them in the town of Assisi alone! ..."

These impish, mischievous, spontaneous remarks had a charitable intention: Sister Euthanase had learned that her young lodgers would soon be paying another visit to the gyno-psychiatrist.

"But," she added, "there is such fervor in this innocent deception, in the end! Can't we rediscover the profound truth of the heart beyond the apparent lies? ..."

At that point, Fouilloux, creasing her forehead, thought that she didn't like Marc Guillard at all. More precisely, she wasn't in love with him. That little piece of filth. What a big wiener.

"And even, finally, faith!" said Sister Euthanase, beaming. "Eleven and eight: nineteen skulls! In seven centuries! Your patron saint, dear Claire, would thus have been ..."

Not in love. He was a kid. But it had excited her atrociously. She would have eaten him all up, that grimy one. She would have messed around with him. They'd have invented all the dirty stuff. Fouilloux had jerked off many a time to Guillard Jr. It was her grandest emotion, the tickleland. She had never told anyone.

Sister Euthanase was smiling from ear to ear at her own skull jokes. The cops and doctors were waiting. Fouilloux's fate was all mapped out, and not for just one day. When you fall into the grip of those who have the right to be virtuous at your expense, you can never get out. Fouilloux risked being loved and understood until the day she preferred to slash her wrists, or fling herself into the water, or strangle someone. To each his own.

"And these nuns are called the Clarisses of the order of the Poor Clares of Perpetual Adoration!" tintinnabulated sister Euthanase, eyes marbles of joy.

She always recited the life of their patrons to those who were locked up in the convent. It uplifted the poor humiliated ones, who were so piteous. They were fewer and fewer, alas, due to the severity of the penitentiary and sanitary administrations. It nearly required a special favor, nowadays, so that the children (girls or— who would have dared think it—boys) traumatized by the great multinational capitalist monopolists could taste the inestimable solace, not admittedly of the divine message (it was not the moment), but simply of evangelical goodness.

"What? Clarisses?" said Fouilloux, perked up. "Wait a minute sister: isn't there a cow on *Mickey* who's called Clara. Huh?"

"Clarabelle! That's right!" answered Sister Euthanase, enchanted. "How amusing! … But that's a pretty name too, isn't it? … Clarabelle! Claire, belle. She must be an American saint."

"A cow, yes, she's a cow who sings," invented and giggled Claire Fouilloux, overexcited.

The sister abandoned her in this euphoria. She had to prepare the other kid.

Guillard had had it up to here. It was the third portage from the old lair to the new. There were still a number of things to move. Oh well, that would do for tonight.

The new one wasn't a construction. Set in the side of a gorge, it was a canopied cave, very similar to certain first-rate prehistorical sites. You accessed it through a sort of slide, partly earth, and partly worn-out hunchbacked stone. All the way at the bottom was the best water, loud and always cold, unpolluted, savory. The gorge was all glutted with wobbly trees, and dense and deformed shrubs heavy with birds.

Despite this wilderness, this was much closer to Saint-Rémi than before.

No one ever ventured into the cave. You couldn't spot any turds or papers or tin cans. There were several vestibules and two rooms, not counting the first shelter under the canopy.

The little Gassés were rather claustrophobic. They would not sleep in the back. Even the canopy frightened them a bit. It could all collapse at any moment. François Boitard rather shared this opinion. The other boys didn't care.

It was surprising that Julien Roquin wasn't there. Had he already left to go fishing somewhere along the torrent (that was an obsession of his), or had he had an accident? No one had seen his stuff, either on the way or in the cave. Yet, he couldn't have taken a wrong turn. And if indeed he had taken a wrong turn, where could they look, where could they call out? He might as well have slid in the water with all his stuff. They'd explore the bottom of the gorge a bit, later on. Everything was so annoying. Guillard almost felt like going back to town. He though about his home. He had a sudden craving for eggs with ham, followed by flashes of nostalgia.

Mr. Seignelet was in a bad mood. He'd had an unpleasant discussion with his colleagues. It wasn't about their work but about morality, education, about the events this July that were against family values. Someone maintained that minors, in principle, were always innocent and irresponsible; they ought to be absolved no matter what they did. Another considered this point of view to be excessive; "one must," he said, "adapt the punishment to the age of the culprits and to the nature of the crimes;

one must reprimand intelligently, uproot the evil without felling the tree, the young tree, the offspring, as the case may be." As for Mr. Seignelet, he did not tolerate these phony allowances:

"Everything you do in this life, you pay for it. It's not complicated. You did that? Good, okay. But now pay. There's no two ways about it; you got to pay. Kid or no kid. You do what you want? Very well my friend, but pay. No. Otherwise it's too easy. *Pay*. That's all."

This rational opinion, which logically evoked the balance of the scales of justice (one for action, one for money), impressed the audience. Nevertheless, the extremist colleague retorted somewhat impolitely; they suspected him of abolitionism and the discussion, veering away from childhood, broached the death penalty. People were getting annoyed. Mr. Seignelet, according to his principle of debit and credit, was applying the law of retaliation: he simply wished that the murderers perish from the same death that they'd inflicted. No more, no less. That made people laugh. Someone mentioned the victims of rape. People shrugged their shoulders.

Things started to go down hill especially once they'd left the office, when the fathers were at the café. By this hour, Mr. Seignelet was usually very tipsy, and today, his conviction and his voice needed some backup. He drank several barely diluted Ricards; declared that the guillotine was not painful; he demanded a real ordeal. His noisy verve seemed to threaten all and sundry with execution. Besides, he swore that for him, faced with the horror of a crime, there were no longer friends or parents, but only men. He would never compromise with his conscience and he would be the first, yes the first, as harrowing as it was (for he prided himself in being a true friend and an authentic father who lived only for his own kith and kin), he would be the first to hand over his best friend or his son to justice if he knew he was guilty. And he would even demand—let him be heard, he would demand—that the law be particularly severe against him. This was the very foundation of morality and of society.

This intransigence displeased his audience. Mr. Seignelet would have liked to be able to prove the truth of his principles, directly. Was there nothing around that demanded justice? Where could they find something to judge, something to punish, immediately, before their very eyes? Someone who'd have to pay, here, pay, now, pay, pay, and pay. To demonstrate the superiorities of rigor.

His position was, indeed, ironclad. Harsh but unassailable. He was right. The café owner himself, despite his prudence, his evasive shakes of the head, was forced to agree:

"Well yes, it's true … We always pay … You have to pay …"

On the way home, Mr. Seignelet's irrepressible judicator momentum continued tormenting him like a rut, an unquenchable anger. During school vacation, he was too often frustrated. In his incursions into the life of his sons, he could sniff out their dubious pretexts, but grasped at straws, flooded with pastis. Even his wife, in this case, swore off backing him. Summer, heat made her nervous enough already, and she wanted a calm husband.

Nonetheless, in order to produce the crimes he sought, Mr. Seignelet improvised homework, tasks, and goals for his children. He thus put them in a position to be at fault. It required a wealth of imagination, but, eventually, he would manage to corner one and make him pay, pay, pay.

His method of inventing laws because he needed culprits revolted his sons. They expected this approach from their mother but not from him. Mrs. Seignelet had crises; the arbitrary was therefore natural for her. But Mr. Seignelet, on the contrary, had systems. They were repulsive, frightening, but they'd grown nearly accustomed to them; it was possible to bend them or to slide on through. It was an effort of aberrant adaptation that Mr. Seignelet had wrung from them; he had no right, no right at all, to hammer together new laws on the pretext that the previous ones were no longer sufficiently transgressed.

The ideal years had been (for Mr. Seignelet) the years of summer homework. In the past, he would devise homework for the use of those of his children who had obtained bad reports in school. One time, notably, Dominique had been obligated to repeat a grade. Mr. Seignelet, at the conclusion of a lengthy palaver with the school, had wrested preferential treatment for the child. Dominique would be allowed to enter the next grade, in the autumn, if he successfully passed a little exam that would focus on the subjects in which he was weakest—nearly all of them, truth be told. His father dedicated several evenings outlining a work program for him that would encompass the entire summer, and then he devoted himself to the delicacies of home pedagogy. Dominique studied alone, during the day; in the evening after dinner, Mr. Seignelet fulfilled the noble functions of private tutor: he would inspect, control, critique, judge, punish, annotate.

Those joys, however, were not without repercussions, for Dominique, after having played for almost three months the delusional role of pupil for his father, remained that timid, terrorized, passive, almost simple boy, malleable to all authority, who would shrivel and sweat at the mere sight of his parents, the way a laboratory dog trembled and whined when he perceived the apparatus to which he had been submitted. Dominique was no longer, so it seemed, an interesting son for Mr. Seignelet: he was too empty. Therefore, from that summer onwards, he was left pretty much in peace, and, very slowly, very painfully, his martyrized tissue and his spirit just barely awoken from the nightmare were regenerating in secret. Now, in any case, the alcohol had too disorganized Mr. Seignelet's brain for him to re-enact, around one of his sons, this drama or these pedagogical tortures. A happiness with no tomorrow—the golden hours of his paternal role.

But today, and thanks to his wife, his fatherly talent and the malign humor in which the conversation has plunged him were about to find nourishment.

"Robert!" squealed Lady Seignelet as soon as he entered.

He was sweating, he was thirsty, and he was falling apart. He listened.

"Look at that. Just look. I won't say nothing, just look!" repeated Mrs. Seignelet.

She handed her husband a book. The title page was torn; it was an old, scrawny, yellowish gray book. Mr. Seignelet opened at random, and tossed in a glance.

"… and to the major perverts we leave the execrable task of festooning their nights with hideous oral sexes."

"Bertrand," said Mrs. Seignelet as sole commentary.

"Bertrand?" said Mr. Seignelet, surprised, in a muffled voice. He had set the book on the kitchen table and continued flipping through it while loosening his shoes.

"… Syphilitic chancres of the tongue and of the palate, oral gonorrhea, infected and fetid gums, lips and throats eroded by venereal cancer, such is the frequent fate of those who, through venality or sensual vice, lend themselves to these pathological vagaries of love, or rather of its dark caricatures … As for the Man who, by a dangerous delirium of the imagination that an excess of desire for his partner would have …"

"I see," murmured Mr. Seignelet.

His wife finally exploded (nevertheless, she somewhat restrained her voice, the subject was too salacious):

"Can you believe it? Fifteen years old! Fifteen years old! Can you believe it! This kid is sick!"

Mr. Seignelet didn't answer. He and his wife were both prudish. They never spoke of "this kind of thing." He had suspected that this day would come with his eldest. He poured himself a large glass of icy red wine and drank it in one go. Then he prepared himself a Ricard. Mrs. Seignelet said: "Here, give me a hit" and her husband gallantly served her some Guignolet-Kirsch. She explained that she had been cleaning Bertrand and Jean-Baptiste's room to the max and that she'd found this under Bertrand's bed, simply put.

This account wasn't exact; she'd been snooping. Delighted by her discovery, or imagining that nothing worse could exist, she had searched no further. She prodded her husband, now, to engage him in a vast general inspection when the children would have returned. No problem, tonight we're eating cold, dinner can wait. Mr. Seignelet accepted. He drank gravely, with a compunctious slowness, until his sons arrived.

He started by taking Bertrand to one side, without brusqueness. There was no reason to slap or yell. What was needed was something else entirely. Mr. Seignelet knew the ropes. Bertrand, dark red, fiddled with his glasses on his nose and didn't say a word. The motive for the inspection thus exposed, Mr. Seignelet took action.

He had an impressive background in search and seizure. It was as if he disregarded none of the hiding places where his children sheltered their secrets but, out of generosity, habitually disdained to inspect them, conceding these petty territories. Till the day, that is, when a serious breach ...

The truth was otherwise. As soon as Robert Seignelet began his searches, his imagination worked on what he perceived, it followed the same path as that of his sons and reached the same ends.

He had begun with Bertrand's stuff. He quickly found the obscene card game, which seemed to him considerably more damning than the medical textbook. One could indeed admit, as a mitigating circumstance, that an adolescent, during certain crises (which nonetheless, he should never have concealed from his father), would research subjects ... that ... well ... But these photographs ... they had nothing to do with anything medical. They signalled, they implied, they ...

Two nudist brochures, now, in full-color. Just perfect. And, alongside, a notebook, a big school notebook.

Mr. Seignelet guessed that what he had here was a prodigious *corpus delicti.* He established a solemn silence; he opened the notebook. Bertrand, seized by madness, dashed forward and tore it from his father's hands. Bertrand screamed and cried in his raucous voice. The galoot was on his last nerve. He was already apologizing, begging, asking for forgiveness, but he wouldn't give back the notebook, a secret diary. Mr. Seignelet, suffocated by the violence of this revolt and the furious and whimpering humility with which Bertrand tried to erase his crime, did not know what to do. He was overwhelmed. Imperially, or like a pontiff, he granted Bertrand the right to keep his thoughts to himself; he even added, in a tone of cold pity, "my poor boy, if you think that there's a single line in there ... at your age ... poor guy, pff ..." He uttered dark and durable threats, on the other hand, in regard to the monstrous, baffling, parricidal disrespect of Bertrand's gesture. The intention could be absolved, or, my God, understood, at least, but the manner of it, the manner, no. What just happened was so serious as to exceed even the remotest possibility of an immediate verdict. Mr. Seignelet reserved the right to make a careful and wise decision on this matter. Nothing, nothing more terrible should ...

Bertrand had crumpled, miserable. He was clutching his stupid notebook, filled with conjugal and professional projects, often cyphered. He had feared the disclosure of these laborious reveries, these weighty projections, these docile secrets, shot through with general thoughts, maxims on what a man, a spouse, a teacher, etc. ... must be, and in what style one must furnish one's household, and what titles and diplomas one ... and what big international corporation ... and if a husband and a wife really cannot (he felt rather liberal on this point), etc. All his miseries under his arm: sixty years of his life to come, under the condition that he succeed, and reach each goal. He would be ashamed to death for a decade. His father hasn't read a thing, admittedly, but that was worse: he has understood, he knew. The notebook was an exact equivalent to the little pack of obscene cards, and it had the same purpose.

Mr. Seignelet remained in the bedroom and rather distractedly studied Jean-Baptiste's earthly goods. In general, the kids (formerly the four sons, nowadays only Philippe and Jean-Baptiste) would typically undergo a body search. The father knew that at their age they didn't have anything very voluminous to hide: some pennies they'd stolen from mommy, or the junk they'd bought with them. The least pocket, the least corner of underwear was enough to conceal that sort of thing. The inspection of drawers, closets and boxes was never fruitful. It was a preamble, a dramatization, before the principal humiliation. Was the stripping and patting down hurtful? Mr. Seignelet didn't think so. A child was just a child: as soon as he reached the age of a certain prudery … the development … Mr. Seignelet gave up. But, up to that point, it was good that kids not consider their clothes or, more broadly, their person, as a domain to which the eye of the master would not have access. To retreat, untouchable, into one's own body? How ugly that would be, and what unjustifiable distrust, what pathological, asocial aloofness on the part of a child—concluded Mr. Seignelet.

A catastrophe allowed Jean-Baptiste to avoid a body search today. His father unearthed the cutlery stolen from *The Golden Unycorn* several week ago. A fork and spoon in heavy and beautiful silver, pressed with the insignia of the restaurant: a sort of goat standing on its back legs, forehead garnished with a long narwhal horn. Jean-Baptiste didn't keep anything that he stole at home. He had forgotten this silverware; he no longer thought about it.

One son a parricide and masturbator, another one a thief. The Seignelet parents were astounded. Jean-Baptiste, his face lashed by slaps from his mother who was beside herself, would be spanked by his father later, after dinner, with pomp and circumstance. As for the silverware, come tomorrow morning he would bring it back himself. He would explain as best he could, and would receive whatever punishment it pleased Messrs. Droole & Sons to inflict upon him.

Jean-Baptiste, despite the instantaneous vigor of the verdict, despite his tears and despite being condemned to a solemn auto-da-fé, was rather relieved. His parents swallowed the explanation he has given for the theft without any suspicion. He had taken the silverware for fun; he had wanted to put them back right after but hadn't been able to.

"… And the beach is off-limits for fifteen days, of course," added Mr. Seignelet soberly, who was submerged by such a bonanza almost to the point of serenity.

Raymonde Seignelet didn't approve this idea of a restitution of silverware. Too theatrical. It would teach him a lesson, but in point of fact, it was his parents who would be compromised. You just don't have a thief for a child, that's all there is to it. There was no other choice but to be accomplices on this one. She would explain it to her husband this evening or tomorrow morning. Not in front of them, of course.

The Seignelet parents were now searching the bedroom shared by Dominique and Philippe. Meager fare.

Except today. Mr. Seignelet, as he was closing a drawer abruptly, detected something that was jolted by the impact and that got stuck in the back. He reopened, searched, pulled out a bundle of half letter size paper, studiously calligraphed: Dominique's poems.

The boy did not react. After the ridiculous scene that Bertrand had just made, he was rather proud of having only this to hide. His father examined it leaf by leaf, ironically, without saying a word, then handed the bundle to Dominique who answered "Thank you." At that very moment a storm broke out behind them. Mrs. Seignelet was ferociously beating the crap out of Philippe as she screamed that he was crazy and sick, crazy and sick, crazy, etc. It wasn't really a beating. Rather it was an explosion of hysteria where the woman, in place of biting the air and clawing the void, blitzed a heap of human flesh. Mrs. Seignelet enveloped Philippe like a spider holds an insect between her paws and rolls it into a cocoon. The little boy's feeling was one of being immured in a barrel full of nails, razorblades and white-hot slabs and being hurled down from the top of a mountain. A variation on the uterus. For an instant, Mrs. Seignelet let go of the child and, flashing on the pile of toys that she has wrenched out, stomped them, jostled them, crushed them under her square and low heels as she screamed:

"Oh, since you did that to me, I'm doin' this to you!"

She repeated the explanation enough to fracture her throat until she had smashed all the toys into a gruel. Then she took her son back under her and ended her anger with the kind of violence that would make you pull off your fingernails.

Later on, the little boy's crime was brought to light. With the help of his bedside rug, slightly shifted from its normal place, he was hiding a greasy stain, as big as a crêpe, which he'd made on the bedroom floor. Talking to himself, he had played shopkeeper: he was selling himself waxes, seated on the ground, and the wax in question was an old tube of oily liniment which had seeped into the hardwood floor. This was what he had "done to his mother."

On the bench, to Joachim's left, were newspapers, magazines: but he didn't dare touch them. Gradually, he deciphered a title. Then he tossed a furtive glance at the cops sticking out above the desks, he leaned to the right and whispered to his cousin:

"It says, *The Crap Cookers*. Did you see it? Huh?"

He pointed a finger to the cover of a racing magazine. Hervé Pellisson repressed a laugh:

"Not crap," he said. "*Crack!*"

"Huh?"

"You don't know, shtt, shtt, you don't know what *crack* is Joachim? At the races?"

"Cracks, like cracking jokes," said Alain Viaud, from the angle on the right. A wooden corner, furniture yellow.

"No, it's horses!" says Hervé Pellisson.

"Horses?" said little Lescot, intrigued. "Craps are horses?"

"Cracks! Cra-cks!" insisted Pellisson.

"If you guys make cracks later on," intervened Mrs. Lescot, "these misters won't be so happy! Be sure to tell them everything alright ducky, alright kids? Every little bitty thing!"

"Since there's nothing," groaned Hervé Pellisson.

"Crap?" said Marie-Antoine, his big eyes laughing.

"Ooooohffff," Mariette Péréfixe lamented.

"But how do they make horses with crap, huh, Hervé?" asked Joachim Lescot.

His cousin tapped his head and hair, screwed a finger into his temple.

A policeman in uniform without his hat crossed the sort

of hallway where they were waiting. He was carrying a pile of folders.

"Hey, you lost something!" Alain Viaud said quickly, while pointing at the floor with his finger.

The cop turned, looked at the ground, frowned:

"What?.. Where? … Huh. What?"

"Duh, it's nothin' nevermind," Viaud answered fast, all of a sudden sensing the imminent possibility of a slap. Out of respect for the ladies present, however, the policeman abstained from commenting upon the boy's joke. He went into another room. He slammed the door to break wind.

Hervé Pellisson was called in. The captain was going to question him. They were here for the theft at Mrs. Arnauld's. She has filed a complaint. A neighbor claimed to have seen Pellisson and the other children hanging around the villa. The investigation even pointed towards the fact that only kids could have committed the break-in.

The idea that her little Joachim, and little Hervé, and little Péréfixe, and little Viaud could be murderers, or thieves rather, made Mrs. Lescot smile. The police were on the wrong track. This neighbor, certainly some old, myopic grinch who hated children, was a true plague of Egypt. Where did he know them from, first of all? It was really incredible, people that you'd never seen, who didn't even live in your neighborhood; they knew you by name. Even if you were a shopkeeper, that was no excuse, and this person was putting his nose where it didn't belong.

"Mommy?" inquired Joachim when Pellisson was gone.

"Yes, cutie. Do you want a bit of chocolate? Kids, do you want a bit of chocolate? Be careful though, I don't have anything to drink. So don't eat too too much, otherwise you're gonna be thirsty! Hazelnuts'll do that to you!"

The little ritual of whispered distribution got rolling. Mrs. Lescot liked Alain Viaud very much; she had never seen him before. She'd have to remember to scold the kids for never inviting him to the café, for snack time, or for a play date. He didn't look too rich, the poor thing. No mommy or daddy. That slight squint of the eyes was so cute, why did they call it cross-eyed. Innocent cruelty, the little rascals. Hervé ought to … And his parents who couldn't get the morning off. They … they thought their son did this. They didn't dare say it outright but it was obvious. That kind of work made you hard. There was a disposition for it after all. If all the workers. No, already as a child her brother … And he found a spouse who … But Hervé was sweetness itself. How he kissed the little ones, and so patient with them. Crap cookers! My chickadee. And they liked him so much in return. What a revolting story. Those thefts, those crimes, the poor police had lost their grip. But still, to be bothering children. Shame. This Mrs. Arnauld and her millions. My little sweetie stealing millions from houses. She was crazy. Crazy. It was the sciences. Education. After a while.

"Yes my rabbit? They are horses sweetie, yes."

"But why? Huh? … Mommy?"

"You just have to look inside, Joachim, no one is going to eat you if you look at the magazine, without crinkling it, gently. Those misters won't eat you! My little darling, cutie pie."

Mrs. Lescot wasn't so sure about that. They weren't very hospitable at the central station. It was as if you were already guillotined before you could say phew. As warm as an ice floe, as the saying went. But all administrations were the same, come to think of it. Looking the part. It wasn't like running a cafe, of course; they might earn less. Night shifts? What were they writing? That paperwork. All that paperwork. You wouldn't believe there were so many murderers nowadays. Character darkens in the long run, that's it.

"That horse crap there cost eight hundred millions!" confided Lescot to Marie-Antoine Péréfixe, pointing to the photo of a horse.

"Really?" said Marie-Antoine.

His mommy looked at the horse without seeing it. This whole business turned her stomach.

"Yeah, it says so here! Eight thousand millions!" said Joachim.

"So, is that a lot?" asked Marie-Antoine.

"It's a horse, isn't it?" said Lescot. "It's gotta be expensive!"

"I'm thirsty!" said Marie-Antoine. He felt his throat as he spoke.

"My little chickadee!" Mrs. Lescot scolded. "You ate too much chocolate! Oh! That's not a good boy!"

"I'm thirsty too," said Joachim.

"Yeah, me too," said Alain Viaud.

The ladies consulted with each other, and sighed. Mrs. Lescot resolved to get up from her seat. Which policeman should she bother? They certainly didn't look gallant. Not even a gesture for a lady who'd gotten up.

Finally, a pencil pusher informed Mrs. Lescot about the location of a drinkable water tap. The children got in a line. The water was tepid, with a metallic flavor.

"Don't drink too much my ducklings," advised Mrs. Lescot. "Otherwise afterward you'll want to go pee, that'll be a whole other story. Oh dear. Don't drink too much. Sponges, what sponges! …"

"Well, I need a piss," said Viaud.

"Me too," said Marie-Antoine.

"Me too," said Joachim, "I gotta do number two."

"Oh dear!" moaned Yvonne Lescot towards Mrs. Péréfixe. "Oh dear, this is a fine mess, the two of us with all these peepees!"

Soon, someone pointed out the toilets. They were repulsive smelling, filthy squat toilets. The children got in line. Mrs. Lescot listened to it flow. It gave her a little urge. But it was the men's room, and so abominable.

"Me neither, oh, I couldn't! It's too much!" agreed Mariette Péréfixe.

The children went back to their seats. They were starting to get bored. They weren't behaving as well. They chitchatted. They were getting along marvelously. Mrs. Lescot thought about the joy it would be, to have three instead of one. But who would make them for her. She no longer knew precisely what form it took. You had to admit that it was by no means handsome. Except her little chicken's little wiener that was so cute, so cute, the little naughtypoo. But it didn't stay that way their whole life through, unfortunately. It would be so nice to love one another with those little white wieners, small, so soft, so soft. Chinese ones they say, the hole. Rabbits. Rats. Given the proliferation. Come on Yvonne, you've got a naughty tongue. Wiener love.

What were they doing to Hervé? Did they even have the right to question him like this, face to face, without any parents, without a … a what. No one knew the laws. Surely they were not going to teach them to you. Their toilets, what pigs. And it was like that everywhere. Cigarette butts. Spit. Dirty people sweat. What a menagerie. What would they do to him?

"It's like going to the doctor's!" whispered Mariette Péréfixe, filled with anxiety.

Mrs. Lescot reassured her. Nobody was sick, thank heavens, and no one was guilty.

"If only my husband could have been here!" sighed Mrs. Péréfixe. "And this one here who's asking for it. Marie-Antoine! Stop moving and shush will you? You idiot …"

"They have to, they have to clear their minds a bit," said Mrs. Lescot to calm her down. "It's this place."

Viaud was in the middle of playing lying monkey with Marie-Antoine, in front of Joachim who was choking with laughter. Mrs. Lescot also knew the game, but she'd never played it with her son because she thought it wasn't so nice.

From his corner, Alain Viaud, at a right angle from Péréfixe, made faces at him:

"Now I'm scratching my nose. You too."

He scratched an ear. Marie Antoine scratched his ear.

"Now I'm scratching my knee. You too."

He scratched his nose. Marie-Antoine scratched his nose.

"Now I'm scratching my eye. You too."

He scratched the top of his skull. Obediently, Marie-Antoine scratched the top of his skull.

"So is this your eye here?" cackled Alain Viaud, gripping a tuft of his hair.

"No, it's not there!" laughed Marie-Antoine Péréfixe blissfully.

"So now you're scratching your … your ding-a-ling."

Viaud grabbed the tip of his shoe. Péréfixe had mimicked the gesture, like before, to follow along. Joachim and Alain were cracking up. A cop turned his head. They didn't see him.

"So," Viaud managed to say, "you're touching your feet!"

And he put a finger in each of his ears. Marie-Antoine, who was beginning to get the game, touched his ear and his foot at the same time. This ridiculous attitude attracted his mother's attention.

"Hey, Marie. Hey. Are you done, you're so stupid. That's a fact. You done? Where are you goin', touching everything. Cut it out. Aren't you done, stop it? … Oh what the heck, it's a sacrifice, but what the heck, and hush up! … And you dummies, enough."

"And now you're touching your butt," whispered Viaud, and he stuck his index finger into his mouth. He sucked, sucked the sugary finger.

Marie-Antoine, laughing, did not react. He was keeping watch on his mother, whose attention Mrs. Lescot diverted.

A door opened. Captain Lorge and Hervé Pellisson appeared. Hervé took a seat next to Mrs. Lescot. The captain called for

Joachim. No, without his mother. It was only for five minutes, they had to check something; it was nothing, of course.

Hervé confided to Mrs. Lescot:

"Aunty, they're nuts."

Mrs. Lescot straightened Joachim's outfit, pulled down his sweater, pulled up his socks, adjusted the zipper of his fly, put two or three hairs back where they belonged. She got up and accompanied the child to the door of the office. With a glance, she discovered that Mr. Lemazier, the famous witness, was in the room. He was a gray old man, small, wily, bony in his loose fitting pants. He looked like a maniac. As soft as she might be, she would gladly have bitten him. Can you believe that dirty old men like that exist? If he ever dared set a foot in her café, the cockroach. She'd squash him like a venomous, stinging critter.

"… No, nothing, aunty," Hervé answered in a low voice. "Nothing. It's that guy, he's nuts. They should lock him up. They can't prove anything. Yeah, in the asylum. Really, you should see the bastard."

Mrs. Lescot was also convinced of it. If you placed side by side her Joachim and this monstrous clawed and cackling viper, this Mr. Lemazier, innocence and wickedness, beauty and ugliness, goodness and hatred of everything. Nasty guy. The asylum, Hervé Pellisson was right. A few good slaps. Old dunghill. And he was proud of himself, on top of everything.

"… And he's proud of himself, on top of everything!" said Hervé, indignant, contemptuous and crimson.

Jean-Michel Cras maintained that it was best to shoot first. Guillard would rather threaten. Cras insisted:

"No, 'cause we're not old enough. Even with stockings on our face they'll get that we're not old enough, they'll do something."

"So we'll shoot in the air," said Guillard.

"No. They'll think we're afraid."

"Shit, but if we shoot inside, from the other side of the counter, it's the upper body we're aiming at. The heart, the face."

Cras and his gang cackled.

"Damn, Marco, you got the willies?"

Boitard was listening to this from a few steps away, with the Gassé brothers.

"Marc's afraid of taking some bastards out, the pussy."

"Why do you say bastards," said Guillard. "You think they make that much?"

Roland Baudière, a brute with a high-pitched voice, yelled:

"No! That's the thing! No. That's the thing! No! That's the thing!"

A sweep of approval. They thought nothing was worse than to sell oneself, for three pennies, to the rich. Maybe for three million pennies … But did the rich ever give that to anyone? No! The more they asked of you, the less they paid for it. Become their facsimile, their asswipe, you'd earn fortunes playing the hall of mirrors. Be their employee, they'd pay you in dog food to do what even the finest among them was incapable of judging and liking. This was because anything of talent got a slap in the face by those who had, as sole talent, the power to buy labor. Regarding crime, that's what you thought when you were a thug from Roche-Notre-Dame, and you contemplated murdering bank employees (because, strangely enough, the bosses hid) since they were merely what an executor of dirty work was to justice: an imbecilic, shabbily cupid, egoistically virtuous machine, which, if you wanted to be free of bastards and of their innumerable foot soldiers, must be pushed into the fire with a kick to the kidneys. But you should only barely touch them, since they stank as much as their employers. You needed years of baths, scrubbings, and scouring to lift the smell and the mark that the hand of the haves would imprint upon you in less than a second. The town boys were naive partisans of mass murder—but they'd have taken their masses *from the top*. They sincerely believed they were minorities, and, to purify the planet of its tyrants, its wealthy, and its high ballers, they no longer believed in revolution, but in gas chambers or atom bombs. These opinions infuriated Marc Guillard. He also expounded overly simple ideas; but he didn't like those of others. The kids from Roche-Notre-Dame seemed to be dangerous anarchists—the kind who murder regardless of their victim's merit; the kind who get suicided by the police with a satisfaction that all the papers reverberate blissfully. Marc was afraid of those opinions that turn you into a marked man (whether you were the executioner or the victim). The boys were going to despise and abandon him. After all Guillard was useless to them.

"No," he repeated, "we can't shoot right away."

"What do mean?" said Cras. "You want to wait for them to call the cops?"

"What? We'd see that."

"What? You think they don't have a system, a direct line for calling that we can't see, huh? You fuckhead faggot."

"Shut up," said Guillard. The wave of anger that he'd been holding back for a while submerged him:

"And why you callin' me that? Did I fuck you up the ass again huh, cherry? You want it up the starfish?"

"What're you sayin'," intervened the shrill-voiced gorilla child, "with your faggots there at your back, you think we don't get it? Whose gonna take it up the caboose tonight, huh?"

With a flick of the chin he motioned towards Boitard and the Gassés.

"You're gonna regret that!" cried Marc Guillard. He tore out the revolver that he kept in his pocket, and cocked it.

The Roche-Notre-Dame gang immediately stepped back to the extreme edge of the terrace that extended in front of the cave, where you could plummet into the torrent, very far below. The boys were a half dozen.

What followed went very fast. One of the boys took out a revolver and fired into the cave. All the boys from Roche-Notre-Dame scrambled up the embankment and reached the plateau, grasping onto the grasses and the bushes. Guillard also fired, but with a wide aim. There were insults, swallowed cries, dust and threats. Eventually, Marc Guillard appeared in the open and screamed at the deserters:

"Bastards, you smoked a guy!"

"That makes one faggot less," answered Jean-Michel Cras, who, like all good captains, was supervising the retreat.

There weren't, in fact, any dead. However, Camille Gassé had taken a bullet in the chest. He had lost consciousness. Nobody knew what do to with him.

His brother Benoît instantaneously fell back into his grand bourgeois tone, and expressed a dignified rage against Guillard the way he would have complained to the director of a travel agency whose holiday package had taken a bad turn. He was a hair's breadth away from threatening him with a lawyer, lawsuits, or calling him a laborer's son. Just in time, he sensed the hostility that his upper-class style inspired; they were more than ten in the cave; even François Boitard didn't rally to these pretentious protests; so Benoît had a fit of interesting tears, as if someone from his milieu, perched on the roof, had been able to see, appreciate, and evaluate his social performance. They took Camille's clothes off. Benoît sulked. There was really a wound, with a real round hole, that they looked at. They listened to the heart. It worked. But how could they stop this blood, and where could they find a doctor without suffering the consequences? Guillard pressed on the wound with a rag. Too bad, he thought, the bullet hadn't found the other Gassé. In that case, would Camille have acted the sissy? Marc doubted it. Camille wasn't the *I-won't-tolerate-that* or the *how-dare-you type*. It was really unfair. The way of the gun, huh. Julien, for starters, was probably already dead. And now this other kid. They'd end up living among brutes. They were fucked.

"I told you, aunty!" repeated Hervé with satisfaction. "They couldn't!"

"Can you believe it? ... And they didn't look too happy either!" said Mariette Péréfixe. "They would have chewed us up and swallowed us!"

"I'm hungry," said Joachim.

"Yes," said Marie-Antoine.

"My little Alain, you're coming to our house, we're all gonna eat," proposed Mrs. Lescot.

"Uhm, no, can't," lied Viaud, "my grandma's waitin' for me."

"My goodness, of course!" moaned Yvonne Lescot. "Let's get a taxi for you, sweetie. That poor Mrs. Viaud!"

"I ain't got a dime!" said Alain.

Mrs. Lescot and Mrs. Péréfixe shrugged their shoulders. Come, come, for a grandmother who was worrying herself into an early grave, they could spare ten or twenty francs.

Alain Viaud gave a false address to the taxi, somewhere towards the north. It allowed him to keep a bill and to get nearer to the new hideout, which he wanted to visit. He bought himself a tube of mayonnaise, a pack of smoked bacon, and a bottle of chilled lemonade in the first grocery store he encountered on his way, just before the twelve thirty or one o'clock lunch break. Then he ate and drank as he was walking—he was cheerful.

"So we're not going to prison?" sighed Joachim.

"Buttercup, my little sweetheart!" moaned Yvonne Lescot as she covered her child in kisses.

Being tired had inflated Marie-Antoine, but had emaciated Joachim.

"Well I must say! Can you believe it! I mean, really!" repeated Mariette Péréfixe, who was nervously clutching a bloated Marie-Antoine.

Hervé Pellisson had wanted to be in charge of preparing the meal. The ladies were going to drink a good little aperitif (Mrs. Péréfixe preferred a merlot or two). Joachim and Marie-Antoine would stuff themselves with peanuts and soda (Yvonne Lescot didn't dare pour her son a beer in front of the other mommy). Hervé would cook, and he would, as was his habit, drink plain iced milk. His aunt had made special purchases. She had reasoned that, if things turned out badly, they'd need comfort, and they'd have to get back on their feet if, after a thousand certainly heroic and dreadful efforts, things went well.

In the fridge, Hervé Pellisson found what he'd been told to expect. He couldn't believe it. He scrubbed, cleaned, peeled. Mrs. Lescot was a perfectly frank person. Ever since she had received the summons, she had told all the regulars about the affair. She'd explained why she had to close till two o'clock, or maybe—if those monsters … you never know—until tomorrow. Now, she was impatient to relate her victory to all of them and to expose the cruel idiocy of the cops. Could you believe they would murder a hundred innocent people at the station, in front of your very eyes, just to hold onto one culprit! (Mrs. Lescot, like all penniless French people, had the realistic conviction that justice was the privilege of the cops, and not the work of the courts.)

"For people who make our kind of money, let's be honest, they ought to be decent!" lamented Mrs. Péréfixe, after a few mouthfuls. "But no! They all think they're God and his saints! They think they are! It's just like the war! It's still the Germans! There you have it! Mrs. Lescot! There you have it! It's starting again! … And we weren't even yay high! I mean, really! …"

Yvonne Lescot got up and went to see how Hervé was getting along. He knew how to work. He planned everything out in his head; he was thorough, clean, methodical, quick and sure of himself. Maybe this was a cafe owner's vocation. Mrs. Lescot would be delighted. She easily pictured herself as a restaurateur.

To nourish without the breast, merely the spirit of maternity. Especially when Joachim would be bigger. Oh, cooking didn't interest him yet, the kitten, not yet! But he already ate well, oh boy. How he spat a veal liver at me because one side had been forgotten a second in the pan! That fine muzzle. One day, he would be the one giving orders.

The ladies and the children had understood that they had to leave Hervé alone. Surely, during the meal, he would narrate his interrogation. When you thought about it, he was the one who had had to put up with the most. To the younger boys, the captain asked terrorizing or vicious questions which the boys didn't know how to answer. The witness, that devil Lemazier, didn't go as far as to swear that he recognized the three little ones (though he'd seen Hervé quite often, when the latter came for his lessons with Mrs. Arnauld). Nonetheless, according to Captain Lorge, the old fart had conducted his own investigation. Once he had assembled his memory of kids prowling around Mrs. Arnauld's front porch and the news of the burglary, he had played the detective and had unearthed the identities of Pellisson's friends, The latter showed up everywhere and, falsely innocent, was always with kids who were younger than he was. Very recognizable, the Pellisson gang, very well known. And the official inquiry had confirmed these damning co-occurrences.

"They must have really grilled him, I mean, really!" said Mariette Péréfixe with compassion; she smelled the first fumes of the rack of lamb, stuffed with pink garlic, that Pellisson had put in the oven.

Viaud slid, butt first, down the chute that descended to the lair. He still had half a bottle of lemonade. He held it in one hand. It was still pretty fresh.

Because of the noise, a guy came out onto the terrace of the cave. It was Thomas Sermaisse, the fat disgusting bastard whose parents were the worst assholes. Viaud hated him, what the fuck was he doing here? Since when was he part of it? At school, he'd get his ass kicked, the scumbag, always trying to cop a feel. Fat ass.

"What side are you on?" squealed Sermaisse with the voice of a pissed gelded fanatic demented fuck. Who did he think he was?

"… You gonna wear your ass in front or behind?" groaned Alain Viaud, disdainful. He squeezed his bottle a bit.

"Fine, go on through," said Thomas. Fatso was chicken.

"So wait, your parents are in there?" said Viaud.

"Hey Millipede, you crazy fool, why the fuck would they be there."

"Milliass faggot, here, if you're thirsty chew on this."

Alain Viaud graciously abandoned his lemonade. The fat kid sat down on a stone, which made the numerous spare tires of his belly into parallel sausages. Then he drank straight from the bottle, which temporarily erased his double chin. Lemonade was good. His parents sold leashes, collars, whips, and knives. To compensate, they ate fat, drank a lot.

"Julien's not here?"

"Hey Millipede, you're just on time. Come have a look."

They showed him Camille Gassé, who was still unconscious and was steadily losing blood.

"You did this?" Viaud asked Guillard.

Marc explained what happened. Now everyone knew that he had a small pistol, and they resented him for not having said so.

Viaud noticed the little Seignelet, Jean-Baptiste. It surprised him. Jean-Baptiste told him why he was there. What a bunch of tales, thought Viaud. "Is there more lemonade?"

Jean-Baptiste had fled his house the week before. Philippe had fallen seriously ill. Mrs. Seignelet had to put him to bed and, soon enough, had to call the doctor. No one knew what the child was suffering from; he refused to feed himself, moaned, and had a fever. What a torture this kid, they couldn't even relax when they were on vacation. Lady Seignelet was mad as hell.

The doctor hadn't been able to formulate a diagnosis. But he concealed this fact. Philippe was smothered in imperative prescriptions; he was gorged with drastic medication. Mrs. Seignelet trusted this doctor, who would never allow himself to say one unnecessary word. He respected families.

Soon after, Philippe's state got so bad that, at eight o'clock in the evening, the Seignelet parents were forced to call a new doctor, since the other was not available right at that time.

According to that practitioner (some vaguely antipathetic dago, you could just feel it, evaluated Raymonde Seignelet), the little boy required emergency hospitalization and surgery. Mr. and Mrs. Seignelet, at first offended by such an enormous accusation, answered roundly. The doctor, flabbergasted, insisted, grew firm, nearly threatened to call the police. The Seignelet parents—one indignant and mute, the other shrieking—had to yield. A nut, it had to be a nut of a doctor.

An ambulance soon took Philippe away. The family car followed. They'd brought Bertrand along as well, for all intents and purposes. But what was it with this quack? Where did all of this come from? Did the law even allow …?

"It's simple," repeated, in a whisper, Mr. Seignelet, "we'll admit it! But if he's wrong, I'll sue him in court! It's simple. He's gone too far. Too far. I'm suing him, that's all. And he'll pay. He'll pay!"

"You're damn right! Damn right, yeah!" squealed his wife, droning. "'Cause this is just too much, just too much! … It's … What is this exactly? Where did he come from, anyway? Oh no, it can't be, oh no! Oh no!"

Philippe breathing easy, in bed in the ambulance without his parents. He didn't feel as bad anymore. No one was bothering him.

The car stopped. Someone lifted the little boy and carried him. Philippe saw the trip through the corridors as if he were someone else.

They put him down somewhere and undressed him completely. They touched him, did other things to him. His parents still weren't there. Maybe it was forbidden. Someone hurt him, but not on purpose. Then, they carried him again somewhere else, and laid him out on something hard and cold. There was a disk of lamps above him, very big but not blinding.

They put something against his mouth and nose; he breathed in some very strong air that had a good smell of medicine. That was his last impression, because he fell asleep immediately. He died during the operation. Mrs. Seignelet, in the waiting room, was seated next to her husband. She was squeezing her ten fingers around her gloves and handbag. They announced the bad news without much consideration. She produced the appropriate gestures and acted devastated, so she'd be discharged of any moral duty. Her husband, who'd turned green, was trembling; his stray eyes seemed to search for a glass of alcohol in the bare, gray-tiled room. However, he took it upon himself, left his wife to the usual condolences, and dealt with the formalities. Pimply Bertrand turned red.

It wasn't a far stretch to think that this doctor was a murderer. You don't get insulted and then be given back a dead son, who was alive the minute before. They weren't going to let themselves be taken advantage of! The bigwigs of the hospital covered for their colleague, no surprise there. And, to top it all off, they expected you to pay the bill. Mrs. Seignelet was suffocating. The savages. The brutes. What about her feelings as a mother? Bastards.

Philippe's funeral took place the day after the next. The weather was good, with some wind. Saint-Rémi's rustic, maritime cemetery was a great tourist attraction. In the summer, it was invaded by visitors and curious travelers. They photographed the ancient tombs, the sculpted stone crosses, the wild flowers, the foamy breakwaters on the dark blue ocean. During the regular funeral time, in the morning, you could smell the baked bread of a neighboring bakery; cultivated or romantic Parisians felt moved by this smell in the fresh air. As for the islanders, they found it rather shocking. They would never have touched that bread.

The Seignelet children, head empty, passively followed the ceremony. The weightless coffin lacked any reality. You couldn't imagine there was someone inside. Their attire was stiff, crêpe stitched to their Sunday clothes, too hot for the season but tolerable, with this wind. For a long time Jean-Baptiste watched a boat leaving for America in the distance. Then he paid attention to the people who were there for the burial, and he noticed Marc Guillard in the group, a little off to the side. Why had he come? Where had he read the announcement?

Guillard wasn't alone. There was also that other idiot Cormaillon, two big boys and a little one whom Jean-Baptiste didn't know as well. He suddenly felt an irresistible urge to join them.

He checked that no one was watching him. He made a sign to Guillard, moved closer to Dominique who was crying and asked him if he wanted to leave with them. Maybe Dominique hadn't understood well, he answered "no." Jean-Baptiste didn't insist. He couldn't talk. He slipped away. The group of boys immediately left the cemetery, making a circle around Jean-Baptiste to hide him.

Once outside, Cormaillon the elder suggested they steal one of the cars that were parked along the wall. Simply for kicks, to make a ruckus. They would get rid of it a little further on.

"No," ordered Guillard. This wasn't the time to kid around or to take risks.

"Once I heard, I knew you were gonna take off," said Guillard to the little Seignelet, who wasn't surprised by that intuition. He has often spoken of this urge to run away; the only thing missing was the occasion, the circumstance that would determine it.

Mrs. Seignelet was annoyed not to have a crypt. They'd have lowered the coffin in one of those decent thingamajigs. There would have been a modern cross, a stone with "Family Seignelet" engraved on top. It would have made a better impression. But they had been taken by surprise. Mr. Seignelet hadn't planned to make this kind of purchase before the mortgage of the house had been paid off. For Philippe, meanwhile, a twenty-year concession would be enough, in the children's corner, which looked good. All the same, Raymonde Seignelet found this kind of inhumation somewhat uncivilized, somewhat sloppy, shameful. And yet the price had been already too high. This whole thing about blew their holiday savings, and their budget for the semester. Yeah, this one had made 'em drool their guts out till the end, you could say that again. She'd said it a thousand times to her husband: four was too much.

"Hey, where the heck did Jean-Baptiste go off to?" she whispered in Bertrand's ear when she'd counted her progeny.

Simone Roquin had decided to confess. Captain Lorge, to whom the case was being reinstated, was delighted. She was jealous, of course. But what a strange way of killing. Simone Roquin told the story. She had quietly murdered her husband, at home. She had taken him by surprise, with a small vegetable knife; then she'd continued to poke him a little all over, because he moved for a long time. She was strong; she slipped on a pair of his shoes and moved him to the saltworks, where she went by car. Well, well. Captain Lorge would simply appreciate it if she could prove all this. Wasn't she just churning out a novel to protect someone? First, had she really acted alone? Mr. Roquin was tall, heavy, and vigorous. What about that knife? On a related note, did she consent to speak of what she'd done with her younger son, Julien, the so-called runaway? Where was the body? Come now, try a little harder. A child doesn't just disappear like that; he doesn't evaporate.

"No, it wasn't boring," affirmed Joachim Lescot. According to him, the morning at the station had been very entertaining. It hadn't impressed him.

"No!" he said. "Mommy!… We had a great time, like little sluts! Yeah! With Alain! He was the one who said it!"

This expression amused Marie-Antoine Peréfixe excessively, despite Hervé's correction:

"Hey Joachim, not sluts, nuts."

He was a bit nervous, but his meat was perfectly roasted. He did not want to tell them about his interrogation, which had shaken him. Especially that old guy, that Lemazier, he was scary. The mothers shared Pellisson's opinion. They still couldn't believe that someone dared to accuse children. Mrs. Lescot declared that if a kid stole from her here, before her very eyes, she would prefer to be robbed naked than to involve the police in it. How inhuman.

"You'll let them steal from us? …" asked Joachim, his imagination fired up. "The whole café? …" He laughed with pleasure. His mommy kissed him.

"You really shouldn't go too far in the other direction, Mrs. Lescot!" answered Mariette Peréfixe. "Otherwise, it's just the same thing! You shouldn't!"

"But I'm not saying really steal from me, really! But I could easily figure something out with the kid without having to go through those people!"

"Who stole from your mother?" said Marie-Antoine, startled. He didn't see anything missing around him.

"Careful my little chickadee, not too much of this mustard, it's very very strong!" said Yvonne Lescot. "Take the other one, in the red jar! Alright, so let's say, for example, that I'm that neighbor, that Lemazier. Fine. I think I've seen some kids hanging around the house where, sure, a burglary …"

"Marie-Antoine, don't drink like a lush! Hey!"

"Well there you go, he was a creepy guy," said Hervé.

"There you go. If I were really sure of what I'd seen, let's suppose, I would ring the doorbell of this Mrs. Arnauld, I'd explain that this was very serious, that I was afraid that some children had …"

"Yeah that's it! That's the thing!" approved Mariette Péréfixe. "We're still people! We're not animals."

"Like I've been saying!" concluded Mrs. Lescot. "A brute!"

"So who was it who stole her money from the lady?" Marie-Antoine suddenly asked.

They'd put a little red wine in his water to make it red. Hervé shot him a kick from under the table. Oh, wouldn't it be just dandy if he spilled everything now, that idiot. Hervé had resolved never to steal again with the little ones. Or only with Viaud, if he absolutely needed a second. And maybe never. It had been a close shave. The mothers ate with great appetite.

"They give back the money and you forget everything," said Mrs. Lescot.

"Yep, a good spanking so they get it in their heads and there you go!" added Mrs. Péréfixe. "What a beast, really."

"Aunty, did he tell you that it was a done deal?" asked Hervé.

"Not at all, dear, not at all," said Mrs. Lescot. "He's continuing his investigation. Can you imagine! His investigation!"

"So we gotta go back again?" said Joachim.

"To Mrs. Arnauld's?" said Marie-Antoine, dreamily.

"My little duckling," Mrs. Lescot answered emotionally, "you couldn't know how right you are! Mariette, do you know that this Mr. Lorge mentioned a dramatization?"

"A dramatization!" cried Mariette Péréfixe. "What! My goodness. I am stunned! Stunned! I am absolutely stunned, Mrs. Lescot!"

"Exactly! Can you believe he wanted to throw our children into the basement through the basement window, to see if they fit!"

"My god! To see if they fit! Can you imagine!" squealed Mrs. Péréfixe. "Through the bars, you mean?"

"The bars. Right. In this lady's basement."

"My goodness!"

"The money wasn't in the basement," remarked Marie-Antoine. "Ouch! Stop Hervé! Ouch! He's doing it, mama! Ouch."

Luckily Mrs. Lescot thought the child was only asking a question; she waited for Mariette to have finished slapping him, then she answered:

"He didn't tell me where she kept it, sweetie pie, I don't know. But does anyone keep millions in their house, really?"

"Millions, my goodness!" repeated Mrs. Péréfixe.

"Hey what if it was him, that old guy, who raked it all up!" insinuated Hervé Pellisson, suddenly inspired.

His aunt directed a headshake pregnant with meaning towards him.

"You never know, you never know," Mrs. Péréfixe commented.

She couldn't have invented that herself. She was quite happy that they'd found a culprit. It lightened the mood of the meal.

Alain Viaud suggested to Marc Guillard that they should tell Dr. Ambreuse. He swore she could be trusted. Marc hesitated. If only they dared take the risk of moving Camille. But that was impossible. Apparently, if you're seriously injured you could die from that. And they'd have to shake him up pretty bad to get him up there. On the other hand, revealing everything to this doctor …

The boys held council. They agreed upon the only reasonable solution. They were going to leave the lair, changes houses once again. They'd leave Camille Gassé here alone. His brother Benoît would keep watch over him. They'd have stuff to drink, food, and money. Viaud would let Dr. Ambreuse know. He would tell her as little as he could. He would bring her to the cave. Then they'd follow her to know what she was doing and to fend off trouble.

Benoît had the choice: he could join the others, afterward, or go back with Camille and return to his parent's house. But they'd probably grill him real bad. Did he at least swear not to give them any names?

Benoît Gassé said that he'd have to give up François Boitard inevitably, since the three of them had fled together. François answered that he didn't care. Besides, if the Gassés left the game, he kind of felt like taking advantage of the opportunity. Or maybe not. He was thinking.

They started moving house right away. They withdrew into their previous lair, so they could store what was absolutely necessary, at least. The rest would be chucked into the water.

Camille was in critical condition. They were concerned that he might die.

As soon as they'd cleared out the cave enough, Viaud left. He wasn't very worried. If the boy died, he wasn't concerned. And the gang wasn't his. Nobody here knew a thing about Julien Roquin, and Alain Viaud wasn't concerned by anyone else.

He dropped by his grandmother's first. He didn't really know Dr. Ambreuse's address. Are doctors home at this hour?

"What is it you want from the doctor?" yelped Mrs. Viaud. "Did you eat yet, you little son of a gun?"

"Yeah," said Viaud. "What else you got to chow down?"

"There's tuna, I made tuna. But it's all dry now, you're not gonna want that. You little pain in the ass."

"Lemme see."

He moved towards the stove, studied the pot, and sniffed.

"Your bottom feeder stinks, it's rotten!" he said.

"Rotten your ass, you good-for-nothing, I'm gonna get you!"

"You old tart, you!" cried Viaud as he climbed to his attic. Such exchanges were commonplace between him and his grandmother; neither of them got upset.

"… And why is it you need the doctor's address?" Mrs. Viaud continued. "You sick? It's not the season!"

"I'm sick, yeah," laughed Alain Viaud. "My ass hurts! I got a tooth growing! A big one!"

He slid down the ladder and fled. After all, he'd easily dig up the address at the post office. He didn't have time to read it for himself, but he'd ask.

Dr. Ambreuse was at home. Viaud explained himself. He said a bit too much, because he didn't quite know how to go about the whole gunshot business. Pauline Ambreuse didn't show any emotions. She said that the wounded boy had to be stabilized immediately; he'd need blood, serum. They absolutely had to alert the hospital. Alain Viaud would wait here and lead them.

The child refused. He swore he wasn't friends with any of those guys. He didn't want to be mixed up in this whole thing. He had nothing to do with it. It wasn't his fault if some asshole from the gang had forced him to do their dirty work. Was he gonna pay for the others, then?

Mrs. Ambreuse reassured him. She promised to clear his name. She understood, she could tell that he wasn't responsible for this, and that he had nothing in common with those unfortunate, stray children. But the little wounded boy must absolutely be saved. Every minute counted. The people from the hospital couldn't spare any time looking for the right cave along the gorge. Viaud had to go with them.

The boy didn't believe her. He hadn't thought it through. Now he was stuck. The doctor had already called the hospital.

"Oh no, oh no!" said Mariette Péréfixe, "you're too kind! This one needs his little nap! Oh yes, yes. And I wonder if I won't be opening this afternoon. That lady with her money, she's gonna end up costing us money! We don't count these things but they add up anyway! The register doesn't fill up in your sleep! And this little one sure needs it, doesn't he!"

The mommies gave each other a hug. They were a little drunk on food and wine. Back in her kitchen, Mrs. Lescot poured herself another coffee. And her little goat, wasn't he sleepy? Oh yes, of course. Oh, Hervé was very kind to put him to bed. He should lay down a little bit while he was at it. She too, despite the coffee, come to think of it … All these emotions, they were no friend to digestion. Gorin's ice creams were too fatty, as well. Creamy, fluffy, you couldn't argue with that, but that was just it. You ate way too much of it, and then you had all this cream in your tummy.

Hervé said he'd rest with Joachim, who had a large armchair in his room.

Several days ago, Hervé had given up caressing his cousin surreptitiously. He felt protected by their crimes and the danger they shared. So last time, he had openly provoked Joachim. He'd kissed him on the mouth and even in the mouth. They took off their pants and everything else. It had come out that Joachim was very fond of these games. He dreamt up that they use their butts. He laughed, he laughed. He wanted to do it again every day, and they would be all naked. In the bedroom, Hervé, once the blinds were closed, softly shoved the armchair against the door.

"Why'd you do that?" asked Joachim, who was laying on his bed fully dressed.

Hervé joined him and unveiled his plans.

These things were truly difficult to do without making any noise. Joachim didn't know how to restrain himself.

"Hey you little monkey! It's not time to laugh now; it's time to go beddy-bye!" scolded Mrs. Lescot from her own bedroom. "Suck your thumb and go beddy-bye. You'll go swimming afterwards! Okay Joachim?"

"You hear?" whispered Hervé, who was licking the little boy's tummy. Joachim was choking with laughter and pushed the head father down. His skin smelled slightly like laundry, which came from his bedding. Mrs. Lescot must not have rinsed it enough, or else she used an overly perfumed brand—probably because of the little plastic gifts that were in the packages and that Joachim wanted. He never had enough toys.

"Put me like this!" said Joachim. He liked it when Hervé laid him down on him and slid his dick between his thighs, and after that, there'd be kissing, and rubbing, and laughing, nose to nose, teeth to teeth.

"Not yet, wait!" whispered his cousin as he sucked the front and tickled the back. Joachim sighed blissfully and took his thumb in his mouth. From time to time he stopped sucking, let go of it and giggled, cheeks vermillion with warmth, if, that is, Pellisson tickled really too much.

The ambulance took Camille Gassé to the hospital. He would probably be saved. Dr. Ambreuse had kept her word. Once they got back, she made Viaud, whom she had taken in her car, disappear. No, she didn't know his name, his address, he rang her doorbell by chance, and she couldn't say anything to help identify him. Besides, he was a brat; he was certainly a stranger to this whole thing.

Alerted by the doctors from the hospital, the police combed every last centimeter of the cave. The harvest was fruitful: the boys had left behind many more compromising objects than they would have suspected. They could do a number of crosschecks already. They were studying an inventory of the thefts and burglaries that had been committed since the spring. It was hard to believe the notorious Gassé brothers gang had made so many hits. It was going to be murder to bring something like this to trial. A hornet's nest. Everyone wished that there weren't too many sons of respectable families involved, and that they'd be able to get a good hold of the culprits.

President Gassé has obtained permission from the sub-prefect, in person, to be the first to question his son Benoît, without a witness.

He conducted this tête-à-tête gravely, by the book. At first, Benoît told him their adventures, Camille's and his, without concealing a thing. The visits to the villas with François-Gérard, the drinking binges, the petty burglaries, running away, etc. He felt ghoulish remorse; in a half-day, he'd certainly matured at least two or three years. His father listened, forgave, erased, overlooked, understood, admitted, and waited.

Then he got to the main point. Benoît had to tell him everything he knew about the thugs: names, activities, plots, and hideouts. Benoît Gassé, naturally, asserted his loyalty. He had sworn to stay silent and not to turn anyone in. They could torture him, put him in prison, but he would hold his peace.

President Gassé knew all about that. He had a long experience in the struggle against scruples, those of others as much as his own. He did not attack his son head-on. There was nothing dishonorable for Benoît, was there, in designating his brother's murderers, those boys from a rival gang? He hadn't given his word to them as well, had he?

Benoît caved in very quickly. What he knew was vague. He lied to himself a little: the police, when they'd have caught the kids from Roche-Notre-Dame, would have no lead whatsoever to find the others. Unless the Cras gang spilled the beans: but it wouldn't be his fault and you'd have to have a warped mind to blame him for it. How could he hide the identity of kids who had all but killed his own brother? It was much too serious, and it was justified. White as snow, already belligerent and furious against whomever would have the bad faith to doubt it.

His father encouraged him gently. Benoît had taken a big step, but was it enough? Did he realize that *he* had committed an act of the utmost gravity in becoming acquainted with these young delinquents? By such an unnatural alliance, hadn't he endangered the life of his brother, his own life, the reputation of his family, and, therefore, the life of his father, him, Henri Gassé? The crimes in which he had participated, more ridiculous than blameworthy, were but trifles. But to have become associated with these ... these ... Besides, was he going to pretend that they had really incorporated him into their group, and that they hadn't detected the essential difference that separated them? Would Benoît even dare affirm that he felt the slightest sympathy for them, the slightest friendship; and that they displayed any of the kind towards him, as puny as it might have been?

President Gassé continued to peck away at the child's resistances till the evening. Family consciousness and class-consciousness were his infallible weapons. He had the intuition that his son profoundly hated his accomplices, execrated the little people, and preferred himself—as he had been instructed to do. He wouldn't persist for long in a pretended loyalty which led him, in fact, to betray the only ones for whom he meant something: his own element, his parents. Mr. Gassé, with perfect patience and flexibility, achieved his goal: Benoît denounced all the boys. He was absolved; no one would ever bother him.

Starting the next day, several police squads raided the hideout that Benoît had indicated and crisscrossed the region. The sub-prefect has begged them to be discreet, but cops have their traditions. They would, however, make no victims, and, apart from a few abusive thugs who'd be rattled more than a little, no one would go crying to mama about some blunder. The papers, with Maurice Glairat in the lead, would congratulate the forces of law and order. The terrorized families took their broods resolutely by the reins, so they too didn't turn into bandits. The holidays continued, well trained, toeing the line.

Julien lifted the corner of the fence that was curling up off the post and slid underneath. Hidden by fragrant shrubs, he peeped into the garden. People were dining in front, on a terrace, under the fluttering light of two or three electric lanterns. The doors and windows of the house were open. The rustling of the waves almost drowned out the conversation.

Julien had noticed that this was an excellent hour for theft. In this part of the island, to the northwest, properties were petit bourgeois; vacationers led a confident and predictable life. Solitary, Julien entered wherever he pleased. He was only afraid of dogs and children.

He quickly located the kitchen. He analyzed the people's movements, and guessed at what stage of the meal they were. In the extreme heat of this month of August, people ate late in the evening. Therefore, the houses stayed open longer, and entering them in full sight of the inhabitants was becoming a game.

The boy crawled to a window that must have been that of the kitchen. He listened to the nearby voices. They were gobbling, guzzling: Julien would be safe. He climbed up to the window and silently leapt into the kitchen. He unfolded a little sack that, after the larceny, he'd be able to strap on his back to keep his hands free.

He was taking good care of his looks. He had even recently gone to the hairdresser. During tourist season, the entire island was full of unknown children; nobody asked you anything. Julien took advantage of it to accumulate rather important supplies. He had established his den on the wild point of a coast, where he discovered the ruins of an ancient abandoned lighthouse. He had staked it out for days, nights, had combed the area a thousand times. The place was secure; the water source excellent.

He delicately gleaned his grub in the low light. These people were gluttons! He opened the refrigerator. And they drank like fish! Julien filled his bag, ears straining towards the door.

Just before he fled, he noticed a flask on the sideboard: he palmed it and smiled. It was ether. He slipped back through the window, flowed through the garden, cleared the fence again and took the sandy road. The night was gentle, peaceful. He didn't have to search for shelter. He sunk into the rocks and the undergrowth.

ABOUT THE AUTHOR

Tony Duvert (1945–2008) is the author of fourteen books of fiction and nonfiction. His fifth novel, *Strange Landscape*, won the prestigious Prix Médicis in 1973. Other books translated into English include the novels *When Jonathan Died* and *Diary of an Innocent* as well as the essay *Good Sex Illustrated*, the last two both available from Semiotext(e).